Beasts Within Our Blood

Beasts Within Our Blood

By

S.N.C. Fletcher

Beasts Within Our Blood
Published by Mountain Brook Ink
White Salmon, WA U.S.A.

All rights reserved. Except for brief excerpts for review purposes, no part of this book may be reproduced or used in any form without written permission from the publisher.

The website addresses shown in this book are not intended in any way to be or imply an endorsement on the part of Mountain Brook Ink, nor do we vouch for their content.

This story is a work of fiction. All characters and events are the product of the author's imagination. Any resemblance to any person, living or dead, is coincidental.

Scriptures taken from the Holy Bible, New International Version®, NIV®. Copyright © 1973, 1978, 1984, 2011 by Biblica, Inc.™ Used by permission of Zondervan. All rights reserved worldwide. www.zondervan.com The "NIV" and "New International Version" are trademarks registered in the United States Patent and Trademark Office by Biblica, Inc.™
© 2026 Simeon Cole Fletcher

ISBN 978-1-953957-70-2

The Team: Miralee Ferrell, Tim Pietz, Kristen Johnson, Alyssa Roat Cindy Jackson
Cover Design: Cover by Riley Kayote

Mountain Brook Ink is an inspirational publisher offering fiction you can believe in.
Printed in the United States of America

Acknowledgments

To Chelsea, who first believed.
To my "kin" who instilled a love of words.
To Amiyah and the rest to follow.
And to Lover's Set, Mar, Clement, and Mary.
You all are my story.

May this adventure be a clear reminder to you, dear reader:
No matter any evidence to the contrary, you were
created with unyielding greatness inside you.

The jungle requires four virtues of a hunter:

- ***The First:*** *Only pursue that which has a fighting chance.*
- ***The Second:*** *Repay the land according to what it gives.*
- ***The Third:*** *Master your Gift. Do not yield to it.*
- ***The Fourth:*** *Never be the cause of prolonged suffering.*

1

Beasts

Solint has yet to lend its rays to color the world below, but even without light to guide us, I already see so much.

I kneel with eyes shut, inhaling the ebb and flow of the lands around me. Sinewed vine and twisted root make up the tapestry of this jungle. Nowhere else do I feel so empowered as I do now; the cloak of thick underbrush acting as my shroud. Beneath this canopy, my very presence is erased from the rest of Spheire, and here, in this unseen place, I am master of a whole new world.

My senses drink in the life teeming around my position. Traces of aurem—the living energy of all things—resonates through my mind. Each unique aurem trace teases its own adventure, all chases I'm itching to pursue. Even after all these hunting seasons, the fullness of aurem still impresses me. As I home in on it, the dark pitch of twilight sky above no longer matters. Aurem paints the world rich with layered detail, even at this tranquil hour.

To my right, I register a heartbeat, always steady, never frenzied. My older brother, Tygon, crouches in his own meditation with the surrounding Wilds. We've gathered now in this specific clearing to await the morning's events to begin. Tygon's bulky outline shifts with little noise to unsnap his shortblade from a sheath at the small of his back. For weeks now, leading up to today's hunt, I've seen him sharpen the skinning tool a thousand-

and-one times. Its edge certainly doesn't need sharpening again. Yet still, he angles the crimson metalwork across stone with slow rhythm. I breathe a bit easier. Between the two of us, it's easily Tygon who keeps composure best, knifework his usual method. I find comfort knowing I'm not the only one a bit tense for what we are about to face.

After a few moments, he flips the shortblade back into his belt and spots me watching him. We share a firm-lipped smile between us, the pressure of the morning's task too overwhelming to allow for anything more. We both know what this hunt will mean for our futures. He and I have learned alongside one another for the whole of our adolescence. Like young lions learning the hunt from their lioness, so too have we devoured every lesson of our den's matriarch. Today, we hope to prove these many teachings were not in vain. Through this all-important test, her principles will make us full-fledged members of the village. By these Wilds we will be made men.

Perhaps in mentally reciting the jungle's four virtues under my breath—the huntresses' first ever teachings—I unintentionally summon our mother.

Muma Kura slips through the treetops overhead before descending into the clearing with practiced grace. The jungle folds over her protectively like a parent sheltering a favored child, and even as she makes contact with the ground beneath the trees, no sound betrays her landing. It is only in detecting her aurem, somewhere between the senses of sight and smell, that I can fully make out her presence.

Our huntress continues to prove her mastery over our surroundings by stalking silent circles around her kneeling sons. We keep our heads bowed as she inspects us. It is the respectful thing to do, and respect is a staple within Beast Master culture. The Wilds bore us and our ancestors before in the womb of her earth. As such, the jungle has given its daughters a simple, yet admirable role: every living soul ever born to our village first learns the hunt from a Huntress.

The woman's voice resonates from the clearing's shadows.

"My sons, I've taught you as well as I could these seventeen odd hunting seasons. So, prove to me today, and to your people, that you are ready for what adulthood will demand of you."

Tygon and I look to each other but keep quiet. I ignore how loud my heartbeat pounds against my ribcage.

After a few more minutes of Muma's encouragements, the test's officiate, Headmaster Lujan, also descends from the trees. This Headmaster will later provide recommendation to the village leaders after judging our performance in the morning's hunt. Ever the masterful huntress herself, our instructor's entry into the clearing is just as subdued as Muma's. I find myself impressed as the Headmaster is closer to our age than she is to Muma's. Beyond age however, there are slight differences between the women only a trained eye would catch seeing them now side by side.

For instance, Muma's stance gives subtle clues about her instinctual approach to hunting. Each day we spent training under Muma revolved around constant readiness, of being able to strike before an opponent or prey ever had the opportunity to react. It is the way a member of our clan—the PanTigris clan—thinks and a tactic borrowed from our lifelong bonded beasts, the tiger. Seeing Muma before us, she is poised as if she truly were a striped cat herself. Fingers splayed. Posture visibly primed. She looks both lethal and eager to prove it with gray-streaked locs falling loose over a slightly hunched back.

By contrast, Headmaster Lujan proves to be the typical PanLeo, proud and direct. Lion's fur is layered over her field garments, and the woman puffs up ever so slightly. Her breath comes easily with pulled back shoulders and hands on hips, her short-edged haircut angled sharply skyward.

Thankfully, never once has the lion-hearted woman lorded her ego over her apprentices. Instead, her teachings are geared toward our integration into the Village as a whole, and as such she oversees a diverse group of students from multiple clans. When Tygon and I raise our bowed heads to meet the Headmaster's eye, it's warmth, gained from years of mentorship, that greets us.

"Faylen and Tygon, you both look mighty ready for the morn'," Headmaster says with a wink before turning to Muma Kura.

"May I take your apprentices?" the younger woman requests.

Our matriarch wordlessly stands aside, never taking her eyes off us as she concedes. After receiving a final good luck gesture from our mother when she touches a hand to her chest, we turn our full attention to the PanLeo huntress.

"Boys, I'm sure you've had the importance of today drilled into you since your earliest Nestling days, but let me reemphasize a final time. The paths you pave after today start by delivering me a clean kill before sunrise. Your mother taught you tracking. She showed you strategy. The ways to cripple and furthermore, to kill. But for the first time, you'll do all this on your own."

The Headmaster briefly gives us each our own moment of steely eye contact.

"The opportunities and roles in which you'll serve our village for seasons to come are founded on what I see in you today." She lowers her voice to a consolatory tone. "I might add too, that I also recognize the unique position you two young men are in. So please, allow me to return to the village leaders with *good* news rather than with heartbreak."

My gut twists at her words because they are painfully true. After the morning's hunt, Headmaster Lujan will stand before Praedari village's clan heads. Her testimony will be heard by the representatives over all the village clans—PanUrsa, the bear-bonded, PanCanis, house of wolves, PanHelos, bonded of night dogs, PanVulpis, the fox-footed, and her own PanLeo too. But at the heart of their company will be my father, the man who's led PanTigris twelve seasons strong. Every one of our successes and failures in the field has, in some way, been tied back to his highly visible position. The older villagers have little shame blaring their opinions over a morning's brew—*how can any leader elevate the people when his or her own household is not in order?* Failing today would mean total humiliation for both the woman who trained us, and the man she chose to ally herself with.

BEASTS WITHIN OUR BLOOD

With our Headmaster's final guidance out of the way, the huntresses retire to the perimeter of the clearing. Their eyes glow from the shadows, then two additional pairs materialize from the dense vegetation. Both women must have called to their bonded beasts earlier, meaning we'll have added witnesses for the duration of the trial.

Alone now with only Tygon at the center of the clearing, whatever transpires next is entirely in our own hands now. I look to him for a bit of reassurance because I realize my knees have started to tremble.

I keep my voice purposely restrained so the sound does not carry through the trees and ruin our hunt before it even begins.

"All right, Ty. Now or never, right?"

He places a firm hand behind my neck, then steps a few paces away to give space for our people's Gift to reveal itself in full.

There are five Bloodlines in this world, ours has made us into children of nature. According to some of our elders, the Beast Master's Gift has made us infamous for unmatched tracking abilities. But this Gift is far more potent than the simple ability to pursue prey. No, I like to think it's in *how* we pursue our prey that keeps us feared across the whole of Spheire.

The predatory changes start off small, as they always do, practically imperceptible to an amateur's eye. However, it only takes a single steady exhale, first from Tygon, then from my own lips, to spark the individual transformations.

When taking on the traits of our beast partners, we first envision the Nodus—our bonded. Every Beast Master has a different story of first encountering their Nodus in the Wilds while we were still yet toddlers. In this moment, I set aside all distractions, doubts, and fears to picture this memory with a clear mind. It's here, holding on to the stillness of the jungle by which our very lives are molded, that the Wild's touch becomes unmistakable.

I register the first effects of my transformation—what our people call the Embrace—shift my physical make-up. Picturing the look of my Nodus's green eyes as it stalks through tall grass, I can feel the predator's sight become my own. Next, I imagine tiger stripes concealing the predator amidst jungle foliage. In response, black lines snake over my arms, legs, and core like unbound calligraphy. My eyes flutter open as the true power of our Bloodline's Gift consumes me. While Beast Masters do not shape shift into exact copies of our bonded beasts, we do borrow enough of their physicality to command the terrain with ease.

The changes continue as I adapt a new physique through Embracing, my form blanketed with muscle mass several times over. Layers of newly formed sinew knit themselves beneath my black striped skin, forming taut weaves of tendon and fiber across my bones. Like some hyper-evolved version of the human form, my skeleton, biceps, and thighs swell together with concentrated density. My feet lengthen to triple their original span, the bones within realigning until my stance shifts forward to redistribute my bolstered body weight. This new stance allows my increased mass to balance effortlessly on the front halves of each foot, and I bend my knees slightly to compress the weight into my calves and ankles. Perhaps as a younger boy, assuming this shape came with a level of discomfort, not unlike a full-body cramp as my form was stretched beyond its limits. Now, I roll my shoulders comfortably, fully capable of directing every ounce of pent-up tension into a killing move at a moment's notice.

What a powerful thing, this human form turned apex predator.

The last tools in my beastly arsenal present themselves by way of all the sharpened weaponry one would expect a jungle predator to have. I flex my fingers back and forth to ease elongated claws from beneath my fingertips. At full extension, their black arcs would match the length of a man's entire forearm and slip through his flesh like knives through twine. However, given that our hunt will begin with travel to the hunting grounds several miles away—a trip to be taken by bounding through the jungle's treetops—I limit my Embrace to keep the claws at climbing length.

With my own Embrace complete, I take in my brother. In normal human form, he has always been a head taller than me, and visibly bulkier. So, standing beside him, even though Embrace makes us both predators, his natural advantages are still present. The width of his upper half commands immediate awe. But outside the obvious difference in size, there's another distinction that we hold secret between us, even going into this pivotal test.

I look from the deep emerald hue of his eyes to the twitch of his elongated ears as they move independently to feed him information from our surroundings. Tygon tries not to look overly concerned when eyeing me back. We both know what he sees though. My eyes are a much paler shade of green, and my ears remain painfully still.

It's something we both agreed could be worked on in private once we clear this test. He didn't want to have to adjust to working with another apprentice for today's hunt and I don't want to be left behind to remedial training. Despite our reasons, we test knowing full well I have a handicap: I've never been able to handle sensing at the level he can. There's just something about the way all that apex instinct battles for control in my mind. I lose track of too many details, and my attention becomes difficult to retain. I've gone near feral multiple times in our practices without Muma. All from having literal waves of information drowning me all at once. So, for now, our plan includes faking a portion of my participation while getting to the actual hunting grounds. If I follow his lead up until then, I can Embrace my senses long enough for the important part—a few minutes of absolute focus to close out the required kill before sensory overload hits me.

We signal our completed Embraces to Headmaster Lujan, but she and Muma Kura remain back in the shadows. Tygon sinks down into his stance and after a moment, springs all tension from his ankles and calves. I follow suit, the explosive move enough to launch us clear into the nearest treetop. Once there, we cup our hands to our mouths and call out in undulating frequencies. High pitches at first, leading into quiet, but steady growls from deep inside the gut. Just as Muma and our Headmaster's beasts knew to join their side, this unique sound signals to our Nodus that a hunt has begun. It's never guaranteed they will drop everything to join a chase, but our odds as human and beast pairing only increase if we work as one. What's more, selfishly I can't think of a feeling better than mimicking our bonded's traits while darting through the jungle's tapestry alongside them.

Per our agreement, Tygon takes the lead, unleashing concentrated energy pooled throughout his legs. Like a grasshopper shooting among creek reeds, I bound away after him, arcing upward to land on a thick branch. It wobbles in receiving my weight, and I'm astounded to see our huntress make the same move a stone's throw away. Muma and the Headmaster move through the trees keeping pace, but somehow, neither shake a single leaf out of place as they rush.

I turn back to the task at hand, drop low to recoil, then slice above the landscape. My arc clears five or six canopies in a single bound. Somewhere below, I see Tygon palm a lower branch. Then, like a rope swing, he flings his legs to accelerate upward.

His release is a thing of beauty. Instead of clearing the canopy head and shoulders first, he corkscrews out of an upcoming treetop completely inverted. Sage leaves kiss his skin as he slips gracefully through them.

If it were anyone else besides my brother, I'd have called this a bit of showboating to catch Headmaster Lujan's eye. But for Tygon, this is all a carefully thought-out maneuver to best navigate the jungle while shoring up for my weaknesses. As he sails overhead, his whole focus is on the ground below. I look up to spot the bright hue of his eyes flickering across landscape in a hundred tiny movements. Before momentum can fully carry his knees in front of his face, he's already taken in so much of the jungle below. Upon landing, a quick look over his shoulder and an imperceptible hand signal communicates he's already plotted our entire course. I just need to act the part and keep to his flank so as to not give our temporary ruse away.

Alternating between far bounds through the air and short bursts on the jungle floor down on all fours, we make quick time through the miles surrounding Praedari Village toward the hunting grounds. After some further distance has been covered, Tygon unspools a long yellow ribbon from his wrist wrapping. It trails behind him, the hunter's signal for the party to halt. With the same control we've demonstrated twisting through the trees, we plant ourselves into our landing spots. Tygon must have picked up on a faint scent below our perch because he quickly descends to converge onto a particular point. Eager to contribute, I lean into my Embrace a bit more, enough to focus on a newly found puzzle piece to our surroundings. The odors all weave together in my mind, instantly sorting useful swatches of information into a clearer picture.

Tygon whispers in the space between us, but I know our huntresses hear every word from their position. Such is the hearing prowess of a fully realized Embrace like theirs.

"Faylen, I think there was a small grouping of Gargan-Elk here a few hours ago. Looks like they started grazing just past the turn of the night." My brother runs a finger across a hoofprint stamped into the dirt. We let the clues carry us around the clearing, nostrils flaring as we investigate the landing.

Abruptly, Tygon's head snaps to focus on a nearby bush. He stalks closer to pick at a seemingly insignificant clump of fur, the color blacker than ink.

"Look here, we've got action real close to the dead of night. See? This is Helos Hound fur."

I momentarily envision the lean-figured Helos Hound, a night dog with long, pointed ears and ever-moving, whip-like tails. The beasts share pack tendencies with their distant wolf-relatives, the similarities there making it all the way into the culture of the PanHelos and PanCanis clans who claim them respectively.

Tygon's call about midnight makes good sense then because according to our studies, Helos Hounds cannot see light. Instead, they hunt by detecting heat with shallow pits along their snouts, temples, jaws, ear tips, and tails. This makes the hounds near impossible to escape after sundown when the jungle has cooled. After all, any lingering heat following nightfall requires a heartbeat. Evidence of their presence here confirms first contact was deep into the night. I wonder then, if the wild hounds might still be somewhere in the hunting grounds ahead. Perhaps steering clear of the jungle's own hunters to complete our own chase is an added element of the Headmaster's test?

I sneak away from the fur snags and scout the beginnings of a trail head. It's a fairly obvious path of crumpled leaves, a discovery that I doubt will win me many points with our proctor, but I refuse to leave all the tracking work to my brother. I breathe in deep, pushing even further into my senses. Perhaps a hint too far once the landscape floods behind my closed eyelids in a world of swimming colors. I clench my eyes to reel back control. Seeing the world is one thing. Seeing it painted anew with the flow of aurem while my Embrace is still imperfected could end my trial hunt here and now if I accidentally go feral.

Thankfully, the familiar scent of crisp water finds me and I cling tightly to it.

I clear my throat. "There's a creek about two miles on from here. I can't make out any blood in the water right now, so those Helos Hounds weren't able to close in on a kill between here and there. Thoughts?"

Tygon kneads a ball of dirt between his fingertips.

"Well, if I had to guess, I'd say the herd of Gargan-Elk didn't fully graze on this side of the waters before the Helos Hounds showed up. Had the grass-eaters gorged themselves, there's no shot they're outrunnin' Hounds. My bet is they made it past the river to the plains beyond and are piled on top of some hill praying for daybreak." He flicks the dirt away. "You know as well as me, Helos Hounds don't care for Solint. So safest place to avoid the dogs would be basking in daylight."

I peel my eyes to the skies overhead and recall a key part of the Headmaster's test. If Tygon and I had the whole day, sure, it would be easy to set up a clean kill. But her deadline was before dawn. That means when the first rays of light break across the land, if our kill isn't down, we fail, no matter how much effort we've put in before first light. We need to move.

I point down the trail. "Let's hurry toward the creek then. The elks probably recovered at the banks to fill up on water. A full-grown bull is going to take hours after that to finish grazing to satisfaction. There's a good chance they let their guard down after losing the Hounds. We should make it just in time to capitalize off that."

Tygon nods in agreement, but just before we step off, a new presence quietly joins the hunting party. As Muma's Nodus, Vai, had found her side back at the clearing, Tygon's Nodus, Cil, stalks up to his bonded. Cil is a sandstone coated cat who's aged alongside my brother. Not quite grown into their adult fangs, neither Tygon nor his Nodus shows the traits expected of a fully matured Beast Master pair. This is obvious the moment they greet each other. Rather than linking up and pressing on to our objective, Tygon finds himself tackled as the massive beast rises to his hind legs to lean heavily against him. I feel some of the tension from our hunt melt away as I snicker at the pair of them. Tygon is a sight to see, trying in vain to escape the tiger's coarse tongue. Apparently, I'm not the only one having a laugh either. I don't need amped senses to hear Headmaster Lujan and Muma Kura chuckling somewhere in the trees behind us.

As the bonded settle down, I find myself listening for a final set of approaching footfalls to signal my own Nodus's approach. The empty silence is telling, and I have to try particularly hard to keep disappointment from twisting a knot in my gut. Such is the way of our beastly familiars. Nodus are partners at best and never pets. While I can hope that eventually my own will join me, the whole point of an Embrace is to take on their traits and be capable of hunting independently.

Still, despite needing to rely on Tygon's help in this moment, there are some parts of the hunt I've made considerable progress on—growth since the last time I've seen my Nodus that I'd like to show him. A whole month now since I've seen my bonded when most Beast Masters see theirs every single day. At least that's what I have observed of my peers in Headmaster Lujan's Elevation class. Out of the lot of us, I am the only one with a fragmented connection to my Nodus and probably the reason I'm so behind my classmates...

But no more. No one will call me lack-luster ever again if I can show I'm good enough today. Nodus or not, I can do this.

Arriving at the banks of the wide creek, the three of us pause to survey the scene. Sure enough, a huge grouping of large hoof prints disappears at the water's edge. On the opposite bank, shoulder-high grass waves lazily in the breeze. I point to the wooly backs of several Gargan-Elks, their tree-span antlers occasionally dipping beneath the sea of green as the creatures graze.

Tygon picks up a handful of pebbles from the creek and maps out a kill plan.

"Okay, Fay, here's the play. I want you to move in a crescent moon around the far-right side of the herd. Your approach will come directly from a right angle here. When you plow into the nearest elk, you'll stagger it for sure. I'm betting he'll run scared straight for center meadow after the initial hit, and that's where I drive forward and take him head on."

He purses his lips for a moment and positions an additional leaf in the mud. "Oh, and that there is my bonded, of course. Cil can act from the outskirts and react to whatever we miss."

Tygon's focus on me becomes penetrative.

"Remember, we've practiced this a hundred times and never once was Muma around to help us. We know this play, Fay. It's *our* play. The kill already belongs to us, he just doesn't know it yet. This whole beautiful morning is ripe for no one but us."

By the Spirits, it feels good to be here in this moment with him. We may be taking some risks going through with this test while disguising my shortcomings, but at least this part feels right. It's impossible not to be drawn in by his absolute faith in the two of us. As he demonstrates the brilliant mind he's growing into, I'm happy just to be here to witness it.

Tygon continues, "Unlike practice though, once you make contact with that elk, our plans can't change. After you initiate, he's gonna' know he's being hunted. So will the rest of the herd. That's the First Virtue for you; we only pursue that which has a fighting chance. I'd rather not have a whole field of ticked off grass-eaters proving exactly how much fight they've got in 'em."

He looks back toward his Nodus but doesn't have to waste

words on the obvious. Mine still hasn't joined.

"And um, hey sorry about Magnus. I know having him around could've only sweetened our odds."

I shake my head. "No, no…I'm ready. Ty, I mean it. Nodus or not, you and I are here together and that's all that counts. It's all that ever has. When I make first contact, I will cut it down."

My brother grabs the back of my neck reassuringly and presses his forehead to my own. At his release, we both face the bubbling river and tread its cool currents. Wading without sound is an easy task as the river drowns out our presence. In the last seconds before the wall of grass engulfs us, I look over to my brother one final time. He's kept perfect pace with my position downstream.

Tygon mimics one of Muma Kura's gestures for when she wants to draw our focus toward securing success, rather than being paralyzed by fear.

He points his first two fingers to the center of his forehead as I've seen her do so many times.

Control my Mind, control the Outcome.

That's what's going to win us the day.

I have a few minutes max at deep Embrace before my limits reveal themselves. Time to make the most of that short window.

I loosen any remaining restraints on my Gift and plunge into the depths of Embrace. As power unbound swallows me up, so too does the meadow around me. The hunter is now fully awakened. A new king has been crowned over these sleeping plains.

2

Motion

The creatures we track are completely obscured from view, but keying in on their scent and aurem, I can follow their movements even through the tall grass. None of the elks give off the unique hue indicating a bond to a Beast Master. As such, any of them are an acceptable kill. Per Tygon's plan, I trek along the right side of the herd, honing onto a single target. This particular grazer has strayed quite some way from the others, nearly opposite the entire meadow from the flock's sentry. The prey will already be ours by the time any alarm can be sent to the others.

Now only a stone's throw from the foraging beast, I wait in place, allowing time for the rest of the party to settle into position. I keep my thighs flexed and ready to propel me forward. I ease my claws out several more inches than I needed to jump through the trees. At full extension, their tips curve slightly, more useful for rending flesh.

I close my eyes, letting the meadow disappear inside my mind's eye. The wavy stalks surrounding me become hypnotic as the sole terrain in my head. I mentally place Tygon's position as well as his Nodus in the backwings. It takes discernable effort to ignore Headmaster Lujan and Muma Kura's aurem at the meadow's far edge. No, not right now...I cannot afford the distraction of nerves that comes with being evaluated.

BEASTS WITHIN OUR BLOOD

Finally, I manage to force the chosen elk into a singular beacon as I narrow my enhanced senses onto the beast. I can register its pulse and breathing from here. It doesn't matter that my time at this level of concentration is seeping away. Done correctly, what I must do won't take long. The rest of the landscape has now faded into mere backdrop. Prey alone takes centerstage and I breathe it in.

Stillness.
Stillness.
Stillness.
Motion.

The grass gives way in all directions around me as I power into a bursting sprint. My calves drive each foot into the ground, my pads compress the earth soundlessly with every stride. The grass thins as I spot the elk in its entirety for the first time. I knew the creature would be enormous—Gargan-Elks always are—but this one's especially so. I can see now why he was confident enough to graze alone. His shag-covered shoulders tower above me, confirming that standing fully erect, the bull would easily clear the height of one of Praedari's Village's entry gates.

Despite his massive size, I carry far too much momentum to consider stopping now. That would kick up a cloud of dust, a dooming signal to the herd, and end the hunt instantly. No, I must commit. Every beast, regardless of its fury, has vulnerability in its vital organs. My claws only have to find one.

Seconds after my initial burst, I have reached the end of my dash and sink low to collect all the momentum I've built up so far. I catapult forward and here, above the grass, the fullness of the jungle truly hits me for the first time. The closest elk is still my target, but the combined sound, scent, sight, and aurem of the other thirty strikes me all at once.

Like a punch to the nose, so much detail hits in too short a time.

While I drive through the air, a wet sensation at the bottom of my feet tries fighting for sensory space in my mind. I ignore what must have been me stepping into a puddle. Whatever, doesn't matter. I steal back precious ground in a sensory war with my mind to commit fully for the bull's back.

But something isn't right.

"Bashtol," I curse beneath my breath. I think I screwed up.

At the sound of that seemingly insignificant puddle, the elk has raised its massive head and spotted me suspended mid-flight on approach for his flank. My claws are only but an arm's distance away when I see the bull's entire hindquarters tense. But I know the bull is too slow to escape my impact.

I slam every claw tip deep into the hip of the animal. I can feel its tendons come undone as the curved points fix me to its bristled hide like anchors. The Gargan-Elk barely has time to bellow in response before I'm onto the next move. I carry my initial momentum with me, aiming to sail over its rear and inflict another damning wound into the beast's opposite hip joint.

Going for this second disabling wound is admittedly greedy, but with Tygon now charging for center meadow, I want to show my limitations don't define me. Yes, I am behind my peers in Embracing my senses, but this, the basic brutality of the hunt...I can do just as well as any other Beast Master. He must know that.

So must they all.

Sadly, success and greed are rarely ever bedfellows, and my misstep reveals itself with cruel immediacy. Before I'm able to secure both hands and feet into the beast's opposite side, the monstrosity rears his giant hindquarters, uprooting my entire grip to his hide. The careful placement of my approach that I'd used to get me this far is abruptly erased. Because I've committed so much of my amped senses onto the elk, I can see every sickening detail as his massive hooves come even with my body.

All I can do is hang here helpless in the air.

In a flash of earthy brown, the bull drives his rear hooves straight into my ribcage. I'm able to tense my core a fraction of a second before the force ragdolls me backward. Unfortunately, this does absolutely nothing to soften the impact as I burrow rear-over-head through the unforgiving dirt.

The elk takes off while I struggle to breathe. With the initial kill plan scrapped due to my mistake, Tygon abandons his run and rushes over to me. He slides in on his knees then grimaces, watching me claw for air. My lungs feel as if every breath I've ever drawn was ripped from me all at once. Even the breeze passes over my gaping lips, taunting with ghostly fingertips.

"Faylen! N-no, are you all right?" Tygon shakes my shoulders hesitantly. His chin quivers in fear.

I nod my head and feel my eyes bulge as I attempt to speak.

"F-finish, the hunt." I croak, reaching out to my hindquarters. I repeatedly pat my hip, motioning at the line where bone meets muscle. Tygon looks at the demonstration bewildered for a moment, then finally catches on.

"You severed its joint!" he says. "Oh, thank the Spirits, I knew you would. That's huge…good hit, brother. Just—just rest here and I'll be back for you when the elk is down."

Tygon wavers in place to look back at me a final time, but I nod the okay. Only then does he bound off in the direction of the beast.

Once he's gone, I'm forced to let the pain in my side truly sink in. My ribcage cries out in painful disagreement but somehow, I manage to sit up, still coated in dust. Short inhales eventually come back to me as I slowly begin to recover. I've lost every trait of my Embrace, my body shrunken back to normal size and all my senses left foggy from the rapid de-escalation.

I stagger to my feet to see the elk rambling about in chaotic circles. Cil has scrambled up onto the animal's back, the muscle-bound tiger using weight to tire out the bull. Our prey has also begun to limp, the toll of my cut at last taking effect. Tygon leaps from the tall grass to collide just beyond reach of the creature's long antlers, an impressive move that expertly pins the bull in place.

Bashtol! This is the exact moment where our hunt would be over if I still had all my strength. With the pair at a head-to-head standoff, one claw swipe at the base of the elk's skull to clear away any padding and a second to sever the spine—he'd be down, just like Muma taught us.

But without me, the trio of hunter, tiger, and bull are

stalemated for a drawn-out moment. Eventually, Tygon's breathing goes ragged and I hear him roar skyward to decry the strain. My older brother has already proven he deserves to pass into adulthood. Truth be told, he's putting in the work of two apprentices right now by controlling the beast in this way. He models literally everything I wish to be in this moment and, at least for his sake, I hope we manage to close the kill.

I also try not to let it bother me how effortlessly he and his Nodus are working in perfect harmony while mine never even bothered to show.

Unfortunately, for his undeniable greatness, even Tygon fatigues. One shaky footfall at a time, I see him pushed back by the elk and its iron will. Three legs are apparently still enough to resist when each spans half the size of a tree trunk. Perhaps that's why that whisper of instinct drove me to go for the second hip joint. Or perhaps I should've worked with what I had and focused on cutting away more of the bull's flank with that initial hit. Either way, the choice is long past.

At last, the kill plan collapses in on itself fully when Tygon has reached his limit. The beast, clearly sensing some give, resurges, bucking my brother aside and turning back the way he came. Wild nostrils flare as the beast rampages—a final desperate attempt to shake off the tiger from his shoulders, the sole remaining assailant.

I feel speckles of dirt pelt the tops of my feet as the bull shakes the earth while driving straight toward me. Twenty odd antler points thrash back and forth with a frenzy, each the individual length of a dagger. The monstrous bone crown sprawls wickedly upward, making me feel stupid for thinking myself king of anything back at the river's edge. Those antlers alone span four or five times my own height.

Impossibly, Tygon manages to stand up from the dirt. He musters the strength to hurl a large stone that smashes into the side of the beast, a decent attempt to alter the bull's path, but it hardly deters his crazed course. A wheezy cry escapes the creature's maw, and the elk re-enters the circle of short grass where he downed me only moments before. With Embrace, I would be fast enough to jump out of the way, but that simply isn't the case now.

Something distracts me from over-thinking my gory fate as I spot Muma Kura disregarding all the rules of our test. She has donned the strength of a fully formed Embrace, evident by her tail trailing behind her as she tears madly across the meadow. Perhaps realizing she'll be too late, she begins to yell some sort of demands at me, but her words are drowned out by dust and thunder.

I let my eyes shut, praying the flash of pain will end before my mind has time to truly process it.

A blur of dark gray streaks across my vision.

In sudden explosion of speed and arterial spray, a giant mass impacts the elk, yanking it off course like a child's toy. The raging bull tumbles across the dirt and a plume of dust clouds my surroundings. I squint into the chaos, trying to pick out what possibly could've reached me in time when my own huntress was too slow to do so.

There, standing over the massive bull, a tiger exceeding its size, grips bits of shredded windpipe between clinched jaws. Solint has lent its first rays over the horizon, and in the dim light, I see familiar smoky fur painted with obsidian stripes. Gray and black, unique colors that belong only to my Nodus.

A lone gray tiger has ever been spotted in the jungles surrounding Praedari Village. So named the Silver Fang by those who actually believe me when I say he exists.

At last, Magnus has come.

Any life the Gargan-Elk once had has long drained away as the creature was clearly dead before it ever hit the ground. Everything from its windpipe to upper ribcage has been pulverized within my Nodus's relentless bite force.

The dust settles around us and full clarity finally returns to my senses. I wonder to myself if Magnus was watching me all along from the very beginning back near Praedari Village. He has never been the predictable sort so long as we've been bonded. Far wilder than any other Nodus I've seen, and that's saying something considering no Beast Master's familiar is truly ever domesticated.

I wonder if he purposely ignored my calls to observe what I might do when acting alone, like any guardian animal would do for its young.

I step gingerly toward my Nodus. It's difficult not to fixate on how long it's been since I saw him last. Aside from his fur sewn into my hunter's garments, I think I've nearly forgotten the feel of him. My fingertips tremble as I stretch my hand out. Anything to reaffirm our bond.

Before I can touch him, Magnus drops the corpse from his grip and stands tall. I'm caught in the untamed tiger's gaze as he looks down at me, piercing green eyes rooting me in place. Perhaps I'm projecting my own emotional state onto the beast, but I glimpse both sympathy and grave disappointment in the giant tiger's stare. Before I can try again to lay a hand on him, he turns and darts away. The tall grass falls in line behind my Nodus to conceal him. My hand hangs rejected in the air and there's nothing else for me to do but hug my painful side. A glance back toward my kin shows them staring slack-jawed at what remains of the fallen Gargan-Elk. Tygon kneels, prying away clumps of dirt stuck to his skin. Muma retrieves basic pain numbing ointments and bandages from her hunting pack and rushes for me. As she approaches, we make eye contact. I have a difficult time reading her expression.

"I'm sorry, Muma. I really am. I thought I was ready."

When she says nothing in response, the silence hurts far worse than cracked ribs ever have.

Truthfully, she doesn't need to say a thing. A crisp wind blows sharp in my face, whispering what this whole blasted meadow knows by now. For all my efforts up to this point, I am hardly the threat worth fearing on these hunting grounds.

Failure clings to me like an old acquaintance I wish I never knew.

3

Hunter's Blame

We gather around the fallen elk, kneeling to remove hunting baskets from our backs. Headmaster Lujan pulls Muma Kura aside to talk privately while I unbutton the fastenings to my holster and unsheathe the copper-toned short blade inside. My hands are still shaky from the encounter, and I drop the knife into the bull's blood. I watch maroon tones consume the blade whole while my reflection gives a judgmental look from within the dark pool. A moment passes before a hand on my shoulder startles me from equally dark thoughts churning beneath the surface.

I don't look up when Muma Kura thanks Headmaster Lujan for her time as she departs. A moment later, our huntress crouches to pull my short blade from the mess.

"Son, you've been through quite a bit today. How are you feeling?" Her voice is more tender than I expected when she hands the carving tool back to me.

Guilt twists its knife into me down to the hilt.

"I failed. When it came time to finally show what I can do, I was the one part of our plan that didn't work." I steal a look toward Tygon. "If it weren't for him covering for my mistakes…I'd be—"

Sweat beads at the back of my neck because I can't stop myself from eyeing the sheer size of the elk's enormous hooves. This close, I can see they are wider than my whole torso, and all I can imagine now being trampled to death.

"Really if it weren't for Magnus, I'd truly be dead."

"It doesn't matter." She cuts me off.

I shake my head in silent disagreement to which she stills my chin with a firm grip. Muma lifts a corner of her leather vest to reveal a fruit sized dent beneath her left ribcage. The wound is covered in old scars.

"This jungle gives us life by way of the plants and animals we take from it. But for the sake of balance, our lives too can be demanded of us at any moment. That is the nature of the Second Virtue." She looks at me for an expectant moment waiting to recite together.

"Repay the land according to what it gives," I mumble.

Satisfied, she straightens her garments and secures a waist pouch back into position. "Faylen, in this life the Spirits were so gracious to give us, there are a few realities we all share. One of these common natures is the tendency to misstep. There's but a single way we separate ourselves from these failures, my boy. You have to dominate each one the moment they show their ugly faces."

I grimace as she applies a small vial of pain reliever to my now blackened chest and side.

"Remember this. Where others hide away from their hideous mistakes, be the one who runs toward it. Sling ropes 'round a blunder and bring it to heel. In time, you'll be stronger for wrangling your missteps than those who only tried to bury them."

The words ring true; but that doesn't make them any easier to swallow. I don't want to be the screw up. I wipe away a creeping tear from my eye as Tygon joins us. He hugs me around the shoulder completely oblivious to the conversation. With an encouraging shake, he guides me over to the kill we must now prepare for the journey home. This meat will be shared amongst our whole clan, no waste even for a hunt meant to test our skills. When I hesitate, he looks bewildered then grins, patting a space next to him at the elk's side.

"Look at that cut through the shank, Fay! You gave that buck one beastly slice, didn't you? Only reason I could head him off for as long as I did." He slugs me in the arm. "Takes real skills. I told ya' you were good to make first contact!"

By the Spirits, can anything dim his light? My failure on those hunting grounds was an enormous one and yet he still finds a way to lend me credit. A bitter pang hits me, but I manage to mask the gloom behind a weak smile. Maybe he thinks my welling tears are in response to seeing how closely I escaped death. But no, this is frustration, plain and simple. A Beast Master's bond to his or her Nodus is the core that defines how much strength can be borrowed from the creature. We train our whole adolescent lives beside these creatures to better learn what to do with their power when we don it. By that count, I should be the strongest Beast Master of a generation. Tigers are already a force to be reckoned with, but Magnus? The fabled Silver Fang himself? He got that name because he is the *only* predator of his kind. The only one seen in the jungle for decades. So for him to be my bonded, I should be capable of practically anything. After all, that's what the old stories say of the last Beast Master who claimed a Silver Fang.

Then again, I suppose the legends never do include a part where *that* particular Beast Master ever struggled. Cool. Thanks, Grandpa. Glad you were just built different.

Reflecting on my Grandpa Ravir brings to memory what my father, Papa Jaole, always calls "an esteemed legacy." The thought never fails to throw a twist in my gut. I'd rather not imagine how Gramps must've easily passed his Hunter trials by the mere act of showing up and instead busy myself with the task at hand. I find my spot beside Tygon where we will carve up the beast. Giving the kill a once over, I notice the area around its ribcage now has a small indent I'd missed before.

After a second glance, I realize that this wound was my brother's doing. Unreal…

Even in his weakened state, his last-ditch stone toss still managed to make a contribution. I'm sure once we open up the chest cavity, we'll find that indent resulted in a bruised or even ruptured lung. The bull wouldn't have made it a mile farther before succumbing to such a hit. All I had to do was not be in the way.

We wait while Muma Kura speaks a prayer to the Spirits thanking them for our fortune during the hunt. I don't understand how she has the patience for gratitude considering Headmaster Lujan probably scratched failing marks in her field notes before she took off. After all, this morning was meant to be our proof into adulthood. How could we hope for credit when the kill belongs to a Nodus? Regardless, our Huntress unfolds a handful of sapling seeds and plants them in the seeping blood at the elk's head.

"May your sacrifice give life to these unborn trees so they may grow to give life also," she whispers.

Once the prayer is done, I take to slicing into the elk's thick hide, following its upper back muscles all the way down to the hip bones. These long strokes will make it much easier to fold and bundle the meat after we package it in leaf wrappings. While we carve quietly, Cil waits patiently in the grass. Muma Kura's Nodus, Vai, whom she had called before we ever left Praedari Village, joins Cil and licks her chops. The two tigers share unspoken communication amongst themselves, a light touch of the noses from mother to child. Neither den mate is in any particular hurry, happy to let us complete the prep work on the elk. This is one of the perks of a relationship between Nodus and Beast Master—the beasts know how reliably the bond produces consistent meals throughout the seasons.

Farther down the carcass, Tygon makes quick work by slicing around each ankle. The knifework provides the perfect groove to maneuver the skinning tip. We'll take the majority of this wooly hide with us. After all, in keeping to the Second, there is little of the kill wasted. This hide will be invaluable for sewing rope, blankets, satchels, and especially clothes during the colder months.

After some time, our field packs are stuffed to the brim. We flip the carcass over to the unbutchered side. This half will go to our Nodus. After our bonded have had their fill, Vai will carry one of the leaf wrappings to her son's younger siblings back in the tiger's den. Anything left will go to the hungry birds already circling above us. And finally, the bull's bones will enrich the soil where it fell, sprouting the seeds we planted.

Muma Kura and Tygon both pat farewell to their Nodus. We gather our goods and walk a mile uphill to the meadow's highest point. When we arrive, Muma unearths a hollow bone from her belt pouch and sounds a long note. A few minutes later, a louder call responds from the surrounding jungle hilltops. I smile to myself as we each unfold a package of fresh fruits and roasted nuts from our packs.

There are advantages to living so closely with the beasts that call these jungles their home. The obvious benefit is we learn to respect the life here and grow to call it an ally. That same untamed life would happily devour any stranger unfortunate enough to wind up lost in this sprawling place. It's why foreigners outside of our nation of Animas are a rare sight to see.

One of those untamed allies has just answered Muma's bird call and speeds toward our meadow now. There, in the distance, I see a blue shape moving fast along the horizon. From this far away, it looks like a blue jay, but in reality, a king of the air has taken flight.

Watching the great bird's approach never fails to steal my breath away.

"Look at that thing, Tygon. Do you know how badly I wanted one of those beautiful giants as a Nodus growing up?" I rise from my spot in the grass and fold my arms. "I mean, could you imagine what Embracing a Qirin would feel like?"

Tygon, who's never shared my enthusiasm for flight, barely looks up at the approaching creature.

"Nope. Thought never crossed my mind. And I certainly wouldn't want some twisted link to one of 'em. That bird-brained monster would eat up all your time and empty the pantry. Is that what you want?"

I sigh at his total lack of imagination. "Oh, come on, admit it. Who didn't dream of bonding to one growing up? Even you used to collect crow feathers as a little boy and claim they belonged to some mysterious black Qirin chicklet."

Before Tygon can deny it this time, Muma Kura elbows her

eldest in the ribs. "Oh, the fool you looked wearing crow feathers around the den while born to a *tiger's* clan. Glad you finally figured out you were scratching up the wrong tree."

Muma looks up at the sky to see the four-winged creature descending toward us at last. I shield my eyes from Solint as the Qirin touches down, blowing grass in our faces as it flutters two opposing sets of massive wings. The giant bird towers overhead, easily twice the size of a full-grown Gargan-Elk. It cocks its head, perhaps wondering which of us had imitated its call. In response, we rip open the packages of nuts and dried fruits, offering the treats to its beak.

It's an interesting relationship we have with these particular animals. Qirin, like a few other epic beasts of the jungle, are unbonded to any Beast Master. Even the feather-bonded up North in Avian Village do not claim these creatures of the Wilds. Stories from the elders say hunters used to be able to, but these titans offer too much raw power to keep bonds with today's Beast Masters. Of course, that begs the question then—considering Magnus is the only one of his kind anyone's ever seen, is our bond somehow an exception to these old tales?

Once the great bird has gulped down our offerings, it stills enough to allow us to climb atop its back. I follow Muma as she steps carefully between its billowing wings. From up here, I admit I feel sorry for the beautiful creature. Being so large, sure, it has no predators, but I've never seen a Qirin have any friends either. As graceful as they are in the air, whenever the giants try picking fruits and nuts on their own, their clumsy rummaging scares off most jungle life in a half-mile radius. Too powerful for its own good. Poor thing.

I lift the shimmering feathers decorating its collarbone and scratch deep until the bird chirps.

Meanwhile, Tygon behind me has tied himself to the bird's ropelike strands of hair, wearing a sour expression.

He purses his lips at me. "Oh, come on, you look ridiculous treating this big ball of feathers n' poo like a chicklet. Quit distracting the thing so we can be off already."

I squint my eyes at him then turn to coo at the bird. "Don't you listen to that killjoy back there, beautiful. I understand how lonely you can get, so let's make the most of our time together m'kay? How's that?"

Tygon's burly hands are death gripped to the Qirin's back.

"Hmph, big ole' bird lives *such* a horrible life freeloading off us. Yet we're the ones crazy enough to let it take us miles off the perfectly safe ground. I'm telling you guys, whoever was the first hunter to come up with this idea was definitely the village idio—"

Whatever complaints Tygon has left are lost to an instant mouthful of gusting air once the Qirin blasts skyward. It only takes a few strokes of its mighty wings for the grazers below to become specks. I look behind me and could break into tears spotting my brother frantically holding onto the bird's hair. His eyelids creep upward into his brow, making him look as if he's never known a night's sleep in his whole life. I grab Muma's attention and we both guffaw at the site of my eldest. Seeing him so flustered is quite the contrast from his usual level-headed self. Considering I'm the one who screwed up today, it's nice to know my dauntless dearest can be at least a tad flawed in something.

Once Tygon realizes I'm poking fun at him, he does his best to reach out a fist to whale on my shoulder. However, the second we hit a stray wind, he snatches his hand back for dear life.

Despite my brother's complaints, I think our village's ancestors were quite smart to look to Qirin for rapid transport from the field. Our full packs non-withstanding, I'm happy to sit back and take in the surrounding skies. I relax watching the massive bird's four wings push vortexes into a sea of blue. The cool air this high up runs through my chest, and I almost forget the panic I felt only a little while ago.

A sigh escapes me.

Maybe everything will work out. Sure, failing today's pass into maturity means I failed this year's Hunter Trials altogether. While occasionally, there has been a surprise second half to the Hunter Trials, I've only seen it happen a handful of times since I was a boy. Better to look forward to the next hunting season to try again. Besides, what's another annual under Headmaster Lujan but a chance to become a better Hunter?

Before I can let my inner cynic answer for me, I look out to the landscape below and try picking out landmarks from our map-making lessons. A twinkling below catches my eye, and I watch the flow of the snakelike river that halves this entire land of Beast Masters north to south. From there I can follow the waterway north to the nation bordering my own—Petrichor, a land claimed by the Bloodline of the Elements—the Weavers. Looking the opposite way, past the wetlands, the river also winds down into our other neighbor, Indom. Stories tell theirs is a Bloodline devoted to the Body, made up of sculpted giant Warriors and cut-throat Blade Masters.

Not like I've met anyone from either of those Bloodlines before, but it is interesting to see just how close we all really are in the grand scheme of things. As the Bloodline of Nature, we spend so much of our time in the jungle that it can feel like its own separate world at times, but from up here, I suppose Spheire isn't as large as it seems from below.

This realization sparks something in me. If the world isn't that large and overbearing, then perhaps the fears I choose to embellish aren't so large and overbearing either. For several seasons now, I've dreaded this day. Dreaded that somehow my unconventional bond with that rare Nodus would see me labeled the failure of the PanTigris clan. At least that's how I'd catastrophized the situation in my head. But Tygon has never once doubted that I have potential. Muma's never stopped saying it.

I look to her now and wonder what's going on inside her head. What looks will she endure when word gets out her sons failed today? That's the thing, Huntresses are the one part of our society that doesn't fail. If it weren't for them, dens would've gone hungry thousands of years ago and never multiplied to form the ties that built Beast Master society. Our matriarchs started as the foundation to our people, and while anyone, man or woman, can be chosen as village leader or clan elder, without these women, we'd have no one for those officials to lead.

I call out to her over the swift winds, and she turns her head enough to meet my eye.

Air catches in my throat, but I force it down.

"I'm going to figure this whole thing out, Muma. I won't let these Trials defeat me. Won't let today stop me..." I pause, refusing to let my voice tremble. "I just want you to know how hard I worked to get even this far. So please, please don't write me off just yet..."

My eyes lower and the image of our stern clan leader waiting at home fills my mind.

"And Papa too. I hope I haven't lost him completely this time."

Muma nods but offers no words. Her shoes are a rough place to be in right now. Another tenant of Beast Master society is our ability to contribute. If you can rely on no one else, at a minimum, you have kin and clan. Clans are defined by their Nodus connection. Only the tiger-bonded live within the Pan-Tigris grove. So, to have weak blood within our ranks...it doesn't bode well for the long haul. Additionally, Beast Masters do enjoy a blessed life within the jungle. But that doesn't mean it ever bends its will for us. The trees do not deliver food to the doorsteps of anyone's den. No—every healthy set of stripes must be ready to pitch in for sustenance and clothing. I must be able to do my part.

I'd thought our conversation over, but a soft tone from Muma finds me through the rustling wind. "Some parts of you may be underdeveloped, but I don't often find a stronger heart in those I meet. Maybe that's all the strength you'll need to find your own way, my love."

I've no words to say after hearing that, and better for it too. The wind picks up through my locs as the Qirin takes a steep downward angle into a clearing beyond one of Praedari's outer gates. Muma and I dismount smoothly, but the instant Tygon hits the ground, he staggers straight for the village entrance. Oh, poor brother. I will pick him up some silk syrup before dinner tonight and make him a calming cup of leaf tea.

Just before the great bird takes flight again for its nest, Muma brings over a large stick leaning against the gate. Tied to the end is a colossal yellow and purple berry. The Qirin lets out an excited flurry of song notes and sways its massive body back and forth to the self-made tune. It consumes the lushalow berry in one gulp and continues its merry jingle. After a few more notes, it pushes off, carrying the harmony back into the Wilds.

Muma returns the staff to the gate and places two shiny coins and a translucent stone into a pouch nailed on the gate post. She turns to me. "Well, I'm sure you know your Papa will get the news from this morning sometime later today. But I think there might be some value in hearing it from his sons first…before their Headmaster."

I gulp dryly.

Muma follows after Tygon and speaks over her shoulder. "Up to you, but that's my two cents. Never said wrangling those failures would be easy!"

Envisioning Papa amongst his clan elder peers steals the taste from my mouth and I am suddenly unable to remember any momentary respite I might have felt flying amongst the clouds.

4

Animal Kingdom

Praedari Village is fully alive this morning, and its people mingle throughout a variety of shops like hornets in a hive. This village is a proud place my people have built into the surrounding mountaintops throughout the generations. Giant stone heads carved into the clifftops stand silent guard over us representing of the clan's primary apex predators—wild bears, lions, hounds, more. Hunters and Huntresses alike walk throughout the village with their familiars in tow.

At the entrance of this village Hub, I see a small grouping of children being counted for morning classes. Many hunting seasons ago, I once stood where they are now, a bouncing little Nestling, barely having learned hunting basics from Muma's home teachings. Forgetting for a moment today's failure, Headmaster Lujan has seen me come a considerable way since I first entered her care.

Now, somewhere in that crowd of excited scamps, my little sister Kleo has started her own journey. She'll try her hand at the essentials—tracking, stalking, and navigation until they become second nature. The girl is smart too, so I have no doubt she'll pass it all with flying colors by the time she tests for adulthood. I've made it my personal project to work with her constantly, giving her daily little challenges and quizzing her with simple recitations.

If I can help it, I won't let her end up where I am.

Through the crowd, a small group of graduated Nestlings, called Half-Points, scurries around us to their history lesson with the village leaders. One of them trips into me and apologizes with a respectful nod. A bear cub stumbles after her and the young apprentice pauses to let her bonded catch up.

I watch the kids with a smirk and Tygon comes up even beside me.

"Ah, now those were the seasons, eh?"

I chuckle and wonder where the time went since I was in their position. Why didn't I listen when grown-ups warned we shouldn't try to grow up faster than we already were?

Tygon exhales. "Can't wait to see how Kleo fairs after she's finished being a Nestling. She's gotten so far already because of the extra effort you're putting in with her, ya' know. Don't think it all goes unnoticed back in our den."

My brow wrinkles sardonically. "At least *one* of us younger siblings has to escape your spotlight. If it's not me, I'm at least gonna' set her up for success."

Tygon rolls his eyes. "Trust me, there's no spotlight, Fay. You forget already that Lujan has definitely failed both of us by now. I'm just grateful we'll get our shot again soon enough. Until then, keep doing what you've been doing. Both in our training and with Kleo. I know our parents are plenty proud to see you growing."

He pauses for a moment to think something over.

"I probably should've done for you what you're doing for her. I was so focused on shielding you from life's punches, I never showed you how I learned to roll with 'em. Better to have been your teacher instead of bodyguard."

I wave off the thought but watch my feet as we walk along. The thing is, he's probably right. I *could've* benefited from a slightly different approach from my brother. But then who was his extra help? Everything he's able to do now, he learned straight from Muma Kura or figured it out alone. There was no doting older sibling to help him get it right. So even though he's older than me by only a hunting season, if he was able to make it independently, I should be able to also.

But I get what he's trying to say. Choosing to focus instead on his earlier compliments, I find I don't really know what to say. Outside of Tygon, I'm not used to receiving that sort of praise.

"Thanks for what you were saying before," I murmur in a sheepish tone. "I didn't consider the possibility of our parents noticing my help. Whatever our little kitten needs, I'm game!"

Tygon is quick to wrangle the back of my neck in his grip. "No matter how this talk with Papa goes here in the next few minutes, you're a good man to me, Fay. I view us on equal footing. We'll hit maturity next time, easy. Like I always say, how hard is it to push past walls when we can leap over trees?"

He probably doesn't know this, but without him to run alongside, I would've lost my way long ago. It's why I have to do the same for Kleo as she advances past Nestling and finds her Nodus during Half-Point afterward. Even on into her own Elevation someday, I'll be there.

Our chatting has brought us into a colorful block of shops with goods swinging beneath various store fronts. These rows of stone, wood, and straw huts are stocked full of mouth-watering fruits, cures of meat traded from successful hunts, spices, and hand-woven garments. A whiff of maplecomb cake kidnaps my senses and I find myself tiptoeing toward the sweets stand. Unfortunately, my carelessness has me trip full-across a stranger's tattered cloak.

With hunter's grace, I easily recover and reach out to apologize. But halfway, I wince and jerk my hands back at the sight of the stranger's scale-covered skin. By the Spirits! I immediately realize how rude my fleeing reaction was, but truth told, the figure standing before me isn't something I'm used to seeing this far north.

A man wearing the faintest hint of reptilian features has me locked in his glare within the cover of a drawn hood. His head twitches in an unsettling way underneath his garments, the whole attire woven over with rust-colored scales. His words are quite literally hissed at me.

"Watch where-sss you're going, cat," he spits. Slitted pupils take me in, darting across the tiger's fur woven into my vest and wrist wrappings. I freeze in place while eyes the shade of yellow jackets on either side of his pitted nose, drink in the sight of me. I stifle a gasp as a see-through sheet of…um, eyelid? Milky pale and visibly wet—slips across his wide-eyed stare. I've never looked at a Reptilix this long in my entire life. Didn't know until now that they even *had* two sets of eyelids until now.

Perhaps sensing how awkward the moment has become, the man peers back toward the direction he was traveling. Abruptly, he stalks away from me, but not before I catch those yellow orbs scouring the Hub's layout. As I watch him skulk off, I steal a final glimpse at those scratchy-looking garments.

Blegh. I feel an itching sensation creep across my bones. No apex-bonded would be caught dead wearing what is, apparently, a scale-bonded's high fashion. Honestly, Beast Masters from Reptilix Village really are a different breed...

I shake my head the moment I realize how prejudiced that just made me sound.

Truthfully, I don't have anything against the Reptilix, but that doesn't mean I'm dying to travel all the way into the heart of the Southern Wetlands to visit their village either. They can keep those itchy clothes and their cold-blooded Nodus too. I turn to find my brother who was patient enough to wait for me. Subconsciously, my finger touches the spot where my arm came in contact with the stranger.

How can anything that calls itself alive have skin that frigid? Agh—freaks the tiger's breath outta' me.

I follow after Tygon through the flow of Hub traffic into Praedari's true centerpiece—the meeting space where our community sorts matters with clan and village leadership alike. We call this time-honored place the People's Hall. The layout of the hall's foregrounds mirrors the rings of a tree, taking inspiration from the surrounding mountainous woodlands.

BEASTS WITHIN OUR BLOOD

I crane my head upward as we enter the cavernous space. I've always been in awe of how high the People's Hall towers above us. Its sheer size mimics the sheltering feel of the canopies and cliffs that shroud us beneath the Wilds. Magnificent columns were even preserved to look identical to the living trunks we hunt within. These trunks stand in matching rows of twelve by four. The floor is made of spacious stone-slab and covered in hundreds of interconnecting rugs. Each is a beautiful hue of hand-woven fabrics that come together to form a perfect union of the many generations who've donated them across the ages.

At the hall's opposite end, our clan leaders stand shoulder to shoulder, but their eyes are all on Praedari's head leader. The man could be sitting on a throne right now, as someone of his stature would easily claim. But instead, I find our Dominant sitting cross-legged on the rugs surrounded by a freshly appointed Half-Point class. These young apprentices are only a bit older than my little sister, and each clings to their equally young Nodus while listening to the man's stories.

Each of the five villages that make up Animas aligns with some grouping of wild beast. Feather-bonded, scale-bonded, and our own apex-bonded, make up the predators of our Bloodline. Hoof-bonded and primate-bonded make up the foragers. All five are headed by their own Dominant and, seconded for wise council by a Sage.

Praedari's current Dominant, Dom Arzen—fondly called Dom, short for Dominant—boasts a sudden hearty laugh with the children surrounding him. After their merry chuckling dies down, one of the youth raises her hand.

"Dom Arzen, my huntress told me a bedtime story last night, but I'm not too sure if she was fibbin'."

The giant of a man motions the Half-Point forward, inviting the scamp to stand tall beside him. He urges her to share with her peers.

She continues, "Well, in her story, she was saying the golden star we see only at dusk and dawn, isn't really a star." She points in a particular direction where I know lies a distant mountain range. "She told me that shining star is really a shrine…and that there's a dragon livin' up there!" The little girl raises a quizzical eyebrow at our Dominant. "Come to think of it, she even says you've been up there to see it with your own eyes."

The girl puts her hands on her hips, "Come on, even *I* know there's no dragons in Animas."

The Half-Points all hush to hear what truth will be confirmed by our village leader. At his side, the clan heads remain perfectly stoic as to not give the answer away. However, from here I can tell a few of them are poor actors struggling to keep a straight face in front of the pure innocence radiating off this future generation.

Dom Arzen's smile flashes broad and mischievous.

"No dragons, you say? Sure about that?"

He guides the young Half-Point's attention toward a tapestry draped from the thatch roof. Its colors are blindingly brilliant, but there's something even more eye-catching woven within the fabric. It absorbs and distorts the light throughout the entire hall.

"Ah, yes, I indeed saw what's atop that distant mountain range. Only the strongest of our people ever get the chance to make that climb to where that golden star of legend is said to rest."

He turns to share a moment of visible respect with the clan heads around him.

"These Hunters and Huntresses at my side who lead your various clans? It was they who put aside any differences to select me for the mountain's call. But if I wanted to accept their nomination as Dominant, I had to make the climb to the range's highest point. 'King's Peak—Where the Dragon Sleeps.'"

Ooohs and aaahs escape the whole Half-Point assembly. A nearby attendant unties a rope, lowering the colorful tapestry into the young girl's arms. She looks like a child clinging onto a fallen star as she strokes a hand across the shimmering dragon scale, its height nearly half her size. Then she cocks her head and looks to Dom Arzen with sudden realization.

"Wait, this is from a Nodus, isn't it? Something super old. Does that mean you met a Beast Master up there too?"

A grandfatherly grin spreads across the man's face, and he applauds the girl's quick-thinking. "Ah, watch out the rest of you. This one'll be the scholar of your class yet. Little one, I didn't just meet *any* Master up there. I met the first Hunter ever, resting in frozen glory."

A reverent gasp spreads throughout the Half-Points.

The scale-bound tapestry is raised back into position and Dom Arzen continues his account of how he knelt before the frozen Beast Master and offered tribute to the first ruler of Animas. It's been an age since I myself listened in as a Half-Point on this same stone floor, but I could never forget this part of the history lesson.

Dom Arzen lowers his voice to a whisper to tell us the exact moment he became our Dominant.

"I marched forward to the dragon inside that golden shrine. Her hide was blacker than night with horns like rays beaming off a red sun. So large was her mass, that it consumed the place, far, far up to the roof. And the teeth she had? Like nothing you've ever seen." He stretches his hands, teetering back and forth as if bearing an imaginary load. The Half-Points mimic his puffed-up appearance until the hall is filled once more with gleeful laughter.

"Even wielding all those man-sized teeth, did you know the great beast's head still lay in the King's lap? That's the power of our Gift, young ones. Our Bloodline boasts a union with nature and the very life that fills these lands. Do you understand what that means for you?"

The Half-Points shake their heads in response.

"Well, here, have a look at this behind me. The King's descendants left for us his final ancient message etched in marble. The words are a reminder for those deemed worthy enough to climb his peak all these centuries later. I took down with me what they said."

Here Rests Our First Sibling, One Eternal: <u>*The Dragon Lord*</u>

Let No Bloodline upon the face of Spheire forget.
Our Power was Gifted to us—Five Siblings in all—
by the Spirits as reward for our Leadership.

Likewise, you too must Lead Diligently. Take a Dragon's Scale, a Testimony to your own strength.
Hone it to Empower—Never to Enslave. We are Servants First, Rulers Second.

"Whether you are this Bloodline's strongest or its weakest, we all share a role in preserving our land. To safeguard these Wilds, we all work hard to achieve the Third virtue—we Master our Gift. Beyond that, strive to be servants of your people before anything else."

With this, Dom Arzen concludes the history lesson, allowing the children to mingle with the clan heads. When Papa Jaole spots us, he politely excuses himself. He motions us to meet him halfway into the great hall. My pulse has already picked up as he approaches. Once close, we fold our hands and offer a shallow bow. This too is a sign of deep respect—especially for his position within the clan's hierarchy—even if it is expressed differently than the reverence we gave by kneeling outright before Muma prior to our hunt.

"Good morning, my sons!" he calls out. "I must be in the presence of Praedari's newest made men for you to be back so quickly from your Hunter's Trial? How was the morn's chase?"

My palms are sweaty as I keep my lesser hand clasped over the dominant one.

Tygon is quick to report the good news. "Yes, Papa, it was a fruitful hunt that will feed our elderly clan members for weeks to come. A full-grown Gargan-Elk fell before us this morning. Muma is back in the den preparing it now." My brother pauses long enough for Papa to turn the brief account over in his mind. The man raises an eyebrow at me when I remain a bit too quiet.

"What have you to say, Faylen? You don't plan to starve your old man of the best details, now do you?" He motions back to his colleagues. "I don't get to enjoy the fields firsthand much these days, after all."

Bashtol. I hate the sudden spotlight. But Muma did say I have to own my failures. Is this really the right timing though? With all these people around who look to Papa for leadership?

I clear my throat. "Ah, right, Tygon said it, sir. Um, I even made first contact with the creature. Nearly sliced its hind leg clean away from it."

The air hangs thick as I know he could turn into his usual inquisitive self at any second. Muma has always been the quiet observer between them, her mannerisms matching her tactics seen in hedges surrounding a hunting ground. She always lets a situation marinate before offering a response. But Papa on the other hand, has always been a truth-seeker. His direct nature fits him well in his role of leader and politician within the village.

Unfortunately, it also makes being his kid way harder than it needs to be.

Not quite ready for the whole truth just yet, I decide perhaps it's best to distract him with some banter about his work. "Papa, how are today's meetings? Any discussion of how the rest of our peers are stacking up in the Hunter's Trial? I know how eager we all are to begin our contributions to Praedari."

Papa doesn't respond at first and I am abruptly reminded of how tall he is. His robe is trimmed with orange fur clippings from his own Nodus and signifies his place as head. A heavy black amulet hangs from his broad neck, also marking him leader of PanTigris.

Another breath later and I am beginning to regret asking about how the others have done on their Trial. It's an easy way to open myself up to comparison. I can hear the question turned back on me already. Were *you* able to summon your Nodus to your side today? How much of the transformation could *you* achieve? And the one I'd hate the most—your grandfather used *his* bond to the Silver Fang to lead this village…are you using your bond to its fullest potential?

Papa eyes me mildly, then I catch a familiar hint of disappointment.

Through tightened lips Papa finally replies, "Be more patient,

Faylen. I am not Headmaster over your training. You'll be informed of the morning's results during Elevation just like the rest. No special treatment."

I stew inside my own head.

Of course, I know that. I am far from some Nestling child. Today, I stood at the doorway to adulthood…to stepping into my matured responsibilities by stepping beyond Elevation into the stage beyond. Pre-Mastery. Speaking to me this way throws all that growth out the window.

By the Spirits, I can't wait to pass the Trials. Just for the chance to force him to recognize my undeniable progress for a change. Any victory to get him to see me for more than just the legacy I carry through my Nodus.

Papa's attention drifts back to the assembly of clan heads before he looks to us a final time.

"Young men, I appreciate that you represented our clan well in today's hunt. I look forward to hearing Headmaster Lujan's full assessment of your skills." He focuses on me. "Faylen, I'm especially proud to hear you landed the first decisive blow despite your…"

He pauses, thinking up the word.

"Limitations."

I wince imperceptibly at this and consider blurting out the full truth before he walks off. That's probably something Tygon would do. But I'm far too heated right now for sincerity. I just want to get out of here already.

So, I keep quiet.

A bell rings from somewhere inside the People's Hall signaling a change in events and I bow in mandatory compliance to my father, then shift to make my exit. As I turn, he calls me again. Tygon has already finished his own acknowledgements and has since stepped away. Despite my anger, I wheel around quickly to avoid even the slightest perception that I've pre-emptively turned my back on our Clan Head.

My father locks eyes with me for a long moment. Then, in rare form, he does something I don't expect. His features soften, reminding me of the man who first held my hand through the trees and taught me not to fear what lurked within them.

His voice is so gentle that it's genuinely alien to me.

"Faylen, I am proud of what you did today. Finally, a chance to prove so many people wrong. I hope you'll be the one to Recite the Chase over dinner tonight?" He nods to himself. "It'll be good for Kleo to hear it from you. It'll be she who takes on our Huntresses' full teachings next, after all. I want her to see that torch passed along."

Bashtol. Whatever that was has caught me way off-guard. Why exactly did I let myself get upset just a second ago? Surely giving up the whole story would've saved me from this fate. Anything but Reciting the Chase while he looks on with pride. That means detailing the approach, the mindset, and of course, the killing strike itself. It's always the privilege of the hunter who truly led the hunt.

That's precisely why I've never done it.

Before I can respectfully suggest that perhaps I'm not the right pick for the Recitation, Papa has already brought me in for a quick embrace.

The man has truly seen so much. His face against mine is a reminder of this as I feel his rough cheekbones covered in pocks and burn scars. His hug can only get so tight as his left arm has been missing long since before I was born. I'm old enough now to realize that his strictness with me comes from a well-intentioned place. He's seen what turbulent times between Animas and its bordering neighbors looks like. In his own way, he just wants me to be ready for whatever the future might hold.

Before I can offer anything else, Papa lets me go and strolls back toward his assembly.

I catch up to my brother and play the tender little moment back to myself. It throws me off to glimpse these delicate interludes with Papa Jaole. Reminds me that even though he can be so unyielding at times, deep inside, there's a greatness he believes I'm capable of.

Yet I often wonder, is it truly me he sees or the inherited legacy of my grandfather, a legend I never got the chance to meet?

I exhale slowly. Looks like tonight is going to be a tough one. But as Muma said, all I have to do is wrangle this failure. In some ways, tripping up just before the finish line has provided me a unique opportunity. How I handle this mistake will prove to my kin that I won't, in fact, end up a permanent disappointment.

5

Discipline

We leave the village Hub for a quieter alleyway, passing beneath a towering tapestry. Unlike the colorful handwoven cloths that decorate the People's Hall and shops, this one shimmers with a foreign, metallic finish. As young Nestlings, Tygon and I would gape up at the mirror-like drapery and guess at its creation. A giant metal blanket that somehow keeps its flexibility. Such a mystery, and that was *before* the moving images started flickering across its surface like morning light across a lake.

These days, I've grown used to these projections and the messages they bring. Currently, one set of images brings to life pictures from far beyond Animas's borders. A cityscape paints itself across the tapestry, a bird's eye view taking us through streets with iron cast boxes on wheels and twisting steel spires that I suppose some people call home. This is about as much of Spheire's capital city, Sanctum, that I think I'll ever see.

Another image stream issues the standard good tidings from the four-member panel that makes up Spheire's global leaders. A Nestling nearby tugs at her Muma's garments and points upward to wave enthusiastically at the giant-sized representations of these leaders. I still don't know by what magic its possible, but their flickering images actually smile and wave back. I observe the girl's mother closely, wondering for a moment what her reaction will be. But as with any other time I've seen the adults interacting with these monumental images from beyond our borders, the response is always the same.

The mother secures her daughter's hand in her own, then lowers her head and shoulders to those beings owning the sky. With her head still very much lowered, she is on her way.

This is probably the closest any of us in Praedari will ever come to meeting the Council—the four hands who, together, maintain a careful peace throughout Spheire and its five Gifted Bloodlines.

I mean to also make my way past the mirrored tapestry when Tygon catches my arm.

"Fay, you're going to miss the best part! Don't you remember? They're showing highlights from the capital this week. The showcase matches at the Discipline of Peace are happening right now. I think someone from Animas is actually up for the crown this time!"

The metallic surface usually displays the mundane sort of information the elders confuse for entertainment, but it does manage to hold my interest with one particular showing. The prized jewel of the Council's reign may be the capital city of Sanctum, but it's the prestigious Discipline of Peace that captures my generation's imagination most. For many of us, there's no higher purpose than being selected by the village to receive an education at this elite combat academy on behalf of our entire Bloodline. Annually, all of Praedari gathers to watch the top grudge matches from the four-year institute. Personally, I never knew the true feats of which a Beast Master was capable until I saw my kind represented there. After several years of military-style training, the heights reached during these one-on-one matches is beyond anything I've seen in the jungle duels and chases around the village. Afterall, due to our quiet village lifestyle, people around here are more likely to talk out their problems before things get too far.

But at the Discipline of Peace a person just might enter a student and leave a legend.

Next up on the sleek tapestry, another bird's eye view, but

this time one showing off the pristine campus catches my breath. The picture sweeps past a central tower, crowned with a massive purple jewel. Then, the landscape drops away with a dive to ground level, bringing two opponents into center view.

On one side, I'm happy to see a representative from Animas. There, standing in a powerful Embrace, is perhaps the largest Primitas I've ever seen. The swollen Beast Master is from the primate-bonded village no more than a day's journey from here. We catch him acting out the first moments of a total onslaught, surging forward to bring the whole weight of his upper half careening down onto his opponent. The whole of him is gorged with muscle in identical fashion to one of the jungle's greatest threats—a silver-back gorilla. Dust clouds surge outward from him as he crashes his mass into his opposition.

Here in Animas, that kind of force would've flattened anything beneath it. Any prey would be pulp after standing in the way of such overwhelming force. But that's the magic of the Discipline of Peace. Nowhere else but this prestigious institute do we get to see what happens when Spheire's Bloodlines collide.

The Beast Master's titanic onslaught is matched in kind by two broad and calloused hands. Amidst the torrent of blows, stands a muscular, and notably, human woman. No transformation, no Embrace, just her and her tattoos. Then again, tallying this fighter's strapping frame and her dark-skinned complexion, I might be oversimplifying a bit.

By these features alone, I know the woman's origin— Bloodline of the Body. A Warrior from Indom, the nation to Animas's southern border. Her's are a people renowned for having perfected the art of durability. Her Bloodline's complexion is said to be a trophy from a life spent entirely within a Solint-baked desert. Even from here, I can see the layers of muscles spiraling together into masses of rippling tendon. With every meteoric overhead smash from the Primitas, her shoulders bulge, easily holding against the relentless assault. When she switches tactics, her dark locs move whiplike following the Warrior's fluid motions. Her hair's unpredictability contrasts the unrelenting focus in her eyes while she angles around the Beast Master.

Tygon elbows me in awe. "Look at that, Fay. I just got to try moving like that one of these days. I mean, really, how do you catch somebody dancing around like that?"

To Tygon's point, I watch as fatigue and realization simultaneously hit the Animas representative. I try to think back on what lesson from Muma's training I would incorporate if I were the one in that ring right now. Nothing useful comes to mind.

It takes a good half minute, but the stone and metal of the arena floor is soon remade into a mess of upturned crags, twisted iron, and dust. Yet despite the Primitas' impressive destruction, everywhere he's cratered the earth, the Warrior had managed to dodge away a half-second before. Now, while he heaves heavy with exhaustion, she remains poised and untouched.

I soon realize there is one piece of Muma's training that I can apply here. It's in the very moment where I spot the Primitas has lost himself. Muma has brought us to countless treetops over the seasons to watch the chase of every sort of creature. In each one, so long as the predator had acted correctly, there was always a moment where the prey seemingly gives itself up to be downed. An exhale of hopeless undoing.

I can see in her eyes that the Warrior spots this same shift in her opponent only a few seconds after we Hunters do; an impressive feat I attribute to her people's learned instincts from a lifetime spent fighting. I watch her ignore the uneven terrain and adjust her frame ever so slightly. The Primitas, too wiped from the quakes he has just created, misses all the subtle cues in her stance. Meanwhile, his opponent now leans deep into her back leg, toes outspread, pausing only for the span of an inhale to collect momentum. When the metal shards around her begin to tremble, it's already too late. I shake my head as her very outline begins to blur.

Her form streaks skyward, birthed out of an explosion. From this angle, I can see the arena spectators in the background. A few of their heads snap up toward the open-aired ceiling to track the speedy movement, but most others are too slow and miss the jump entirely. By the time they catch up, the Warrior has already pivoted in mid-air. She almost appears to float before careening downward from that gut-wrenching height, bringing heaven with her behind a cocked fist.

I truly pity that Beast Master because if he sees this move coming, he certainly isn't acting like it. He may have made an impressive show of force moments ago, rearranging the arena floor, but it's the Warrior who turns it to dust in every direction once she craters him deep into the earth below. The air following her fist crackles across the arena seconds later as though her hands were formed of thunder. Immediately, Earth Weavers burrow into the ruined stone floor with hopes of recovering the Beast Master's broken form somewhere within.

The projection brings the Warrior into view now that her victory is complete, and as the arena cheers, I can't help but wonder what that must feel like. To have such perfect command over that much power that it bends to your will. To be an unquestioned victor.

I think of my own dormant power, the greatness supposedly available to me through my bond to the only Silver Fang seen in the jungle since my grandfather's time. A tie so unique, I've had to figure my way with the Nodus entirely on my own. I find it frustrating that this rare connection should have lent me the kind of strength that would humble doubters and enemies alike by now, yet here I am. Truly, I should already be what my father expects of me.

Perhaps the Discipline could also teach me how to do what that Warrior just did—surpass simply winning and losing for genuine greatness.

I catch Tygon staring at me once the recap of the fight is done. There's something in the way he looks at me in moments like this. As though this is the very second I'll awaken some mythical version of myself. Fortunately, his anticipation doesn't leave me with a sense of anxiety afterward. Because I know somewhere in his eyes, I am already great. My brother has the rare ability to look at me, and everyone else, with the promise of what we could be. It's just who he is deep down.

I abruptly clap my palms together. "Ty, we should get going, eh? Muma's not going to be happy if we don't help her cook after such a huge kill. Let's get home."

He nods in agreement, then something captures his attention.

"By the Spirits, speaking of a huge kill. Check out the hunting party coming through."

I crane my head around to watch a procession slice through the Hub. There, a group of six athletically built Beast Masters weaves toward the meat market, each carrying a whole deer slung across their shoulders. The reactions from the crowd are telling on their own. Every one of us can make out all six kills were made cleanly, with no bruising and minimal claw marks on the hide. These hunters did their work with admirable skill.

The party makes their way through the alley, and I get a clearer view of the wolf-bonded hunting pack from PanCanis clan. They walk in step, but at the helm, boasting wolf's fur woven into his garment, a curly-haired apprentice my age leads his siblings to the butchers. As pack lead, he holds his head high. His focus reads "I'm on a mission" to me. His body language reenforces this as he lowers his shoulder, carrying the deer in one arm to clear a trafficked chokepoint between us. I duck away from Tygon, a bit further into the crowd to avoid eye-contact as the wolf-bonded nears. But once the pack's lead is within arm's reach I see my chance.

A well-aimed twig beneath his fourth and fifth rib usually does the trick.

I poke the make-shift weapon out from amongst the passersby and hit my mark.

The boy may look the part of an epic hero with that deer slung over his shoulder, but all that goes out the door when a ticklish guffaw escapes his lips.

The wolf-bonded freezes in place, eyes wide at the sound he's just made. I take the moment to skulk away, using the crowd as cover.

Once I've made a bit of distance, I call over my shoulder. "So that's the famed war cry of the wolf, eh? No wonder you only howl at the moon when the village is already asleep."

Apparently, I didn't make my moves fast enough because five bodies box me in all at once. Musk, sweat, and wolf's fur—all trophies from the hunting grounds—cling thick to their skin. Clearly, this is what you get when you mess around with a clan that holds to an established pack structure. It's always a bit intimidating to see them move as one like this. I detect Tygon has quickly rejoined me. The pack's lead, however, takes his time to enter this impromptu huddle. The wolf-bonded squares up to look me dead in the eye.

"I don't think I heard you quite right through the crowd, catboy? Care to repeat yourself?" he says, flicking the tiger's fur on my shoulder.

We stare at each other for a long second, both of us trying to out-macho the other.

Neither of us wants to lose the silent battle, but slowly I wrinkle my nose at him.

Finally, I can't help but murmur. "Oh, Zahk, I hate to be the one to tell you, but this tough-guy act needs some work. Please return my goofball friend. I seem to have lost him?"

Zahk's composure goes out the door then and a huge grin tears across his face.

"Darn it, *Amio*," he says, calling me his 'valued friend'. "I overdid it again, the whole alpha wolf thing, just like you said, huh?"

I wave to our flank, the small huddle of siblings awaiting his command. Their confident postures alone, and the kills they carry, speak volumes to their prowess on the hunting grounds.

I wink at him. "Hey, I'm just trying to keep you humble, wolf pup. People 'round here might get the wrong impression that you're some kind of amazing hunter or something."

We both chuckle and Zahk gives a wordless signal to his party. His PanCanis kin— brothers, sisters, and wolf Nodus—all progress in the direction of the butchery. When they pass by Tygon behind me, each offers him a head nod of mutual respect.

Zahk pulls me into a quick embrace, and we clasp forearms, pounding our breasts while stomping the earth.

I thumb toward the deer limp across his shoulders. "Gorgeous kills you all found today. You'll put the rest of us to shame."

Before he can reply, a huntress behind him says. "I wonder who he's got to thank for that?"

That voice instantly melts me to my core, and I imagine I probably look the part of a total sap peering past Zahk to meet the playful gaze of his sister. Hoisting her own deer, larger than her older brother's, Lunis brushes past us with ease. I try thinking of something, literally anything spunky to say in the moment, but flirting is another underbaked skill in my arsenal. Then again, no one in all of Praedari could quite catch my tongue the way this one does.

The worst part? She knows it too. Probably has for a handful of seasons now.

Zahk looks between me and his sister with narrowed eyes and clears his throat.

"Hi, Lunis," I manage through limp lips.

Lunis shakes her head, then cuts her brother a look with hazel eyes, the shade of sky on an overcast night, then sidles up beside me. The hairs on my forearm prickle at how close she comes.

Since my heart and mind are tumbling over each other to see which will make the bigger fool of me, I never find a smooth opener for the girl. Graciously, Lunis doesn't seem to mind as she brushes wavy curls from her face.

"How'd the morning's hunt go, boys?" she says, looking to Tygon as well.

I purse my lips. "Uh, not too bad. Really, not too bad at all. In and out of the hunting grounds with the quickness. How 'bout yours? I'm sure the six of you pulled off something epic out there."

Lunis smirks at me. "Ah, yes, the perfect deflection, Faylen. Somehow you've managed to tell me absolutely nothing about your hunt." The girl brushes shoulders with me to tease. "Always a mystery with you?"

Judging by a wrinkle in Zahk's brow, it seems as though some invisible barrier has just been crossed and he drills an arm between us.

"Ahem. Well, that's *enough* of that. Lunis, cut the kid a break please? You spin him up like this every time but it's me who gets stuck hearing him go on about it for the next week and a half."

I gape at him in complete horror, but he keeps on talking…

"'Ooooh, Zahk, d-did you see? She touched my elbow! I'll never bathe again.'" He mimics me in an insultingly high voice. "'Oh, and we're totally gonna' get married too someday cause wolves and tigers get along like so easily.'"

Thanks, bro. Why not just go ahead and kill me right now? Seriously, if brown skin could manage a blush, I'd be twenty shades purple by now.

However, just one glance at Lunis eating this up with the village light's dancing in her eyes is enough to make the embarrassment well worth it. She truly is the sweetest flower. Before I have the chance to dote on her a little more, just like that, the tender moment is over. Lunis waves at me, adjusts the sizeable kill on her shoulder and turns to follow her siblings into the meat market.

Once she's gone, Zahk is left shaking his head at me.

"By the Blood, you're completely hopeless, man. How many jungle beasts have you stared down, yet we get barely two sensible words out of you for my sis? That huntress is gonna' eat you alive, you know."

I stare after her dreamily. "Yea, you're probably right. Maybe you could set us up or something. That way I can get on with my happily ever after already."

The kid knocks me in the shoulder so hard I almost topple over.

"Amio, did you forget I'm bound by literal bro code? Last I checked, you still need her older brother's seal of approval. I may have barely a hunting season on her, but Alpha earns the name for a reason. You won't be changing my mind anytime soon, catboy.

"

He jogs backward to catch up with his pack.

My heart flutters as high as the animal faces carved into the surrounding cliffs, but my head hangs low enough to clean dust off the alley road. He's right. Friend or no, what have I done lately to earn his, or anyone else's, approval? Tygon retakes my side following the rejection while I watch the pack round a corner at the end of the long alley to disappear fully from view.

"Come on over here, lover boy," he says with a consoling pat. He steers me back toward the PanTigris grove. "No huntress, least of all a wolf-bonded, is ever going to want a scrawny scrap who also can't cook. Least you can do is help your chances in that area, so let's not miss our dinner date with Muma."

He's right, of course, but that doesn't make me sulk any less while following him home.

6

Arduous Account

My stomach rumbles as I sit at the wooden table of our roomy den. My kin bustle around this space carved into the base of the tallest tree in the PanTigris grove. Music and laughter from the other tiger-bonded kin trickle into our kitchen and I contribute by strumming a tune while the final preparations are made. Muma Kura has made fine work of today's harvest from the hunting grounds. Adding to my musical strumming, the air is layered thick with a harmonious swoon thanks to her rich stew. Vegetable broth sets a steady melody with its fresh essence, while charred elk meat drives a spicy tempo. A few accents from Muma's secret spices swirl with all the rest and my mouth waters at the whole ensemble.

The rest of our kin bring cloths, bowls, and spoons to the table while Papa Jaole leads into a different song on his panpipe. After listening to a few beats for the rhythm, I follow along, plucking the strings on my balalaika. His heavy foot falls give timing to our pace. In this moment, it's hard to spot the rigid clan head in him at all. Right now, he's just Papa.

He closes his eyes, leaning back while the music takes him. Sometimes, on evenings just like this, Muma will even lend us her voice. Our huntress can sing a tune with as much grace as she can fell prey. As I strum along, Papa sways next to me in small circles. For once, his missing arm is no longer a handicap as he only needs a single hand on the palm-sized instrument to lull sweet notes into our den.

I look down and examine the strings of my polished ashen-oak balalaika.

Papa pauses and asks, "Do I need to restring a few of those for you?"

"Oh. Uh, no," I murmur, unsure of exactly when he'll expect me to Recite the Chase. "I still have that hook-ring you got me a year ago, so I'm good, thanks."

Papa nods and leans back again to continue the tune, stress lines nearly gone from his worn face. It seems like forever ago since I've seen his brow absent its usual tension. Watching him like this in rare form reminds me of stories Tygon used to tell me. Back from a time just before I can remember, when Papa was a crafter prior to his election to Clan Head. Tygon recalls Papa even owned his own stand then, whittling away all sorts of wooden goods when our huntress wasn't calling him into the jungle as a chaser.

My hands move gracefully up and down the neck of the carved balalaika. With each shift, my palm slides over a small groove in the ashen oak. The notch is an engraving I've worn down over a decade spent playing the small instrument. The letters, "Jao" and "T" for Tigris, can still be read though if I look closely enough.

By far, this balalaika is my favorite possession. Its rounded edges are inlaid with tiny sculpted faces of jungle animals on one side and rare spring blossoms on the other. Papa Jaole even managed to place notches into the back side of the neck. Over the years as I helped Muma with hunts, he would fix a piece of bone from the most difficult kills into it.

I pause to look at the collection of ivory bits laid alongside one another in the back of the instrument. My thumb passes over the empty holes nearest the body where I've yet to complete the collection. I thought I'd have filled all these slots seasons ago, but frankly, Papa's criteria for trophies has become much steeper after I hit Elevation. For instance, simply helping in the chase was no longer sufficient. I needed to be the one to land the decisive blow.

Muma Kura calls us all to the table as she carries a large pot. I hang the balalaika on its wall hook. I suppose it'll have to be in the next Hunter Trials that I take my shot at another Gargan-Elk and add its antlers to my collection.

Muma asks who would like to deliver the prayer and though it's an open request, all eyes eventually creep over to our kin's little kitten, Kleo.

She looks up at us, eyes full of pure innocence.

"What?" she says.

Muma Kura barely holds back a smirk while Papa wears no expression.

His question is direct. "Little one, have you been practicing anything in your Nestling classes that you'd care to share with us tonight?"

It takes a second, but finally the dots connect in Kleo's mind, and she bolts to her feet. Her tiny hands clasp together as tightly as they can, held a breath away from her lips.

"Spirits of old, take this humblest prayer,

We thank you for home, for love that we share,

Though aurem has parted to feed us this day,

We remember the land, we shall always repay."

When she's finished the prayer, Kleo releases her hands upward as though she'll physically push the words to the skies. Then, one at a time, we each dip our bowls into the pot and wipe the edges with cloth. All hands wait folded until Muma takes her first spoonful.

After she nods to herself satisfied at the taste, Papa begins the dinner conversation, "Children, what new adventures did you pursue today?"

Little Kleo blurts out something unintelligible through a mouthful of bread before Tygon shoots her a wide-eyed look of warning. She gulps the bite down and buries her head in her chest. Her curls fold over her face, masking a timid peek around the table.

Perhaps trying to save our youngest kin any extra scrutiny, Tygon takes lead by tackling the probing question. He goes on for a little while, carefully avoiding all talk of the hunt by detailing the fight we'd seen on the tapestries above the village Hub instead.

As he reaches the end of the retelling, I place a tender hand atop Kleo's still bowed head and attempt to coax her from her shell. I stroke her bushel of curls until she finally looks my way.

I nod to her then and motion up toward the dinner table.

"Kitten, I believe you had something you were trying to tell us?"

Kleo's eyes sparkle at the gentle lead in and she lifts her face. "Oh, yes, yes I do! Today, our Nestling teacher said I showed the calmest aurem while keeping the most still out of the whole class! She said that means if I can keep calm on my Nodus Quest, like I do in meditation, that I'll stand out to my future bonded super easy!"

Muma beams a huge smile at her daughter and claps enthusiastically, "Ah, my baby. That is so good to hear. Keeping a calm sense of mind is rare, especially at your age. But it's a calm aurem that invites our Nodus to trust us during that first meeting in the Wilds. It works the same way as every beast is drawn to the banks of still, rather than rushing water. Keep it up and you'll be a young tigress leading the hunt in no time at all."

My end of the bench begins to teeter as Kleo swings her legs giddily beneath the table.

Papa rests his spoon and wipes the corners of his lips. He tilts forward to look eagerly between Tygon and me then clears his throat. "As I remember, Faylen, we get to hear you Recite the Chase tonight, mm? Do tell us how you cut down this delicious meal!"

He sits back already satisfied, patting his stomach as a compliment to our efforts. His pockmarked hand cups Muma's own as he thanks her for matronage over the hunt. She returns the warmth with a quick peck on his scarred cheek.

Tygon looks over at me to offer some encouragement, then I begin.

"Well, kin, today we pursued no ordinary beast. We met Muma and Headmaster Lujan early before Solint awoke. Then we cut toward the plains and, obeying the First Law of the Jungle, we faced off against a formidable Gargan-Elk."

Kleo tilts her head to the side and then her eyes gape wide. "By the First, that means you were going for something with a fightin' chance. Does that mean you really tried for a big one?" She stretches her arms above her head. "With antlers taller than Praedari gates? No way…you're foolin'." She squints in suspicion.

Tygon pipes up, "Nope, just look at this kiddo." He pulls the elk's wooly hide from a tanning strap, stretching it out until it spans him entirely. My brother even stands atop a chair to further emphasize the hide's fullness and still half of the skin rests on the floor.

Kleo is out of her chair instantly, crouching to the floor to take the hide between her fingers.

An arm's length above where the elk's tail used to be, Kleo runs her hand over a tear. "Is this where you got to make the kill mark, Fay?"

Those of us who have hunted before all chuckle. "No, kitten." I put a hand over hers to trace the incision. "You'll wind up a scrawny huntress trying to kill anything by aiming a finishing blow at its tail."

Tygon kneels beside our little scamp. "But that doesn't mean you shouldn't disable a beast anywhere you can." He looks up at me then. "You really should've seen him today, Sis. Right here is where your brother Faylen leapt on top of the buck's back and sliced his tendons clean through." He demonstrates the hit by touching her across the hip bone.

She only has eyes for me in this moment, looking completely in awe and cooing like a young owlet seeing the twin moons for the first time. I try to memorize the look for later, these precious few seconds where she somehow sees a hero in me in the same way I do Tygon. Spirits help me, what I wouldn't give to always earn this look from the girl.

"Wow, Faylen," she finally says in a whispered tone. "You must be really strong then. Just like Grandpa Ravir."

At this, my eyes immediately dart to my father's, then to the floor. I catch myself too late and hope I didn't give away any hint to my inner shame. We return to our seats and continue the meal.

It's obvious Papa is fully invested in the tale now as he leans in my direction, grinning large and clapping me on the shoulder. Meanwhile, my palms have begun to sweat. I know what's coming.

"So, Son, tell us. How did you force the bull to fall? It must've been amazing to watch you in action considering you had the skill to nip him the way you did on first contact. All the way up the flank? That's no easy task."

A long sigh escapes my lips, but I play it off by blowing on my stew. Just as I realize I'm hesitating for far too long, I meet Muma's gaze. She nods subtly, reminding me of her earlier words.

Only one way to separate myself from failure—I have to own it.

I plant my spoon in the stew with sudden conviction before standing up. I snatch up the corner of my hunter's vest to reveal the injury beneath. My side is shaded deep black, trimmed by mottled purple edges. Dark red blotches are sprinkled throughout the heavy bruising. Kleo drops her spoon to the floor and Papa gasps.

"Papa, I got kicked by that elk full-on today." I pause, clenching my jaw slightly. "The bull heard me step in a puddle on my approach, but I still went for his back anyway. Once I was up there on the flank, I tried to make it better by landing two strikes, instead of just the initial one. I was so close to landing it too and had the second one struck, I woulda' crippled him then and there. A short climb to the shoulders. A double-fisted strike at the base of the neck. The beast wouldn't have made it ten strides. But instead, he caught me and left me in the dust."

The man's face has gone completely statuesque, somehow more withering than the familiar look of disappointment I'm used to. I begin to stammer, to try and add even the smallest bit of context to soften the news. But these are the Hunter Trials we're talking about. Mine and Tygon's passageway into adulthood. There is no softening this.

I pinch my fingers in front of my face. "That close, Papa. I was that close to claiming total victory and making good the rest."

The table goes quiet as I tuck my vest back into my garments, sitting down onto the bench.

After a minute, Papa eventually breaks the silence—his voice is surprisingly calm. I don't understand how.

"If you live each day by how close you were to accomplishing feats, those margins will build up, until one day, you wake up and see just how far off you are from what could've been done with your life."

I stare straight ahead, trying not to let my face betray my emotions.

Papa continues undeterred yet keeps shockingly cool-headed. "So then, boy, how did the elk die? I'd hope that with two capable Elevation apprentices working together to ascend into maturity, we aren't here enjoying the fruits of a hunt carried by our huntress."

Tygon opens his mouth to try and offer me a way out, but I shake my head at him. My mistakes, not his. I will not be spoken for. Not this time.

"Magnus was tracking me in the wings of our kill plan. He slaughtered the elk to rescue me from his stampede. Snapped the bull's neck in a single bite." My voice fades as hardly more than a whisper.

Muma looks down to her hands and closes her eyes in a long blink. She looks so tired.

Papa knits his lips together firmly.

"So. Ensure I understand correctly. As a young man, hoping he'd graduate into adulthood, into his Pre-Mastery a few short weeks from now…not only did the prey down *you* but your Nodus did all the work? Do you think the Silver Fang will feed you and care for your future family too?" His voice rises to a sharp note. "Have you not been trained to take in the whole environment around you? A puddle? Even Half-Points can watch their steps!"

My knuckles are white nobs by the time my composure slips. "You think I—"

I stumble over my words, fuming.

"You think I could spot a puddle in all that grass? I could barely—"

Curses. Why now of all times do I have to be a fumbling mess? A second later all I've held back comes bubbling to the surface.

"—I did every. Single. Thing. All that I could to focus in on that hit and it was a good one too! But I guess, just like every other bit of good I might do, it's not enough, is it?" My fists drive into the hard wood, but already I regret the outburst before my bowl stops rattling.

Papa's eyes flash frigid warning as a dangerous green hue flickers through them. A low but unmistakable growl resonates from his throat.

I'm quick to lower my head, staring straight into my lap.

Occasionally, once in a handful of seasons, you hear of a fight breaking out between parents and their offspring. The stories always end with the same warning. Our parents' union is what keeps the den safe. It stands together against all threats within this jungle. Rebellious children are no exception. Far better to be harsh to one child so the younger siblings won't repeat the same mistake after seeing what happens to the perpetrator.

Muma grabs Papa's hand, giving it gentle strokes. She murmurs something in his ear about progress still to be made and me having a genuine heart. After a seeming eternity, Papa's glare leaves the side of my face. I brave a look with the hope the brown hue of his eyes has returned.

Muma offers me an out. "Faylen told me on the way home that he gets it. He understands why his Mastery is so important for the clan…for the village altogether."

I take the hint and raise my head with due caution. "Yes, Papa, I haven't forgotten."

Papa stands up slowly and moves behind me. He places his heavy hand on my shoulder and squeezes it in a familiar pattern. "Faylen look at me."

I'm terrified to look, because in truth, I can't take any more scolding. Emotionally, I've been rubbed raw and have hit my limit for the day. All the same, I rally, turning to him. I can't help but take in every deep pock mark and twisting scar across his hardened face.

Incredibly, his voice is softer than expected. Less the Clan Head, more the bedside storyteller. "Son, there is so much riding on you and your brother. Times aren't the way they were when I was your age." He pauses, looking up into the high ceiling of our den.

"We need young Beast Masters like you to go beyond Praedari's gates and be this Bloodline's ambassadors to the world. To venture to places like our capital where you might even graduate the Discipline of Peace. The time of war between nations is in the past, but we only keep it that way by having our voices heard beyond this village. Strong ones like you must speak in our stead—that's the way of tomorrow—the only way the Council will ever hear us. Our village relies on you for representation, for a future." Papa holds my chin. "It's a challenge I wouldn't give if I hadn't the faith you'd be strong enough to meet it."

Papa returns to his seat with a loud exhale.

He looks between my brother and me with steady focus. "You will be the leaders we could never be. In a world that keeps shifting further from the one my generation grew up in. And frankly, that's a good thing I think. Spirits know the old ways left fractures across Spheire. Violent fractures that tear and hunger." His hand slides over his chest, stopping where his missing arm used to be.

"This old stump knows the tale, boys. A gift to me from one of Petrichor's Fire Weavers. I was barely a few years older than you, Tygon. Back then, times weren't as…civil as we got 'em today. We had our share of problems with our neighbors to the North."

He grinds his teeth. "While my bicep was being roasted to the marrow, it didn't matter that that Weaver's father and mine were probably allies some twenty years before when war consumed the world. All he cared about were the claws and fangs in front of him that he was foolishly convinced were meant for him."

I'm transfixed by his words. Papa rarely goes into details about how he got his scars, only the meaning behind them. And he certainly never mentions a time where we were more than just neighbors to the other Bloodlines. Allies? When? During the Great

Bloodline War? I want to press him, but none of the older villagers ever breathe a word about that. This is the most I've ever heard in one sitting.

Muma touches her hand to her lips. "The only ones who are going to be able to safeguard the peace we now enjoy, and that the Council has nurtured, are young fighters like yourselves. For the sake of Animas, we send the strong ones. The ones with good hearts. We need them to steer our people into tomorrow."

Tygon and I bow our heads with understanding. We've heard before what our abilities mean to the future of Praedari.

There's a lingering moment of silence and Papa looks like he's wrestling with whether or not to say something more. Eventually he knocks a finger on the wooden table.

"Boys, your Headmaster briefed us Clan Heads today on the passes and fails in your Elevation class. I didn't think anything of it since per her report, you two were counted among the passes."

Tygon and I look at each other incredulously.

Papa strokes graying hair under his chin, "I see now, that your hunt was a success based off a technicality. The elk did fall, and your huntress didn't participate." He pauses, then glances at me. "It just so happens your Nodus did the closing work. But still, you managed to keep the killing blow within your overall partnership."

Papa shakes his head grimly. "I'm not too happy about it, but this will allow you both to participate in the Hunter Trials' second and final stage."

There are so many emotions going through my head right now, but pure joy isn't exactly one of them. Rumor has it the second stage of the Hunter Trials, a rare occurrence in itself, is always much harder than the first. Awesome, I managed to scrape together a win today on a technicality. But how will I fare on a round two where the difficulty is ramped up?

At last, looking to lighten the mood, Papa brings his panpipe from his robe and thumbs toward my balalaika. The scolding is over for now. "Muma, what do you think about some singin' and dancin' over a few bowls of dessert?"

Muma Kura erupts in a sudden but impressively long high note and Kleo stands up, breaking into the animated imitation of partner dancers she's seen in the People's Hall.

Tygon thumps me in the shoulder with his fist and points his finger up, tracing a circle in the air. It's the signal we made up at a younger age for "let's go out tonight." After the kin is off to sleep, we'll run off to our secret hangout.

I uncover a tray of silken honey rolls I bought earlier when shopping for stew vegetables. After grabbing fresh leaflets, I pour a glass of milk. Kleo tiptoes away from the music and hands me my balalaika from its hook. She sneaks a gentle hand to my side, but when I wince, she jerks her hand back. Her eyes go wide with worry. Before I can reassure her, she rummages through a pouch dangling from her belt. She brings out a handful of lullaby buds and holds them out to me above her head. She plays the part of a tiny healer well and has always worn that medicinal pouch every day since I sowed it from a cotton hare's pelt for her birthday.

"Promise you'll put those lullaby buds in your milk and drink it all?" she says, her lips trembling.

I hug her, holding an armful of her bountiful curls to my waist. I feel a damp trickle as her tiny shoulders shake gently. Poor little thing. I've watched her be the first one to run to another Nestling's side with bandages if they get so much as a scratch. I can only imagine how her little empathetic heart broke when she first saw my bruises. My own eyes begin to water with a sense of compassion. I wonder from whom she learned all this absurd sensitivity…

I look down at her plush swirls and chuckle to myself. Kneeling down, I wipe the tears from her cheeks.

"Kitten, I'll drink every drop, okay? Doc's orders, I promise. Nice n' slow too."

She lets me pick her up as we join the others in a ring of floor pillows and blankets.

Papa and Muma didn't have to say it, but there's another reason I need to get my mastery under control. I put Kleo down next to the hearth and begin to strum away on the balalaika.

I've got loved ones who may need protecting someday and this kin needs more than just one capable son to help look over it.

The Hunter Trials continue. This is the second chance I cannot miss.

7

First Nodus

My kin spends the rest of the evening performing little acts and jigs, all to the tunes of Papa and me. Eventually, full stomachs and high spirits get the better of us, and we each climb up to our individual nooks carved into the walls of the den. Typically, the canopy at the top of our tree is our usual sleeping spot. It's strung up with comfy hammocks, and I keep mine expertly stuffed with plush down plus fallen leaves. But a downpour began shortly after the meal, so Muma made the call for us to sleep down here instead. It's certainly cozy below in the den, but if I had to pick, I'd choose snoozing outdoors every time. It's the countless little things that make up the night sky that still my mind after a day like today—the breeze, the distant glimmers, the all-consuming vastness so much greater than the sum of my problems.

Still, the nooks do offer a certain sense of security once one is tucked away beneath a blanket. Carved high into the den walls, my own niche feels like a hideout only I know. Throughout the seasons, I've made a decent collection of fur paddings, filling every inch of the nook with some sort of cushion. Papa has even taught me enough woodworking to carve a tiny ledge for candles, a book, and a cup of milk. As I curl up in a nook corner, hoping at least for a short nap, I wish I could bring the night's sounds directly into this little cubby. Nothing would be more calming than the jungle's serenade romancing the moons above.

I toss and turn in the soft plumes, nearly forgetting to listen for three quick snaps—the signal from Tygon that it's time to go. What I do hear is the rain trickling down the bark outside. Its ghostly whisper calls to me like hushed words between lovers before a first kiss.

By the Blood, what would I know about kissing? And why am I always this melodramatic before drifting to sleep?

There's no fighting it now, though. In the privacy of the dark, my thoughts drift to Lunis. My mind revisits our meeting in the Village Hub earlier today. It paints a picture of her smiling face and, like magic, the worries and fears from my botched chase are suddenly impossible to find. I imagine her and I riding atop a Qirin to visit some of my favorite hideouts amongst the carpeted greenery below. We could skip along the banks of the Birth River that halves this jungle territory, hand in hand until I dip her low and bring her in for that long-awaited kiss...

Three snaps at the tip of my nose snatch away the image of Lunis and I stare at Tygon staring back at me. His square head has never looked more like an Elevation punching bag.

"Hello, snooze goose. Wake up already!" Tygon badgers in a low tone, hanging one armed from the ladder to my nook. "We move out now, brotya. Time to pounce."

I crawl down the wall after him.

Brotya. A grin creeps across my lips. We haven't used that so regularly, not since we were middle-aged boys. A brotherly adventure like tonight's must have recalled the old nickname between us. A heartwarming feeling takes root in my chest for all the trouble we used to dig up back then.

"You, Ty know I can actually pronounce 'brother' just fine now. We could probably pass that nickname down to Kleo if we wanted to."

Tygon hushes the thought as we sneak out the den entrance. "No shot. That's always been our thing. Plus, I used to enjoy hearing you stumble on your words as a Nestling. I could see the effort you were putting in. Makes the nickname extra endearing all this time later. Don'cha think?"

I roll my eyes at his over-sentimentality.

We leave the quiet grove toward the outskirts of the village. A stone tiger's head watches us depart, outlined by the backdrop of night sky. The usually crowded pathways are dark and empty now. In the village Hub, ours are the only feet to pitter-patter across the wet cobblestone. I raise my hands to the downpour, inviting the warm rain to wash over me. Tygon sways back and forth in the shower like a wind-caught stem carrying dandelion seeds. For a long moment, we let the sprinkling steal both years and expectations away from us.

We dance on slick stones.

We hum long-forgotten tunes.

We laugh in ankle-deep puddles like children who don't yet know what the world will soon demand of them.

Outside Praedari's gates, we Embrace into our wild transformations only enough to gain night vision. Through our glowing eyes, weaving vines and creeping insects all come into focus. The twin moons too have stroked new colors across this woodland canvas.

Beginning our journey in the same way young Nestlings learn to do, we pause to steady our aurem before leaping through the trees. Better this than to accidentally attract some flying night predator that, despite our enhanced senses, we'd likely fail to sense swooping from so far above.

"Brotya, let's move!" I call, dashing away first to leave Tygon in my dust. I add some extra incentive once I've claimed a small lead. "Last one to our spot buys breakfast in the morning!"

Tygon goes suspiciously quiet before I detect a sharp uptick in aurem behind me.

"Hmm, well in that case…" he murmurs.

Bashtol, that peacock upped his Embrace that quickly? I scramble for the treetops, but he sails clean overtop of me. I'm not kidding when I say time freezes too as he spins past me. He turns just enough to give me a swindler's crooked smirk, then vaults off a branch and through the canopy ahead of us.

Where he would normally cut through smoothly, this time he leaves behind a generous clump of leaves to pelt my face.

I narrow glowing eyes at him.

"Oh, two can play that game!" I shout after him, but all I hear is cackling as the distance grows between us.

Finally, Tygon echoes back through the trees. "Hey, Fay? I'll take two bags of juniper berries with my buttered toast in the morning, please. Thaaaanks!"

A new tingle streaks through my hands and spine, a sure tell of a rapid muscular Embrace. My sharpened senses go fuzzy as I trade awareness for raw power.

Tygon continues his jest. "Actually, scratch that. I forget you're probably broke from buying Lunis more gifts that you're too chicken to actually hand over. Not too late to open a shop with all that inventory you keep hidden beneath your pillow."

My mouth hangs open a little at the fact that he knows about my stash. Plus he's having a grand ole' time pulling the string out of my satchel...

I wet my lips like a starved cat that's corned a mouse. Something hungry inside me *wants* him to keep talking a big game.

I push every inch of my swollen frame into the ground.

When I fire into the treetops, the launch is different from Tygon's and even Muma Kura's.

My soles leave a small crater behind me. I let the sudden outburst carry me three times the height of the canopies below. Every bit of the jungle is a blurry carpet beneath my feet. I am practically flying.

Unfortunately, without my senses attuned, I can't exactly make out Tygon or much else below. This is one of the deeper muscular Embraces I've ever taken on, proving my solo sessions out in the woods haven't been entirely useless. Several times a week, I sneak away to an old picnic spot that our kin used to frequent. It's a spot beneath towering waterfalls and I use the slippery terrain to practice whole jumps up and down the rapids.

The speed I've gained from my exercises is truly amazing, but I don't always see the ground rushing back up to meet me after I've jumped.

Thankfully, that isn't an issue this time. Tygon and I picked our hideout years ago near the Birth River. Where the river spans its widest breadth, it feeds the largest tree known to these jungles, the Seed Tree. Considering I recognize my surroundings, I know the famous tree to be a half mile away. More than enough distance for me to land safely somewhere in the river's depths.

I feel gravity gently tug me toward the jungle below. Where Tygon has probably made a good ten or so leaps to cover this distance, I just did it in one. As I'd hoped, I'm beginning to comet straight for the Birth River. The light rain has kept up throughout our little race and now beads of water evaporate on my cheeks as swift air whizzes past my face. At least the river can't soak me much more than I already am.

I crash into the river's depths, the cool surroundings immediately churning into a storm of bubbling air around me. My locs whiplash around my head as I recoil on the riverbed. I push a second crater into the ground that launches me toward the surface, my vision even more of a blurry mess until I return to the night air and wipe the water away.

Nearly back on land, I clamber to the river's edge and look up in time to see Tygon beating feet a hundred mets behind me. The farthest outstretched branches of the Seed Tree arc overhead and I can make out the massive trunk. Tygon speeds up as he realizes I'm not a washed-up piece of driftwood on the shore. Meanwhile, I scramble over the river rocks, losing my footing a couple times. *I am so close!*

"Ah! I can make it!" I howl.

Tygon's hefty footsteps are suddenly horse hooves behind me. Tomorrow's breakfast is on the line—who cares that he's the fastest runner in our Elevation class. I power into my strides, but my legs protest as if I'd been hiking the whole day beforehand. Waterfall exercises or no, my body is not used to the level of amp I just experienced. Plus, I'm usually resting between sets up and down the rapids.

But I ignore my body's pleas. No time for fatigue now.

I strain my arm forward, all but hobbling the final mets to the great tree. I don't need heightened senses to feel Tygon's breath on my back. I inhale deep and let loose a crazed outcry.

Only one more final surge, that's all I need!

Before true exhaustion racks me, I feel a rough texture in the palms of my hands. My legs instantly turn to jam, and I fold over into the dirt, laughing senselessly between heavy breaths. I look over to see Tygon touch the tree in second place.

He collapses beside me, tossing up fallen leaves around us. Rain drops bounce off our heaving chests and we chuckle until we're both hoarse.

"Okay Shiny Stripes," my brother wheezes, tugging at gray fur woven into my wrist wrappings. "Where was that on our hunt for Headmaster Lujan this morning, eh? No wonder Papa leans into you so much. There are fully matured Beast Masters back at the village who couldn't pull off the stunt you just did."

I catch my breath and sit up to ease the last traces of Embrace from my shaky body.

"Yeah, but think about what that really means. Every day I wake up, I've got these massive footfalls to fill because of all that supposed potential. I'm my own worst enemy!" I blow air noisily between my lips.

After a few moments, we recover enough to stand up and dab off in the rain.

"All right, how 'bout we find our usual few stones and head up to the spot?" I ask.

"Sounds good, let's do it."

Tygon and I have been collecting glowing rocks from these riverbanks since our first youthful nights in the Seed Tree. The pale stones are a common find along the river, we just need to head to where the river swells. There, the water sloshes up onto the shore, painting portions of the riverside in luminescence due to deposits of shining blue rocks. Since the tides cause the light, we named the stones "lightides." Down the river, I spot a patch of them, and we jog away. I palm the brightest one I can find and wipe it clean on my vest. Once back at the Seed Tree, we make the climb to our hideout with ropes made of hanging vines.

Our secret perch sits about halfway to the top—a converging point of several thick branches that overlook the rest of the jungle. A rusty chisel awaits us hanging from a nail and I grab it, gently carving a couple small grooves into the thick bark. Then, we finesse our lightides into the wood. Having dried off since being picked up at the river, the rocks have already lost their glow, but as I step back to see our spiraling collection, Tygon takes a capsule of water from his belt and douses the mosaic.

"There, now that's more like it. What do ya' say, Fay? Think we're up to four hundred by now?"

I nod and catch the blue spiraling pattern reflecting in his dark brown eyes.

We sit back, reclining on leather mats we've nailed into the branch. If I can truly call any place in all the world my favorite, this would easily win. I close my eyes, soaking in the silence. The rain is little more than a sprinkle now, but distant lightning has taken to the clouds in an orchestrated dance. Streaks flicker through the sky, spotlighting distant lands near the horizon.

I point to where the crackling strikes the earth. "You think that's over in Petrichor?"

"Oh, yeah, that straight shot north from here? Most definitely."

I watch, almost as if anticipating something spectacular to happen across the border. "I wonder then if there's any Storm Chasers out tonight."

Tygon chuckles to himself. "If Papa's stories are to believed, then yes. Every time there's a storm, one of that Bloodline's lunatics is running around hoping to get struck."

Thunder rumbles behind distant clouds.

Tygon rustles beside me, propping his head up with his hand. "So, back to that leap you made on the way here. Lemme guess, you had no clue where you were landing?"

I bite my lip for a second. "Kinda. I knew I was within range of the river. Beyond that, no. Same as every other time. There's so much power surging through me when I Embrace. I can handle parts of it, but when I try piecing it all together…" I wave my hand aimlessly through the air.

Tygon keeps quiet as I rest my palms in my lap, thumbing the handle of my short blade.

"The worst part is I know what it's going to take to get there. Our Gift is all about the perfect marrying of senses and strength, but I don't know how to force that union. I do know I have to control them both equally."

My brother plays with a strand of worn leather and I can tell he's now trying to problem solve. It's his default as the older brother.

"Maybe you'll catch up on that part once you've hit Pre-Mastery?" He offers.

I flick the button strap of my hunting knife. "Nah, I hear the Pre-Mastery mentors are more severe than our Headmasters now. If I take too long to figure this out, they'll sniff a fake in their ranks in a heartbeat. And truthfully, I hate to say it, but that's if I get past the second stage of this year's Trials in the first place."

Tygon clicks his tongue. "You're right. I still can't believe we managed to pass on a technicality. Who knows what they'll throw at us going forward."

I exhale in frustration and shift to look at him, "Brotya…how did I manage to get this far behind you? You should've seen yourself this morning. You were everything I wish I was." I pause for a long time. "I really wish I'd have gotten to meet Grandpa Ravir. Or even inherit a journal…heck even a single letter from him. Anything to have helped me with this whole Silver Fang thing."

Tygon wraps his massive palm around the back of my neck. "Ah cheer up, Shiny Stripes. If you scream your nightly prayers loud enough, maybe they'll make it up to him in Everrealm and he'll send you down a carrier pigeon!"

I roll my eyes but can't help but grin.

Tygon looks out over the trees. "In all seriousness, I do wish you had some kind of answers. Magnus is so rare, the only one of his kind in more than half a century. I don't envy the spot you're in."

We sit quietly as the Birth River roars far beneath us. I lay back, letting its rushing course filter through my soul. A sigh escapes me and a new thought wave bubbles up to the surface.

"Someday, I'm going to do all the things I'm too afraid to do right now."

"What do you mean?"

"Well"—I hold up three fingers while emotion clenches tight my throat—"first off, I'm going to stop being so afraid all the time. I'm sick of it." I clap my hands together firmly. "Second, I'm going to do more with myself. That way I can *be* of help rather than being the one who always needs it."

Tygon nods in agreement.

"And third, while I'm at it, I'm going to be more truthful in my feelings. In fact, I think I'll even bring Lunis to this very spot someday and spill everything I've ever thought about her."

Tygon raises his eyebrows at me. He keeps silent though, leaving room for me to press on.

"I tell you what, once I'm down this path, I'm never going back. I'm so *done* with this mediocre chapter of my life. Like enough with this bashtol version of me!" I pound my fist into my chest and hold it there.

The perch goes quiet as thunder rumbles to fill the empty space.

Tygon strokes the clumps of tiger fur lining his wrist wrappings. He looks down at the stripes and then out over the jungle. I see deep reflections in those brown eyes.

"Faylen, did I ever tell you about the first Nodus I tried to bond with?"

I mentally step down from my soapbox and recall for a second. "No. Never. I knew Cil wasn't your first, but beyond that I never wanted to pry."

He sits back down and brings out an extra lightide from his pocket. He rolls the dark stone around in his fingers.

"When I went on my first Nodus Quest, I thought it'd be me who'd find the Silver Fang. I had no clue what to look for, but hearing Papa's stories, I hoped he was somehow still out there. I was too young to know just how rare the tiger truly is. Anyway, I went out, armed only with a hunch. Thought that if I went opposite of the normal hunting routes, maybe I'd find him." He raises his eyebrows in a quick sarcastic motion, flicking my Nodus fur. "Turns out it was never to be since he randomly walked up on you one day to choose you."

He presses on, "So, there I went, south—toward the border. Never found the silver cat of course, but what I did find was a den some sixty miles out from Indom. I heard these little mews calling from this den and when I knelt inside, there was the tiniest little cub soaked in blood."

I close my eyes, imagining the scene.

"The Bloodline of the Body is no joke. Indom's got those brawlers…those hulking Warriors we saw in the Discipline fight today versus the Primitas. It's also got these killers, Blade Dancers they call 'em. Apparently, the latter become masters of death partly by practicing while poaching all across Southern Animas."

I can't help but stew in anger. There is no honor in that. There is no virtue in creating some lucrative business or even sport out of death and suffering. There's a reason our people abide by the First. A kill must have its fighting chance. Even in trapping, so long as there isn't suffering involved, there exists an element of fair play. You have to outwit the beast you're attempting to trap. But sending a sniper's arrow through an animal's eye socket from a mile away? What chance would any creature have at that, man or beast?

Tygon tugs at his wrist wrappings so tight I fear he'll lose circulation, "The cub I found was alone, it's ma cut down in the entrance of her den, a good portion of her skin was missing but the rest was untouched. When I looked inside, I saw multiple nest dugouts too, so I knew the mom had several kits, but the only one that hadn't been taken was this little one."

"When I tried to move the welp, he cried out in pain. That's when I saw he wasn't just covered in his mother's blood. He was leaking out too."

I've only seen my brother cry in a few instances and it has caught me off guard every time. It's the same now as I watch tears pool onto his open palms.

"I-I tried to bond with him. Thought that somehow; by doing that, I could sustain his tiny heartbeat. Just long enough to run back to the village, y'know? Of course, I had no clue that the bonding process itself doesn't have any special healing properties," he says.

"Faylen, h-his faint little pulse it was *so* weak. I tried…oh Spirits I tried everything, even stilling my aurem to match his so somehow he'd know it was going to be okay. But it was just too, too low." His jaw locks from the painful memory. I can barely watch him like this, those boulder-like shoulders quaking with regret.

"Before I knew it, his aurem disappeared completely. That was when—I was just—he was just…" Tygon wipes angrily at his eyes. "Gone! Dead and alone in that lonely den. A cold, tiny lump of a thing that didn't get his fair shot at life."

His voice cuts to a whisper and he looks at me with haunted eyes. He stabs an accusatory finger into his chest repeatedly. "All I could think of in that moment was, what if I could've been better? What if I had actually known what I was doing and sensed him sooner from a greater distance? Could I have made my way to him and he lived? Could I have made any difference?"

My heart washes over with sympathy as Tygon's expression morphs from a pit of sorrow into a sudden emboldened ascent. How can he possibly look this much like Papa?

"You know what I learned that day? I learned that if you beat yourself up about what you can't do, you will never catch sight of what you can do. A hunting season later, I went on another quest and I found a different cub. I named him Cil and from then on, I swore to be the best I can be. Nothing else gets to die ever again because of my uselessness."

Tygon draws me into a deep hug, "So please, Faylen. Don't give up. Out of everyone, Magnus chose you. I truly believe that's got to count for something. We're all backing you. Even Papa…"

I sniffle a choked response. "I know, but I'm still afraid of all these—"

He shushes me, making the hug all the more secure. "You'll find your way in time. I promise. So long as you keep looking for it. Just remember. Papa's harsh, but do you know in comparison, he's never been as hard on me??"

I shake my head, and he cradles my face in calloused hands. "That's because he knows you're the son who'll be able to do the kind of stuff the rest of us can't even dream of."

He pats my cheek. "Half-mile leaps are just the start."

We sink back into our mats and Tygon unties our blankets from the tree. After a deep breath, he settles in, allowing me space to think.

"What do ya' say, Fay? Should we get some rest? It's been a long day." He smiles at me, offering my blanket.

"All right, brotya. Thank you for sharing your story. I really didn't know. It makes me want to get past all this and really, you know, become something."

"You'd better. Kleo looks up to you more than she does to any of the rest of us. Plus, after these Trials are done, I'm definitely going to the Discipline of Peace. If I'm gone and you don't join soon after, that makes you oldest in the den?" My jaw drops slightly at the thought. Just how far ahead does he think? Tygon chuckles at my expression and shimmies into the mat. In a few moments, I hear the deep hum of contented snoring. I look out across the shadowy landscape. Lightning arcs down amidst the rain, piercing the earth tens of miles away.

I lean back and watch droplets fall past our perch. A slew of thoughts streams into my mind all at once, though fatigue has begun to slow them. I allow myself a new fantasy: envisioning what it would be like if I were the one to walk the halls of the Discipline of Peace in Sanctum. Somewhere within that vision, I feel a new calling. Praedari might've taught me to be a great hunter, but after seeing the epic fights in the Hub today, I can't help but wonder if perhaps there, I might learn to become something more.

A champion.

Still, before I get caught up in something so far-fetched as studying in lands far from Praedari, there's something more immediate I need to deal with. The second stage of the Hunter Trials—a chance I thought had vanished the moment that elk put me in the dust.

Facing this challenge, I wish I knew what it was like to control power instead of it controlling me. I wish I could have that feeling...that feeling of being in full command.

My eyes flutter as sleep rushes to find me. Shards of lightning cut through the black, prancing through the clouds to end their performance somewhere over the flatlands. Petrichor, our northern neighbor, lights up past the border, summoning each strike to touch her rolling hills and knolls like a starved lover. The raindrops whisper sweet good nights to me and darkness wraps me in warmth. The last spark I see is a rippling column crackling over the horizon. I'm too tired to fully register lightning doesn't work that way, though.

Odd. In all my years, I've never seen it shoot back *upward* into the clouds.

8

Elevation

Two days following our rendezvous beneath the Seed Tree, Tygon and I find an enveloped parchment at our front door. The envelope has the Elevation Class stamp and a note from Headmaster Lujan falls out once we open it. Apparently, all apprentices have completed their hunts for part one of the Trials. Those who successfully passed have been instructed to report back to the Elevation dojo tomorrow for an impromptu briefing where we'll learn what to expect in the final event.

    I rise early the next morning, earlier than the rest of my kin. I quickly throw on my hunting vest and cinch down my fur-lined wrist wrappings. Considering we slept in the open-aired canopy, I'm thankful the branches do not give away my escape as I dart through them toward the den below. I don't intend to be here long, just a quick snack before I head off for warm-up exercises at the dojo.

    After a loud noise from the kitchen, I realize I won't get the den to myself this morning.

    I hear another noisy clang and peek through the den's curtains to see Kleo has beat me here. "Eh, kitten, what are you doing up this early? You've got quite a bit before your Nestling class, ya' know."

    My little sister startles at the sound of my voice, her sea of curls a total mess.

"Ssssh, you're so loud! You're gonna' get me in trouble. I wanted to try doing my hair to look nice for class today."

I mosey over to her makeshift workstation, the den's meal table turned staging area for a braiding experiment gone wrong. It's hard to keep a straight face seeing her at the epicenter of such a mess. "Gotcha, well would it be a big deal if I gave you a hand?"

The small girl squints suspiciously, eying my hunter's get-up. "Aren't you trying to get out to the dojo?"

I crook an eyebrow at her. "What, and you think those dusty punching bags will grow legs and run off before I get there? Come on, let's knock these braids out and you can give me the downlow on *who* you're trying to impress."

Kleo inhales sharply and tries to protest the claim, but I've already flanked her and begun to part her curls into individual sections with a comb. She waits patiently as my fingers work. Repeatedly, I extract three small strands and intertwine the outer most strands over the middle one. Soon, her bountiful curls have transformed into a crown of intricate twists. I'm surprised how quickly we made time until Kleo comments why.

"Thank you, brother, for fixing me up like this. And it's not just today, either. You've done this so many times for me—ever since I could remember! Now look how good you are now."

I peek outside the den window to see dawn has yet to birth its fullness over the ever-watchful stone beasts. Good. Still have time to make it to the dojo for a short session.

I bring Kleo in for a tight hug and land a kiss on her newly fashioned styling.

Wishing me luck on the day, Kleo whispers a prayer into her palm then locks it in a fist. She circles the closed fist around her heart and pounds once. It's mornings like these that I know I'll miss when I must grow up and leave this den.

A bit later, I arrive at the Elevation dojo to find I am the only one on the grounds at this hour. A fledgling Solint peeks timidly over the horizon and casts shadows around this open-air space. The dojo is large enough for fifty students comfortably with plenty of room for practice strikes and acrobatics without swinging an accidental fist into another's face. The floor, made of packed earth, is shaded a dull red hue, partially from time worn clay stomped over by countless apprentices throughout the generations. The other reason for the color is no doubt, the equally countless practice duels. Even in a setting dedicated to learning such as this, our bouts are no stranger to blood.

Fortunately, when I come here alone, I don't have to see the faces of those who've donated my blood to these grounds. I can ignore the number of times I've been dragged unconscious to the sidelines or clawed to permanent scarring because I refused to kneel. This time lets me focus on something I can always control: my form which is the foundation of every great hunt.

A contraption is set up in a far corner where the earth is much less worked. It's a simple device that most apprentices have forgotten outside myself. Looking similar to a massive tent post planted into the earth, the central beam supports angled metal beams on either side. The triangular metalwork holds a large, rusted hook at the center. Nearby, an equally neglected punching bag filled with compacted rock lies in the overgrown grass. This dojo boasts many a training tool—from flying targets to battle dummies with spring works at their core—but no one ever uses this classic leather-bound sack besides me. I sling the heavy bag onto the hook and step back.

"Hello ole' bruiser. Another round, eh?" I whisper.

Bruiser has never been one for words, but I swear some its stitching twists into a sinister grin.

The next thirty minutes of Solint's rise, I devote only to conditioning my shins. Over and over, I slam them in alternating sets. At first, the pain is enough to make me want to give up. But I push past this world into a whole new realm. One I can only enter once I've called my pain by its true name:

A Lie.

Pain itself is not a tangible part of this world or any other. It cannot be held or stuffed into a box. No, pain is a violent reaction of the mind. Same as fear. Same as anxiety. Luckily, the mind can be dulled and even restrained. Just ask the drunkard's bottle.

I may not have yet mastered control over fear and anxiety, but through practice, I am so close to forgetting pain. It helps when I Embrace a bit to numb the senses in favor of strength. Next, fear will be my conquest. After all, what is fear but the mind's escape route away from pain? To me, anxiety is unease when forced to face those fears. By conquering one, I weaken the others' hold on me; it is all an interconnected web.

Ten minutes more and Solint has fully risen. Its light reveals the harsh work I've done to myself. While my shins were strong enough to resist breaking skin across the practice bag's coarse surface, the rapid-fire assault in the final repetitions has made my hands worst for wear. I Embraced a hint more, gaining a slight covering of muscle to continue giving the sack a real beating. Now, my knuckles trickle a steady stream as I face-off for the last exercise.

Despite the fatigue of the morning's routine, I drink in a bit more of my Embrace. This sharpens me into something more lethal than before. Bones like small cutlasses slip from beneath my fingertips as I stalk 'round the bag eyeing five or six hardly noticeable seams across its texture. These small grooves and only these will be my targets. A clean swipe through them and I'll be rewarded by catching no additional fabric. Conversely, a sloppy strike at full strength would mean yanking a knuckle or two from the joint.

I kick the bag forward and it flies upward. At the height of its swing, I reel back and ready my stance.

The first two practiced swipes follow one after the other seamlessly.

Swipes three and four are clean kills as I dodge around the bag with a backswing.

At the fifth, I backflip to deliver an overhead hit to the bag's highest point.

I land knowing this next one is the last and most important. I need to drive all claw points directly through the center and counter the bag's momentum all at once. The same sort of thrust I should've delivered to the Gargan-Elk. The killing blow that could easily push a non-hunter's heart through the backside of his ribcage. Done right, once I've hit my mark, the whole contraption will come to an abrupt standstill.

The world seems to slow as I watch the bulging leather swing and spin. I debate amping my senses to gain accuracy in the hope I won't miss. But the trade-off would only rob me of the strength needed to make the death strike.

I stick with raw power and trust my practice.

As the bag hurtles within arm's reach, I drive into my lower half, twisting to drive my arm forward. I imagine I must look like a wild version of the Warrior I saw fighting in the Hub the other day. I tuck my chin to my chest, putting all I can into this moment.

With barely any distance left, I register footsteps behind me. I'm immediately made aware of how much light is in the sky overhead. Bashtol, I lost the time. Is class really beginning so soon?

I feel these distractions tugging me off center. My eyes beg me to look away at who might be watching. The tawny leather blurs in front of me and suddenly I'm taken back to the hunting grounds, waiting to fall victim to the elk's hooves all over again.

Somewhere within, however, routine anchors me. I have crafted this motion and embodied it whole. This win is already mine to claim, I only need bring it to heel.

I cut through the noise with claws dipped in midnight. Five tips plunge past fabric and stone until I'm shoulder deep inside the leather.

I'm shocked to find something soft and velvety this far into its core. When I rip my elbow back through the thick hide, shreds of a fake heart hang from my claws. I smirk to myself. Odd…I wonder for how many Elevation classes this thing has been hidden here, waiting for someone to strike true.

I hear the approaching footsteps again, but don't have time to look up before slow applause fills the empty dojo.

"Bravo, bravo. Looks like you *can* tear something to shreds so long as it can't hit back. What an inspiration. Come, tell us, how'd you pull it off?"

Bashtol.

That condescending tone soon reveals its source in the form of a massive PanUrsa boy standing at the center of the dojo. Borust, an oversized monster of a teenager stands there amused, grinning over at his much smaller cousin, Kip. The two idiots cajole one another as though commenting on my practice session is the comedy routine of the season.

I wipe the strands of fabric off my forearm and look around to see if anyone else is in the dojo. Spotting no one, I quickly release my Embrace to return to normal. This is one fight I've tried avoiding growing up, but one my bullies have managed to rehearse all the same. On multiple occasions, where the Wilds have been blessed with ample rainfall, I've found myself at the bottom of a muddy ditch by their ambush. Once, after I'd exhausted my energy on an unsuccessful track and chase, these cousins found me. They ripped my hunting vest away, stomped my gut into a misshapen mess and tossed me limp and convulsing into a growth of thistle-fleece. Took me half a day to slowly crawl my way out of the forest cactus and I wear the marks across my back to prove it.

Borust seems to be reminiscing on one of these horrors as he hunkers toward me. His bare feet plod the worked clay and pause over a spot darker red than the rest. His cousin Kip moves in, matching pace with him, the two fanning out to encircle me. Borust traces my glance down at the blotchy earth and looks to me with a crooked grin.

"Ah, you're remembering some of the good times we've had too, eh? Right here dueling, I had you ready to lose half your guts out the bottom of your scrawny rear. Shame Lujan went and stopped that match. I'm sure I coulda' gotten some fine huntress to come give me the world after a show like that. I really was an alpha that day."

Kip darts around my backside and I lose him for a moment beyond my periphery.

His voice is more coarse than broken glass. "Well, look on the bright side, 'cus. Neither Lujan or that soldier brother of his are here to keep you from finishin' the job this time." The younger cousin spits at my feet. "Honestly, Cat, you'd probably have been dead long time ago if it weren't for other people always stepping in to save you."

Borust produces some over-the-top version of laughter from his dry, split lips and rolls his shoulders.

"Ya? Well, the way I heard it from my Mum, he'd have been dead this very *week* if it weren't for Tygon. Couldn't even handle his proving hunt on his own."

That's one thing I always hated about Borust. For having nothing in that empty skull of his, somehow he manages to always be in the know. Probably the benefit of his Muma being the minutes keeper of the village leaders. To make things worst, his blasted Pops is the village crier too. Their's makes the *perfect* pairing of a woman who hears everything and a father who spouts the same, it's no wonder their son turned out to be such an obnoxious piece of work.

When the boys have stepped within twice arm's reach, I realize I have a decision to make. Perhaps I've avoided this fated fight long enough. At least, that's my prevailing thought until a low, cavernous growl cuts off our conversation.

"And here I thought I was clear. You'll not touch him."

I almost feel a swell of hope at the welcome interruption. Almost.

Unfortunately, it's no savior who has joined our company.

The voice continues. "The day he falls, it won't be at your hands. You've had your shot many times over."

If I weren't frozen by the pure ice in the adolescent's voice, I'd probably have time to relish the comical stiffness in Borust's and Kip's backs. The pair immediately backs away and looks around to source the voice.

Yet I already know where to find him.

Behind us, high in the trees, it's not the glowing brown eyes of a PanUrsa that oversee the dojo with a vulture's watch. No.

Those eyes hold the familial green glare of one from my own clan.

Beneath the speaker's perch, a large section of uneven stones makes up the dojo wall. Our guest descends to them without a trace of lost footing. He then pounces from the shadows to the dirt below with hands in pockets, a cloud of dust masking him for long enough to shroud all but those glowing eyes for a moment longer. Finally, the newcomer approaches.

The blood-red tiger's fur sewn across his hunched shoulders is the first thing I see as he stalks directly for me. Then, I see him give barely more than a tilt of his head and a scarred crimson tiger with only one eye vaults effortlessly over the dojo wall to fall in step behind him. The pair stop inches from me on either side, close enough for me to detect the scent of raw, uncooked blood fresh from a kill on their breath.

"Hello, Faylen. It's good to see you made it through the hunt."

I don't know why I look to Borust and Kip first before swallowing hard and lowering my gaze downward. There, beneath my eyeline I meet those green eyes that should, in any other world, designate this boy as my ally.

But Dourn has never given care for ties he could not twist into some sort of advantage. Ever since my father was elected Clan Head over his father several seasons back, he has viewed us on unequal footing. There's been nothing between us for him to find advantage in. So instead, he's found contentment reminding me my supposed superiority is only by proxy of my father's position.

Dourn looks me up and down in the long, drawn-out way I imagine a lover might to a long-lost flame. It'd be almost flattering if he wasn't stroking a blood speckled claw tip back and forth across his chin stubble as he did it. Spotting something on my fur wrappings, he gives a slight frown and tracks my path back toward the disheveled corner where the punching bag lies broken. He squints his eyes, inspecting the damage, then cuts a look back to me.

"Hmm, getting stronger, I see. Very good…you'll keep it up, yes?"

The hairs on the back of my neck raise as he saunters past me, patting me almost friend-like on the shoulder as he goes.

"I'll need you at your best on the day I choose to ruin you. Pride of the PanTigris and chosen of the Silver Fang? Your den curries move favor than it deserves—high time we had ourselves a new golden heir."

He needs say nothing more as he steps off, his thugs scampering away to stay beside their keeper.

Solint now shines bright in the Elevation dojo. Having arrived here so early, I made it to my kneeling spot well before the others. The tense morning has wracked my nerves though. Even as Zahk and his wolf-bonded enter the grounds, I barely look up to see his frantic waving. Eventually, Headmaster Lujan steps out from her quarters, her living space hidden by a curtain within the dojo's central building. She looks over the rows of students then holds out her hands. The clearing goes quiet as we wait for her to begin.

"Good morning, Elevation Oak. I'm proud that each of you made it to this glorious day! You've done what some in your age group couldn't. An impressive feat considering you were mere children just a week ago and now are halfway to joining us in adulthood," she says.

My tongue feels a little dry at the way she casually phrased that. Are we really supposed to be ready for adult life so soon? How did childhood disappear so quickly? I look around at everyone else who are seemingly unphased. Makes me wonder if the sentiment is just a me thing.

The Headmaster looks across our assembly. "Tomorrow you'll set off on the final portion of the Hunter Trials. Even I don't know all the details but expect their duration to last the better part of a week. Some of you may still have prep to do so I will release you shortly."

"I'd suggest you use the time wisely to stock-up. Gather any last supplies you might need, but don't overdo it," she says with a wink. "These are the Hunter Trials, not Pack Mule Try-Outs."

The class chuckles in response.

A voice hisses behind me. "Heh, maybe there's still time to sign up for a future without hunting. Everyone here knows you didn't earn your spot like the rest of us." Borust's pitch sharpens to a squeaky whine. "Oh no, I lost control again. Oh gee, my Nodus did all the hard work for me. I'll be old and gray and *still* in Elevation!" The jeer is followed by high fives, no doubt to Kip.

I exhale and keep my head perfectly still. I hope the tension in my shoulders doesn't give my anger away. Those bearish grunts only ever get worse with a reaction. I've learned that the hard way over the seasons.

The Headmaster continues to discuss the significance of tomorrow's event, emphasizing that while most of us will go on to Pre-Mastery, we should note, not everyone is expected to pass this far more difficult trial.

A low burp rumbles behind me, followed by a foul breeze that clams up the side of my face. More chuckles from the blockheads behind me.

"Here's an idea, I bet the trials in Tauris Village will be way easier than dealing with a hunter's challenges. All they do up there is eat grass and make cow pies. Sounds perfect for someone like you who can't hunt or Embrace for crap. If you go, I'll cheer you on myself." Borust's voice hangs wet and thick in my ear.

A few seasons ago, this whole morning's nonsense would have sent me careening over the edge. Somewhere along the way though, I had to find ways to cope. Being so far behind in Nodus control when compared to my peers, I haven't had much ground to stand on when getting made fun of. I used to allow Tygon to help me, but at a certain point, having him fight this particular battle wasn't going to cut it.

My fists are clenched and pinned to my lap. I freeze in place, breathing slowly, but maintaining flawless posture for the Headmaster. While my knuckles go white, I'm reminding me of the only time I planted them into Borust's drooping face. I was a lot skinnier back then and ended up hardly bruising his jaw. After the blow, I ran as fast as my little legs could carry me, speed being a PanTigris' advantage over a PanUrsa. Still, he didn't forget. If I thought getting dumped in muddy ditches was bad, what they did to me by the time I let my guard down at a watering hole was much worse. Suffice it to say, I've drowned before. Don't know why I never told Muma and Papa but I should have. I didn't want them fighting that battle for me either even if it was the right thing to do. I suppose at the end of the day, I did and always have blamed myself first. Given my Nodus, I figure if I was able to Embrace the way I'm supposed to, I probably could've ended this circus act a long time ago. I could've sent all four of the PanUrsa lowbrows Borust had with him that day running. I wouldn't have been force-fed dirt and animal scat between dunks beneath the waters, all under Dourn's watchful eye from high up in the trees 'til I passed out.

I relax my tense shoulders, the mockery behind me having faded for now as our Headmaster walks through the rows. The lion fur weaved into her cloak moves in unison with the commanding swagger of her steps.

"I expect great things from each of you. I believe in each of you. Together, we've done something special here in Elevation Oak. I know mine will be the top class over our sister Elevation classes, but only if you stick to the lessons. You've worked harder than Fir and Willow's apprentices and I think that will show itself this year. Watch out for one another if the challenge calls for that." She meets each student's eye with a reassuring look.

The huntress moves back to the front of the dojo and pivots toward her kneeling class.

"Let us Elevate for Praedari!" she shouts with a sharp voice.

"Let us rise!" We call back in unison, our echoes filling the clearing as we end with a collection of animalistic roars.

Our Elevation ranks are dismissed, and I spot Tygon break away from the first row to chat with a couple of his friends. I scan the group for Zahk and see him gearing up to leave with his pack. He waves me over before turning to continue his conversation with a nearby student. I only take a few steps in his direction before getting shoulder checked hard by Borust.

Despite being knocked back a few steps, I whip around

coming face to face with him.

The brute seems amused, his wispy haired beard as poorly maintained as his patchy eyebrows. Musty breath blows in my face, the smell of tar beans assaults my nose and waters my eyes. Borust spits a thick globule out on the ground, splattering my foot. His cousin chuckles a few steps behind us, but Borust continues staring me down while replacing the tar beans with a fresh supply from his pocket.

I spot Tygon running over past the boy's shoulders, but I shake my head briefly. He stands there, gritting his teeth with visible fury. I know what he's thinking. He wants to help, but we've been over this. There are certain moments I must be ready to stand firm alone. I refuse to back down, and I already heard Dourn's command this morning. They aren't allowed to hurt me. This small moment of not backing down is something I need for me. To face him after so long.

My fight, not Tygon's.

I crack my neck, tilting my head while glaring first at Borust, then Kip who's stepped closer. I reserve a special flavor of contempt for Dourn who's still seated on a rock, watching the moment unfold. I can see a leashed violence in him, brewing in his eyes. For whatever his cronies have done to me, I fear Borust and Kip haven't been severe enough for his tastes.

A new voice joins us. "Leave him alone. I'm not afraid to put something into that empty space where your brains oughta' be."

The browbeaters smirk at the threat and I see their aurem flicker slightly, signaling a desire to Embrace and brawl. I'm so tense that I flinch when an unexpected arm hooks around my shoulder. I look over to see Zahk leaning against me. He gives me a wink, then inclines his head toward the aggressors, an amber hue glinting in his eyes. He and I stand in unison, ready to up our individual Embraces as necessary.

From my other side, I smell an aroma of ash-wood leaves. I know Lunis is there before I even see her because I'd recognize that scent anywhere. She hand sews all her shirts with ashen oak fibers. When she's next to me, I can feel the righteous anger.

"Need me to repeat my brother's warning with a picture book? Move, Borust, or be moved."

She shakes her arms loose before snapping into a huntress dueling stance to prove her point. Her eyes are consumed by the exact hue of sap lit by flame. Her glare penetrates into her newly acquired targets and the corners of her lips turn up in a grin.

"Your move boys," Lunis says. "Heck, I could use the exercise before tomorrow's Second Trial. Which of you lightweights wants to be warm up?"

I see them trying to do the math on being called 'lightweights' despite the size difference between PanUrsa and PanCanis. I hear the beginnings of a misogynist slur birthing from Borust's lips, but Kip elbows him nervously to cut him off. It isn't worth finding out whether their size or her skills would win out in a duel. Every Beast Master learned the chase from a fully matured Huntress. As the Wilds would have it, a hunter will usually always command a higher degree of overall brute strength depending on the clan. But our more graceful opposites have always held the best techniques and physique for gutting a foe. Disrespecting a Huntress, even one in training, could have quick and morbid consequences.

Borust stammers, then recollects himself. "Big talk for someone defending a dirt-stain like him. You realize he didn't earn his place here like the rest of us? Even now, you're standing in the way of an honest fight between men. Faylen has no right to be here, and I'll be a fangless fool before he's counted as my equal."

Zahk flicks a middle finger in front of the blockhead's face. "Well here's something you can count instead." He nods toward me. "My boy here is amply ready to handle his own business, just you wait and see. Til then, shove off."

This nearly sends Borust over the edge, but instantly Zahk whistles a sharp note. All around the dojo, those members of his clan who are also in Elevation snap focus our way. At this, Kip abandons his cousin, practically falling over himself backpedaling at the pack's unspoken blood promise.

With his cousin in full retreat Borust shifts nervously too, eventually turning to run.

Then it's only Dourn poised at his rock. Even beneath the pack's watch, he only has eyes for me. He seems completely unconcerned while gently scratching behind his red tiger's tattered ear.

Lunis steps forward in his direction. "What, can't you see? Your goons all turned tail. How 'bout you join them?"

Dourn glances at her for a moment before settling eerie focus back onto me.

"It's a little sad, Faylen. Here they've spent so much time around the worst of our clan, that they think they've an understanding of what a tiger can truly do." He rises from his seat and steps off toward the dojo exit pausing to smirk directly at me. "Just know when the time comes, I'm not beneath killing dogs to get to you."

With the trio gone at last, Lunis releases her Embrace, blowing on her claws like hot coals while they retract.

Zahk pulls me away and I thank them for the support. I didn't want anyone to step in, but at least I stood my ground.

Lunis looks me over. "Always happy to look out for a friend, Stripes. Just take care of yourself, okay? We're not always going to be around." She crouches to collect her things, stroking a curl behind her ear. I stare a bit too long and she takes notice. With a cocked eyebrow, she holds eye contact. Then she rises, nods with a knowing smile, and jogs for her pack.

I have a mental flashback to Tygon teasing me about all the gifts I've bought for her and never given.

I should buy her another one.

Zahk squares in front of my face, squinting at me. "Ahem, Mr. Not Yet Approved. I can hear your romantic gears turning. Bad news, they're rusted over from a lack of use."

Busted.

Fortunately, since the young wolf wears a smile constantly, he's pretty bad at the whole intimidation routine when it comes to me. Takes him only a second to break out in laughter.

"I'm just steppin' on your tail, Stripes. But really, if you need help with those guys in the future, just holler. They'll be back, I'm sure—'specially that little creep."

Wow, what a perfect title for Dourn.

I nod thanks and look to change subject. "Hey, you and the pack headed out for Trials prep? If not, I was thinking we could visit that watering hole you showed us up north to polish our fishing lessons. Never know what skills might be useful in this second trial. I need to practice that trick you taught me."

Zahk digs in his pocket then picks up a thick stick from the ground.

"No, I won't be able to join this time." He unspools a string and winds it around the newly acquired stick. "Just remember, you need something like this to use as a rod. Not that insignificant twig you snapped on our last trip."

"Oh, shove off," I laugh.

He tosses me a pouch that clangs metallic when I catch it.

"Pack these with your other prep stuff. Finest fishing hooks this side of the jungle. Had 'em smithed just this morning."

His pack calls him over and we clasp forearms for our usual handshake. I look for Tygon and find him chatting with a friend. He finishes his conversation, and we leave the dojo.

My brother doesn't wait to bring up the stand-off.

"Fay, why didn't you let me jump in there to help you? Three on one? How exactly is that fair?"

I shove my hands deep into my pockets. "I don't want to ask for help, Ty. Zahk and Lunis kinda' just came in and surprised me. I let them be good friends." I pause to collect my thoughts. "You know I've been thinking about what happens when I'm rescued. Like how Magnus saved me from that elk."

Tygon nods, as we head for Praedari's Northern Gate.

"I didn't gain a lick of experience from that. All I did was stand there and be rescued," I say. "I want to be the type who stands tall, regardless of if the odds aren't in my favor. Back there, sticking my chest out when Borust wanted to see me shrivel? I took something from that." I pound my breast.

We reach the Northern Gate and Tygon pulls a bone whistle from the post. He calls a Qirin and I put some coins into the pouch. He grabs the lushalow berry rod.

"Fair enough. I don't like it, but I suppose your decisions aren't up to me. Just be careful."

I thumbs up agreement.

"Anyway, moving on, Headmaster Lujan was right. We've got prep to do." He looks down at his bare feet. "I really need new soles for my combat lugs. Figured we could get some armor hide scales to do the trick? Those hoof-bonded Beast Masters up north always sell the sturdiest footwear."

A Qirin call echoes into the clearing as a flock of much smaller birds erupts from distant treetops.

I watch as the great beast bursts through the clouds. "So long as we don't tee off another giant Elk while we're up there, I'm game. It's been a good while since I've been that so near to the Petrichor border. Tauris Village it is!"

9

TAURIS

Despite the usual grumbling from my brother, we ride via Qirin onto the long dirt road entering Tauris Village. A farm girl tending a feeding station, hefts a large basket full of fruit on her shoulders, and the feathered creature delights at every juicy morsel. We thank the farm hand and drop some change into her tip jar.

I tap to catch my brother's attention, waving my hand over our surroundings. "Ty, this place is magical. It's so easy to forget how unique each of the Beast Master villages really are."

Tygon looks as mystified as I do. "Don't get me wrong, I love all the trees surrounding Praedari, but it's somethin' to see all this grass in one place. This valley looks like it could spread all the way to the sea!"

That's not even the half of it. The village sits at the bottom of a bowl-shaped meadow protected by circling layers of grass-covered cliffs. Taurins call this area the "Ascending Fields" because of the land's layout. We are surrounded in all directions by what looks like a giant set of stairs carved into a mountainous basin. Various crops grow atop each distinct level—tuberous vegetables and rice patties here near the bottom, fibrous stalks in the middle, and the bowl's lip is lined by hundreds of thousands of fruit trees.

We stand at the lowest level where the main road stretches

for miles toward the village entrance. On either side of us, lines of dirt come together to form a comb-like pattern. A brawny farmer drives a tri-plow with his Nodus, a heavy Iron-Crown bull. The creature moves slowly but with palpable strength as it pulls a yoke attached to three plows. The Iron-Crown's horns arc, forming six points in total at the end of the thick bones. Four points angle menacingly front for offense, the other two curve over its spine to protect the back.

The farmer tips his sweat rag to us, and we bow respectfully since we're walking through his land. Praedari and Tauris may lead hugely different lifestyles, but creatures like his Nodus have always been safe. Huntresses teach us to observe the aurem of a potential kill before the chase begins. Bonded animals give off a distinct hue that we can recognize. As such, despite our many differences, Taurins never have to worry about their grazers falling to any hunter or our bonded.

I raise my eyebrows at Tygon as we enter a monumental stone archway marking the Tauris Southern Gate.

I whistle at the scale of the construction. "Brotya, you know, after these Trials are done, imagine we somehow make it to the Discipline. Do you realize we'll be facing Masters just like that farmer? Like the people who built this place? I mean did you see the horns on that guy? We've got claws n' fangs—"

"Plus speed and good looks..." Tygon machos a hero's pose.

I roll my eyes. "Right, so claws, fangs, speed and imagination...in our arsenal. How does any of that get past an Iron-Crown's defenses?"

Tygon echoes, "Imagination," a few times, throwing my words back at me. Then he considers for a moment. "To be honest, let's say we did end up making it. I doubt facing others in our Bloodline would be my biggest worry. It's the rest who we haven't had experience against who'd be trouble."

"Hmm. Really?"

Tygon nibbles his lip. "Think about it. You ever think about what the other Bloodlines out there can do when we see them up on the projector? Rumors say the strongest Warriors in Indom are supposedly as durable if not more so than the Masters in this here farming village. I can't remember the last time those punch-happy Warriors weren't on top of the graduation rankings."

I study him for a moment, wondering if his usual confidence is going shaky in the face of the Trials. Because realistically, of the two of us, he'll probably perform well enough on them to earn some clan leader's recommendation for the Discipline.

We navigate through the marketplace quickly due to its convenient layout. Unlike our village Hub which is set in layers of rings, like a tree, Tauris's shopping district is set in long rows, exactly like the fields they grow crops in. Crisp aromas hang in the air—plump fruits, rich vegetables, and freshly winnowed grains. The shopkeepers all wear a certain look of earnestness and every one of them stands proudly over their crops. We stick to the outer rows where the non-farming vendors heckle us with friendly persistence.

One of them steps closer to prod. "Oh, son, looky here, so big 'n strong. Probably could use a fresh coil of rope, am I right?"

"Ah leave 'em alone, you scoundrel." Another merchant moves in for the pitch. "Sade's the name. What you young hunters really need are these one-of-a-kind straw hats." The skinny man shimmies the accessory onto his head with one hand while shoving a sample in my chest with the other.

He smiles with a wink. "You see? Just like that, instant-shade! That's why I call 'em 'Sade's Insta-shade Straw Hats'. Only available here!"

Tygon gives me the wide-eyed older brother look. *Don't you give in to this smooth talker!*

Agh! This is another thing that always makes me uncomfortable…I hate turning people down. I bolt from the stand, not even having the decency to say, "No thank you." I know how stupid I must look awkwardly shuffling away to avoid further confrontation.

We finally reach the sole shop and wake up an older man. He kicks his feet down and we hand him our worn combat lugs. He gives each pair a onceover, then looks down his chipped spectacles at us.

"Pardon me, but I've got ta' ask you Hunters something first before I service ya's. You won't be using these here lugs to make any trouble 'round the village here, yes? You know good 'n well that our farm animals, ev'ry one, are strictly off-limits. Been that way for centuries and my shop won't help if ya' plan to shake that up."

Tygon bows his head impressively low. "Elder-buck, we wouldn't think of it. Just want the best shoes in all of Animas for our tests to ascend into adulthood. Maybe even snag a Discipline seat afterward. We'd be forever grateful."

The craftsman huffs, waving Tygon to stand back up. He flicks a stalk of wheat back and forth over his missing teeth. "Well, you're in luck. We just groomed fresh scales off a herd of armorhides not too far from here. Their Masters did us a real solid." He opens a stone chest. "They been dryin' in the heat box for a week now. Reliably tough yet completely flexible, exactly what y'all are lookin' for."

We offer the old man eager grins as he bends over his workbench.

"I been getting a whole host a' business this past week. Younguns' just like you boys came down from Petrichor in droves, some justa' hour ago! Imagine clogs from my little ole' shop being worn all over the North?" He shakes his head with an old-timer's hearty chuckle. "Guess that's the power a little 'world peace' can have. Gotta thank the Council for good business, I suppose."

The old man maneuvers his set of needles like a knife through butter, looping fibers into leather as cracked and worn as his steady hands. When he's done, he seals his work with a thin layer of tar-bean extract. Apparently, mixing the gooey substance with clay results in a pliable mortar that won't wear down for quite a while. Realizing that this pungent paste is made from the same stuff Borust basically grazes on is enough to turn my stomach though.

We try on our newly remade shoes before packing them away and I give the shopkeeper a handful of colorful stones. We thank him for his help and no sooner have we turned to leave are the man's rickety legs kicked back up on his worktable. I smirk seeing him lower one of Sade's Insta-shade hats over his face for a snooze.

Since we've got a few hours before dinner, Tygon and I decide to grab a quick snack before strolling past our fishing spot on the outskirts of Tauris.

We find wooden stools at a nearby snack stand and I look up to see a shining metal tapestry streaming new images, identical to Praedari's. With a full mouth I grunt to snatch Tygon's attention. It's an odd thing because unlike the typical capital city or Discipline of Peace images, something is on display we don't often see—real-time developments of another nation.

"Is that—is that Indom?" I ask. The background in the hazy pictures is full of sand and dunes, a landscape I'm positive is exclusive to the Warrior's desert-filled lands.

"Has to be," Tygon says. "According to our map classes, only place drier than that in all of Sphere is the Wastelands on the other side of the continent. Nothing lives out there."

The Bloodline of the Body's desert landscape is soon replaced by a pale woman with short blonde hair and bulging forehead veins. Her bangs are outlined in a sleek black trim and her shoulders look like sharp daggers beneath her collared shirt and jacket. For some reason, she is positively furious before even saying a word.

I point at the image. "Hey, Brotya, look, it's one of those…eh. What did you call them last time?"

"Suits."

"Right, right, sooots." I chuckle at the funny word. People in Sanctum dress so weird, honest. That get up she has on is somehow uglier than Reptilix garb but at least theirs is probably comfortable…to them.

I slurp the remaining drops of syrup from my snack. "You know"—I say between licks—."Muma and Papa are right, the outer world does need people like us in it."

"Oh? Why's that?"

I motion toward the woman who is now shouting about something. "Non-hunters will be stuck in some horrible fashion choices if us PanTigris boys don't teach 'em a thing or two. No fashion beats tiger stripes."

Tygon smirks. "And here I thought I was the one with all our imagination."

I wipe the sticky goodness from my cheeks and elbow him.

While Tygon finishes his snack, the images shift to focus on a small desert town. Thick smoke rises above the buildings as the citizens huddle in masses on its outskirts. The bird's eye view stops abruptly once charred bodies are pulled from the collapsing buildings.

"Tygon, look! I knew it! Those rumors from our elders were true. Mysterious fires have been cropping up all over the place outside of Animas. Thank the Spirits they haven't cropped up here."

Tygon eyes the chaos silently. "Feel bad for those townspeople though. Bet they didn't even see it coming."

"I know. But if it keeps happening, the Council will find out who's responsible. You heard Pops, the Council's kept us safe since even he was young."

Suit lady's puckered face is back on the tapestry and her bony shoulders tremble in righteous fury. When she slams her fist onto her table, I can't help but pay attention.

"Our leaders will never hear nor bend to the demands of murderers. These fires are blatant acts of aggression that will be met with the true power of Sanctum! Until every one of you so-called Libertas Heirs is dead!" She froths at us so intensely that I feel phantom spittle on my cheek. After a moment, she composes herself, returning strands of wild hair to her perfect bangs. Then she sneers, directing a knife-hand toward an unseen audience.

"Listen to me. You Libertas Heirs will never get whatever it is you're trying for. Our world is finally at sacred peace and you cowards will only lose your lives by killing the innocent. My advice? Surrender to the Council while you still have a chance. Despite your crimes, they can still be merciful but only to those who yield. Spheire doesn't need to re-open its violent chapters." She pauses, nodding justly to herself.

Suit lady continues, "The five nations that make up this world will never give in. No Bloodline will be swayed when the Council has kept us safe for fifty-five years. Think about that. Their power is unmatched, and they will root you out. Sooner or later, they will expose you. They will uncover your sins."

Tygon shifts next to me uncomfortably as if he knows what to expect next.

"And if you even *think* there will be another outcome in all this madness... Well, perhaps your comrades will educate you otherwise."

The projection shifts to something I haven't seen before. A vast prison courtyard in Sanctum where a line of twenty man-size capsules made of thick glass are bolted into a wall. Prisoners stand in each of the pods, shackled to the bottom. Just as the images sweep out enough to reveal the entire line-up, water begins to fill the tanks simultaneously. The prisoners inside wear matching bandanas as they yell and pound on the glass, yet no sound escapes the thick barriers. The men and women are each wrapped in a gray flag, bound to their chests with rigid rope. The flag is hard to make out, but I see an embroidered black emblem—a scale being crushed underfoot by an angel holding an owl. The stitching reads 'Libertas Heirs'. Every prisoner struggles in their bonds as the water slowly fills the small capsules.

Tygon looks away from the projector and pulls me in the direction of the North Tauris gate.

"Come on man, let's go. I've been seeing these pop up in the last couple weeks. Trust me, you don't wanna' see where it goes."

When Muma was sick with the crud and Papa couldn't hunt on his own, we would secure our dinner by Zahk showing us fishing holes just like this. Sometimes the ponds he picks out have been a little out of the way, but with him you never know. His favorite spots are usually to the north of Praedari. Says the fish are more gullible for some reason. He's even taught us a few tricks to catch a bite without a rod—just a bit of string and a hook.

We arrive at a lake set within the first layer of the Ascended Fields. It's a beautiful patch, full of dense trees, almost like a miniature Praedari set into the valley floor. We enter the woods and Embrace to buff our leg muscles.

I scale a canopy hanging over the lake and turn to Tygon with twinkling eyes. "Bigger splash doesn't have to clean the kitchen tonight?"

"Brotya, you're on. I've got you by at least thirty pounds."

I roll my eyes. "Ahem, I think you're forgetting something, scrub. It's not the size of your butt that wins, it's the technique!"

I jump from the perch, falling fast toward the water below. I pull myself into a tight ball before hitting the surface. However, as I submerge, all the hair on my arms stands on edge and I feel a sharp warning pang creep over the back of my neck. There's a tinge of electricity to the air bubbles swarming me and I worry when Tygon doesn't plunge in after.

I flail to the surface, water marring my vision, but my other senses help fill in the blanks. I put the clues together and gain back vision in time to see orbs of water levitating over my head. The electricity from before is much more intense now, like the feeling before lightning halves a nearby tree.

Elemental Weavers are here.

I clamor to the banks near my brother. In front of us stand three Weavers from our northern neighbor Petrichor. Two of them—boys—move their arms in small patterns. Orbs of water follow the path of their hands. Behind the pair, a girl my age stands wearing a tightly woven black braid and magnificent blue, white, and gold trimmed robes. Her eyes cut from Tygon to me repeatedly. Her stare settles on me and she looks me up and down. Her iris' burn as if they were poured directly from Solint's fiery surface.

"What're you Praedari hunters doing this far north? Need we remind you, this is a neutral part of the border," the girl calls to us.

Bashtol. I can't help but think of Papa's missing arm. I know that Weavers like these probably aren't all bad people, but who does she think she is? Despite being all the way on the outskirts of another Beast Master village, we're very much still on Animas soil. The Bloodline of Nature lays claim to this space. How dare a girl from the Bloodline of the Elements question us on our rightful land?

My nose wrinkles into a sneer. "I could ask what a buncha' Petros are doing this far south? Need a map? We're still in good ole' Animas last I checked."

Tygon whispers behind me, "Dude, cool it. Not looking for a fight, not with these guys."

As if to suggest otherwise, the girl's robes surge with power. The ground beneath her plumes into flames and she hovers in the midst of them. She twirls upward in a full revolution, rising higher as the firestorm rages under her feet. When she faces us again, she's floating half a tree's height above the ground. The flames reshape into a pair of overlapping disks, spinning like the spokes of a giant wagon wheel. The glow in her eyes fixates on me and my hair rises once more. This time, sparks dance across her fingertips. The sparks connect, crackling into blinding streams of lightning, and I blink in total disbelief.

"I am Ilysia of Petrichor, Fire-into-Lightning Weaver and apprentice to Storm-Caller, the Grand Legioness Audra herself. I will be Spirit-forsaken before if I wind up on a hunter's plate tonight. Now leave before I blot the memory of you from Spheire...there won't even be ashes left for your family to collect!" Light snaps in jagged angles around her.

Her threat rubs me all the way wrong. My eyes flash green and rage paints faint stripes over my skin. My vision narrows until all I see is a mouthy girl looking down on me. I think about what it would take to jump up to her. Might be a little hot on the way there, sure, but in a second I could crater that cocky matchstick into the bedrock beneath this lake.

However, it's Tygon who catches me off-guard when he abruptly grabs my arm and flings me back toward the tree line behind him. He stands between the Weaver and myself. "You're one of the Stormchasers we saw over the border last night, aren't you?"

The girl raises an eyebrow, then huffs haughtily at the question. "Was quite a show wasn't it? I could give the encore right here, if you like. Your companion looks like he'd enjoy that."

Tygon looks over his shoulder, shooting me a warning. "No, no, my brother and I were just doing a little shopping in Tauris, probably the same reason that brings you here. We're not looking for a fight. In fact, we only came to the lake to cool off with a dive. We didn't see you below. I'm sure seeing two Beast Masters pop out of nowhere got you, eh…pretty heated."

Her flaming eyes register the pun joylessly, but after a tense stare down, the electric storm around her fizzles away.

"I see. In Petrichor, our Bloodline is taught you can never be too safe when you're in the jungle. Not every *beast* is so willing to back down."

I catch a brief ripple in Tygon's jaw. In Animas, there's a thin line between man and beast. We view our proximity to wildlife with pride—but for some reason, other nations don't seem to share our perspective.

Makes it a whole lot easier to look down on us.

I brush myself off, itching to leave the lakeside altogether, but not before glaring up at the Fire Weaver. Tygon's already turned his back to her, heading for the tree line. She descends to the earth, and her gaze never once leaves my face.

She points to the combat lugs on our belts and calls out, "I suppose you've got some sort of test coming up too since they're happening in all the nations. Good luck, and maybe, who knows, I'll be seeing you at the Discipline someday."

I've certainly been called gullible before but even I can hear the sarcasm dripping from her voice.

We exchange looks for a few more seconds. My eyes return to normal shade. The girl adjusts her lengthy braid and straightens her shoulders with a deep breath. She smirks at me, exhaling a long breath of trailing smoke. The dirt beneath her sparkles with embers. She raises her chin at me and whips back around to her two companions.

My fists are clenched and trembling when I catch up to Tygon. Curse the Elements.

I shake my head. "I don't care how many times it takes to pass the Hunter Trials. Someday, I'm going to make it to the Discipline of Peace. Apparently, the world needs a fresh reminder of what Beast Masters can do. I can't wait to show them all."

Tygon marches silently, his determination driving each step in righteous indignation.

"Me too, Faylen. Me too."

Part II
Hunter Trials

10

RULES OF THE CHASE

The day has finally come and with it the crossroads of my future...

Tygon and I are up and buzzing around the den before even Papa Jaole is awake for clan duties. We stuff our faces with meat-filled buns and jellies that Muma prepared the night before. One of Kleo's hand drawn doodles lies on the wooden table—her two brothers wearing victory wreaths on their heads. A note beneath written in barely legible scrawl reads, "Good luck, be amazing!" Next to the parchment are two small arrangements of jungle lilies and several freshly stitched bandages for each of us. I breathe the lilies in deeply, reveling in their ability to rouse even the groggiest morning haters. With our meals completed and a final check of our minimalist gear, Tygon and I set out for the village Hub.

    We arrive to the People's Hall just as its open-air floor begins to fill up. Parents, mentors, and excited Half-Points alike all chatter about their hopes and predictions for this season's event.

    One villager comments to another, "I hear Elevation Willow has the most promising hunter apprentices. That old Canis Headmaster of theirs seems spry as ever, taking his students for mountain runs twice a day!"

    Another retorts, "That's nice and all, but my cousin's got a whole poucha' coins down on one of Headmaster Lujan's scrappers. Not a bad bet for the lioness to have the first ranked

Discipline nominee if you ask me."

"No, no, not a chance! She is talented, a ruthless huntress—no argument there. But Lujan's the youngest of the three instructors. Poor thing, she just 'aint got the seasons on her that the other two have. That first Discipline prize won't go to Oak."

I chuckle inwardly hearing the bystanders. Headmaster Lujan was good enough to be a top twenty graduate of the Discipline of Peace eight hunting seasons ago. "Ruthless" is underselling her a bit. I was a little kid when I saw one of her duels with an Indom Blade Dancer. He was master of the bow, sending volley after volley at the young Lujan. Finally, she'd had enough and plucked three arrows from midair. She hurled them right back at his ambush position—pinned his legs clean through to the perch he was hiding in. Even the Mending Corp was unable to fully mend his severed tendons, and he left the Discipline soon after.

Inside the People's Hall, I take my position, kneeling at the front section of the large room. Tygon settles beside me.

"Ty, how we feeling?"

He inhales slowly, rotating his shoulders opposite one another. "I feel real good, brotya. We've come a long way and worked our butts off. Lujan's last speech has me hyped up too. Fir and Willow aren't ready to meet our best. I can feel it."

I glance over at both groups on either side of our apprenticeship. The rows of students from Elevation Fir and Willow kneel in absolute silence, many with their eyes closed in quiet meditation. Some of the others have their Nodus with them, petting the beasts as if to soothe their nerves.

I catch a rare sight in one of the rows of Elevation Fir.

"Well would ya' look at that? Only on a day as special as this would you catch the ever-elusive PanVulpis out in the open."

Tygon follows my gaze to the grouping of Beast Masters clothed in autumn-colored furs. "Wow, I think that's literally the most fox-bonded I've ever seen in one place. They aren't going to be easy to deal with."

I suck air between my teeth. "True, but I'd still rather chance a fight with one of them over a few of these other bruisers. I've seen a PanVulpis Embrace once, he wasn't so big afterward."

Tygon chuckles. "You of all people are underestimating size? They're the nimblest in the village, and probably as light-footed as any on Spheire. To fight one of them is to end up fighting yourself, I bet."

"Huh. That's probably right. Forgot about that."

"Not to mention *if* you find one in the first place, you're facing traps woven into traps woven into further traps. They've perfected that method of hunting for how many generations now?" He clicks his tongue. "Yeah…no thanks."

I look behind us to see the hall now packed to the brim. Each Clan Head stands before the large mass, between the crowd and the last Elevation rows. Muma Kura and Kleo stand near Papa. Our kitten waves to us, proudly pointing us out to Zahk and Lunis's little brother, Rani. Muma and Papa both nod, placing their first two fingers to their foreheads, signaling focus.

"Clans of Praedari, welcome to the big event of this annual's Hunter Trials!" a voice booms from the stage in front of us.

The noisy crowd hushes instantly and the rhythmic beat of drums shakes the floor mats. Our Dominant does a ceremonial welcoming dance and we clap along with the drummers' cadence. Once the greeting is finished, the brawny musicians cross their sticks over their chests. At centerstage, Dom Arzen stands with his hands toward the crowd.

At his side, sitting motionless, is his Nodus, Elokai, the Helos Hound. The ink-black dog is a stark reminder of the night's terrors. Her vermilion eyes scan over the Elevation rows taking in the bonded beasts' heat signatures. Few Nodus return her gaze.

"Brothers and sisters, today we celebrate the forging of our village's future. The fighters, huntresses, keepers, and leaders of tomorrow sit here in our very presence!" The Dominant waves over the Elevation youth.

He gives each group a distinct moment of attention. "Your Headmasters have gifted you the tools you'll need to thrive in this challenge. No matter its course, remember, the skills you need have already been engrained in you from your earliest days."

The boulder of a man waves over his second, Sage Ophis, to join him. The ancient man moves smoothly in the drapes that form his leaf green robe. Once at centerstage, Dom Arzen surrenders the foreground. The Sage raises his ancient looking hands, lifting a carved wooden totem to the crowd.

"Behold children, The Manifest of Maturity!" the elder announces. "Each of you began your journey as a Nestling, learning what a proud Bloodline you belong to." His hand passes over the totem's bottom carving, a bird's nest painted with tree leaves.

"From Nestling, you went on to become Half-Points. Here your lives as bonded truly began. You found your Nodus. You spent the rest of your time at this stage growing alongside them." Ophis touches his bony fingers across the animal cub faces sculpted into the next tier.

"Now you sit before us as a testimony to your development. You are seasoned apprentices, with strong bonds, ready for examination. Ready to Elevate and prove mastery with your Nodus. After this Trial, you will be Pre-Mastery apprentices, ready to find trades and dedicate full service to our great village."

Tygon squirms giddily next to me. Among many dreams he has shared with me, the one he tells most passionately is becoming an Elevation Headmaster. This usually gets him going on for half an hour.

I've heard him say before, "I can't be a sponge forever," and "What good is all this learnin' if I never pass it on?"

Sage Ophis returns the Manifest to a shelf. He points to the tapestry above the crowd.

"Be inspired. Just as our Dominant was forged on the sheer face of King's Peak, so this week, you will also be forged into future leaders of Praedari. You. Are. Champions!"

The entire hall erupts with fanatical applause as the drums once more reverberate through the floor.

When the crowd quiets down, the Sage signals for the clan heads to join him. Three men respectively from PanLeo, Canis, and Vulpis step to the stage, each with their clan's crest adorned over their garments. Two Elite Huntresses of PanUrsa and Helos join them and stand like heroines, their heads held proudly over the assembly. Papa Jaole stands alongside the other five leads.

The Sage waves over several attendants who bring a cage, a small chime, and several long strands of new leather.

"Listen closely. I will now give the rules of this Trial's challenge," the elder shouts.

Every student's eyes are fixed with undivided attention, not wanting to fall into early disadvantage by missing a detail.

He holds up a leather strip. "Each of you competitors will be given one of these belts. You will be sent into the Domain of Bones with these wrapped around you in any fashion of your choosing. There's only one rule in wearing them—the belt must be visible at all times."

He hands the strap back to the attendant. "You will pass into Pre-Mastery if you complete a six-day survival challenge by returning to the village with your strap and that of another. You will fail if you return with only your own or none at all."

Tygon and I look at each other confused. Surely it can't be that easy. All you have to do is lie low in the woods and practice basic survival skills to protect your own belt? Then once most of the week is up, sneak up on someone while they rest and snatch their belt. Shoot, six days isn't even that long and the easier the task, the more apprentices will pass into Pre-Mastery. I've never heard of a Hunter's Trials without steeper stakes…

The old man's eyes sparkle in bemusement, chuckling at our apparent confusion.

"For those of you with aspirations to attend the Discipline of Peace, you will have to meet one of two conditions. Your first option is to return to the village with any "blooded" item."

A pair of attendants step forward holding two examples of the thing he's speaking of.

The first attendant passes a small cage to the elder. The Sage lifts it up toward the hanging lanterns above and I see a hare twitch its nose between the bars.

"As Elevation students and future contributing members to our hunting lifestyle, you must know when and when not to kill.

Just because we have power does not mean we can gratuitously impose it over the creatures and villages around us. Fairness—that is key to the Wild's First virtue."

He walks with slow steps, holding the creature in easy view for all three Elevations.

"Fifteen hares will be released into the Domain of Bones at random times during the six-day period. Around its neck you'll find a collar soaked in deer blood. For every release, we'll also sound the Behemoth-Drum."

He continues, "If you kill the animal, we will know. Upon inspecting the collar, the scent of its blood will be quite obvious. You will then be disqualified instantly and sent back to your Elevation to learn self-control." A gasp escapes our ranks and Tygon looks at me. Complete disqualification? What a risk! It'd be better to not go for a blooded item at all. My palms begin to sweat because this task would be especially hard for me. Controlling my instincts is hard enough when I give in to the Silver Fang's senses. Holding short for something as fragile as a hare? Poor thing would be left in ribbons if I chased it.

Okay, that's the first way to gatekeep the Discipline of Peace. Well played.

The Sage clears his throat. "Keep in mind that the moment you claim a blooded collar, you are allowed to exit the Domain, so long as you yourself escape being targeted while claiming the strongly scented totem. If human blood is detected in addition to the deer's blood, that's allowable and the duel's winner will be honored. That is only the first "blooded" route to the Discipline though."

Sage Ophis returns the cage to the attendee who, in turn, hands him a tiny chime. The metal instrument gives off a quiet ring when the man shakes it.

"This is the second "blooded" option. Another fifteen of these cloth-wrapped chimes will be found dangling from trees in the Domain. If you find one or perhaps, defeat someone carrying it through the jungle, again, you can immediately return to the village with the chime. Present your belt alongside it and you'll be accepted as a Discipline candidate."

The Sage croons a sly look over each Elevation. A grandfatherly grin stretches his wrinkles as he shakes the tiny instrument a final time.

"A soft melody here in the hall, a clamoring alarm amongst the trees, children."

He hands off the chime and returns again with the leather strap.

"Now, moving away from the blooded items because eventually, their numbers will run out. Here is the only other way one gets to the Discipline of Peace."

"As you know, our village has sixty seats to the Discipline, same as all the other four bonded villages of Animas. Between the thirty blooded items, that means there are still up to thirty seats to be claimed. Those remaining thirty seats will be perhaps the hardest to earn."

He pauses, letting us whisper amongst ourselves for a second.

"Any apprentice who returns with two belts taken from his or her peers while maintaining their own will claim a seat. But this only applies to the first thirty to present these trophies."

I lean over to Tygon. "I knew it couldn't be that easy."

Tygon and I sneak a look around us to catch Borust and Kip scratching their heads at the rules. We snicker quietly at the pair when I accidentally catch Dourn's attention. His lips twist into an unsettling smirk. I shiver and turn away, feeling his gaze still on me long after.

Dom Arzen steps back to centerstage.

"Thank you all for coming to this opening ceremony. Remember that we will host a Selection Festival for all successful apprentices after tallying the Trial's results next week. Dutiful Headmasters, this will be the last command you give to most of these fine youth. Direct your Elevations a final time."

After a swift bow to the large man, the instructors each turn to their classes. Headmaster Lujan chants, her voice is a roar louder than the other mentors, "Let us Elevate for Praedari!"

Oak, Fir, and Willow snap to their feet, bellowing from their chests, "Let us rise!"

Our lioness calls out, "Give your farewells to your families now and head to the Domain of Bones within the hour. Bring only what you need and remember that does *not* include food! The jungle will provide you shelter and sustenance over the next six days. Don't get caught trying to sneak in something you shouldn't."

Tygon looks to me as the hall erupts into hoots and hollers.

"Well, Fay, it's finally time. I'm ready to see what I'm made of. You?" His hand finds my neck.

"Brotya, let's get 'em."

11

ENTER THE DOMAIN

After a final few encouraging moments with our kin, Tygon and I head off to the Praedari Southern Gate. The Domain of Bones is a few clicks from the village, in a mostly untouched area where the jungle collides with a long rock formation. The range of white stone rises above the tree line like the jungle's spine—full of wild dens, burrows, and tunnels of unknown length that most Masters avoid altogether.

We walk each in our own thoughts until I break the silence.

"I don't know how I want to approach this, Ty. Getting belts off two other students seems like a big risk, at least for me. If I get into a fight without full Embrace, I'm not sure I'll win that."

Tygon holds my forearm, pointing to the gray fur sewn into the wrist wrappings, "If there was ever a time to figure out this whole Silver Fang thing, this is it, Brotya. I've seen what you can do. When you get into those woods, your only weapon will be your bond to that animal. Considering it's Magnus we're talking about, I'd say you're walking in here with a pretty huge advantage." He releases my arm. "You have many strengths, and they'll only end up as disadvantages if you let 'em be."

I reflect on his words for a few moments, following Tygon through a narrow portion of the trail.

"Hey, Ty, had you thought about what you're doing for food? I plan to stick to fruits and nuts, anything I can pick really. Figured they'd leave less of a scent to track."

He wrinkles his bottom lip. "Shoot, I might steal that. I half thought I'd be looking for insects. Your plan is better. I'd hate to wind up like some of these jokers. They'll wake half the Domain trying to hunt a kill like it's just another day."

Up ahead, we see the crowd of Elevation students gathered around a wooden sign reading, "Stop Here." A couple minutes after we arrive, our Headmasters appear from behind the sign. The PanCanis Headmaster leaps to a low branch nearby and shouts above the noise.

"Elevation students, the Trials will begin shortly! Listen as your name is called and remember your post!"

We quiet down to hear our names being listed off along with a number.

"Iden, Post Two. Evet, Post Six. Karnash, Post Five. Zahk? Zahk, are you here?"

A wolf's howl answers, and I can feel my friend's enthusiasm from here.

"Yes, Headmaster Wilk, I most definitely am. I checked in with Headmaster Lujan."

"Ah, good then. Zahk, you're at Post One."

The older man continues his assignments. I try to place where my friends will be entering the Domain's circular layout by their Post numbers. I get a good picture when imagining the posts as hours on a timepiece. My ears perk when my eldest is named.

"Tygon, Post Three, Dourn, Post Seven, Borust, Post Six. Kip, Post Six."

I shuck my tongue inside my cheek at learning the titular trio has managed posts so near to one another. I catch sight of them on the opposite side of the crowd, Kip and Borust jostling and punching back and forth like children. Dourn stands behind them, never moving his folded arms. I know those three will be entering this thing close enough to link up and cause trouble.

"Lunis, Post Nine. Nalin, Post Eleven."

I wish the man would just spit my name out already, I'd love to pair up with any of my potential allies. However, with Tygon being at Three, Zahk at One, and Lunis at Nine, my support system is all over the place. Of the four of us, I'm the only one with a target on my back.

"Faylen? I'm not sure I saw you come in, young man—you made it, yes?"

I wave my hand above the crowd. "Um, yes, Headmaster, I'm over he—!"

"Dibs on the free belt!" a snide voice interrupts from clear across the throng.

Laughter breaks out from my Oak fellows sprinkled throughout the grouping. A few members of the other Elevations try to hide their smirks—clearly, more than just my own apprenticeship is in on the joke. I catch Dourn studying my reaction as he looks at me between a gap in the crowd.

"Ahem, that'll be enough of that!" Headmaster Wilk commands, eyeing the assembly but unable to pin the source of the heckling.

"All right, where was I? Mmm...oh yes. Faylen, Post Seven."

Bashtol. That striped prick is at the same post as me. I'll have to work especially hard to get away from the entrance quickly then. Otherwise, I'm sure my enemies might track me down in minutes, just for the sport of it.

After all the names and posts have been listed, the Headmaster rings the first bell signaling for us to depart to our assigned locations.

Tygon grabs my shoulders and brings me in, whispering softly, "You stopped letting me fight your fights a long time ago." He pauses, looking me dead in the eye. "Today, that's got to pay off. I'm going to be on the opposite side of the Domain, and I won't be looking for you either. I'm afraid if I try searching you out...well you never know who could be following as we close the distance."

His brow wrinkles as he tries to weigh his options one last time. I know he's right though. Should either of us leave our aurem detectable enough to find the other, we risk being discovered by an aggressor first. Or something unpredictable and hungry within the Domain. Partnering up is not the Trial's objective and ignoring that is a sure-fire way to be washed back.

"Ty, I'll be okay. I got this. I'll try to be the first one to a blooded item and sprint like mad to get outta' the Domain early. Who knows, maybe both of us can be sleeping comfy in our hammocks by nightfall if we do this right."

A sliver of ease softens Tygon's worried expression. "That's a good plan. Do that. And if you see those losers out there, even one of 'em, run. They won't be looking to play fair and I'm sure they will find each other in the woods pretty quickly."

I shake my head. "Lucky. They can get away with that. Most people detect a PanUrsa's gross butt funk and they head in the opposite direction cause it's a tough fight."

"Exactly, so if you sense that they are anywhere near, get gone. Don't play into their games."

The bell rings again to hurry any stragglers and Tygon breaks away toward Post Three. I inhale slowly, trying to steady the whirlpool turning my guts to mush. I trudge forward, following the group headed to Posts Six and Seven. My head is an unapologetic swarm of anxious thoughts when a charming voice cuts through the haze.

"Well, hello to you too, Stripes. Warm greeting you've got there." Lunis swoops in front of me, catching me off-guard.

"Oh, um, hey. I didn't see you. Sorry, all this has me a little out of focus."

Her eyes, the exact hue of smoky pearls, study me intently. She points her finger in a circular motion, gesturing to the surrounding forest.

"Ya' know, I don't think any of this is what's got you unfocused. I think it's a few runts who'd probably be terrified if they knew what you can really do."

I blink repeatedly, surprised by her words. "*I* barely even know what I can really do. How would you, or anyone else for that matter?"

A new warmth sparks through my fingers. I look down and see Lunis holding me in a firm, yet soothing embrace. My hand nearly drops off my arm.

"I've got a quick story for you before I run off to my post.

Did you know that about, say, ten years ago, there was a rampant flock of venom-bats terrorizing the village?"

I can barely register her words, fixated instead on the looming palm sweat I'm about to bathe this poor girl's hand in.

"My papa once told me that those venom-bats were terrorizing the night sky back then, picking off anything they could get their fangs on."

I snap back to reality to see her unearth a familiar pendant from beneath her hunting garments. She fingers a pale-colored lightide pendant thoughtfully and I can't help but gasp.

"My parents made sure none of us went out at night for a month or so before the bats were confirmed to have migrated back to the border. So, imagine my surprise when this messy haired little boy hands me a moonstone brighter than any a traveling peddler has ever sold."

I pause for a moment. "Okay, two things. One, you ended up calling it a moonstone? And two, how do you still have that after all these seasons? I thought the boys around here would've showered you with far better gifts than that by now."

She cocks her eyebrow at me with laughter in her shoulders. "I called it that because you can only see the glow at night. And of course, I kept it. I always wear this when I need to channel bravery. You were barely a Half-Point, yet you ventured so far from Praedari to bring this back to me. Defying of the night creatures all the adults were so terrorized by."

She stops in front of me, her observant gaze dangerously close to unveiling my every secret wish about her.

"Faylen, I don't think you were afraid at all to brave the darkness back then because your inner light shone brighter. You have never had any fears...until you let others put them into you."

The reality and truth of her words sting. I always admired how direct she can be. On numerous instances now, I've witnessed her being far wiser than her years should allow.

"I'll leave you with this, Tiger. Zahk has always called you a stand-up guy. Back when you two were little boys, he'd strike a champion's pose almost every night at our dinner table. He'd wave his arms all around, telling tales of his adventures with his best friend." She pokes me in the chest.

I smile to myself, reminiscing on some of those good times.

"My parents always asked Zahk if he was gaining anything from all these adventures to make him a better member of the clan. Every time he'd throw his head back and point to the sky, saying, 'I'm always tellin' that striped catboy, somethin's only unthinkable if *you* never think it!'"

She lets go of my hand all too soon but takes a moment to fumble for something in her pocket. She presses the item into my hand.

"I know tigers and wolves probably aren't naturally occurring friends, but promise you'll wear it anyway?"

The huntress turns toward her post, and I open my palm to see a polished wolf's tooth tied to a bit of decorative string. The charm is absolutely gorgeous with intricate patterns carved into the surface. I know the polish alone would've taken ages.

"You amaze me, Faylen. Every day. Good luck, and I'll see you at the festival afterward, okay? Look out for yourself!"

I wave back toward her...*oh please, please brain, don't leave me hanging. There's got to be one smooth thing you can say here. Literally just one.*

I cup my hands around my mouth and hear myself say, "Thank you for kind stuff!"

What. In. The. Actual. I swear some days I might have brain damage.

"—I meant *words*. Thank for kind words!"

The gorgeous huntress tilts her head to the side for a second while I freeze in place. I'll bury myself alive right here and now before I shout nonsense at her a third time. She flashes a smile more captivating than a shooting star and disappears to report to her post. Once I'm sure she's out of sight, I dance a quick jig then proceed on my way. When I arrive at Post Seven, I stand in a single-file line with the other students. I'm distracted by mentally replaying the charming moment with Lunis when a tousled head of dark hair turns around and I see Dourn's beady eyes glaring up at me from below my nose.

I look down on him. How did I never realize how little he was? Or how little he should matter to me? Perhaps his whole murderous vibe has been nothing more than an overdone act this entire time.

"Please don't go getting yourself downed out there in the Domain too quickly, Faylen. Your blood is mine, and I've got six long days to claim it. Do me the favor of at least making the chase a little interesting."

I pretend not to hear him, but he steps closer as though he skipped the Nestling lesson on personal space.

"I have such great plans for you."

I raise my eyebrows sarcastically to show threats have failed to register. I also blow air out of my lips, perhaps a bit intentionally into his face.

"Well too bad for the both of us those plans of yours didn't include mint leaves. But in all seriousness, Dourn, does this whole routine not get a *little* exhausting for you?" I shrug him off. "Whatever, can you move out the way? You're slowing up the line."

A popped vein in the tiny tormentor's brow betrays his otherwise calm demeanor. I'd revel more in the small win of frustrating him if I weren't also looking past him at the line in front of us and the looming Domain beyond. I mean, really. I've got far bigger things to focus on than him. I chuckle inwardly at the unintentional pun. The boy is truly insignificant compared to what lies ahead.

The next bell is the final one and with it the line in front of us begins to shorten. Each student breaks off, lost to the dense screen of trees in intervals of forty-five seconds. After only eight in the line have gone, loud roars can already be heard in the woods we face.

How in Everrealm did fights break out that fast? This Hunter Trial could turn out to be a blood bath far shorter than six days.

Dourn is up next and when his interval sounds, he walks

slowly through the post to the nearest tree. He turns to lean his shoulder on it, looking directly at me.

"Move your butt, kid. Gon' ahead! Get further into the Domain already!" the proctor calls, checking the sand left in his miniature hourglass.

The boy skulks into the brush, marking an 'X' in tree bark with a claw-tipped finger.

At last, it's my turn and I count down in my head while considering my options. I could Embrace my senses and maybe be able to track any aggressors, but then my muscular buff won't be that strong. Or I could go with the power boost, take the early risk and worry about sensing later. That would leave me open to Dourn's approach and just about everyone else hiding in these trees.

I calm myself. My mind is made up.

There's an eternity of silence as I wait the last couple seconds for the bell. I'm ready to face this challenge. I'm ready to shake off my insecurities, even if it means faking the confidence at first. I'm ready to ignore the cretins who wish me ill and accomplish something for myself.

Lunis is right, I'm the one who let them come into my house and give fear a home.

Time to put my plan into action—find a strategic, but safe place, sniff out a blooded item, and get out. I have a real shot here if I don't become my own greatest obstacle.

The interval sounds and my leg muscles drive compressed energy into the dirt. I feel clods of grass linger on my shins as I sail above the trees. In that moment, all I see is the Domain.

Who cares about Dourn's plan. Mine is to make this place my own.

12

HATE

A few hours have passed since I left my post yet the trees around me have been filled with constant shrieks, enraged shouts, and ferocious roars. I've been lucky though. To my surprise, I've managed a largely uneventful morning. I decided early on to find a place where I'd see any aggressors coming before they could spot me. At first, I considered hiding in a tree, but since leaping through the canopies is our people's main way of travel, I needed a better option. For the moment, walking around on ground level offers plenty of escape routes. But with flat ground also comes little cover.

    I am headed for the spine-like ridge jutting above the jungle. I know it's pocked with small burrows and miniature caves, so I figure picking one and leveling my aurem will make it harder to be singled out. Finally, arriving at the long formation, it takes some time to climb and find a good spot. The sediment covering its surface is made entirely of loose rock that crumbles at the slightest pressure. I slip a few times but finally leap to a large burrow using smaller ones as footholds. Now I just need to sit and wait long enough to catch my bearings and memorize my surroundings. This will make my eventual kill plan only that much more fool proof.

    I poke my head out from the miniature cave, forcing all my Embrace into my senses. A new world of sound floods my ears, further defined by a spectrum of scents. Half a mile away, I can hear two Beast Masters locked in a grapple, both trying to quiet their grunts as to not attract a stronger opponent. I breathe deep, letting my mind match the nearby aromas to familiar ones I've memorized on chases with my kin.

A sweet note in the wind paints a picture of dewberries. The crisp smell of water faintly drifts past my nose. Good, I've already located a drinking source and won't need to stumble around the Domain recklessly to reach it. I look toward the body of water and see a flock of white birds perched in the surrounding treetops. One of them takes flight and, after soaring in several slow circles, disappears beneath the tree line. A swooping flock means they are aiming at something. My bet is there's a fine fishing spot nearby too.

I check my belt pouch and pull out its minimal supplies—a small razor, Kleo's bandages, a thimble-sack of pain medication, flint, and four iron hooks wrapped in thin twine. I carefully place the valuable resources back into their pouch. Fishing will be a quieter alternative to chasing prey and, considering how bright Solint is overhead, I might not even need fire to dry out the meat.

I can do this!

The Behemoth-Drum sounds in the distance, interrupting my thoughts. No way…someone is done already? There's no doubt—that was a long drumroll which means someone found a blooded chime and turned it in. A seat to the Discipline…claimed just like that. What crazy luck to be done with the Trials in a mere few hours. I wonder how many foes they had to fight off to reach it first and walk out with their prize.

I sigh to myself. Well, fifty-nine spots left for the Discipline. It isn't my number one goal right now, but I figure I'm here, I might as well try. Plus, nabbing a blooded item and evading thereafter means a quick way out of this Domain. Less time for Dourn and his cronies to get their hands on me. For that perk alone, I'm game.

The only disadvantage of holing up inside the ridge is that Solint's light bakes the outer surface like an oven. I'm forced to slink farther into my hideout or otherwise lose precious moisture to the heat. Unfortunately, hidden in the cave's depths, I can't keep an eye on my surroundings. In the enveloping darkness, a heavy yawn finds me. Well, we are at peak daylight anyway. No sense exhausting myself now when I can just as easily set out closer to dark…

I wake to a growl ringing in my ears. It jolts me up and I spring to my hands and knees, trying to keep a low profile so as not to show through the hovel's opening. The growl rumbles again. Thankfully, it's just my discontented stomach protesting a lack of food. I peek outside my hideout, listening carefully for any clues of an ambush. I only find silence. Good.

I climb down the ridge, carefully placing each foot before moving my weight to the next hold. This cursed descent of fifteen mets is such a vulnerable position. I am relieved when my combat lugs finally meet the gravely earth below.

I head in the water's direction, pushing leaves and branches out of my face. Leaping through the branches would be far quicker, but that flock of birds has me worried. I'd hate to snag a branch near their perch and send the entire area up in white feathers. Observant apprentices would be following my heading in seconds.

I walk into a grove rich with flowers and hanging fruits. Behind a thick brush, I find the patch of dewberries I'd scouted out earlier. Thank the Spirits!

I unroll a small folding satchel from my pocket and fill it with handfuls of the delicious fruit. Oh, Tygon, if only you were here, this spot would be perfect for both of us. I shove a few of the energy-rich berries in my mouth, continuing to pluck handfuls until the leather bag bulges.

At the sound of pattering feet nearby, I freeze every muscle. Without moving, I sweep my eyes from side to side, trying to find the source. I pivot toward the brush to protect my back. The patter has stopped, and I can't help but feel eyes watching me. I gulp down the few remaining berries still in my mouth and snatch the satchel drawstrings shut. I've got to get out of here without leaving a trail to my hideout.

I wait a couple more seconds before Embracing into my senses. I try to home in on one specific aroma—sweat, every hunter's ultimate tell. At first, the only moisture I smell is my own, but then a foreign tinge of salt registers in my mind. I'm shocked to realize someone's been so close this whole time and I was too distracted to notice. I seek out their aurem but only detect the faintest hint of brown…or maybe its red? I can't tell for sure, and I won't be waiting to find out.

I enhance my muscles only a small amount, choosing to prioritize my senses instead. I bound into the nearest treetop, then to the ground, then back into the branches. Maybe by being unpredictable, the potential threat won't have a clear trail to my hovel.

I recollect my momentum on the ground and commit to a full-on sprint. Safety is but a short dash away! From my hideout, I'll have the advantage. High ground—from there I can wait and listen. If any pursuer follows me, I can spring an ambush using the ridge's layout to my advantage. As I enter my stride on the straightaway toward the rock, I begin to breathe a little easier.

I realize too late how foolish it is to let myself mentally relax.

A sharp pain shoots up my leg, and I tumble into the fallen leaves and dirt. I'm not so worried about a potential injury as I am for the crashing noise I've just made. In fact, the discomfort isn't full-on agony…it's similar to a bee sting. I look down at my leg to see why—a line of wooden teeth sunken into my skin.

Wait, is this a trap?

I pull the teeth from my leg, the pinch identical to removing a stinger, but it's what I see at the wooden tips that unsettles me. Each barb is laced with a light pink liquid with a faintly sour odor pluming up from the substance. I pocket a tooth to examine later back in the hideout.

My mind races to figure out the next move. I have to act carefully considering a PanVulpis has also decided to make camp in this area. Who knows what mystery plant they've just put into my bloodstream? Shoot, who knows what kind of secondary snags are in the greenery around me? What if this was just a bothersome decoy meant to send me in another direction for the real deal?

No sooner had the thought entered my head does a sinister sight come into view. Because I'm sitting on the ground, I can see a tripwire mere inches from my nose. The thin bit of dark green twine would be impossible to see from any other angle than this. Of course it would be the exact shade as the jungle floor. I follow it into a branch above and see a small pouch of dung-a-lews hanging from a wooden pin.

I chuckle at my luck. Back home, it takes days to scrub dung-a-lew juice out of your skin, and in the meantime, only the most loving kin would tolerate the smell.

Unbelievable luck. A Master with fuller Embrace and thus more speed, would have burst right through the first trap. After losing their footing to that barbed foot clamp, they would have slid headfirst into the wire.

I shake my head and thank the Spirits once more. *I won't forget your fortune.*

I make my way whole and untainted back to my hideaway. I'm too exhausted by the close call to open my bag of fruit. Even my stomach has long forgotten its hunger for now. I listen intently for the smallest clue that another apprentice is nearby. I'm having a bit of difficulty concentrating but chock it up to frayed nerves. After a few more minutes ensuring the coast is clear, I skulk back into the dark recesses of my hideout.

I finally take to the dewberries, but find every handful is somehow heavier than the last. I feel dragged lower into a slump with each bite. Despite the overwhelming fatigue, I force every berry down until the bag is empty. I slap myself hard then think to re-examine that wooden tooth. I'm struggling hard now for any scrap of focus, then finally understand the genius of the PanVulpis's trap. The trap was meant to incapacitate and mark a victim simultaneously. Anyone else in the trap would've been so busy focusing on wearing a fresh coating of dung-a-lew pulp that they wouldn't have noticed the teeth in their leg. As such, the full dose of this mysterious pink mess would've set in near instantly instead of the smaller amount that is affecting me now.

I laugh to myself, imagining being passed out entirely, some light-footed fox following my newly acquired scent and lifting the belt from my snoring body. What an easy play.

A short drum beat echoes in the distance.

Oh yes! A hare has been released! I hesitate for a second, weighing my current condition, but decide to risk the safety for victory. If that hare is nearby, I can be out of here within the hour. Blast that sneaky Vulpis and his sleep trap. If I find that collar, the fluid's effects won't have time to get any worse.

I wobble to my knees, shimmying down the ridge as fast as I can. On the ground, I Embrace my senses to their limit, pushing past the swooning haze. A wisp of deer blood finds me—bless the Spirits, it's strong. That means it's not too far away. I boost my climbing muscles and make a jump for the nearby treetops. I stumble over the woods, forcing my focus so hard a headache stabs my brain. But no matter, I'm on my way.

As I leap through the branches, I'm careful to place my weight, shaking the branches only slightly. The tendrils of scent thicken into an unmistakable trail. The hare is moving sporadically, but it's only a mile out from my location. Hope sets my heartbeat a flurry. Could this really be my chance? Adulthood *and* the Discipline of Peace in one fell swoop? Here I come!

I pause high up in the next canopy, slapping sense into myself once more and taking in my surroundings. No, I'm not making the same mistakes twice.

If getting knocked on my back by that Gargan-Elk has taught me anything, I can't fixate on the end goal by overlooking the steps leading up to it.

It's a good thing too that I've stopped here. Otherwise, I might not have caught the slight noise of leaves crunching underfoot. The steps are intentionally slow, like a hunter trying to mask their presence. Whomever they are, this particular apprentice isn't even tracking in the direction of the fast-moving hare. As long as I can leave the immediate area without a sound, they will be none the wiser I was ever here.

I settle into my stance once more, preparing to lose the stranger by blasting away from the perch. I ignore my burning temples, ready to spring off when I hear something that seizes up every muscle in my body.

"Ya' sure he was in this area?" a familiar voice questions through the branches.

"Are you questioning me?" The scorn in Dourn's voice is more sinister than I've ever heard it. There's a note of desperation I can hear from him too.

He growls harsh over his shoulder. "I saw that striped whelp leave our post and head this direction. We're in between him and the starting position. He is close, I cannot be mistaken."

"Okay, but we been searchin' out here for almost a day now. The trials might be half over by the time we find him, and we still gotta' get ourselves some blooded items," Kip whines aloud.

I hold my breath, cold disbelief at what I'm hearing. The first day is nearly over and they've committed all this time just to hunt me down?

There's a moment of silence as the party comes to an abrupt halt before a sharp slap cracks amongst the surrounding trees. There's a large thump as Kip topples over into the dirt.

Dourn pauses to stare down the much taller Borust. "What, got something to say? He wouldn't be on the ground right now if you had shaped him up a long time ago. Stand aside."

Borust shuffles back and Dourn looks down his nose on his weeping underling. I can feel his irritation from here when he suddenly crouches to eye-level and grips Kip's chin none too gently.

"When we officially started this trio, we had just one mission, and you agreed to follow my orders because you desperately needed leadership. Otherwise, you were on your way to flunk these Trials for a second time. Weren't you?" He pauses and Kip stifles a sniffle. "With me, you two have become terrors of our class. But finding those blooded items is not your destiny. Not the Discipline beyond either. Our agreement stops at getting you a pass and nothing more. Fail me, however, and I promise you'll join the village cripples."

Dourn moves his hand to pat Kip on the cheek, then saunters past the PanUrsa pair with clear determination. Borust watches him, then looks as though he's weighing helping his cousin up from the dirt. It doesn't surprise me when instead, he trots away through the underbrush to follow his leader like a lost dog. Kip stares after his cousin, looking on the verge of tears. Then he rises with fury in his eyes. Of all things, he curses *my* name before running off to rejoin the rest.

I hear Dourn somewhere below. "Just one more day boys, we'll hunt him down. And when we do, I will do what I do best."

The woods go quiet for a second as if every tree were waiting with bated breath.

"I'm curious to see if he'll still be PanTigris's 'chosen of a generation' when I take his hunting away for good."

The trio passes underneath as fear ravages my mind. I try to return to the safe place of Lunis's encouraging words but can't remember a single one. This thing gripping my gut is different than anything I've felt before. Even when the trio are long gone, Dourn's threat repeats in my head as if he were whispering it in my ear. I squeeze my hands to my head but still can't blot out his voice. I suddenly envision every time I've caught him gazing at me longingly. Even when Borust and Kip were off bothering other people, Dourn's only ever had eyes for me.

It goes beyond a strong dislike for me. He nurtures sick hatred for everything I am.

The jungle reclaims its silence, but my mind knows anything but. My skin is clammy and sweat-drenched. Eventually, I wretch onto the branch that holds me. Losing the berries only intensifies the sleep trap's effects on my brain. The tree shakes as I continue to dry heave, hunched over in the leaves like a shrew. I tremble as though winter had suddenly erased this warm summer evening.

I only have one simple joy…that none of my loved ones are here to see me like this.

13

Lured

My mind can hardly process what just happened, especially not the fact I'm being purposely hunted down. Terror has me in its paralyzing grip and I no longer have the blooded hare's trail. It takes every ounce of mental strength to redirect myself to my hideout. My joints are mush. My limbs? Stone. But eventually I manage to run. And crawl. In all honesty it's hard to tell which I'm doing—my body is moving like a puppet with knotted up strings.

Back at the cave, I drag myself deeper into its shadows than ever before. I hope Tygon, Zahk, and Lunis are having better luck than I am.

My head hits the cave floor and the low ceiling swims in front of my eyes. There's no fighting the effects of that fox-footed's trap any longer. I'm unconscious just as I hear multiple long drum rolls echo through the night.

Daylight shines bright enough to turn my burrow into a skinner's hotbox. I squint my eyes open, then startle awake. Solint only burns that bright at its high point in the sky. Goodness, half the day gone already? My stomach rumbles angrily as though it had its own voice—*Hello…I've been waiting for you this whole time*—it seems to protest.

I think back over what I can remember, trying to estimate how long I was out. There's no way to know for sure, but I know I heard drumrolls while I slept. I hope I didn't dream them. Nine drum rolls in total—six long, three short—that's how many I faintly picked up. That means six hares and three chimes respectively are good as gone. Add that nine to the hare I was chasing before the terrible trio showed up, and that takes ten total early tickets out of this place off the table. I've got to find a blooded item or my remaining options will be slim.

We only found out near our posts that anyone finishing early with two belts from other students will not be signaled with a drumbeat at all. This makes it harder to know the exact number of apprentices left to fight once the blooded items are gone. So, either I fight two random apprentices for their belts or sit in this Domain for the full six days and snag one at the last minute. I shake my head at the latter. Dourn will definitely find me if he has a whole six days to do it.

I sigh, secure my belt pouches and gather my supplies. What a position to be in. Not to mention, the Sage just had to make things a bit harder this year. Even removing the Discipline from the equation, I still have to face down at least one apprentice and claim their belt by the time this is all done. I can't afford to waste any more time.

Okay. Enough worrying, I need to get to work. I creep toward the hole's entrance. Poking my head out, I scan the area for any obvious changes. I breathe deep, trying to pick up on the water's scent once again. It's refreshing aroma finds me, coercing me to leave the hideout.

As I trek toward what I hope is at least a small river, I look back to my hideout. It's been a relatively safe place, especially compared to the absolute chaos I've heard from the center of the Domain. The problem is, there's nothing to find out here but another trapper's setup. While this side of the Domain has seen less action, I can't afford to be passive the whole six days. I might still have my belt by the Trial's end, but I won't pass this way.

Once I break the tree line before the river, I Embrace into my advanced senses. No giveaways suggest the presence of potential enemies—no scents, no wisps of aurem, no snapped branches. Against all odds, for this moment, I might actually be alone at the river. Instead of waiting around uselessly for the next drum to signal a blooded item, I decide to make this given opportunity count.

I pick up four thick twigs from the tree line and a hand-sized stone. I take the first twig and snap off a portion of it. Splitting one end with my razor and threading a length of twine into it, I tie off the contraption with a few knots, securing line to wood. Finally, I drive the improvised fishing rod into the moist soil near the river, finishing by covering the setup with dirt. The hidden device looks promising, now all it needs is a little bait. Fortunately, I'm able to pocket a handful of grubs with minimal digging. I repeat the process, adding bait to each hook, until I have a large section of the riverside covered. Zahk would be proud. All that's left to do now is wait.

Hiding in the tree line's underbrush, I try to sniff out any hint of deer blood. What crazy luck it would be to somehow find an unclaimed chime all the way out here! However, after a couple minutes huffing and puffing through the nearby woods, my search proves unfruitful.

I sit back in my spot, watching the branches sway rhythmically. A timber-mouse high up in a tree feasts on a nut. Its chubby cheeks quiver with rapid chewing until its meal is devoured. A hint of jealousy stabs up from my groaning belly.

I edge back to the water to inspect my lines. Not a single one of them is taut with the feel of a catch. I let out an exasperated breath. Perhaps another half hour and my luck might change. Back in my waiting spot, I watch the mouse clean itself with sporadic motion. Wow, what a great life that little dude must live, this one tree being his whole world. What would such a simple creature have to fear when its home provides both the security and all the food it could ever want?

For some reason, Dourn's threat sneaks back into my mind before I'm able to block it.

I grimace at my current situation. I'm hungry, yes. But I've really got to get moving. Staying in this open spot too much longer is bound to expose me eventually. The jungle chooses now to illustrate this point with cruel timing. The poor timber mouse is sliced to ribbons in the bloody talons of a hawk neither of us saw coming.

Newly motivated, I trot back to my fishing lines, flicking each of the strings. Three of the four respond with a promising twang and I reel the lines in to find a fish thicker than my forearm at the end of each one. Yes! If I can find a spot where Solint is baking a rock nearby, I'll be out of here with a full stomach in no time. Full energy for more than a day with a catch like this means I'll have an enduring advantage against anyone I meet in the Domain.

I head for the underbrush and slice into the clammy flesh to gut my catch. I carve out thin strips of meat and wrap them in nearby leaves, making for easy carrying in my foldable satchel. The leftover guts at my feet reek something fierce. Admittedly, being around their stench was always my least favorite part of fishing. My growling stomach urges me to hurry as I dig a small hole to bury the putrid entrails. No sooner had I started do I hear a troubling sound nearby.

"Ugh, Borust, how long are we gonna' be out here? How do we even know he's still in this area? It's our third day, and we still got ourselves to worry 'bout."

I roll my eyes. Going on three days, really? I knew that cursed Vulpis trap stole a stupid amount of time from me.

The larger PanUrsa and his cousin trudge clumsily through the underbrush about a quarter mile away, snapping twigs and vines without a care in the world.

"Eh, let's just do what boss said. He told us we'd be done lookin' today if we just split up this one last time. Ain't no point in peeving him more in the state he's in. He's already got his blooded item so I'm just happy he promised us some easy fights so we can pass these Trials too. I'm so ready to be done."

Unreal. That puny jerk actually has a blooded item and could have been out of the jungle by now, but he's so bent on making sure he gets his hands on me, he's willing to risk it all.

Kip pipes up, "Fine, can we at least check over that way then?

Stripes wasn't by the river at dawn, but I could at least use a drink and a dunk."

"Okay, have it your way. I smell fish 'round here anyways and that's got me hungry. Maybe we can paw a few outta' the water."

I look down at my incomplete hole in the dirt. I'm not so worried about covering my tracks as I can make a break from these guys pretty easily. Speed being a PanTigris's advantage over a PanUrsa, running isn't the issue…but positioning is. If their trio has split up, Dourn could be anywhere. If I barrel straight into him or he detects me anywhere nearby, he's going to call his pals right over to close me in from the rear.

I huff with frustration, sinking back to slouch against the tree. I look around my immediate area, trying to think of some strategy to escape this bind. Why can I never seem to catch a freaking break? Lunis's charm brushes up against my hand as I struggle to devise a plan. I palm the talisman gently, looking over the intricate carvings. Closing my eyes, I whisper for help. The leaves sway above me like a thousand tiny witnesses.

When I open my eyes, I hope for something amazing, like Tygon being there. Or maybe Magnus. Instead, there are only trees. It's then that reality truly sinks in. Whatever the solution is, I've got to figure this one out on my own.

At the trunk of a nearby tree, I notice a pair of Riverbank-ants fly into a hole, carrying food for their colony. I look down at my charm, conjuring up an old memory. My eyes snap back to the little creatures.

Hold up, now there's an idea!

I scramble to my feet and scoop a handful of the fish guts into my hands. I trot carefully over to the nearby tree and drop the entrails at its roots. I turn back to my unfinished hole, making three stealthy trips until a mound of innards sits at the tree's base. I take an especially slimy piece and trace a line from the roots up to the insects' nest. In just a few seconds, a trickle of Riverbank-ants streams out, descending onto the pile of guts.

I smile to myself. Muma always emphasizes the importance

of giving back to the jungle after taking life from it. She taught us this Second virtue, and I hear her words now as if she were next to me. *"Sons, always search out creatures that are like Qirin. Those giant birds love fruit more than anything, and though they are kings of the sky, the jungle made it so that they'd need our help to get what they love most. Always look for ways that you can be a helping hand to the beasts of these woods. You never know what favor will come back to you in return."*

On one of our earliest fishing trips, Zahk showed us how the remaining fish guts could be covered in dirt to hide their scent from animals. But when Tygon and I went on our own trips, we remembered Muma's teachings and would use the remains as fertilizer to bury seeds with. This habit led us to discover yet another secret.

I stand back, watching the Riverbank-ants swarm over the new food source. Fish is the favorite food of the winged insects, a meal they will travel up to a mile to enjoy. Ironically enough, the persistent critters are unable to swim. As such, they typically make nests near bodies of water, while settling for a life of nuts, seeds, and fruits. But they're always on the lookout for washed up fish. Watching them feast now, I rub my hands together excitedly. My plan is starting off strong!

I hear a pair of footsteps approaching a few hundred mets away. From their hefty weight and the sweaty stench of bear butt-funk, I can tell it's the cousins. Bashtol. My plan is great, but I'm not ready to spring it yet! I focus on my aurem to avoid letting it spike. This plan has one chance to work, and if I pull it off, those two oafs will be out of the picture for good. Then, I'll only have to worry about Dourn, whom I might manage to avoid altogether.

I crawl through the underbrush tying all four lines of fishing twine to a nearby tree. I leave a forearm's distance between them and the jungle floor below and run the lines off to a nearby trunk. I smirk at my sudden slyness, perhaps I've got a little PanVulpis blood in me somewhere. Finishing my own version of a trap, I climb to a nearby canopy that has a concealing view. Now, time to set the bait.

"Tygon?—Er, where are you, my brother? I am over here, fishing. Fishing by the river!" I shout.

The jungle goes quiet for a second.

"Shh, shh, did you hear that? That moron is nearby! I knew it…and I *knew* I smelled fish!" Borust tries to conceal his excitement.

"Finally! Now Dourn won't be able to ride me so hard. I'm socking that cat in his stupid mouth too before the boss gets here. Shoot, we don't even got to worry 'bout Tygon too since Faylen's lookin' for him," Kip hisses.

"Righto, so let's catch him quick before his brother shows up."

Clearly, neither of them are focused enough to pick up on my scent. Their aurem are way out of control, lighting up the nearby area like signal fires. After a moment, a set of footsteps stampedes toward my position.

"Head straight for that fish smell. It's got to be him!" Borust whoops, plodding through the thick underbrush.

I peer through the canopy to spot the duo for the first time. They rush the area with wicked determination, and their sweaty scent is heavy. I hear a familiar twang, much deeper than the ones to signal a catch, and watch the two dolts fly forward. They slam into the ground, carrying every bit of careless momentum into the pile of fish guts.

The boys cough up their lungs when inhaling the strong odor. Their skin is covered in slimy ilk, sealed in by a layer of dirt and leaves.

"Ugh, *gross*! What in Everrealm is this crap?" Borust shrieks in a higher voice than I thought him capable.

Kip tries to shake the gunk from his arms but much of the mess has caked into his fur-sewn vest. "At least we know he has to be around here. If he was gutting fish here, he's close. I just know I wouldnta' tripped so hard if I hadn't run into your giant butt."

Borust drives his meaty fist into Kip's arm. "Shut it! You know there's vines evr'where in the jungle. How was I supposta' see 'em?"

I snicker to myself as the second portion of the trap sets in. That smell will make them easy to find for the next few days should they show up near me again. But it's the insects that will send 'em packing.

"Wait, h-hold up…Kip, your neck. Are those…*Riverbank-ants*!"

The nearby trees erupt in one-part roar, one-part shriek, and one-part manic sob. In only a few seconds, I can see the first wave of ants has already made contact. No matter how the boys swat their arms, the palm sized insects refuse to unclamp their notable jaw-pincers from the cousins' now fish-flavored flesh.

As the second wave of winged terror is making its way to join the first, the two PanUrsa rip through the brush at top speed as best as their burly Embraces will allow them. It's a clumsy show to watch though, the pair slamming into trees as often as they do each other, each time slowing down enough for more ants to claim another few inches of uncovered skin. After a few minutes, all that's left of them is the low rumble of distant chaos and the occasional bear's yelp. I snicker to myself, holding the lucky charm in my hand. Okay, Lunis officially gives the best gifts. I thank the Spirits and adjust the tally. Two down, one to go.

We're even on the board, Dourn, and your cavalry isn't coming.

14

BLOOD DUEL

I wait several minutes in the canopy to sense any additional newcomers to the area. Once confident that the scene is clear, I scamper down from the tree and trot lightheartedly to the river's edge. I scrub the fish guts from my hands, letting the smooth current wriggle between my fingers. Had those two PanUrsa found their way to the river, they could've washed at least some of the scent away. That might've helped lose the Riverbank-ants, but would've played perfectly into my back-up plan—attack while they rolled around in the water.

I stand up, shake the moisture from my hands and scan the banks for a sunny spot. In the end, I'm grateful a surprise attack on the cousins wasn't in the cards. Ambush or not, someone would've certainly heard the commotion of me taking on two Beast Masters at once. With their bounty in tow, escaping with their belts would've also been much riskier.

A quarter mile down the river, I stumble upon a tranquil bend dotted with several large stones. Solint has baked them all hot to the touch—the perfect make-shift oven to crisp my thin strips of fish. Knowing time still isn't completely in my favor, I quickly unpackage each leaf wrapping and lay the pieces side by side. If the rock surfaces were a bit warmer, the promising morsels would have probably sizzled immediately. After four of the stones are covered with fish, I stand back to admire my work. I wish Zahk was here to see this catch! Maybe this student has surpassed his scraggly teacher.

I find a stick in the dirt and plot out how long this catch will last me. Three fish, plus some berries I pick en route to the Domain's center. That'll last at least a day and some change assuming I Embrace a few times along the way. Today is the latter half of the third day, so this catch will get me through to the start of the fifth. Perfect, with sustained energy from a full meal when most apprentices should be surviving off bare scraps, I should be out of the Domain before my supply runs out.

I inspect the mouth-watering strips and can tell they'll need at least fifteen more minutes before they're cooked through. I decide not to waste energy in the sunlight and find a shadowed spot beneath a thick canopy. Comfortable, yet alert, I keep my feet under me but lean my back against the trunk. I'm suddenly aware how perfect a spot like this would be for a first date —a gurgling river in front, a shady canopy overhead, and a picnic sizzling away.

I pretend to put on my most "attractive" face, cocking my eyebrow so far it almost hits my hairline. I fluff the fur on my wrappings and pop my collar. Finally, I snap my fingers at a nearby brush, dazzling it with a toothy grin.

"Lunis…well, hello there wolf-lady. Here's a little somethin' for those beautiful wrists which are attached to…" I pause waiting for something smooth to enter my mind. "*Bea-u-ti-ful*…hands."

I coo, reaching toward the plant to slide a makeshift bracelet of weeds around it. A thick beetle leaps off the leaf, thunking me on the forehead before buzzing away annoyed.

I grunt, swatting the stupid brush away. Great. My brand of charisma doesn't even work on shrubbery. Maybe one of these days, I ought to ask Papa the trick he used to win Muma's favor over all the other eligible hunters. Huntresses are the ones who pick their life-long mates after all.

With the fish still baking by the riverbank, a couple rays of sunlight break through the swaying leaves above me, kissing my eyelids with gentle warmth. I close my eyes for a quick self-check-up. It's been an eventful day, and I should tune in with my body for a meditative second. The moment this meal is done, the search continues for a blooded item. If I'm not lucky enough to find one, I'll have to face a hunter, maybe two. I have to make significant progress today. Losing a day to the PanVulpis trap has put me at a huge disadvantage—I need to make up for lost time.

I've barely collected myself for a minute when my eyes flutter open. I hear the light crunch of pebbles in front of me. Someone is here...

I catch a distant motion, but don't have time to fully react. I'm only able to move my head mere inches when a huge chunk of rock explodes into dust on the trunk behind me. My eyes snap to abrupt focus while my pulse picks up to a furious tempo.

Cruel laughter, like I'd imagine of a young tyrant, pierces the air around the riverside.

"You should've let that hit, Faylen. Would've made this next part a whole lot quicker for the both of us."

Dourn squats down by the rocks where my catch used to be. He scoops a handful of strips over his mouth before dropping my hard-earned catch into his greedy lips. Oil drips down his chops and he smears the grease across his chin with his forearm. The last pieces of the meat, he throws to the dirt for his Nodus.

"I've been lookin' all over for you, Faylen. So excited to finally have an uninterrupted moment alone with you. I've been meaning to clear the air between us for"—his voice oozes like burning tar—"let's call it the final time."

The boy's tiger flanks me slowly, cutting off one of few escape routes. By himself, I know the wild beast wouldn't harm me in the woods, but he's here with his Master. The two are going to work in unison, no matter the target, so long as it's a strategically reasonable kill. I'd call my Nodus too, but frankly, I don't know if Magnus would even show up. To try would mean taking my focus off the immediate threat by shouting through the trees. Instead, I rotate with careful steps to keep both boy and tiger safely in my periphery. It's then I decide on a new tactic: shifting this uneven fight back to even odds.

"Well, congrats, you finally found me. But what say we keep

this a fight between men? You and your troop dogged me just the other day for letting my Nodus win all the glory in my proving hunt. If you're the better between us, prove it."

I watch him consider this point. At last, Dourn gives a slight head nod and his crimson familiar growls a deadly threat before taking off for rear positioning.

Immediately I drive my feet into the earth to stand my ground. My lips tighten and I crack my neck. The space between my shoulders goes tense and is consumed by a wave of tingling pricks. Dark black stripes swirl over my brown skin, my eyes flash with light green aura. Claws snap from my fingertips and my muscles engorge. I ease this strengthened form onto the front halves of each foot. Once done, I step forward to issue my challenge.

It is unsettling to see Dourn watching with half-lidded eyes as he lets out a bored sigh.

"Even when you should be at your strongest, you still can't help but be an embarrassment to our clan. You and I both know you're missing a few things."

The boy takes no time at all matching my Embrace. He even pauses long enough to gloat, then surpasses it. The differences between us are all too obvious. The weight of all that extra sinew and tendon sink him several inches into the dirt—a clear sign his muscular Embrace is a good deal denser than my own. His human ears are lost to a layer of fur, replaced seconds later by twitching tiger's ears atop his head. This marks another advantage he has over me. For just as I've witnessed my own brother's ears move independently to collect information from all angles, Dourn's move the same now. His claws grow several inches longer than mine on both hands and a wicked set rips through his combat lugs to carve the earth. A coarse tail whips behind the boy's back, compensating his balance. Dourn crooks his neck within the fortress of his shoulders. A pretentious smile snakes across his face, and as it does, two lengthy fangs reveal themselves behind his lips.

He makes a big show of flexing different muscle groups and

I envy his clear level of control. I wish I could match the depths of his Nodus bond. I've never taken on Magnus's full power and certainly can't risk trying it now. Maybe there I would find the strength to beat him. But without practice, I could just as easily don so much muscle, that I collapse my skeleton in the process.

Dourn waves a hand over his nearly perfected form. "Well, whadya' think? Might not be the Silver Fang's bond, but hey, look at it this way. After I'm done beating it out of you, you won't have it either!"

I've had enough of his mouth. Thinking to catch him by surprise, I break into a sprint toward the river where he stands. Pebbles and leaves kick up behind me. A full out leap would've given me the advantage of the air, but I think this approach is the better opening move. Leaping at that speed always leaves me exposed with limited perception.

Dourn's eyes are a lush green and with his senses, I suspect he has perceived my dash thoroughly. A huff under his breath suggests he understands my limitations. The boy compresses his leg muscles for half a second before propelling forward to meet me. His launch explodes a cloud of dirt clods and heavy stone high into the air behind him. His approach is quick, making it difficult to detect his charge. In fact, portions of his body are a blur as he heads straight for me. I slow to brace into my stance and absorb his impact as our bodies clash. A loud snap from rapidly compressed air escapes the space between us as we collide.

I try to get an angle on Dourn as his hefty momentum resets, darting in and out of his range in circular dashes. Going from two feet to all fours and back, I close in, claws reaching out to drink his blood. But with every swipe, I fail to find him in the space he'd occupied only a second before. Weaving around him this way feels like chasing a ghost. I gain nothing but a slew of painfully close misses. Meanwhile, Dourn is grinning, hands folded behind his back. He sees it all clearly.

I am a moth, and he is a flame—getting close means nothing when he is untouchable.

I switch strategies, focusing on making contact with a slew

of quick jabs. This time, I celebrate when a few of them connect. But I quickly realize he is in full control of where they fall. A jab to the shoulder, a light strike to his chest, a drive toward his face—all slapped away with the back of his hand. Finally, I throw in a feint then commit to finding the bridge of his nose. The hit is good but comes at the cost of a devastating hammer fist to my jaw.

I fall to a knee but quickly regain composure. Our huntress didn't raise no one-n'-done son. Surprisingly, it takes Dourn a few extra seconds to recover from the hit I landed on his nose. My trained instincts kick in, for within those brief seconds, I see my opening.

This time, I abandon nearly all precautions and lunge for the boy, claws extended on either side of his torso, looking to sever any muscle that will even the fight. At an arm's length away, focus returns to Dourn's face. Though he isn't as Embraced as a fully Mastered clan member, an arm's distance is more than enough space for him to react. He ducks, disappearing from my approach path, letting my body tumble into the earth.

I punch my claws into the ground to slow my momentum and whip around, protecting my back from the enemy. A clod of dirt slams into my face, caking my eyes, nose, and mouth. I cough hoarsely and rub my eyes to regain vision. Dourn guffaws and the sound echoes.

"Didn't expect a child's move to work on you so easily. A dirtball to the face? You're lucky I don't dig your grave and bury you in it right here and now! Would anyone even miss you?"

Just as I'm able to see again, a python's grip locks around my ankle. My leg almost pops out of socket as Dourn slings my whole body from the dirt, over his head, and back into the hard ground on the other side of him. My head is abuzz and the taste of iron floods my mouth.

"You are every ounce the loser I've chocked you up to be. In fact, I think I'll give you a bit of an advantage. Since we're so mismatched, how 'bout I give you an extra Gift? The ability to know the future!"

A sharp pain drills my spine as Dourn drops his elbow into

my back with the entirety of his dense body weight. I don't mean to, but a raw scream escapes my throat.

He tussles my hair while sitting on my hips, pinning me into the dirt. "Shut up, Faylen. Cry if you want, but no one is coming to help you all the way out here." He clears his throat. "Now, I said I'd let you glimpse your future. Here's how the rest of this little blood duel of ours is gonna' go."

I squirm under the boy's weight but he's sitting right on my center of gravity. I'm completely stuck, writhing in the dirt like a worm.

"I'm glad the Domain was the second Trial we had this annual. After today, I don't want you simply being sent back as an apprentice. The way I see it, I have the unique opportunity to rob you of your entire destiny in one go." He smacks the back of my head making my eyes blur.

He continues as I cough up dirt. "My destiny you might ask? It's to do something great. Like going to the Discipline of Peace and returning to this village a legend. But thing is, leaving for glory means I won't be around to keep you low in the mud where you belong. I need to give you a lasting reminder of the failure you truly are—someone who never deserved our clan's admiration."

"You think I want it?" I spit through gritted teeth. "They ride me with higher expectations than anyone else in our generation! How is that a good thing for me?"

Dourn pauses, considering the argument but ultimately dismisses it. He scoops a handful of dust and sprinkles it into my locs, then holds my face to the ground.

"It's funny. I really could just end you here and now. Trust me, I'm considering it. Who wouldn't believe that you died to some beast somewhere out here in the Domain?" He pauses long enough for me to realize he has a point. "Next, I've thought I'd make you match your old man by ripping a limb off you. That one-armed hack never deserved to beat out my Pops as Head of the Clan. But truthfully, I'm feeling in a more creative mood today. As I said before, I've plans for you."

My heart pulses inside my chest, if only I could get a bit of leverage. I try putting my elbows underneath me to allow room to buck the boy off.

He presses on unimpressed. "I've decided, why take just one arm, when technically I can take all your limbs. Ruin you so badly yet leave your parts intact so no Mender can ever put you back together. You'll be no hunter then. Just a cripple stuck watching life in this village pass him by."

Finally, I gain an angle on him, pressing against the ground with both hands. I only get a couple inches from the dirt before my rival punches me in the shoulder blade, nearly knocking it out of joint. I collapse back to the earth, and he chuckles sarcastically at the attempt.

"I end your story here and now. No clan will claim you. No young apprentices will seek you out."

He lowers his lips to whispering distance of my ear. "No lady-wolf will want your seed."

I snarl, unhinged in the soil, flailing about to no avail.

He scoffs at the struggle. "Okay, okay. Gee, have some patience! You're right, enough foreplay. Let's begin! Where would you like me to start? Oh, I know. Remember that feeling after you've been running all day and your legs are limp?" He pauses and shifts his weight, then drives his claws into my upper thigh scraping bone. "Consider running to no longer be your problem after I've given you a few more of these."

I try not to cry out, I really do, but it's too much. Tears stream down the bridge of my nose as the boy finally stands up, allowing me to breathe in again. My gasps are uneven and I'm afraid to break down into chest heaving sobs in front of him.

"Get up, Faylen. I'm going to pull you apart by the joints, but I won't have my victory soiled by you weeping in the mud. I want to hear the sounds you make when the ugly truth sinks in." He spreads his arms out to our surroundings to highlight how utterly alone the two of us are. "You're no hunter, and it's your turn to be the prey."

I stagger to my feet, limping unevenly. The holes in my thigh have blood trickling down my leg, but I'm lucky they are punctures instead of full-on slashes. Dourn could've severed the tendons all the way down if he'd wanted to. I imagine that'll come later, but for now, he's enjoying drawing this out.

I carefully edge closer to my foe in a fighting stance. I keep my weaker leg forward to allow my strong leg the defensive position. I hold one set of claws in front of my face and the other cocked behind my ear, an imitation of Muma's own fighting stance.

Dourn's eyes flicker like a snake from my face to my thigh. I don't have time to blink before he spins into a turn, sweeping my injured leg entirely from beneath me. My upper body swings forward to catch myself.

Sadly, I never hit the ground.

Dourn completes his turn, slamming an enforced fist straight upward. The air around his knuckles snaps as he drives them full force into my cheekbone. My vision fogs over and I feel my body tumble, then roll uncontrolled. When I teeter back to my knees, I'm all the way back to the tree I started this fight under. My skull aches. My leg throbs. My body doesn't respond when I tell it to get up.

Dourn stays back at the banks, pelting me with skipping stones like I'm target practice. After a few land, his haughty expression droops into boredom once more. "Somehow you've managed to make even the act of pulling you apart a disappointment. Maybe I'll find my fun elsewhere. Let's end this. " He snorts and spits at his feet. "Enjoy the rest of your crippled life."

I glare at the boy's nonchalant demeanor. I'm no threat to him, not at this level of Embrace.

He ignores the hostility in my eyes. "Speaking of the future, by the time you see me coming back from the Discipline, this village will be my oyster. After my father, I'll be Clan Head one day. But ya' know what I was thinkin' about before that? Becoming a good 'ole Elevation Headmaster. I'll show all the youngsters how to really take down an opponent. How—like me—they too can be the best."

I try to focus on the endurance sparring sessions Tygon and I drilled at our hideout. My lungs scream their disagreements as I slow my breathing, exchanging short breaths for long inhales and exhales.

The goon continues, "Say, won't your bratty little sister be in Elevation 'round that time? If she's anything like you, I bet she'll need someone to hold her back a few extra seasons."

My breathing slows but my fists tremble.

"Shoot, I wonder how fast your entire kin would implode in on itself if she just happened to not make it back from a hunt one day. We all know just how dangerous the Wilds can be, after all." His eyes reflect a murderous glint.

Kleo's precious face flashes through my mind. In an instant, a stream of all the people I love overflows through my head. This turd isn't just threatening me, he's thrashing my life and the people who make it worth living. Do what you will to me—threaten my people though, and you will pay.

He pouts. "Really? Still nothing from you? All right, have it your—"

Dourn never finishes that sentence. The Embrace that takes me is the most intense muscular amp I've ever had, easily surpassing my half-mile jump transformation. I still don't have the extra features the boy wears, but my fibers are twice as compact as his. A faint shade of gray spills into the spaces between my darkened stripes. There's only a single drawback—since strength has overtaken me, my senses are gone except for enough focus to see a small circle where Dourn's navel is.

Good enough.

I surge forward, splitting several trees behind me with explosive force and my footfalls leave a trench in their wake. Dourn's reflexes prove too slow for him to so much as flinch by the time my fist is an inch from target. Moving this fast, I have all the time in the world to see him blinking dumbfounded at the tree line I've left behind in ruins.

My knuckles slam into the boy's abdomen, twisting his gut into a fleshy vortex. We travel forward together as my momentum carries us into the river's shallows, well past where Dourn stood planted a second before. I extend into the fullness of my punch as we slow but snag his vest to keep him from tumbling away.

An animalistic growl takes control of my throat and my voice is jagged glass when I speak.

"Oh, no you don't fall away that easily Dourn. It's I who has plans for you. This time, let me tell you your future. My loved ones' names will never pass those lips ever again."

The fangs in my mouth twist into a dark grin.

"Now enjoy the rest of *your* life wearing a new face."

I jerk Dourn's collar toward the ground, yanking his whole torso downward. With a measured twist of my core, I fuse a hardened kneecap with his ugly maw. His nose turns to pulp that drains down my upper thigh as the blow molds his skull.

I watch the green in his eyes flicker as his Embrace threatens to leave him altogether. From his reaction to the earlier hit, I figured this spot would be his undoing. It was only a matter of reaching it.

Yet somehow despite his eyes nearly rolling in his head, unfortunately, he's still in this fight.

Dourn squints to rein in his focus while staunching his newly inverted nose with his hands. He spews both blood and wild threats from split lips at an impressive rate. The enraged hunter lists every person close to me that he can remember and assigns them every manner of unholy fates I'll never unhear. But I've already warned him once. So by the time he details the ways he'd ruin Lunis, my mind reels. He tilts his head back, trying to use gravity to slow the bleeding.

The predator in me only sees an exposed underbelly left open for a second time. I can almost picture the wriggling innards within.

My growl morphs into human voice again. "I may be prone to my mistakes, Dourn, but this has only taught me not to make them twice. Clearly, that's a lesson you've yet to learn."

The rock surface beneath my combat lugs splinters as I power into a low squat. Tiger's instincts beg me to open my foe up. My claws demand his flesh. At the last second though, I reel back enough control to slam my fist up into him instead, driving it at a higher angle than the first gut punch. My forearm spikes deep into the boy's diaphragm, nearly sending his lungs through the bottom of his throat. He spews bloody vomit before hurtling through the air, landing in a heap at the water's edge. His chest heaves to find wisps of air but his Embrace has disappeared completely.

I fall to my knees and suck in hoarse breaths. Okay. That one took its toll. Lying in the mud, I watch the slight gray drain from my trembling hands. I can't believe I was able to change this much. I may have just unlocked the higher levels of the Silver Fang's strength.

After a few moments of recovery, I trudge over to Dourn. In the end, I somehow managed to keep from slaughtering him. I can't say he'd have offered me the same consideration. I turn him over and inspect his clothes for the leather belt. As I rip it from his torso, the blooded chime he'd kept all this time teeters from his pocket, but alas, before I can reach it, it's swept away by the current. Even floating around the bend, its scent is strong, but I'm far too exhausted to chase after it.

Dourn's Nodus tries edging closer to his Master. I can tell the crimson tiger wants to challenge me to protect his bonded, but after my display of power, the animal knows it is not the Alpha between us.

Seconds later, my Embrace leaves as well, but first I drag the unconscious lump of a boy back to the tree line. Dourn responds to the sudden movement by unwittingly upchucking the remains of my catch. I dump him in a nearby patch of dung-a-lew berries, making sure a few pop their oozing slime to release unbearable stench over his clothes and skin. In the unlikely chance he manages to recover and foolishly continue the duel, I'll be able to smell him a mile away.

In addition to my own self-defense, I'm also dooming him for the rest of the Trials. He won't sneak up on anyone else. His Trials are thoroughly undone, and I have doomed him. He will be held back to apprentice …maybe this time he'll learn not to obsess over what he mistakes for a weaker opponent.

I limp away, trying to ignore the pain radiating through my punctured thigh. There's so much I need to find before nightfall arrives—a replacement meal, water, and shelter to recover until dawn.

I look down at the second belt around my waist. I could leave right now back for my hideaway, but I'm more determined than ever to make that Discipline spot happen. Still, I have to consider I'm worth more in this moment than I was an hour ago. If an opponent takes me out, that's an immediate two belts for them. Meanwhile, I would leave these woods wearing none and without a blooded item.

That's not going to happen though. No one gets to stand in my way anymore, not after what I just accomplished.

15

Awaken

This morning following the brawl is the most painful I've ever had. Solint sends its rays over the horizon to meet me where I've made camp a mile past the river. It seems to mock me here on the fourth daybreak of the Trials, mercilessly baking me while I grit my teeth with every move. The gouges in my leg barely allowed me to sleep. Any shut eye I did manage was cut short by nightmares of chasing a blooded item against an endless and freezing river current.

As the sky finishes changing out of her star-sewn nightgown, light reveals bloody bandages clinging to my leg. I sit among the roots of a nearby tree and take out the last of Kleo's bandages. The good news is I was able to find a cloudberry shrub before yesterday's sunset. These shrubs are covered in white buds, the bulbs known for their sticky nectar. As Half-Points we are introduced to self-medication—treatment using what the Wilds offer us. These particular buds are one of our first lessons. When exposed to air, the nectar forms a web-like mesh—perfect for sealing wounds. Last night, I filled up my pockets with extra to get me through the remainder of the Trials.

Looking beneath my bandages now, I see blood is no longer seeping freely. The first of my three dressings didn't last long. Dourn certainly did a number on the back of my thigh, and it was all I could do to wrap up the wound before the obvious scent gave me away. In similar fashion to the fish guts, I had to dig a hole to hide the wrappings soon after I'd put them on.

As I apply my last bandages now, the breeze rustles a nearby bush, loosening a cluster of nuts to the jungle floor. The chestnut morsels roll lopsidedly against the side of my leg, and I desperately pop a handful into my mouth. Their savory flavor cleanses blood from my pallet, and I'm grateful to have something in my stomach since Dourn swiped my catch and I was too exhausted to search for food after our duel.

A tiny nose wriggles through the leaves in front of me, followed by two round eyes, a fluffy head and a pair of long wispy ears. A twin-tailed hare edges out from its hiding spot, drawn to the treats I've only just found.

I chuckle to myself, whispering to the hare, "Nice joke, little guy. Let me guess which Spirit sent you at a time like this? Was it Comeo?" I'm referring to one of Sage Ophis's legends about a Spirit who enjoyed watching early human life so much, that he renounced Everrealm and became a traveler gifting humor to Spheire.

Of course, my luck isn't good enough for my new visitor to be wearing a blooded collar. Regardless, I reach out to the little creature, and it walks over to my outstretched hand and takes a nut carefully. It's not lost on me how easily he would make a meal, but I let him devour the morsel in peace. Then, the hare is off, back into the underbrush, wagging tails behind him.

Burying my soiled wrappings, I follow the hare's example and leave the rest spot as well.

Yesterday wasn't a packed day for only my bullies and me, the Behemoth Drummer has been busy too. Of the original fifteen collared hares, ten are off the table leaving five unclaimed. My pain was at its peak when one after another, a number of the creatures were released into the Domain. Later, I heard seven short drumbeats sound through the trees, confirming that grouping of collars were turned in. Throughout all of it, I was too busy trying to keep quiet while the cloudberry nectar stung my wounds. Now, only five collars and five chimes are left. I've hardly got two days to find an item and I would hate to try to fight another student for their belt in my condition. Time to move, noon on the sixth day is rapidly approaching.

Solint is well past its apex as I trudge along, knocking back my last thimble-sack of pain medicine. The minced flower petals go down easy with a swig from my waterskin. I plan to continue on this side of the river, following its bank farther into the center of the Domain. I've kept keen senses on the woods so far, searching out any waiting apprentices, yet the farther in I go, the more on edge I become.

My ears perk up when a short drumbeat sounds—the signal for a collared hare. I freeze in place then doubletake when the faint smell of deer blood meets my nostrils. The scent is light, but it's steady. The hare was let loose from a post near me. Finally, a shot! I take off in the scent's direction, the concern for my leg somehow melting away between excitement and the medication taking effect.

As I run, I Embrace further into my senses, allowing the deer blood to highlight into a swirling stream of red ahead front of me. I scramble to the top of a nearby tree for a better overview of the landscape. The wispy scent snakes through the woods, then diverts like a straight path toward the skeleton-like ridge a mile away. My mind scrambles as I realize it's headed back in the direction I camped out the first few nights. Apparently, the critter and I have similar instincts when it comes to staying safe in the Domain of Bones.

The wind tosses my locs as I fly through the canopies. I make as little noise as possible with every jump. Intangible scarlet strands hang in the air beyond my reach, converging as I close the distance to their source. I try to sense for any other Elevation apprentices, but as I suspected, none are between myself and the animal.

A few minutes go by and I'm finally at the base of the looming stoneface. I scan its surface, there are hundreds of burrows here and who knows which one the critter could be in. No matter, the little guy is nearby and that's what counts. I inhale deeply, trying to at least narrow down a section the hare could've crawled into. The smaller holes dotting the ridge look like shallow standalones from down here, but I know in reality, most of them are interconnected deep within the rock like an anthill.

The trail seems to stop near the summit. As I climb, each foothold becomes more difficult to find with the weakened strength of my injured leg, but at least the pain dampener is doing its job. I'll take reduced speed over discomfort any day.

At the top of the gravelly slab, a sweeping view of the Domain spreads out before me. Looking toward the center, I can see the direction of the post Tygon would have been near for the last few days. My predictions of heavy conflict in that heading are confirmed as three distant figures leap above the treetops. Two of them slam into the third, flinging the person back down through the canopies. I shake my head, glad that's not me—I've faced enough tough odds for one week.

I focus in on the deer blood once more. The smell is thick. I'm right on top of the hare. It's just at the base on the other side of this hulking ridge.

I'm about to scurry down the opposing rock face when a sight catches my eye. At the base, massive footprints cover the ground, leading to a line of collapsed trees. The trail of destruction draws toward the left, the fallen trees extending a couple miles before breaking into a large clearing where no treetops are left standing.

I don't like it. The only thing that can move through the jungle like that is a monstrous creature no Master would dare go near. In fact, the only way most hunters encounter one is by running into its clearing on accident to find they've wandered into one of their trampling nests. I don't know anyone who's seen the fabled Saberhorn up close, and I don't need to be the first. Headmaster Lujan has warned many times that being anywhere near these epic beasts is a quick ticket to Everrealm.

For now, the hare can wait, until I get a better sense for where the creature is. Thankfully, their large bodies mean they're also too heavy to climb so I'm relatively safe on this perch. As exposed as my outline is atop this ridge, I'm pretty sure it's the safest place to make an escape if need be.

A few moments of scanning the jungle below and I see a massive horn curve out from among the treetops. There, a mile away from its trampling nest, the Saberhorn rears up on its back legs. The mammoth beast is larger than any living thing I have ever seen. Before its body slams back down into the jungle, I can see its moss-shaded hide covered in overlapping thick plates. The monster's back is encased like a jagged version of a turtle shell, providing evidence for why they haven't been prey to anything since dragons ruled the skies.

The creature lets out a shrill boom from its mouth that sends every bird a mile around flocking into the air. It rocks from front legs to the rear ones, pounding thunderous vibrations all the way to the ridge beneath my feet. Trees collapse around it, and I wonder if that will be a new spot for a trampling nest.

I click my tongue behind my teeth, grateful the monstrosity is so far away, but keeping caution in mind. I'm just going to grab the hare, secure the collar, and be gone before anything changes. I look up again to see a few apprentices jumping through the canopies a mile away from the Saberhorn. Apparently, I wasn't the only one on this side of the Domain looking for the hare. Too bad for them, they came from the wrong side of the ridge. The Beast Masters fly through the trees, shouting to one another as they make distance away from the stampede.

With their focus solely on leaving the area, I'm free to turn my full attention to the hare. Like them, I too will be gone once I claim my prize. That monster can stay over there, I will stay over here—everything will work out just fine so long as we each mind our own business.

I poke my head into the first few burrows below me, sniffing out the deer blood when I hear a distant roar spike into a high-pitched shriek. That's the sound of searing pain, meaning somebody must've gotten into a nearby tussle and taken an unplanned hit. So many blood duels…the celebratory stories told at this annual's Selection Festival are going to earn many toasts of maplecomb-mead. I can't wait to hear how Tygon did, and find out how Lunis outsmarted someone this time...or see her dance in the dancing circle—

Another roar interrupts my thoughts. It begins with decent power but ends once more in an agonized shriek. I pause to home in on the aurem in the area. Whichever apprentices are dueling over here must be fighting like crazy. At first, I don't sense anything other than the specks coming off the pair fleeing the Saberhorn. Then as another roar sounds, I see a small uptick. It's an auburn one.

My mind races through the possibilities, eliminating each one until a single fear remains. PanCanis aurem matches the auburn shade of their eyes during Embrace, but it's usually more distinct than this. Images flash of the times I've detected the wolf-bonded Masters...their aurem was more obvious because they run in packs. Duh.

This is the Hunter Trials, so there are no packs.

This time, the wavering roar only sounds for a second before slicing the air in its high pitch. Only females can hit that kind of frequency. It can't be a coincidence that the sound is coming from the blip of auburn aurem. My heart nearly stops as I place the huntress' location right at that Saberhorn's new clearing.

Oh no. Lunis.

I Embrace into an immediate muscular boost and bound off the top of the rock formation. In mid-air, I try calling out to Magnus. I was afraid his presence would tip me off before, but if that's Lunis, who cares about being discovered. I'll need every bit of help I can get, even if he's nowhere near big enough to take on a threat this large. If growing up bonded to that creature has taught me anything—he may not always come when I call, but he's usually not too far away. I'll have to hope this is one of the times he shows up. Like a guardian angel with selective hearing.

I still don't have a plan by the time I arrive near the scene of the Saberhorn's destruction. I can barely stand considering the earth quaking all around me. I try to sense out any living beings nearby aside from the Saberhorn and immediately pick up the auburn aurem again. No doubt about it. I know this exact hue…it's definitely Lunis.

Through the tree line, I glimpse her for the first time. She's Embraced into her bonded's traits—a pair of pointed ears lays low against wavy hair, she bares long pearly fangs, and two sets of lethal claws hang ready to slice. A light layer of gray and black fur covers the back of her neck, arms, and back, ending in a bushy tail. Then I see it.

A scarlet flow streams from bloody gashes in her shoulder, side, and leg. Above the tree line, I can see the Saberhorn's ivory spike towering above the canopies. Its tip glints with a red sheen. The beast begins to charge at Lunis, but even with her injuries, she's nowhere near done fighting. She heaves a large stone onto her shoulder and hurtles it at the beast with devastating aim, sending the stone straight through its wrinkled eyelid into the softness beneath.

It howls in agony, rampaging in a circle before restarting its charge toward the mismatched opponent. Lunis can only limp to a crag in a nearby boulder, shimmying inside the crevasse. I can hear her praying the titan will somehow miss. The Saberhorn levels its tree-sized horn to obliterate the girl's feeble stronghold.

Time seems to freeze as my world crashes in around me. I have never felt more incapable in my life and no kin, no brother, no friend, no Headmaster, and no Nodus can help me. As the jungle spins chaotically, my mind sinks into the depths of emotional madness. I try to Embrace further, but through the fear and desperation, the transformation can't find me. A soot-stained demon claws into my brain and whispers hoarse truths I already know—the power that came to me when fighting Dourn wouldn't be nearly enough here. To save Lunis, I'd need the kind of legendary strength the previous Silver Fang's chosen possessed. Imaginings flash before me of Grandpa Ravir's wartime feats—him facing off against an army single-handed. It only serves to fuel my devastation. I am nowhere near accessing that level of power and I haven't discovered the secrets needed to get there.

BEASTS WITHIN OUR BLOOD

The jungle trembles as the Saberhorn closes in some one hundred mets from Lunis. The trapped girl's hyperventilated sobs ring so loud in my ears because I know I'd be too slow to reach her.

In the frozen space around me, a new presence emerges. I look to my flank to see Magnus standing there solemnly. His cool green eyes examine the scene in front of us before turning to fixate on my twisted face. The giant gray tiger stares through me, the hint of disappointment more resolute than usual. He expects more?

"What in Everrealm do you want from me, you stoic cat? You know darn well I can't do anything here when all I wish is that I could! She's got maybe another thirty seconds, and my friend is gone!" I scream at him.

His eyes hold mine for a moment before shifting to gaze at Lunis. She may be far away, but her tears are so clear I could practically wipe them from here. A pit forms in my chest as I watch her head shake uncontrollably between trembling hands. Her Embrace is starting to fade from the blood loss. She whispers to herself fears of death and has every right to do so.

The tiger peers into my soul one last time before he turns to inch closer to me. Both eyes churn in their own unique storm of glowing emerald. A low growl hums from deep inside his chest and I can almost hear the interpretation.

I understand his message.

No one is coming. My kin couldn't help me even if they were here. The Dominant and Sage couldn't either. Even Magnus can't strike the rampaging monster in a way that would stop its attacks. A chunk of rock to the eye hardly slowed it and the beast simply wears too much armor. In all of Animas, only the Silver Fang's chosen could take this battle. At some point, I have to stand up or no one will.

With twenty seconds left, even Magnus's speed now wouldn't matter to yank the girl from the rocks. A single force balances the equation needed to safeguard her life. A single factor. The inner strength I've been granted by a power higher than myself. Its full potential in this moment will only ever be realized through me.

I am the one Magnus chose.

I am the instrument.

I have been called.

Tree leaves whisper around us as I bury my forehead in the giant tiger's chest, engulfed in the warmth of his gray fur.

"Thank you, Silver Fang," I whisper.

With a breath, midnight stripes rip across my body. A deep gray hue rushes over me, scattering the brown of my skin. My bones cry out as the monumental weight of a million tightly packed fibers bears down upon me. Then, my frame evens out as I feel my skeleton expand to match. Savage claws arc out from my fingers and toes, the tightly fitting combat lugs turned to shreds as my feet expand seven-fold. A thick coil snakes out the back of my hips, and I feel a new sense of balance as my tail whips through the air. My eyes glint like polished jade.

I capture this moment in time. My body is at its greatest power, dwarfing what I felt when I drove my fist into Dourn's gut. The transformation has compressed the earth around me, and I now stand completely immersed in a freshly made crater. Where I only put cracks into the ground beneath me before, it takes a graceful leap to climb out of the hole I've carved into the earth by my presence alone. Magnus meets my eyes, and I detect only satisfaction and expectation from my Nodus. No matter what happens, in this instant and for the first time, he and I are one. I hold onto the sensation, hoping today won't be the last time I feel it. But tomorrow is not my concern. Only one thing rings in my head to describe the feeling I hold in my hands.

Titan's blood coursing through human veins.

Emotion still clouds my thoughts, but I must keep a clear mind if I'm to steer the full mastery of the Silver Fang's power. I don't have time to think further on it, so despite a haze around my vision's edge, I simply go. My surroundings seem to shimmer back to normal and I blur through the canopies, instantly soaring above the jungle below. My senses pinprick, then expand, magnifying this entire side of the Domain's tapestry into my mind. *Wow, is this how Magnus perceives the world?*

For the first time in my life, I feel like I can truly see.

Solint's rays bounce off every surface beneath me far brighter than before. I can see the particles of dust launched from each step the Saberhorn takes. I can see the individual scales that overlap to make up its armored back. I can see the cracks and vulnerabilities that age has etched into each one. I can see through its hide and muscle into its thumping heart.

As I fall, accelerating toward the animal, my own rage mixes in with the flow of heightened senses. They feed off each other. The jungle rushes forward to welcome me as I dive for the clearing. I have claimed power, yes, but everything I've gained is admittedly too much for the boy I am. Faylen becomes lost. He can hardly remember his purpose for fighting, only that a target exists. A dormant beast has control. Faylen may be approaching eighteen seasons old, but in this moment, he is little more than a small child holding reins to a storm.

Lunis

I can't help but cry as I hear the Saberhorn charge outside my hideout. I know these boulders aren't enough to keep me safe from the giant's horn, but I didn't have anywhere else to go. I'm freaking out. My body hurts from the gashes that crazed titan gave me while I tried to jump away. Didn't mean to bother the overgrown brute. I had no idea I was between it and its trampling nest. I only wanted to get to that hare and go home to my wolf-kin. I'm not used to being so alone like this. I dunno' how the other clans get so used to it. My kin, my pack...that's all I've got in this world, and I wish more than anything that they were here.

I hear a new roar detonate the air outside my hideout. I peek my head out from between the rocks to see a gray streak fall from the sky and collide with the horn of the monster, forcing its head off course from my direction. My ears almost bleed as the Saberhorn cries out in surprise. It scrambles to regain footing and plants its hooves to fling its head. The gray and black shape grasping the massive horn is launched clear into the forest behind me. *I watch it fall, but whatever it was is lost to the trees, only the sound of its tumbling through the distant woods remains.*

The angry creature turns its last good eye back at me and it blows dust clouds from its snout. Bashtol! That could've been my chance to escape! Before I can make a move, the Saberhorn charges again.

I watch the folds under its neck tremble back and forth as the creature barrages forward. With its horn lowered, the bull splits the ground between us. I don't stand a chance.

I'm so sorry, Muma and Papa. Zahk, my siblings and PanCanis. I—

A breath later and a muscled figure appears beside me. His whole body is gray and covered in glossy lines of starless night. The air around him hums with power, occasionally distorting in a way that seemingly defies the breeze. Waist-long black locs streaked with white weave into a cluster that rests behind his thick shoulders. He turns his shimmering green eyes to me.

The face this Hunter wears is so familiar to me...

"F-Faylen, i-is that you?"

I know the slight smile that appears on the Beast Master's face. Unbelievably long claws are poised at his fingertips and he raises one to point to his breastbone. My hand slides up to the warm moonstone pendant dangling over my chest. Those sage eyes offer a promise for protection before the Master stands-off against the incoming beast. The humming sound around him reverberates into an all-time low when he sinks into a leaping stance. I hardly blink and he's gone. Only tranquil silence and shattered rock remain in the space he once stood as he flickers through the air.

The crackle that breaks across the Wilds a second later and the shockwave that follows bows every tree around this clearing. From here, it appears the gray streak has collided with the Saberhorn's wide skull, resulting in a meaty snap from within the beast's neck. The raging bull no longer stampedes, but slumps to the ground, dragging its armored hide through the dust. Its body begins to lose speed as it slides toward me totally unresponsive. A slow huntress is a dead huntress and I certainly don't need *instructions. This time, I'm gone from the crevasse while I have the chance.*

When the creature's momentum stops, I see its good eye bloodshot and rolled into the back of its head. There is no neck left to be seen as the throat section is entirely blown out, driven deep into the beast's scaly body. The collision must have imploded the titan's spinal column somewhere inside the chest cavity. Well, I'll be a tender-pawed pup. I didn't know Saberhorns could be killed outside a dragon's blaze.

The Beast Master pulls himself out from within the corpse and stands atop, striking it wildly until the horn shatters at the base. It falls into the earth like a logger's tree, trembling the ground. The Master does nothing for a moment, then heaves his shoulders and tosses his head to the sky. Thick dreads of savage hair whip around him. He blasts a roar into the clearing and what's left of the trees surrounding us quiver down to their roots.

Blood loss begins to take its toll and my vision darkens. My Embrace left me a while ago and my thoughts are now a tangle worse than morning hair. Who knows, maybe I'm imagining everything I've just seen...but deep down, I don't think so. I know what I saw.

The Silver Emperor has returned to Animas.

16

Mender

There's no way this was me...
I peer around the clearing that held so much chaos mere seconds ago to see it has somehow gone completely tranquil. Despite standing amongst a sea of fragmented bark and leaves. Despite a dead Saberhorn at my feet...It's difficult to truly believe I was the cause.

I look down at my skin to see the fading signs of a typical Embrace—no gray, no tail, only faint black stripes. I try recalling anything that happened after my leap through the trees, but everything following that instant is blank. Once I accepted that I could not control the newfound power, it expanded to consume my every thought, leaving me shoved against the outskirts of my own mind.

The sounds of strained breathing nearby snap me from my confusion, bringing back my purpose for being here to begin with. Behind me, only a few steps from the boulder crevasse, Lunis shakes, trying to hold herself up. Her eyelids flutter and her toned shoulders quiver before she crumples down to her knees. Blood streams from her gouges and the brave huntress can hardly lift her drooping head while inspecting her injuries.

I'm there at the girl's side in seconds, scrambling to catch her before she falls over entirely. She's slow to recognize me, but after a moment, a faint smile breaks through layers of caked blood and dirt.

"H-hey, Stripes, I knew—I knew that was you." She nods at the Saberhorn's remains. Even such a small gesture causes her teeth to grit.

As my face scrunches into worry, a moment of clarity flickers into her eyes. She huffs under her breath to lift an arm to my face. I think she's about to caress my cheek, but in typical Huntress fashion, she lightly pushes my face away. One part to check me over, one part to redirect my anxious expression somewhere else. I unfurrow my brow slightly, acting more confident than I feel, and she accepts the small win.

She inhales sharply. "It's okay, I'll be fine…I will. I'm just glad you made it when you did. A minute later and this ole' girl would've been in Everrealm."

I absolutely refuse to picture the thought. Her eyelids close with a long exhale, as though she's fading into a much-needed rest. I look her over and know immediately that survival treatment isn't going to cut it. She needs real care from the village healers. I take the leftover cloudberries out of my pouch and squeeze the nectar into her open wounds, hoping the mesh that forms will hold off the bleeding until then.

"I was up on the ridge, looking for that hare when I picked up your aurem. I'm so happy I made it in time." I fold her arms over her chest, prepping her to be carried. "Lunis, I'm going to get you out of here, okay?"

The girl gives no hint that any of those words registered, but after collecting her legs and hardened torso into my arms, she mouths noiselessly. I put my ear to her lips and wait.

"I-I only took one belt. I c-can't leave yet," She raises her hand to lift the fringe of her vest, showing her original leather strap and a second one secured against her skin.

I see. Whether or not she intended for the Discipline, that hardly matters now. The real problem is we aren't at the full six days for the Trials to be over. Neither of us is allowed to depart early with the number of belts we have. I don't even have mine anymore after facing the Saberhorn. I hesitate, thinking over my options. I could make camp and search us out two blooded items for an instant exit. That plan isn't great since I could hardly find one for myself. That and Lunis needs help now. She might not bleed out fast considering the quickly forming mesh, but the material will only hold for so long.

My mind is made up as I stand, settling the girl's weight evenly in the crooks of my arms. Lunis's wavy hair falls gently into her face and a sense of calm eases across her grime-caked features. Steady breaths flow from her blood-stained lips. She never once gave up, never surrendered to her foe. No one deserves this moment of reprieve more than she does right now.

"Don't you worry about that second belt, darling," I whisper, knowing the words fall on deaf ears, "Somethin' tells me you'll be just fine."

I cradle her head to protect from whiplash and burst through the treetops, heading straight for Praedari.

When we finally arrive at the village Southern Gate, I sprint straight for the Nurse Dwelling. I slam and kick at the door, expecting a pretty-faced girl around Tygon's age to answer. It's always fun to tease him about her after we run errands out here—this sweet healer being one of only a few people who has ever flustered my eldest. Instead of her face, however, a boy a bit younger than myself opens the door and shows us to a fur lined cot. I look around for older, perhaps more experienced healers, but the dwelling is empty. The boy hurries out of the room, returning a couple moments later with several pouches, a neat stack of cloths, a sharp blade, and mixing supplies.

I watch curiously as he empties each small pouch, dropping minced flower petals, leaves, and herbs into a shallow bowl. Clearly a well-practiced expert, he mixes and grinds the ingredients with rapid finesse.

He looks up with a snap. "Get me that over there. Hurry!"

I follow his pointed finger across the clay hut to a sealed jar of aquamarine liquid. I grab it and hand it to him.

"No, you pour it. And do it slowly while I keep grinding." No sooner had I started do his eyes go wide. "Hey, s-slower! Spirits help us, that's a whole jar's worth of Angel Tears you're holding! You waste our delivery, fresh from Hayvin this morning and I don't know what we'll do." He murmurs something under his breath about the rare liquid needing a whole month's of his Bloodline's prayers to produce.

If this boy weren't helping Lunis, I would've certainly rolled my eyes. We're lucky to have a wanderer from the Bloodline of the Soul living in our village. Indom is our closest Southern neighbor and this boy's people claim lands further still called. His people live much closer to the capital Sanctum and the Discipline than Beast Masters do. As such, I don't know why he's grumbling at me now. How could I know the mysterious intricacies of the boy's healing? I, for one, have never seen so much Angel Tears in one place before. Sure, I've seen a vial or two used to accelerate the growth of a new tree, but not a whole jar. I surrender the thought, ignoring his unblinking stare as I concentrate once more on the pouring.

"Are there other healers here? Maybe your eldest sibling?"

He glances around the room as if just giving thought to the other workstations for the first time. "Hmm, I don't know about the others volunteering here, but I'm standing in for my sister, Puri. She had to take a Qirin ride out West. Another wandering Mender there required her aid in Avian village."

"Mending? Is that what you call your healing Gift?"

He smirks, shaking his head as if I'd said something absurdly simple. His hands continue to fly while he accomplishes his work.

I peer at the engraved amulet hanging from his neck. Confusing symbols disappear and reappear in a swirling fluid within the circular pendant, forming a beautifully complex pattern of interwoven spirals. I can't read the symbols, but I know what they are. You'd be considered lucky to learn even a few words of

Essence Tongue from someone born in Hayvin. The Bloodline of the Soul claim to be bilingual, speaking the same language as everyone else on Spheire, but a separate dialect too. It's been said that Essence Tongue is only known by his people—the Spirit-Born—used to meditate through the plains of Everrealm itself.

The healer catches my befuddled look at the magical-looking token and snaps his fingers in front of my face.

"Hey, Hunter, focus. Save yourself the time, I don't need you rupturing vessels in your eyes trying to read Essence Tongue. It's just a name—reads Orin."

I look back to Lunis, grateful she's sleeping peacefully. I hope this mending will stop her bleeding soon.

"Orin, was it? So, are you just sorta' passing through until Puri's back?"

The mender finishes mixing the solution and soaks the cloths in it.

"Yes, I rotated here from Primitas Village. Jumped at the chance to see what life was like in Praedari before my Wandering time is up and I head back home to Hayvin."

Orin scoops the bottom of the bowl, spreading the substance over the prepared cloths.

He addresses me again. "You, boy. After I'm done here, make sure you find the girl's kin and bring them over? You did well to come to our dwelling first, but her loved ones need to know she's in my care. After a few hours, she can finish resting back in her own tree."

I barely hide a smirk. *Boy? You're younger than I am, ya' squirt!* No matter. A Mender's journey is clearly far different than a Hunter's. I can only imagine the things he's seen in his time wandering the world. According to stories from Puri, where Beast Masters' lives revolve around hunting for the sake of the village, most from Hayvin leave their nation for many seasons to strengthen their mending skills for the needy. After a period living abroad, the Spirit-Born can return home to their people and elect to attend the Discipline of Peace.

Orin cuts into Lunis's vest and belt loops just enough to expose each wound. With tender hands, he begins removing the cloudberry mesh.

"Did you apply these out in the Hunter Trials?"

I nod, watching him rinse the blood and dirt from the deep gouges.

"Mmm, fantastic work. It is a little basic, but you may've saved your friend a couple weeks of recovery by stopping the bleeding, not to mention her life."

Orin pats each cleaned wound dry and applies the now glowing paste before applying bandages. Lunis's forehead wrinkles momentarily in her sleep then her whole body eases into a state of relaxation.

The young Spirit-Born begins cleaning up around him. He re-wraps unused herb pouches and stores them in a cubed basket.

"Do you have to pick all the plants you use yourself?" I ask as he scurries around the side of the cot.

He looks up at me. "Sometimes we get pre-packaged portions from the Healing Corps at the Discipline of Peace. They have a great set up there that I wish to see myself someday. However, there are some advantages to living within this beautiful jungle. It provides that which you simply cannot find anywhere else."

He pulls a vial of dark red flower petals submerged in clear green liquid from a pouch of many vials strapped over his thigh. Even with the lid corked shut, I can still smell the strong scent the Slumberrose within gives off.

"Try finding stuff like this anywhere other than Animas. You probably won't! Nowhere has an array of plant life like your land has. It's fascinating the variety your people have access to here." He wrinkles his brow as though just remembering something. "Now, Hunter, erm, what exactly was your name?"

"Oh yea, 'spose we never made it that far. Call me Faylen."

"Ah." He says, thinking it over. "Perhaps you can help me with something. I overheard from some elders in Primitas that there is supposedly a Beast Master in your village with some sort of rare bond to what they called an 'Epic beast'. In the same way sort of way, the Qirin are impossible to bond with except this fellow has managed to claim a pet called a…Pearly Fang? Could have sworn they said an old man fifty years back had a connection with one, but that doesn't seem right to me—"

His unfamiliarity with my village is honestly so cute to watch. At first I want to correct him, that Magnus is certainly no pet, but I'd rather let him ramble to hear what other absurdities he might spit out.

I give him thumbs up. "Mmm, yes, Pearly Fang is definitely what you're thinking of."

His eyes go wide with wonder and at that I can't keep up the act anymore.

"Okay, sorry, I just had to. You heard right, such a hunter exists, but he's certainly no old man. That was my Grandpops, but the current *Silver* Fang happens to be with me. When he's in the mood."

Orin's eyes light up and he moves quickly to my side, suddenly poking my body, tugging my ears, rousing through my locs.

"Ooooh, I see," he mumbles from behind a magnifying glass he's seemingly whipped from thin air. "No wonder the beast chose you, I can sense you've got quite a bright Resonance—"

"Wait, what? What's a Resonance?"

Orin swoops in front of me and places his hand over my hair, pressing his thumb into the center of my forehead. His thumbprint begins to warm then abruptly burns hotter than a match. I didn't get a good look earlier while he was working, but the boy's forehead, breastbone, and forearms are all etched with faded moon-shaped tattoos. When I inquire, he calls them "Luminares."

These luminares look identical to ones I've seen from one of the Council members on the moving metal tapestry in the Hub. She's called Exalt Danika, and I see her most often giving speeches at the start of the Discipline's showcase matches. The only difference is where she has a line of six full moons, Orin only has two full and one crescent moon on each arm. Both Spirit-Born share the same white dot on their foreheads.

As he continues pressing his blazing thumb to my skull, those tattoos illuminate with visible energy. As if his bones were made from Solint, the energy flows up his forearms to his forehead and back again. After a few seconds, the glow increases, nearly blinding me. Orin lets me go as I stand there swooning, feeling as though I'd just levitated up to the ceiling.

"Beasts and their Masters find each other out in the woods when you are young, right?"

I try to nod but it comes out looking like more of a head swirl. A dizzy sensation churns my stomach into a whirlpool.

He wags his finger, "Yes, with a Resonance like yours—I believe that word translates to aurem for you folk in Animas? Anyway, with what you have, that rare beast must've been drawn in like a beacon. Animals are ancient relatives of the Spirits, after all. But it's the rare ones like your Nodus that are much closer, more like great cousins of the Spirits who first inspired their forms."

The room finally stops spinning and I'm able to focus back on Orin. He beams a fanatical smile. Before I can complain, he plucks a tuft of fur from my wrappings, squirreling it away for unknown shenanigans before stopping beside me. He does a double take when seeing my damaged leg and gently pats along the thigh.

"Faylen, what happened here? What kind of snake bit you that you're able to walk into our dwelling all the way from the Domain…carrying a girl with you, no less?"

I hold my tongue, crafting my words carefully. I've decided that I'm going to keep a lot of what happened in the Domain to myself. No one would believe I downed a Saberhorn, especially when I don't remember the whole event myself. I don't want it getting out that I handed Dourn a new perspective on humility either. Someone might piece together that I gave my belt to Lunis and I'd like at least one of us to have passed these Trials.

"Look, Orin, if it's all right with you, I'd rather not talk about it. Let's just say there were a lot of fights this annual, and I got into my fair share."

He pats me on the shoulder. "Good enough for me, now hold still, this won't take long."

Without another word, the boy conjures a glow between his palms so bright, he could be a doula hand delivering new stars into the room. A warm sensation spreads across my leg. For a terrible second, searing agony shoots up my femur. However, before I even have time to yelp, it is replaced by a soothing feeling—like the first moments stepping into a scented bath.

"Sorry, Faylen, I know that initial part burns a bit. Since your wounds are small, the muscle strands are still close together, I'm able to stimulate these to grow into one another once again. Getting the layers moving so suddenly comes with certain pains, unfortunately."

A few minutes go by and my leg feels better than new.

"Well, I suppose you should be on your way to the girl's kin to let them know her whereabouts. Keep an eye on that leg, or rather, don't push yourself too hard. The connections I made are still fresh and if you aren't careful, you could rip the seams open again. Just take it easy."

I bow to the young Spirit-Born and let him know I'll bring by a few coins for donation later. He nods and joins his hands in front of his chest to form a circle over his breastbone. He bows deeply while maintaining the hand gesture to finish what I gather must be a typical greeting in the Bloodline of the Soul.

I'm able to breathe a bit easier knowing that I made the right choice taking Lunis out of the Domain. It's only a short jog to the grove of trees where the PanCanis live so I take off at a slow pace in that direction. On my way, I pass the People's Hall to see the clan heads just starting an evening meeting with Dom Arzen and Sage Ophis. A dirt-covered Elevation student rushes into the open-aired building and delivers something to the attendant inside.

I can easily make out a belt and a tiny strand of red cloth, a blooded item. Bashtol, I'm not looking forward to walking in there later empty-handed. Rescuing Lunis forced me out of the Domain with about a day and a half left in the Trials. Without the saving grace of a blooded item, leaving early is sure to mean instant disqualification.

I sigh to myself. Well, it can't be helped now. I suppose me and Dourn are going to have plenty more time to get re-acquainted since we'll both be held back in apprenticeship.

17

HARD TRUTH

I make it to the PanCanis grove in no time. The moment I gave my report to Lunis' parents, they dropped everything to rush straight for the Mender's dwelling. But right before the den's huntress left, Muma Rylia swept me up in her arms, making sure her gratitude was known. It's no wonder Lunis and Zahk have such big hearts with such a warm presence as this at the center of their lives.

    The couple made such quick time that on my way back into the village Hub, they're passing me to return home. I spot Lunis cradled like priceless treasure in her father's arms, and he gives me a grateful head nod. Still dazed from Orin's treatment, Lunis doesn't seem aware of much. However, our eyes meet for a moment in passing. She manages a slight wave, gifting me a hopeful smile. My hands almost sweep across my heart to offer her a lover's gesture—the smallest token to assure her she'll never once leave my thoughts. Seeing her this way sends tremors through my heart, like any person who's done all they can to shield a loved one from hard times. In the end, I betray my heart and settle for simply returning her wave.

    At the front steps of the People's Hall, it's clear the meeting I witnessed in session earlier has concluded. Only a couple clan elders remain, staying behind to converse with a small group of village workers. I walk in and nod to the attendant who rises from her chair to acknowledge me.

"Welcome back, young Elevation apprentice. Congratulations on being one of those who made it back early! So, what do you have for us?" She opens the lids to the baskets in front of her.

I squirm uneasily seeing the collection of belts and blooded items. I really hadn't planned this part out. Why are the honest truths always the hardest to admit?

"Er, well, ma'am, I have my—"

A meaty hand clamps down onto my shoulder, patting and rubbing in a familiar pattern. Oh no, not now. How I wish the hand had jostled the back of my neck instead.

"Now that's my son, back so soon with time to spare! What luck my meetings kept me late today so I could see you complete the Trials. I thought I'd have other errands to run, but I see the Spirits had other plans."

I look up at Papa Jaole, trying not to give away a sense of helplessness. Papa continues, completely oblivious to my fraying nerves.

"A day left in the Domain and here you stand. That's the Silver Fang's chosen for you." Papa Jaole claps my back while winking at the attendant. She smiles pleasantly at him, then looks to me, holding out her hand patiently.

I'd take another week of hunger and fatigue being chased and bruised through those trees, over enduring this twisted nightmare. I genuinely don't see a way this gets any worse—

"Brotya! I knew it, I knew that was you! I bet I would've beaten you here too if I had run just a bit faster!" Tygon says, laughing in between heavy breaths.

I nearly toss my head back in outrage but remember the importance of composure. I avoid the attendant's eye by looking to the nearby columns in front of me. Directly overhead an ugly banner waves lackluster in the breeze—the Spirit of Humor, Comeo. He grins down at me from behind a grotesque playright's mask as though having a laugh at my expense.

Really? Your cruel jokes, now? You Ancient Trickster, I'll burn dung-a-lews at your next tribute offering for all your poorly timed guiles this week.

The attendant clears her throat snapping me from my silent fuming. "Young hunter? Are you ready? What did you bring us?" The attendant raises her hand a bit closer as if I'd somehow missed it.

I open up my hunter's vest, motion to my barren midriff, and fold my hands politely in front of me. "Ma'am, my sincerest apologies, my humble return is all I have to present. I have nothing else to give you."

She takes in my words slowly and looks me up and down before gently shutting the lids of the baskets. But if hers is the face of confusion, it's nothing compared to the absolute bewilderment of my kin.

The attendant clears her throat quietly. "Well, young hunter, you may not know this. Perhaps you were so exhausted from the Trials that you lost track of time, but it's only the evening of the fourth day. There is still tomorrow and the half day after before the Trials are concluded. And you certainly shouldn't have come out empty-handed…"

Papa Jaole leans forward in disbelief. "D-does that mean he's—a double fail for leaving early and without his original belt?"

The attendant looks at me with heartfelt regret. "Yes, I'm afraid so. Exiting the premises means he had an unfair advantage over the other apprentices still trying to survive by masking their aurem within the testing grounds."

Tygon looks down at the ground before placing two leather belts plus his original into the basket. He raises his eyes to mine before stepping in. "Ma'am, I'm sure my brother had a reason that clears all this up. He's worked so hard for this and I belie—"

"Enough!" Papa Jaole's voice echoes loud enough to halt conversation clear on the other side of the Hall.

"Tygon, go home now. You will not be coming to your brother's rescue this time. Today was his chance to become a grown man and he's had ample training to do it. So, there'll be no hiding behind you! Now move!" Papa's hand flies rigid from his cloak, pointing out into the Hub.

Tygon nods his respect but hesitates a moment to give me a look of encouragement. His tight-lipped expression says it all. "*I hope whatever the case, it was worth it.*" After he dips out into the crowded circle, Papa edges to the side of the table.

"Well, Faylen, you had something to say?" His fist trembles , but his eyes lock with mine revealing a fragile hope in my decision making. Despite visible fury and confusion, a part of him still clings to faith in me.

I run through my options. Telling anyone about a Saberhorn at this point is going to sound like rehashed folks' tale. Feats like that haven't been heard of in decades. Not since Grandpa Ravir's time. Even those stories are based in his prime, a phase of life I am nowhere close to achieving. Not to mention they happened in the backdrop of a global war...

The other option is to say nothing, but that seems stupid. I don't need people jumping to conclusions. I may have just gifted Dourn some fresh perspective and a new nose to match, but his aren't the only loose lips that could twist reality if I say nothing. Before someone claims I left because I was too afraid to face another day of the Trials, I'll write my own story with the truth.

I puff out my chest. "I saved my friend from bleeding out in the Domain. Lunis, Wolf-Bonded of PanCanis, was hurt badly in a fight. I detected her aurem nearby and when I found her, she had significant wounds. But her prowess was undeniable, I'm witness to that. And since I couldn't care for her completely on my own, I didn't bother looking for a proctor and instead brought her straight to the Nurse's dwelling."

The attendant chews her lip, thinking over the new information.

"I see, that is going to be...rather challenging to sort out," she murmurs.

I look to my father, ready to hear a speech that will start off by acknowledging my efforts. But soon afterward, I know his words will turn critical and harsh, ending in admonishment for having failed to persevere until a better solution revealed itself. After all, *"A true hunter anticipates the unexpected, Faylen. You must remember the three A's, Accept, Adapt, and Adjust."*

Insert finger wag and stern paternal look here.

I prepare for the worst until I'm taken by surprise when instead my shoulders are wrapped up in thick folds of embroidered garments. My cheek rests on the cool PanTigris crest hanging from Papa Jaole's neck while I try to figure out what is happening.

"Giving yourself up for the sake of others? There isn't a single trait I'd rather have demonstrated by a son of mine. Forget the rules, forget the Trials. You may still be an Elevation apprentice to the village, but you're as much a man as they come in my book. That's how you represent PanTigris, my boy."

I stand there awkwardly in shock for several long moments as we embrace in front of the attendant. Papa holds me close with his sole arm. He doesn't need a second one to communicate how proud he is. My mind races, trying to commit this moment to memory, to remember its soul and its heart. For so many seasons I've waited for this exact affirmation. I might not have full control of my Silver Fang inheritance. Despite reaching my peak to save Lunis, the power is still very much an enigma. But perhaps I have something even more powerful to my name—the discernment to make good choices. That's got to count for something.

Papa's grip finally loosens, and I sneak my wrist wrappings to my eyes to dab away trickling tears. However, reddened eyes immediately give me away as he tussles my locs with his hand. We laugh together for a moment when I catch a droplet curving down his own scarred cheek.

And here I thought the man had long forgotten how to cry.

Papa winks at me before turning to face the attendant. "Ma'am, I appreciate your time and consideration in this odd matter. I'll let you and the other Trial staff handle informing Dom Arzen and Sage Ophis. I am sure the other Clan Heads will be called in to discuss the way forward, so I'll see you then."

The attendant clasps her hands and bows respectfully. "Of

course, I hope we can come up with a fair solution for you, young hunter." She slides down the table to help an approaching apprentice.

Papa and I walk toward the Hall's entrance.

"Son, I'll see you at home later. Take a breather, you've been through a lot—I can tell." He turns me around to get a look at my bloody trousers. Spotting the size of the crimson stains, he raises his eyebrows.

I shrug. "Yeah, it was a heck of a Trial this year, but I did my best. Even set a few of my classmates straight."

Papa's eyes twinkle. He fiddles in the pockets of his garments and hands me a few clear pink crystals.

"Gon' buy yourself a little snack and some recovery fruits for energy. Snag you and your siblings a few items from the vendors too while you're at it. The traveling merchants should be setting up for the Selection Festival right about now." He rummages in his purse, bringing out a fist full of round beads. "Here, take a bit more, might be time to get yourself a new dancing get up!"

I can't believe how many shining pieces are sitting in my hand right now! I'd have to do a month's worth of mine and my sibling's chores to get this many, and most of them are 'glistenin' pinks' at that! Who needs more bracelets? I could give Muma Rylia a small dowry for Lunis's hand right now.

I think for a second and take back the thought. Lunis would need time to come up with her half-dowry to our Muma Kura as well. And then there's the small inconvenience that I've never actually admitted my feelings to more than Tygon and the jungle trees. The girl can't *choose* me if she never *hears* me say the words. Awkward staring is not effective communication.

I bring myself back to the present. "Thank you, Papa. I'll see you at dinner."

I stuff the little gems into my pocket and take off through the crowd. I've got to get myself something flashy for the Festival. While I duck and dodge, I catch sight of Zahk standing near the Hub's edge. I call out to him when I'm within earshot.

"Amio, you made it out early! Good for you. Hey, did you hear about your sister?"

Zahk clasps my arm, giving his breast a brief pounding followed by a few foot stomps.

"Yea, Stripes, I just came from seeing her, actually. Thanks so much for looking out for her. When it comes to girls, you punch straight zeroes on the board, but I'm sure this'll bank you major Lunis points for once. Add a few from my Muma too!"

I swat him in the shoulder. "Punching zeroes? Really? Big dog, you gotta' keep that level of honesty to yourself."

He shoots me a devilish smile. "Truth hurts. You're a tough hunter, you'll get over it." He laughs as I fumble a decent comeback.

"All I'm sayin' Fay is this. My sister is a lot more impressed with the size of your heart than the bulge in your biceps." He flicks my arm. "So, with those goose eggs, I think you're in good standing."

I cut him a look. "Wow, you're on a roll today, aren't you?"

He winks and shrugs.

I roll my eyes. "Amio, if Lunis is waiting for me to figure out the right moves, she's going to be waiting a long time. I'd need to meet the Spirits firsthand and beg their aid before getting so slick."

Zahk chuckles at the imagery. "Sounds like a trip to Hayvin then to me. Save me a spot 'cause I'll be heading there to beg alongside you. Between the two of us, I think I have you beat in hard odds of finding that lifelong partner."

I look at him smugly. "Oh really, and exactly how do you figure that?"

He eyes the beastly stone monuments in the far-off cliffs and reflects for a moment. "Muma Rylia has always said I'll ally with somebody out there…" he waves his hand whimsically.

"Out where, outside Praedari? Don't tell me you're going to try allying with someone in another village. You know those ties don't work out between kin too well." His daydreaming suggests to me he isn't listening. "Oh, come now, snap out of it! What're we talking about here? Falling in love with some Tauris farm girl? Say she comes home to meet your kin and poor girl sees leathers everywhere? There goes the wedding!"

Zahk laugh inwardly, pointing up at the metal tapestry with views of Sanctum behind us. "No, man, somebody out *there*, in another nation, in another Bloodline. I've always been drawn to all the unknowns in the other lands. I think traveling Spheire and finding my life's ally is just the most natural path for me."

My mouth flies open. What kind of terrible friend must I be to not have known this before now?

"Amio, good luck with that, seriously. But a few things…" I hold up a finger. "One, I nearly got turned into a crisp by a Weaver before the Trials so, those are off limits." He rolls his eyes but lets me continue. I hold up a second finger. "Two, it's worth mentioning the Bloodline of the Mind. Back in our map making classes, we learned they live on the far side of the Wastelands. So, if your adventures take you that far and you call me begging for a visit, *you'd* better be buying the ticket."

Zahk scrunches his face into a sour twist. I mirror the expression right back at him. We're a half-second from tussling in the dirt when a banner with giant red letters scrolls across the bottom of the metal moving pictures, stealing both of our attention.

LIBERTAS HEIRS MEMBERS SUSPECTED AT LARGE. COUNCIL WARNS ALL NATIONS TO BE ON THE WATCH FOR SUSPICIOUS ACTIVITIES AND ESCAPED CONVICTS. REPORT ALL FINDINGS TO LOCAL LEADERS.

Zahk shakes his head at the screen while I pat him on the shoulder.

"Bashtol," I murmur. "I just hope none of that nonsense ever makes it our way. Hard to imagine it gets through all the dense Wilds, but still. We've got nothing to do with all that Council, Sanctum, and Libertas mumbo jumbo."

Zahk stare a long while at the images before turning to me. "Hard truth is we're headed to the Discipline, amio. This kind of stuff might have more to do with us a whole lot sooner than you think. We'll see pretty much every corner of Spheire represented there," he says quietly.

I nod, contemplating our possible futures. Then I remember the reality of mine. "Actually, about that, I got disqualified for leaving the Domain early to help Lunis out."

Zahk's hands fly up in disbelief. "Wait, are you serious? Uh, no. You saved someone's life. That's bear scat dude. If they don't sort this mess out *fairly*, I'll start the blasted riots myself."

The crowd bustles around us as we stand silent for a few moments.

Zahk grabs my hand before putting his palm to his heart. "Catboy, if it makes you feel any better, no matter what the elders decide, I think you're a pretty standup guy. Spirits know not everyone woulda' risked their neck the way you did. And at the cost of an instant DQ? Unthinkable for most, but unsurprising knowing you. You've always had heart."

I smile at him. "Funny you should say that. I heard this cute little story before the Trials about a wolf cub who used to preach about the 'unthinkable.'"

Zahk looks at me, cocking his eyebrow in confusion.

I whirl around into the crowd, heading to the clothing alleys. With my head thrown back and a finger pointed to the skies I shout, "Lunis said it looked something like this? Ahem, 'somethin's only unthinkable if *you* don't think it!'"

Zahk's eyes widen as he remembers the line. "W-wait, Faylen! What else did my loose-lipped sister tell you? And when *exactly* did y'all two run off to have this conversation, huh?" He tries to chase me but I'm too quick. I hear him rambling somewhere behind me, "I still don't remember signin' any paper's saying you could date my sister!"

I side-step back and forth before disappearing fully into the crowd. "Your signature's in the mail, wolf-boy."

I chuckle at my temporary victory and dart away. Perhaps now that I've talked the talk, I should walk the walk. Time to get some gear that would impress the gorgeous huntress on the Festival dance floor. Assuming of course, that she's properly healed up by then. If not, I'm bringing the Festival to her by dancing on her doorstep.

As I pass through the alleyway for my favorite clothing shop, I can't help but overhear some villagers talking behind me.

"The Council is going to come down hard on those escapees once they find 'em."

Another voice chimes in. "Come down hard? Pssh, everyone of them is getting the tank for sure. Animas best stay out of it like we always have been. We don't need that drama in our woods."

"Ha, and the other Bloodlines call us savages. You know I never understood that. The quietest of the five and perhaps the ones who keep most to ourselves."

"Plus, we aren't the ones going around blowing up houses and starting fires. Some real savages, am I right?"

The two villagers pause for a moment before one of them pounds his fist into his open palm.

"Still, I hope the Council can nail the Heirs and get this chaos under control soon. Even if we are removed, I want to know who's behind it all. Find out what they're really after. I swear, they better not be riling folks up toward another Spirits-cursed war..."

I stoop into the clothing store away from the noisy crowd. Zahk's warning of all the new people I would have met at the Discipline comes to mind. The combative academy seems worlds and futures away now. Completely foreign. Maybe even a little threatening too when I think about it.

I reaffirm my personal resolve. If the Council is searching the Heirs out, and the Heirs are hurting people, then that makes Spheire's leaders the good guys in my book. That means anyone doing well at the Discipline would also be supporting what's good in some small way. The Council has kept things peaceful for quite some time and any effort to maintain this is a worthy one.

I'll have to leave that endeavor up to Zahk and Lunis for a while and join them at the Discipline when I've proving myself here in Praedari. Still, I'm realizing just how little I know about the other nations and Bloodlines. Beyond a bit of map making classes, not a lot makes it past the trees.

Good for Zahk though, he sounds excited about it all. I hope he's careful. Who knows who's waiting out there in this big, crazy world…

Part III II

Loghis
Bloodline of the mind

18

Rebirth

Somewhere Far Beyond the Jungle's Reach…
"Daughter of Intellect, we will now begin the planned procedure to remove your arm and shoulder."

A middle-aged man stands in front of a panel of large parallel screens mounted into a wall. Behind him, a team of assistants hunches over a series of smaller screens, organizing holo-images and schematics, then swiping the data to the main panel. The older man adjusts his white lab coat and collects the swiped information, constructing a virtual model of the upcoming amputation.

He turns away from his screens and walks over to the middle of the room. Flashes of pale green and digital blue flicker through the air in random patterns, casting the man's expressions in shadow. He stops before a specialized gurney at the room's center, studying the projections streaming above it. He places his hand through one of them and it turns solid green.

A computerized alert sounds, followed by a programmed non-human voice.

"Anatomist Victor Veis, you are cleared for amputation procedure. Awaiting sequence start command."

The Anatomist stoops closer to the bed to meet the eyes of a young woman previously hidden beneath the projections. "Daughter, ignore the computer's formalities. Simply call me Victor if it puts you at ease going forward." His expression shifts into a gentle smile. "Now that my team's precautions are completed, we need your final approval to get us on our way. Please, start your identification prompts and we will begin."

Around the operating space, busy hands freeze as every set of eyes fixates on the young woman at the room's center. Only the electric hum of screens and machinery can be heard within the cavernous space until she speaks with a commanding confidence.

"Commence."

The inhuman voice recites its programmed lines.

"Subject Name?"

"Althea Regis," the young woman states coolly.

"Subject Age?"

"Eighteen Annuals."

"Subject Proclivity?"

"Erudite."

At this response, whispers fill the air, along with oohs and ahhs amongst the attendants and observers. So, the rumors were true.

Althea could hear the hushed tones all the way from where she lay on the surgery table.

"How rare! To have shown aptitude in all four high Minds and at such a young age? She could've been a queen before—"

The inhuman voice continues, unconcerned with the girl's supposed significance.

"Please specify the classification of procedure to be given on this date—Day: 96. Centum-Season: 4th. Annual Cycle: 10,110."

Althea replies, "Classification: This will be my third body modification. Subject volunteers for complete amputation and enhancement of right arm, shoulder, and required rib cage reinforcements. Further synaptic and spinal tethers approved."

The voice acknowledges. "Daughter—Althea Regis—thank you for your cooperation. Anticipated recovery time: four days. As you will likely still be unconscious at the four-day mark of your recovery, Happy New Annual in advance, best wishes on the procedure."

Althea looks up at Anatomist Victor with a smirk. "Since when did you update smart-gurneys with a personality? They recognize the holidays now?"

The graying man has busied himself adjusting a separate panel with hundreds of dials but manages a quick chuckle.

"It's your generation of Mechanic Mind who keeps coming up with the craziest new things. My father's era developed a way to extend the Loghint's lifespan by fifty percent. Yours figured out how to create semi-sentient portable companionship. I suppose one of those companionship updates made its way down here."

A young boy whips back around to his small screen, failing miserably to hide his guilt beneath shrugged shoulders. A couple of neighboring attendants give him an accusatory look.

Victor stands up, adjusting his coat once more. "Daughter, I will be placing you into a partially aware stasis. You will not feel any of the pain from the procedure, but your mind will register all that is happening. Over the decades, we've found this is simply the best way to do it. Since the brain is still processing each step of this significant body alteration, it tends not to go into lockdown and cause total rejection."

Althea nods, "Agreed. You know, I studied the manuals of your work when I was younger. *'Enhancement Science'* was essentially a bedtime story I'd read to myself. Better to be awake for all this than to sleep and find oneself half-paralyzed."

The Anatomist makes a slashing motion across his shoulder. "Half-paralyzed and without an arm in some cases. Even Medic Minds can't help the brain recognize the original organic material once removed with one-hundred percent success. If this modification doesn't take, there's no guarantee we'll be able to reconstruct you to your former self. I'm sure you understand the risks, then?"

Althea looks from the Anatomist to the ceiling. "It's not like I have much choice, we both know that. I may have engineered some of the specifications myself, but let's not act like this amputation is my idea. It isn't."

The man's eyes don't carry much in the way of outright sympathy, but he does pause for her benefit. He knows who is funding this whole operation. Althea's lying here was out of atypical circumstances to say the least. Someone high up had a job that needed doing. His role was nothing more than to equip her to do it.

"Well, Daughter, if that is all, then let's get this underway."

All the attendants work furiously as digital symbols stream across the parallel screens. Victor dons a metal headband with clusters of tiny antennas on it. He slips on a pair of fitted chrome gloves covered in nodes, all converging into spirals at his fingertips. After a few seconds, his brown eyes change color to surge with an aura of digital blue. The headband matches the hue, followed by his gloves.

Victor lifts his hands in front of his face then slowly brings them together. Five large metal arms above the gurney move in insect-like fashion to mimic the motion. Together, they twist through the air until converging their laser-tipped points over Althea's right arm.

The young woman eyes the sparkling points for a long moment then holds her other hand out to an older mistress standing at her bedside. "See you on the other side, Protectorate."

The mistress caresses Althea's outstretched hand. This limb will remain untouched flesh and bone; the older woman grips it firmly between her two metallic palms. "No worries, Daughter. Today, you will truly join our people. I'll watch over you after the Medics take you in."

Althea nods to her, grateful for the encouragement. The older woman kisses her hand.

"We will await your arrival. Welcome to Rebirth."

"Yes, ma'am." Althea settles back into the gurney, adjusting her head until the sensors align with the symmetry of her face. "Put me in stasis."

With a nod from Victor an attendant presses a sequence of projected buttons on the gurney. A measurement indicator highlights onto the parallel screens and a dial on it rises, changing from red, to yellow, to green. The indicator inches closer to the center of the colored dial.

Victor calls out, "All right, thank you. Hold her consciousness steady at mid-point and keep those pain restrictors flat. I will not have anyone coming into full-functioning consciousness mid-operation this time! Oh, and could someone please start my symphony?"

The room's atmosphere sweeps through with melodic beeps, pitches, and vibrations, pulsing into a rhythm of electronically tinged notes.

"Ah, now that's the good stuff. Here. We. Go!"

He waves his hands, then levels them out completely flat. His fingertips pinch, flick, and dash all to the music like a conductor. Only with this maestro's every movement, ten laser points, two per massive arm, sear through Althea's muscles with a brief hiss. Beams of bright red light dart around the green and blue accents illuminating the room.

Althea watches with partial awareness as this portion of her birth body is erased away. It won't be the only relic of the past she'll have to leave behind to complete the work awaiting her. Today is only the first step into a highly uncertain future. It's like the Protectorate said as she offered those last words of encouragement…

This truly will be Althea's Rebirth. Into what, she considers, remained to be answered.

19

REDEMPTION

Althea comes to beneath a disoriented haze. Her surroundings become clear as her corneas and lenses calibrate, rotating and shifting until both eye augments are in sync. Her recovery room is on a high enough floor to allow a breathtaking view of distant fireworks blossoming over the landscape. The city of Redemption was always beautiful to Althea, a far improvement to the slums and outskirts she knew growing up. But it went deeper than appreciation of simple scenery and the architecture of this place. To her, Redemption held a certain…promise to it. It didn't matter how unkind the past had been toward her countrymen, this city was a testament to their hope. It was her Bloodline's—the Bloodline of the Mind— second chance.

She smiles to herself as giant projections dance amidst a night sky painted in fluorescence. Well-known figures from the story archives hover between the tall buildings and children below point up to their favorites, perched on the metal plated shoulders of their parents. For a moment, even Althea is overtaken by youthful wonder when one final pair of electronic puppets twirl in unison, higher than all the rest.

"What a tribute, King and Queen Regalia. You look amazing this annual," she whispers to herself. When she hugs her knees into her chest, reveling in the sight, she feels the tug of cords still connecting her to diagnostics arrays monitoring her recovery. Althea pays the blinking sensors no mind, smiling to her countrymen on ground level. She leans away from the gurney until cool glass kisses her skin. "Happy New Cycle, Redemption. Here's to another step forward, until we've left all our shadows behind."

Once the flickering royal couple waltzes out of view, Althea turns slowly to disconnect the clear tubes of bio-tethers. She hesitates though when eyeing the wire bundles feeding into her freshly operated shoulder and spine. Reminded of the full extent of the surgery, she studies her new augment that replaced her dominant arm for the first time. Her right arm perfectly reflects the view outside, casting vivid colors around the room. The seam connecting the augment to her body, is so well crafted she looks like she was birthed with the thing. Althea brings the enhancement closer for a better look, running a finger along its smooth, polished fibernetic alloy. With a double blink of her eyelids, projections transpose above the new arm, highlighting a slew of specifications and features. She catalogs the schematics appearing within her visual augments, sorting them for future viewing.

"Impressive. I can barely feel the added weight." Althea flexes a thousand synthetic tendons, one hundred at a time. She rotates the wrist joint a full one-hundred-and-eighty degrees, then touches each finger to her thumb with a metallic "clink." With full responsiveness confirmed, she continues the wrist rotation for several three-hundred-and-sixty-degree revolutions like a drill.

She chuckles. "Good, looks like I'll have a new trick during my next Combatives session. Marshal Sevarick won't be submitting me to anymore of his favorite wrist locks ."

As the young woman spins her hand in fast revolutions, a small pod lights up on a nearby nightstand. The egg-shaped object hums a tune before hovering into the air and zipping over to rest on a small port above Althea's metallic wrist. The gadget rotates its head around, matching the revolutions of the new hand, beeping gleefully with each new turn.

"Blooper! Hello, little friend."

"Blooooooop!" the tiny companion responds, its giant eyes flashing brightly.

"Well, what do you think? Good enough to get me through my assignment?"

The bot looks up and down the new right arm, emitting a laser pointer from its head to trace the distinct angles. After the scan, it turns to blink the laser at Althea's unaltered left.

"This one, I insisted on keeping. I wanted to preserve a piece of myself for all my future creations. I don't care how many sensors they pack into these things"—she wiggles her alloyed fingers back and forth—"nothing beats the feeling of natural touch when tinkering on a new design."

Blooper tilts its head, then claps four elliptic disks that make up its arms. The bot displays a projection from its chest, showing a moving picture of a scale, then a flexing bicep.

"Oh, right, the weight, let's see. If I memorized the most recent data charts correctly, Medic and Anatomy charts document a human arm as six-point-five percent of one's total body weight."

She stands up, wincing as the cold floor bites at the soles of her feet.

"Goodness, I know an Agriculturists' job is to focus on farming the essentials, but couldn't they harvest a few more fibrous plants? Metal floors everywhere with no carpet seems like a bit of an oversight, even this far past the Wastelands."

The little bot hugs itself, shaking its head back and forth to imitate a shiver. Of course, she knew this was just an act. Althea never installed temperature sensors into her small companion when she built him.

She flicks the egg-shaped pod. "Oh, shut it, clunker, you can't get cold, remember?"

Blooper blinks its large eye cameras innocently before letting out a pre-recorded version of Althea's laugh.

"Anyways, comedian, these fifteen pounds of metal are a good fit. It's near double the weight of my birth arm, but it's a lighter load than the conditioning cast I've been training with. A whole annual cycle in that thing…I thought I'd never be freed."

A red light blinks from Blooper's torso while he emits a question mark prompt.

"No, no. I'm a little sore, but I don't have any more side aches in my obliques. Must be the pain-blockers. Plus, the Anatomist did masterful work integrating that support brace into my ribcage."

The door to the room slides open and Althea's older mistress enters the room with two young nurses in tow. The pair of medical workers rush to the side of the bed, one pressing a sequence of projected buttons, the other disconnecting the cluster of bio-tethers still attached to Althea's augment. Each time a coupling is removed it breaks contact with a sharp hiss. After closing out the bedside projection menus, the nurses shuffle away as quickly as they'd come.

The woman nods to Althea before inspecting her body. "Welcome back, Daughter. Good to see you."

"Likewise, to you, my Protectorate."

The older woman holds up her own metal arms, dulled by decades of use. Pistons all the way up to her neckline compress and decompress when she offers a slight grin. "I know when I first received my own enhancements, I was dying to know what all I could do with them. Should we begin the demo sequence and see what firepower you have been given?"

Althea nods and her eyes glow digital blue as she extends her arm, stretching her fingers before her. The streaming lights inlaid beneath her fibernetic skin surge with energy, illuminating her arm like Redemption's streets below.

"Prodigious!" the girl says, amused. "They look almost like natural veins."

The current channels up and down her arm in a thousand rivulets as though she were reinventing lightning itself.

After charging up the power, she allows a series of detailed diagrams to stream through her enhanced visuals. Each one provides instructions for utilizing her augments. While she takes a moment to internalize the information, the far end of the recovery room shifts into a fully functioning demo range. A ballistics dummy arises from the farthest panel in the floor and a hundred sets of sensors click into place within the surrounding walls and ceiling.

The older woman steps back, holding out her own metal arm, beckoning Blooper to hover over to her. The bot relocates, then spins its head to watch the show. Althea's hand rotates like before, then retracts seamlessly into the wrist compartment of her arm. A two-pronged device slides out to replace it. Once fully extended, the prongs fold and duplicate, suspending an "X" of crackling light between them.

"Oooh, a Voltraic Disabler. It looks to be the same model that comes standard in Security Force's lightning javelins," she says with complete fascination. "And what's this? They included my suggestions to add a ranged feature?"

With this realization, Althea squares her shoulders, whipping her arm forward. Nearly invisible cables follow the momentum to snake through the air, launching the intersecting prongs to the opposite side of the room. When they sink into the skull of the dummy, the figure's simulated flesh melts away in sparks. Althea focuses for a moment, attempting to spike the voltage. In an instant, the dummy's whole top half bursts into a cloud of smoke and it teeters off its podium.

The older woman's eyes go wide. "For the sake of Everrealm, what kind of monsters do they expect you'll be fighting off?" She thinks for a second before continuing. "Ah, never mind, I suspect you'll likely need that and more for what lies ahead."

Althea retracts the extended cords into her wrist as the demo range resets, presenting a second hapless dummy for her to explode. Any remaining smoke from her previous victim is quickly scrubbed from the air. Althea notes a satisfying click once the Voltraic Disabler slides evenly into the depths of her forearm. Then, the next weapon reveals itself—a lengthy rod that extends double Althea's arm span. She traces a half arc above her head, impressed by the elongated reach.

"Trigger," she says.

At the command, particles ionize a crisp blue from the rod, forming a translucent blade of humming energy.

Althea whistles with a grin. "Boosted."

The Protectorate squints disapprovingly at the use of her slum slang.

Althea grimaces at her loose-lipped slip up but continues to study the new feature. "A weaponized version of the plasma-torches we use for construction. Never thought I'd see it beyond my blueprints, to be honest. Perhaps I could apply to be an Architect now. Build a few bridges with this thing."

The Protectorate chuckles at the prospect of the complex tool hacking away at such a simple task. Althea's blinks twice to catalog the rare sight of the woman smiling.

"All right, round two." She levels the vibrating blade at the dummy and takes off with a sprint. A small reactor powering her arsenal spins up in between her shoulder blades, propelling her forward.

Her advance triggers an ambush and from the walls, a hoard of mannequins, all wearing iron plating, rush the girl. She tracks their movement with her visual augmentation, calculating their exact convergence point. Her body modifications surge in unison as she lifts into the air, to execute a perfect triple spin. A high-pitched hum cuts through the air and shadows dance across the walls. When Althea lands on her knee, sparks sprinkle across the metal floor behind her and the hoard of armored figures clatters to pieces. Althea inspects the blade a final time to see neon letters stenciled near the hilt. They spell out the name she'd given the invention: Lucent Edge.

The older woman eyes the charred target dummies scattered across the far side of the large room. Althea can hardly read her expression and only manages to catch her words by reading the woman's lips using telescopic vision.

"Perhaps...she might actually do this."

Ignoring the burning temptation to ask for clarification, Althea instead sheaths the Lucent Edge back into her wrist. She places her weight into a defensive stance, holding the augment in front of her head. From each side of her forearm, two halves of a buckler shield lock into place.

With no warning, a hard-shell gatling gun materializes from the ceiling and sends rounds straight for her head. Althea ducks low behind the shield as it absorbs the assault, reducing what should be the impact of searing heat and metal into nothing. With a whir, the gatling clicks back upward into the ceiling tiles.

Althea kicks hot brass out of her path and looks the compact armored piece over. "Twenty reinforced layers of condensed Boltsteel. I'm amazed they cut a deal with the military Strategists to acquire this much of the alloy."

The Protectorate waves the though off, though they both knew the deal was only possible due to ample negotiating and politicking by the older woman.

"Yes, Daughter, one might find that alloy is *usually* reserved for our Zephyr Carrier fleet, but you would be surprised how far a bottle of forty-year-old whiskey will get you."

Despite a lingering look from Althea, the woman goes tight-lipped. Althea was old enough to know that a highly coveted alcohol such as whiskey—a rare output from the Agricultural district—was far from the only favor her Protectorate called in with the commanders of the Loghis Intelli-Fleet.

Blooper, wanting to be a part of the conversation per usual, projects a formation of giant ships hovering over the Redemption skyline. Each Intelli-Fleet carrier is seen equipped with a menacing looking solar cannon affixed central to the airship's bulkhead like the war machines were built around a burning inferno.

Althea resets her arm, restoring the metal hand into place once more. Finally, she inspects the underside of her forearm to find a small button. She's surprised to see the last of her enhancements hidden there as an inner compartment opens, ejecting four folding racks, each with twenty tiny slots. Althea traces her finger over the empty arrays with a whistle. "Four magazines for a total capacity of eighty Micro-Rounds. Imagine loading that much Tempertite into this thing. I could fell a skyscraper with that much suppressing fire."

The Protectorate keeps an emotionless face but raises her chin. "Good, they've made you into a weapon. I'd almost say you could singlehandedly win a war."

Althea is unable to leave that one unaddressed and opens her mouth to question the older woman but is cut off before her inquiry can begin.

"Daughter, I am glad to see you're so well-equipped for your mission. Oh, and I almost forgot to mention—Happy New Cycle."

"Thank you, ma'am. Maybe you'll share with me your age this time? Or perhaps some new piece of your story?"

The Protectorate pauses, fractions of an emotion playing at the edges of her face. But just as quickly, whatever she might have been thinking is hidden back beneath the veil.

"We…must be going, I'm afraid. The panel will assemble to brief you soon. We must get you tailored and prepped considering these new modifications."

Althea mulls over the suggestion. The woman was right, of course, but that didn't excuse the brisk change of subject. Why did this always happen the moment she ever tried learning even the smallest details about the woman? *Didn't the Protectorate know how much she meant to her? How unfair that the only person she had left in this world was seemingly happy to remain at arm's length?* In the end, she placed a mental note to return to the topic as soon as possible.

The Protectorate clasps her arms behind her and walks over to the door panel.

"Protectorate Release Authority."

The doors accept her credentials and slide open, letting in the sounds of the busy Medic Institution. The pair take a glass elevator down to ground level, then walk through the central rows toward the exit. Althea looks around, taking in the sights. Organization is a highly valued virtue in the nation of Loghis. Even with hundreds of people in the lobby moving about, the quadrant schematic of the Institution bay eliminates any congestion.

They take a seat in the out-processing row, allowing wall sensors to scan them for contaminants and any defects the attendants who visited earlier might have missed. Althea sits patiently and a Senior Medic smiles at her before kneeling to inspect the broken arm of a young boy who has yet to have his first augments.

"Well, well, young intellect. What did you do to yourself this time?" The man asks, reaching into the pockets of his coat. Its cuffs are ringed with four glowing red stripes to indicate his seniority.

The young boy holds up a rust-covered wrench with pride. "My father is an Mechanic workman and my mother an Agricultural specialist. Sometimes, they've been working all day and are so tired by the time they get home," He wipes a dirt stain from his cheek, then looks the Senior Medic straight in the eye. "Well, I found a broken heating line beneath the house, and rather than wait for my parents, I crawled under the basement and fixed it myself. Just got a little stuck on the way out, that's all."

The man nods, patting him on the back. "So, your parents are workers then? You know, that's something to be very proud of, right? Loghis needs her Civic Minded, people just like you, because you reach the fixes no one else can. You are our Bloodline's backbone."

The man beams at the boy, pulling of all things, a newly polished chrome wrench from his pocket. The boy's eyes light up as he examines the tool with his good arm. The Senior Medic speaks in a hushed tone, "Every Loghint is an Arkitech. A builder of the future. Whether they are one of the four high Minds like myself, or Civic Minded like you, remember one thing. We must all work equally hard. That is the dedication our Mother Loghis deserves."

The boy pumps his bony arm, clenching the glimmering trophy. He pauses for a moment, then places two fingers to his temple. The tiny Civic boy looks hopefully at the middle-aged man, eager to have earned a confirmation of his potential.

Althea hides her smile behind her hand at the Medic's response. With clearly exaggerated gusto for the boy's sake, the medical professional squares his shoulders, returning the two-fingered salute to his own temple. The man's visual augments light up, and though the boy won't undergo his first enhancements for a couple more annuals, no digital lenses could shine brighter than those eyes do now. The child gasps in awe as though he'd just received a medal for valor.

The contaminant scan completes, and Althea follows behind her Protectorate, thinking about the symbology just used between the man and the boy. A warm memory blossoms into her mind—a memory of when she first learned the gesture herself. She closes her eyes, hoping that maybe this time, the exact sound of her mother's voice will be easier to recall...

"We give this sign to one another as a reminder of our shared purpose. It is through toil and sweat that our four high Minds: Strategic, Medic, Chemic, and Mechanic reach their potential. This individual pursuit for greatness is called Ethos, and every person's Ethos feeds their own knowledge. However, we as a people still fail if each Loghint does not remember to connect their pursuits to that of another. Never hoard your accomplishments, Althea. Let your knowledge and strengths be the foundation to build up another. That is how Loghis evolves and always has. It is why ours, of the five Bloodlines, is the only unconquerable Gift."

The city air rushes into Althea's face as she walks the crowded streets behind her Protectorate. The sky has gone mostly dark, the colored hues fading in favor of Solint's nightly retreat. Admirably, the ongoing Annual celebration has hit its full swing, yet the teeming streets still maintain their perfect order.

The Protectorate turns to Althea before entering a walking Stream with the other travelers.

"Daughter, we will exit the Stream twelve markers from here. A tailoring hand is waiting for us there. He will outfit you in a new set of garments better suited for your augments."

The pair fall in behind the rushing lines of people, their journey accelerated by the moving pathway carrying them along the Stream. After a few minutes of travel, a banner projection shimmers above the hurried walkway.

"Your Work is Your Redemption!" one blinking image reads.

"Four Minds form the Intelligent Eye: Loghis' Defense Against a Ruthless World," reads another.

Althea looks over the side rails and gasps in amazement at a nearby intersection. Despite the festivities to bring in a new annual cycle, a crew of Civic workers is busy tunneling into the ground to access a ruptured pipeline. The grime-stained group are all smiles and laughter in their hole, despite toiling at such a late hour. Their faces are painted over in dirt and sweat, making it difficult for

Althea to make out anyone's eyes. For a brief moment though, the crew's leader—a woman seemingly her same age—makes eye contact.

Althea waves and shouts. "Thank you for your work, fellow Arkitech! May your toils be met with just reward!"

The woman removes her sooty glove and offers the two-fingered salute. The streetlights glint off her dented iron-plated enhancements.

"And you, sister, in whatever work may be asked of you, present or future, toil for Mother Loghis!" She puffs her chest before turning back to her small team.

Althea's own heart swells with a matched sense of pride. Her mission may be a mystery, but it was hers, nonetheless. The people of Loghis had endured a harsh enough fortune over the past few decades…

It was comforting to know everyone's work still counted toward a better tomorrow.

With only a couple Stream markers remaining, Althea taps the older woman on the shoulder. She turns with an inquisitive look.

"Protectorate, I haven't forgotten my earlier point. I don't know what task will be required of me tonight, but we both know I will be far gone from this beautiful city. Who knows how long we'll be separated, so while I can, I intend to pursue answers."

The caretaker looks up with visible fatigue, closing her eyes for a few seconds.

"Daughter, you know what the Supris Generals have ordered. They ordained our relationship after finding out I was caring for you in exile. We are lucky enough they couldn't send operatives to confiscate you immediately back then. It allowed you and I a few precious years to search for your mother. Don't test their patience."

Althea cocks her head. "And? What about their ordinances over us? What do the Supris Generals have to do with all of this anyways?"

The older woman's eyes tell a painful tale as she looks to her younger. They plead with her to let hidden secrets remain as such. She sighs. "The Supris Generals instructed me long ago on what information you needed to know. When we moved to the outskirts on this side of the Wastelands, it was for your benefit. Besides, what does the past matter when you're meant to play such an important role in our future?"

The irises of Althea's eyes rotate counter to each other as she bites her lip in frustration. Finally, she erupts, "Skyelle!" Her own voice surprises her as she's clearly abandoned all proper manners by shouting her Protectorate's name. "What do those old men know that you aren't telling me? By what you've just now said, the Supris Generals of the Crown's Hand have been pulling the strings to my entire life since I was a child. Since I am no longer such—a *child*—you have no right to steer me around the truth!"

Indignation sparks across the older woman's face, matching a pluming fireworks overhead.

Where Althea expects a scolding, surprisingly, Protectorate Skyelle's eyes soften rather quickly, and she looks instead to the sky. She studies the colorful magnetic particles expanding and reshaping above the city.

"Look up there, Althea. What do you see?"

Althea fumes thinking herself ignored once again. She surrenders and takes in the grandiose view.

The air is filled with flickering banners of different colors, each of them displaying an emblem. A royal Tri-Crown with an eye at its center rests over a mallet and wrench crossed in the background. The whole emblem is framed by a rigid gear. Loghis' national crest disappears into the night as the women pause in silence.

Althea whispers slowly. "I see nothing but the faded remnants of a past no one seems brave enough to explain."

Skyelle shakes her head. "Daughter, it is certainly not bravery that stills our tongues. It is pain…and it is loss." Her fingers quiver as they reach to her lower neck to graze a black web of scar tissue burned into her skin. "The world has taken so much from us, Althea. Your Mother included. Yet, despite the trials heaped upon us, our Bloodline always finds ways to overcome."

Althea instantly regrets her outburst, reaching out to the older woman, but the attempt at comfort fails to register. The Protectorate's eyes are now painted over with a haunted shade.

"We strive against the dangers of this world, but the unfortunate truth is that despite our efforts, we are a people robbed of what was once ours."

Blooper hovers over to the older woman, collecting several loose strands of graying hair and placing them behind her ear.

The Protectorate straightens up, sudden fury taking root in her eyes.

"I was a young girl, around your age, when our homelands still belonged to us. The accomplishments of our people…" She waves to the Redemption skyline that reaches for the stars above them. "If you think this is beautiful, this city is but a cheap copy of our Mother City, Diligence."

Fireworks boom above the buildings, filling a moment of silence between the pair.

Althea strokes the woman's fibernetic skin with the back of her hand, choosing her questions carefully. Perhaps now is the time to finally uncover her longest-standing mystery.

"Protectorate, then—what was it? What changed that our people came here and built Redemption? Where is our true homeland…and why aren't we there now?"

Skyelle's nose twitches and her eyes flash to meet Althea's.

"Exile, Daughter. The Scattering."

A few heads around them turn to look the Protectorate's way, then shake in shared rage.

"Daughter, halving a people—splitting mother from father and child from parent—is akin to killing them. It was a hard-enough blow to this nation's heart. But further condemning one of those halves past the Wastelands? That was enough to break the nation's body."

Skyelle touches the scarring on her neck once more.

"And yet, worse still…we, the half that remained spent twenty years in slavery. This is what broke our nation's soul."

Althea stares in disbelief at her caretaker.

"Tw-twenty years? You never once told me it was that long. The history archives hardly discuss the slavery period at all and there aren't many memorials from that time."

"Because we weren't permitted to build any." The woman spits.

Althea looks away as her keeper's eyes smolder, but she continues. "Think Althea, what better strategy to keep a robbed man from knowing he's been stolen from than to swipe history from him too? We're lucky to be able to commemorate King and Queen Regalia and their fallen family at all."

Hushed voices nearby whisper upon hearing the royal names of the same couple whose puppets I saw waltzing past my room earlier. "Blessed be the Beloved Majesties, may they rest in peace as the Crown's Hand guides us into a better age." The people say.

Althea and her Protectorate finally arrive at their marker and make for the tailor shop. After Althea is measured and weighed, new garments are printed in a three-dimensional weaving machine. The Protectorate holds up a digital token which the tailor scans with his augmented eye. He winks his other unaltered eye as the pair leave his shop.

"Protectorate, what am I in all this? What do the Generals in the Crown's Hand want with me considering everything you've just told me?"

Skyelle calms a trembling fist and puts her hand to Althea's heart.

"The sickly roots of this world must be yanked loose and burned in the fires of the sun. Daughter, you will be the hope of our Bloodline reborn and return what was robbed of our people. Only then can Loghis rebuild."

Without warning, she steps away to speak into an earpiece Althea hadn't noticed until now. "The preparations are complete. She will be in the Chancellery within the hour."

Althea imagines the intimidating tower at the city's center and takes a small step in retreat. The older woman turns slowly around, beckoning toward a pitch-black alley.

"Skyelle…w-what is this?"

The woman's expression is cold steel as she lets a beat of silence hang in the air. Althea can feel her pulse quicken, but her keeper simply raises her hands to the city around her.

"This, Daughter, is our chance at true Redemption."

Althea stands motionless, suddenly unsure of the older woman's intentions.

"Now come—it's time we take back what the Council has long since stolen."

20

Mischief At Midnight

Althea paces the length of the glass corridor that makes up the Chancellery foray.

"Remember your Ethos, remember your Ethos," she chants to herself, hoping to maintain her usual air of confidence. After all, being cross-examined by a board of aged officials was hardly more formalized than the standup tests and recitations she'd been acing for over a decade now. Blooper sways from side to side while tethered to her shoulder plate. The bot plays a calming track, a collection of recorded rainstorms. Althea closes her eyes, reveling in the white noise. Even if downpours were almost non-existent on this side of the Wastelands, the rushing sound was still her favorite.

"Thank you, Blooper. You have always been good at flatlining my nerves."

A warm orange hue emits from her companion's tiny core communicating *You're welcome*, followed by blinks of gray—*Just breathe.*

Althea exhales slowly while looking out over Redemption's midnight view. The city is a sprawling blanket of lights from her vantage point, a glass corridor set within the Chancellery's ninth floor. Hundreds of walking Streams with thousands of markers fill each city quadrant, every one of them teeming with enthusiastic travelers. Her viewpoint overlooks the tops of all nearby towers too—Althea traces their sharp curves up to the stars above.

Beautiful. This was a view meant for kings and queens...

She looks up through the glass ceiling to see a small cube hovering atop the Chancellery. Where the rest of the tower is radiant—a beacon illuminating the surrounding structures—the room-sized cube above somehow hangs weightless in utter darkness.

Althea studies the black cube with telescopic vision, recalling history lessons of the Chancellery's purpose—the original structure was a gem at the center of Diligence, the capital's heart where Loghint kings and queens could fully appreciate their countrymen's Ethos. She nudges Blooper, waking the bot's sleep cycle to take pictures of the view for later analysis.

"Did you ever imagine we'd be this close to the throne room, Bloop? Zoom into that box up there please. I'm positive that's where the royals once sat."

The gadget chirps then guides its laser pointer to a set of art pieces hanging in a nearby display case. Althea moves closer, curiously studying the collection of old paintings.

"It says here that the cube houses 'The Galaxy Thrones.' Up there is a replica built to memorialize the throne room of the same name, the one we left behind in our original lands."

A painting of the throne room floor, notably much larger than the commemorative cube above her, shows two jeweled seats set amongst interlocking circular gears. Gems and metal disks make up the floor and walls, forming a gleaming tapestry not unlike the innerworkings of a pocket watch. A caption on the bottom of the painting indicates The Galaxy Thrones reoriented each day to mimic the position of the planets in Spheire's solar system.

Althea finishes inspecting the other items in the display case before returning to the opposite side of the corridor. From this height, she can see the same view held by the ever-watchful eyes of King and Queen Regalia's memorial statues. The giant figures cast in polished bronze reflect the Chancellery's light. The King and Queen both hold hands and point across the horizon in the compass heading of Loghis' homelands. Around their outstretched wrists are three thin lines of gold. An exact match of those golden bands projects around the couple's temples like spiraling wreaths.

"The Tri-Crowns," she whispers to herself in awe. Althea had spent what felt like an age digging through old archives to learn more about the royal heirloom. In the days before the Scattering, it used to represent the powerful lineage of her people. More recently, some in Loghis have resurrected the symbol to mark resistance against oppression from the Council. Their philosophy follows one line of thought—what right did the Council have to assume rule over all of Spheire when the Tri-Crown existed? It provided a time-tested legitimacy to whomever would rule Loghis, negating the relevance of its current foreign leaders.

Althea watches the golden projections rotate slowly around the statues' temples. She finds herself humming a bedtime tune her mother would whisper to lull her to sleep.

Children be Minded, Our Purpose is Clear,
With Ethos our Weapon, no Loghint knows Fear.
The Tri-Crown appoints, our Bloodline Adheres,
This Naton preserved for Tomorrow's Frontier.

It wasn't until Althea studied the laws supporting the Tri-Crown that she was enamored by the role it once played in her society. The golden wrist bands were built with sensors that could detect a distinct genome in the biological code of its wearer. Not only could the device sense the rare proclivity for all four high Minds within a royal candidate, but it could also trace connections to ancestors in Loghis' history who had accomplished significant feats. Heroes and heroines, wise leaders, fierce debaters and brilliant scientists alike—the pedigree of these figures could all be traced by the Tri-Crown.

Once a candidate matched both criteria, the artifact would be awarded to him or her upon the ruler's coronation. Small augments that only matched the frequency of the Tri-Crown would be implanted into the temples of the new ruler, allowing database like information to be accessed at any time. The implants would also sync with the capital city to feed real-time updates about problems within its districts. Should a certain quadrant report the rise of a pandemic, the heirloom would be alerted. Were the city limits under breach from an unforeseen threat? Within seconds the ruler would know. As an added measure, the best kings and queens would share this data stream with the Crown's Hand to allow the Strategic Minded Supris Generals and Marshals to help with preventative problem solving. In this way, Diligence was a "smart city," and the royal family were one with it. In turn, their constant attentiveness was rewarded with an unwavering admiration from the Loghis people.

A voice interrupts Althea's reading, "Well now, don't tell me it's the Generals' infamous 'Nuke' in the flesh. And here I thought the rest of us were never going to actually meet you."

Althea turns in the direction of the voice to see a tall, slender young man with jet black hair and a cunning half grin. Whereas the backlight of Althea's eyes matched most citizens—digital blue—his eyes were the same color as a patch painted down the middle of his hair—brilliant gold.

"Excuse me, Brother, do I know you?"

The dashing stranger leans against the glass with a cavalier expression. "Mmm, not yet. But Althea, we all know who you are."

Althea feels her irises begin to spin as she assesses the scenario, slightly irritated at his withholding manner of conversating. The newcomer is quick to pick up on the hint and starts to backpedal.

"Hey, hey, hey, no need to stare down a Loghis *brother* like that." He holds up his hands innocently. "Here, Nuke, let's have civil introductions first? You can call me Clintis P."

"Clintis P.?" She says, emphasizing the abbreviation. "I'll be sure to remember that by the odd choice of last name alone." Althea crooks her neck feeling a spur of irritation. "And introductions aside, what is your exact purpose for continuing to call me that? You've said it twice now."

The boy cocks his eyebrow giving Althea the impression their every word is somehow a move on an invisible chessboard. "What? Nuke? Do you like it? It's what a few of the other candidates started calling you when we heard about you. Rumor is, having you with us will provide that extra…boom." He makes an animated sound effect, spreading his hands apart to mimic an explosion. Clintis chuckles at his own joke, then catches Althea's unamused reception.

"Ah, well, maybe a sense of humor isn't one of your specialties."

The girl snaps back, "Nor comedy yours."

He smirks while nursing an imaginary injury. "Ouch."

Althea glances down at her enhanced arm. "Besides, your moniker makes no sense. They may have put an entire arsenal inside here, but a nuclear device isn't one of them. Sure, I might engineer some adjustments here and there, but I have no intentions of adding anything that destructive."

Clintis crooks his lips, pointing from the arm to its owner. "That's not the nuke, sweetheart. You are."

Althea walks over to him coolly then, studying him close. She juts her chin like a razor toward his neck, keeping her voice low. "Listen here, I do hate to be redundant, but for you I'll make an exception. My name is not optional. It's Althea Regis and I wouldn't suggest you push me further."

Clintis steps to Althea's side after noticing her clenched metal fist.

"Whew, well aren't you fun? Look at us, starting off on the right foot already." He makes an attempt to backpedal the tension with raised hands. "Fine, keep telling yourself whatever you want, but I'm no fool. I've heard the secrets they keep about you behind closed doors."

Althea narrows her eyes at him. She's tempted to inquire precisely how the little deviant knows what's been said about her behind closed doors but imagines he's crafted a way.

Clintis shrugs nonchalant, "Anyways, I know an ace-in-the-hole when I see one, Nu—"

He chokes back his words. "Sorry, dame, it just has such a ring to it."

Althea looks at him, keenly aware he is easily within her striking distance. She imagines how proud her Combatives instructor would be to hear how easily she duped a foe larger than herself. Or perhaps her new enhancements could use a live fire subject…but alas, she lets all tempting ideas pass. No, she was minutes away from being screened by the Crown's Hand—an official board possessing several centuries worth of collective knowledge. She hadn't the time to react to the whims of some unknown mischief maker.

She purses her lips. "What exactly are you doing up here anyway, hmm? I'm sure you could be stirring up trouble anywhere at such an hour as this."

Clintis doesn't make any attempt to stifle a sarcastic grin. He holds up his arms in front of his face like a performing actor. Both arms are complete modifications fashioned like Althea's own procedure but made of featherweight fibernetic alloy and covered in tattoo-like designs. He jabs the air with perfect form then dives backward into an effortless one-handed cartwheel. He winks up at her before lifting to a single finger, both of his golden legs pointing upward, reflecting the Chancellery's outer lighting. He tumbles neatly back to his feet, like a gymnast, twirling to lean back against the wall as though the whole maneuver had never happened.

"Sis, I'm thinking with all this training to my name, I'm here for a mission brief. Same as you."

Althea considers the new information. She certainly hadn't ruled out the possibility of this mission being a multi-person task, but what could she possibly have in common with this wild card? She decided to press for the additional information that her Protectorate chose to omit.

"Of what Mind are you?"

"A good bit of Strategic and a dash of Chemic, if you must know."

Fantastic, someone who can outsmart most opponents and euthanize the ones he can't. What kind of task did the Generals have in mind here?

"Do you know why we've been chosen for this? Or rather, what precisely *this* is?"

Clintis thinks for a minute, tapping the bottom of his metal forearm against the glass. With each tap, a small *shink* cuts the silence and a tiny set of triple pronged syringes slides in and out of his enhancement.

"Honestly, I couldn't key you in on what you're looking for. All I know is the other two-hundred and ninety-nine of us have been getting tested somethin' fierce over the past annual. Unlike a certain someone who I'm told has had it pretty nice around here with one-on-one training."

That little rogue! How did he know so much about her? If the Generals were setting her up, she'd at least wish to know their motivation first. Before Althea could assault him with a line of further questioning, the door at the end of the corridor slides open, announcing the arrival of the elevator with a monotone ring. Inside, Skyelle stands waiting.

"Come, Daughter, the panel is ready for you."

Althea steps to walk away, allowing not a single ampere of brain power to linger on the beautiful young man. Clintis, however, has other plans.

"Really? No goodbye? No good luck?" he chides. "Come on, Nuke, you'd think the Generals would pick me someone a little nicer to work with."

Althea drives forward, ignoring the comment. *You'd think the Generals would pick me someone less unbearable to work with.*

Once inside the elevator, it begins a slow ascent. Althea and her mistress are headed to the stop just below the Galaxy Throne memorial. Her Protectorate looks over her garments, inspecting every inch for any unaddressed flaw.

"Let's review one last time for a few possible test questions," she says. Skyelle thinks for a moment before speaking again. "What are the five nations and their respective Gifts?"

Althea smirks at the overly simple recitation. The five Bloodlines were a child's memorization: Mind, Body, Soul, Nature, and Elements.

Mind - "Loghis, Obtainers of the Complete Knowledge.
Body - "Indom, The Body is the Weapon.
Soul- "Hayvin, The Spirit Born.

Nature- "Animas, Mimics of Beasts.
Elements- "Petrichor, Weavers of the Storm."

The Protectorate nods approval, "Good. As you know, your Combatives instructor, Marshal Sevarick, will be on this board. He has already advised the members of his observations of your Strategic prowess. Let us anticipate a question from him."

Althea threads her fingers, focusing on the lessons learned from the harsh instructor.

"You have entered one-to-one combat with a physically superior opponent. During her first strikes, you observe a weak spot in her stance and wish to exploit it. How would you calculate the force of impact you are able to apply to the vulnerability?"

Althea considers her answer for a couple seconds. "The calculation for ascertaining my force of impact in shorthand is the division of kinetic energy by distance. More specifically, force equals point-five times mass, times velocity squared, all divided by distance."

The Protectorate, having not been born Strategic Minded checks against her pocket notes to confirm the response. "Good, flawless delivery. How about this scenario?" She flips through her notes before continuing.

"You have deployed on a campaign into the nation of Animas. You find your patrol ambushed by a fully transformed Beast Master from the Bloodline of Nature. With only the ascertainment that he is bonded to an apex predator such as a lion, wolf, or tiger, how would you disable this combatant to give yourself the competitive edge?"

Althea thinks through the layered scenario carefully. She starts off slowly. "Disabling such a threat would have an infinitesimal window for execution due to the target's speed and aggression. However, Beast Masters with, um, Nodus? Yes, with Nodus like those are most susceptible to a disruption of—"

The elevator stops and its doors open to reveal a dimly lit room with a long walkway leading to its center.

The Protectorate whispers, "Good luck, Daughter. From here, your fate is your own. Do well in your task for Mother Loghis. I know you will make her proud, and so I will be also."

Althea keeps her composure steady, giving the woman a brief nod of respect. The eyes of the Crown's Hand are already on her, and she feels there can be no room for any perceived imperfections. She embarks onto the walkway, the strips of light on either side becoming the only source of light once the elevator closes at her back.

Althea holds her head high when she reaches the room's center. The board sits at a half circle table above her, the dim lighting in the room concealing their faces. The only confirmation of each member's presence are eleven pairs of glowing blue eyes inspecting her through the darkness. On the periphery, Althea notices an unknown but well-built twelfth figure without visual augments is also here, shrouded beneath a heavy hood. Althea returns her focus to the others, keeping still before the board's presiding member.

After nearly five minutes of agonizing silence, a stream of light illuminates the face central to the crescent shaped board. A hardened older man with a severe jawline stares down at her. She tries not to fixate on the gash-like scar across his forehead, matched by the discolored burn marks etched into his otherwise gray bearded chin.

His voice reverberates around the black room as though he were the mouthpiece of a storm. "Althea Regis, Daughter of Intellect and Erudite of all four high Minds. I am head of this panel, Supris General Pierce. Welcome to the Crown's Hand. Let us begin your long-awaited cross-examination."

21

Icebox

Following the General's introduction, the room illuminates to reveal the rest of the panel.

It curves around Althea's periphery, and she only recognizes a few of the stern faces. A momentary glance to Marshal Sevarick earns her a tight-lipped greeting. She studies a few of the others quickly and realizes she doesn't know all the matured women but guesses them to be older than the Protectorate. These hardened Matrons wear as many scars as their male counterparts, adding to their venerated appearance. Only the hooded figure remains in shadow.

General Pierce sits forward, shifting enough for Althea to now see a crest hanging high on the wall behind him. There, a golden Tri-Crown rests in the palms of four hands. The two center hands are simple human ones cast in iron, the third forged from spare augment parts. But it's the fourth hand gripping the headpiece that makes Althea's stomach lurch. It is crafted entirely from hundreds of human bones, a clear hearkening to a skeleton. The message though subtle, is clear. Whomever wears the Tri-Crown might not deal so directly in death, but the Crown's Hand was certainly versed in it.

The iron bearded man lets his irises spin slowly while taking in his newest subject. General Pierce presses a button, initiating a recording device and speaks. "Althea, I will begin with your first question."

She steels herself, wondering from what field of study her opening recitation might come from. The entire panel is difficult to get a read on, especially considering Althea never could find much information on the organization in the communal archives. They were an utter mystery until recent studies granted her access to higher-level records. She remembers the importance of remaining flexible here since the members could be from any area of society. Agriculture, engineering, education, defense and others beyond—their backgrounds were diverse; thus, any topic is game. She empties her mind so as not to accidentally miss some minute detail.

"Why do you believe you have been called before us today?" he says.

Is he serious? What kind of essay question is that? I don't even know where to begin! Her thoughts must have unintentionally betrayed a foolish micro-expression across her brow. Several of the Matrons squint their eyes, catching the misstep and scribbling furiously.

"Supris General, while I have spent the last annual trying to piece together what you could want with someone like me, I was unable to arrive at any meaningful conclusions. I don't know what task you will put me to. However, rest assured, my upbringing—like any other Loghint—was filled with Ethos building. I am ready to comply for our nation."

If it weren't for slight movements of the General's beard quivering in the conditioned air, she could swear the stoic man had been swapped out for a bust. His face gives away no clue to whether her answer was sufficient or not. In fact, this most distinct feature lends him a presence that matches the room around her. From the dark gray metal of the panel's table to the austere violet lighting, everything in this room seems so...cold.

For the next inquiry, Marshal Sevarick leans forward, pointing from her periphery. "Give us your definition of a birthright."

Althea skips past the written definition, trying to align herself with whatever subtext the panel might be searching out.

"I believe this to be authority belonging to a person or entity by which claims to certain privileges can be made. These privileges exist by the simple fact said being exists. Despite the preferences of others, but perhaps not completely in spite of others, the pursuit of one's birthright is earned simply by breathing."

The Marshal wrinkles his bottom lip. "Good answer, Daughter. I'm sure you could go a step further to say that sometimes one must be willing to die to claim such privilege?"

"Of course, Marshal."

A needle nosed Matron on the other side slams down a gnarled relic of an augment into the metal panel. "And what of the reverse? What of the requirement for *others* to be made to die for the attainment of such privileges?"

Althea considers for a moment. To her, logic like this was always a slippery slope, the underlying philosophy behind it far too easy to abuse.

"Matron, I submit that such a cost as you've described should only be implemented when the proverbial bill is high enough."

The woman looks at her quizzically. "Explain."

"Let us say a sector in the agricultural district has suffered a great famine. If a father has run out of food and his children are on the verge of starvation, but the man's new neighbor moves in with a household and stores of nutrition, I believe—"

The general leans in, reminding Althea of the coiled motion a desert cobra makes before ending a prey's life.

"—I believe the father must be willing to fulfill a certain level of misdeeds to pay the bill of keeping his loved ones alive. All peaceful means should be expended first to ensure the neighbor can also maintain the well-being of his family. For example, asking to share the resources at a reasonable apportionment. However, in the end, the father must be prepared to commit certain calculated and measured violations as necessary."

The chilling answer earns several nods around the room though for Althea's part, she can hardly believe the words that just escaped her.

A woman, noticeably younger than the rest of the panel, clears her throat. Her straight black hair frames her delicate face, but Althea has never seen a fiercer pair of blood red eyes. In some ways, she reminds Althea of a younger General Pierce.

"Daughter, it is heartening to see what our Bloodline's progeny are willing to do for their country. This patriotism is cut short, however, when one considers their toil contributes to a nation without her own sovereignty." She pauses, letting her point ripen in the silence. "As you know, Mother Loghis, along with the rest of Spheire has been under the rule of the Council for a little more than a half century now. From what you've learned, what is the Council?"

Althea breathes easy, finally a simple pull from her history sessions. "Matron, where all five nations and Bloodlines used to have some form of self-governance, the Council assumed control nearly six decades ago, veritably removing previous power structures entirely. For a brief time, most Bloodlines were permitted to maintain their leadership with figure heads installed, but soon after the Council's full reign was implemented and all national powers were reduced to local, much smaller levels."

"Good, you seem to know your books..." The flex in her acute jawline sends a chill down Althea's spine. "But tell me something that isn't written in the textbook's pages—what happened to our King and Queen Regalia?"

A flash of anger strikes behind the inquisitor's eyes and Althea tucks the observation of it away for later. There's no denying the similarity between her and the General now. In fact, the cruel judgement in Pierce's stare is identical to hers and no wonder. The man and what could only be his daughter—are clearly cut from the same cloth.

Althea chooses her next words wisely. "Matron, regarding the fallen King and Queen—after the Council took control of Spheire, they found the royal couple guilty of an undisclosed, large-scale wrongdoing. Though these allegations were only accusations at first, the King and Queen, along with the small children of the royal family were all seized and publicly executed. They were the first the Council ever put to 'The Silent Bath.'"

General Pierce's lips twitch into a hateful scowl—the burn marks in his beard adding a new shade of sinister to his vengeful look. "May they rest easy in Everrealm." The oldest members of the panel are visibly seething but repeat after him. Althea wonders if some in their ranks would've been young peers with the fallen rulers long ago.

After a few moments of silence, Pierce holds up a finger, signaling the questioning would be concluded with this final inquiry.

"Daughter, from an authoritative standpoint, what benefit does a governing body stand to gain by monopolizing and standardizing higher education?"

Althea immediately understands his intent, the light going off in her head. She finally has her first real clue toward a possible purpose for her being here.

"Consolidating a people's education allows for a reliable stream of information to be issued out to the masses on a routine basis. If I may reference my Protectorate, she stated earlier today that it is easier to keep what was stolen from a robbed man by swiping his past from him as well. In a way, streamlining education allows for only a certain version of historical events to be told."

Once again, no cue either way from the steely-eyed man. She covertly glances over to Marshal Sevarick. His tightly lined buzzcut accentuates the deep frown wrinkling his face, but he offers a nearly imperceptible nod of approval.

"Young Erudite, you've answered well, and I believe the members here all representing the four high Minds agree to the confirmation of your role within our plans." The General scans the half-circle, looking for any signs of disapproval. "Your task is as follows."

The man brings up a small projection menu on the desk in front of him and presses a series of virtual buttons. The wall behind Althea sparks to life, showing a feed from the screen in Redemption's shopping district. Most of the time, the marketplace projector installed by the Council is blank. The older Loghints had figured out how to interrupt the foreign stream ages ago, turning it on only when Sanctum representatives were expected for inspections.

On the wall, sweeping views of a beautiful campus loop alongside still pictures. Every ten seconds or so, the images freeze, and a three-dimensional scan of the recorded structures uncovers blueprinted versions of them. The schematics are collected at the end and data points drawn from the information flash onto the screen. A final number zooms to the center of the projection: three-hundred.

"Daughter, it's been exactly fifty years since the 'Great Bloodline War' ended. The Council built Sanctum on the backs of our people and when that wasn't enough, forced them to go against a high law in Loghis."

He rewinds the stream to a clip of Sanctum. In it, workers are repairing the supportive beams of a bridge. He presses a few of the menu buttons and brings up a side-by-side clip of similar work being done in Redemption. "What do you see? What is the key difference here?"

Althea studies the images carefully, not seeing anything at first. Then, it becomes unmistakably clear. "A-are those robotic workers?"

The entire room shifts in their chairs, disgusted by the sight.

"Indeed, they are. Loghis law prevents our society from becoming lazy enough to leave our work to the hands of automatization. We have always believed that to create a being to work in your stead robs first your Ethos, then your mind as it has nothing left to challenge it. Without work, we lose ambition."

He pauses the clip. "Regardless, all that slave labor from decades past was funneled into a final source, the construction of the Discipline of Peace. And after forty years of filling the minds of Spheire's elite children, the Council has finally come for our own."

A giant image of a Hayvin woman consumes the wall. Her hawk-like glare is made no less intense by the fact it's simply a projection. Exalt Danika, member of the Council and Head of the Discipline, beams from the screen, the illustration of ultimate power.

"To put it plainly, this is the first time Loghis has been allowed to, or rather required to, send the Discipline tribute. You will be one of three-hundred envoys we have selected to represent us," the General says.

Althea looks at the campus pictures before turning back to the panel. "To what end will we attend this institute? What possible strategic edge do we gain by sending the brightest of an upcoming generation away from Loghis?"

General Pierce smiles for the first time at the question. "You can let us worry about the strategy. But understand this. No plan this panel concocts will work without first being equipped with information. All three hundred of you will report the ins and outs of both The Discipline and Sanctum. Your proximity to members of the Council is also being considered for exploitation."

Althea nods. That's smart, using the requirement to their advantage.

"The final component, however, is for Strategic Minded only."

The panel goes still, waiting on the General's every word. It's the first time tonight all eyes haven't been on her.

"Using your words, girl, there are certain bills that must be paid. However, Loghis has paid enough. The Council will assume the costs of its actions, by force if necessary. The future may give us a unique opportunity to challenge Exalt Danika's authority. Ideally, the other nations will stay out of the way."

He pauses, running a metal finger through his grayed beard.

"Perhaps, not only will they remain uninvolved, but it is our hope our rebellion will stand as the inspiration Spheire needs to throw off her shackles entirely." He pauses, his threaded fingers resting over tightly pressed lips. "But we know better than to leave any strategy to hope. As such, you and the other Strategic Minds will be sent to assess the current readiness levels of the other Bloodline's finest."

General Pierce's tight-lipped grin is harsh and joyless. "In whatever you are required to do, track, collect, and report. Every hour of every day will gift us with a better understanding of the capabilities of your classmates. The Crown's Hand will handle the rest."

The projector minimizes before fading away and the panel looks back to Althea. Each member settles back into their chairs. Althea notes that never once did the muscular hooded figure move. The lights fade then, obscuring them all once more in shadow, yet the General remains illuminated.

"We look forward to seeing what you can do for your country, Daughter. You are dismissed."

Althea steps back, bowing low, then turns to walk down the walkway toward the elevator. At its doors, the General's voice echoes out once more.

"So I am entirely clear, Althea, there are many cogs to the success of this plan. A good portion of them are already in motion, even outside this room. Have pride in this distinct honor. You have been called to be a part of something so much greater than yourself. We will send for you in the coming days."

Althea steps into the empty elevator. She looks back up, committing the room to memory with a final glance. The crest glints in the violet light. She notices for the first time, the unyielding death grip the skeletal hand has on the Tri-Crown. The room's lighting is completely dimmed, and all eleven pairs of blue eyes hang like apparitions in the darkness. If the interior's cool metallic vibe had sent minor chills down her spine before, the sensation is nothing compared to the panel's penetrating icy stare.

Althea shivers imperceptibly as the doors close and the elevator begins its descent with a hum. Alone, she lets out a breath, exhausted by the encounter. This wasn't the type of panel she was expecting from the Crown's Hand—she had no way of knowing how merciless and calloused time had made her country's leaders.

Redemption reflects off the metal of her arm prompting Althea to press her fingertips to the elevator's glass walls. She wonders if all Loghints share the hardened souls of their leaders, if history has seared vengeance into all their minds...

Althea closes her eyes, whispering words to a faithless prayer—hoping without confidence that her countrymen have not inherited their leaders' frozen hearts.

Part IV
A Changed Tomorrow

22

SELECTION FESTIVAL

The Pan-Tigris Grove
"Come on, come on, *come on*! I've seen snails in the Wilds faster than you!" Kleo grunts while shoving me out the den's exit. She switches tactics, flanking my front side. My kin stand around and chuckle, watching the girl dig her heels into the floor, trying to yank my hand through the curtains.

I stick my tongue out at her. "Call me slow all you like, but putting on this new dancing outfit was really hard!" In truth, I'm excited whenever she's excited, and the Selection Festival is definitely worth getting stoked for. The village holds different festivals throughout the seasons, but there's always been something a little more magical about this one.

Tygon snags our youngest and hoists her up on his shoulders. She squeals, delighted, enjoying the new sense of height.

"Tygon, can I ride your shoulders during the ceremony?" Kleo pleads. "I don't wanna' miss anything!"

Tygon claps her on the knee gently. "Well, if you'd have eaten all your fruits n' vegetables by now, you'd be tall enough to see for yourself!"

Kleo huffs, crossing her arms dramatically.

"I'm kiddin', kitten, but I still won't be able to help you tonight. After all, somebody's going to be on the big stage." It takes a moment before Tygon looks at me sheepishly. I shake my head to confirm I haven't been offended. Why would I be? He deserves this proud moment—even if it means our paths diverge for the foreseeable future. Tonight, my big brother will represent both kin and clan as a selectee for the Discipline of Peace. With his superior mastery of our people's Gift, I'm glad that between the two of us, he will be the one to go.

Muma Kura inspects my outfit, and I catch a twinkling in her eyes as she murmurs something about me looking just like Papa. She adjusts a white strip of cloth around my head—the same accessory the village's ceremonial dancers and drummers wear to keep their hair in place. I'm more interested in its other purpose though—keeping sweat out of my eyes. I've got big plans for this evening and can't leave any room for mess-ups.

Tonight, I am going to show Lunis the way we PanTigris boys learned to dance. Papa Jaole showed me a few of the moves he used to get his first dance with Muma. Sure, his style was horribly outdated—like seriously ancient—but I figure I can mix in my own vibe to make it work.

Papa Jaole swoops into the den, carrying a satchel on his back packed full of seating mats. "Kin, let's get going. I was just with the other clan heads overseeing the set up. The Hub is beautiful, and we don't want to miss getting a good spot in the Hall to see our boy!"

Tygon humbly accepts Papa's hug. This is a big moment for every kin who gets to send their children to the Discipline and represent our people abroad.

We leave the grove together and Kleo holds my hand as she skips along the walkway to the Hub. The path is packed with excited villagers and yet even over all the chatter, the booming music from the festival can be heard.

"Brotya, I like that get-up you've got goin' on. I'd say several young huntresses will choose you for a dance tonight," Tygon says, raising his eyebrows and shoulders to the beat rustling the leaves above us.

"Pssh, I'll be lucky to get the one and only dance I care about. Tonight's the night I catch Lunis's eye!"

"Well, at least you have those gifts you've been stocking

away for her all this time. That'll make you a bit more enticing," Tygon says.

I freeze in my tracks as blood rushes to the tips of my ears. "Wh-what? You're supposed to bring gifts to land a dance? Papa, you never said anything like that!"

Papa laughs. "Son, sometimes the only thing you need is some sweet moves and a bit of love. When I asked for your Muma"—he imitates that first invitation, strutting as he walks backward while popping his shoulder rhythmically—"I sure didn't need no shining jewelry to get the right answer."

Muma smacks his hand playfully before cozying up beside him. "Boy, don't listen to this 'ole kook. He'll have you looking a fool's fool out there. Only reason it worked for him in the end certainly wasn't due to any skill on his part…I was feeling unusually merciful that night."

Papa plops a sloppy kiss on her forehead. "Eh, that's all details nobody wants to hear. Point is, it worked, and that's how you little crumb-snatchers got here. So just go for it boy! Let loose and do what comes naturally."

I consider naturally running my butt back to the den to get my bracelets. But we're already so far up the path, I decide it's not worth it. Plus, what Papa said was right, this place is too beautiful to miss. "Wow, would you look at that," I whisper to myself.

The entire inner Hub sparkles with light from thousands of wire frame baskets, each with a candle inside. Every wick is made of various plants and roots to offer a unique tint to the space. Like a spiderweb woven through a prism, the streams of light glisten into an intricate pattern—all converging at the center where the People's Hall stands.

Through the Hall's open-aired structure, I can see a thousand villagers mingling, laughing, and telling each other stories. On the stage in front of them, Dom Arzen shimmies back and forth, stomping double time to the drummers swinging like madmen beside him.

We head straight for the Hall and place our floor mats in one of the middle rows. A PanVulpis kin seated next to us waves 'hello' and we lean over to greet them. I ask their eldest son, a boy around my age, what Elevation he is from.

"I was in Elevation Willow," he replies. I try my hardest to recall if I know his name. Fortunately, he saves me before I embarrass myself.

"Name's Tanner. You'll have to remind me of your name, but I definitely have seen ya' before."

I look at him confused. "Uh, yea, I'm Faylen, from PanTigris. When exactly did you see me? I must not have been paying much attention, sorry."

Tanner snickers under his breath. "Let's just say had you been rushing a bit faster through the woods, I woulda' been able to get out of the Domain a lot sooner than I did. I haven't seen a stink n'sleep trap fail me yet 'til you came along."

I think back over the past few days and it finally clicks. "No way, the dung-a-lew trap in the Domain? That was you? You know that sleep nectar had me out for a whole day? You sneaky fox."

"Ooh, the highest of compliments. Thank you!" Tanner bows with exaggeration.

After a few more minutes, the drumline's rhythm slows while each strike increases in power. Every kin quiets down as Dom Arzen prepares to speak. The Dominant and Sage both take their positions on stage.

"Praedari Village, what a night we have in store for you," Dom Arzen booms. "We not only thank you for being here, but let's also put our hands together for tonight's true reason to celebrate!"

The hall breaks into applause as the leader motions for those accepted to the Discipline to stand tall. The noise doubles as whoops and hollers fill the room. Excited kin toss streamers into the air, signifying what clan their child will be representing in Sanctum. After a few moments, the uproar fades and everyone turns back to the stage.

"Before we really get down to our merriment, let's take a moment and remember why we are here. This nation, this Bloodline, the people of this village—we all share a Gift. This very Gift will be on display every day at the Discipline and you young hunters will be charged with representing it well." Dom Arzen motions Sage Ophis to the front of the stage.

The elder steps forward. "Children, we can never forget where our strength originates from." He holds up his hands, gesturing to the hanging banners along the columns. Each of them is adorned with a different Spirit and no two are the same shape or color scheme. The Sage brings his hands together over his head, pointing at the giant banner above him woven with the dragon's scale.

"The First Beast Master—The Dragon Lord—was the eldest of the Five Siblings. Ten thousand hunting seasons ago, Spheire was a young world and humanity was just beginning to blossom." He closes his hands together, forming a small circle.

"The Spirits also lived on the face of Spheire, but in their own lands. Our ancestors and the Spirits lived separately, but in peace. At least, until the Spirits detected a disturbance approaching our budding world." He balls his fist, smashing it into the hand holding the imaginary circle.

"Wherever there is harmony, eventually there will be Chaos. This presence floats amongst the stars, waiting to confuse progress and, if left unchecked, consume life. The Spirits understood this and approached humanity to seek an ally, an intelligent species with capable bodies. They hoped we would join them and align against the darkness. It was thus the Five Siblings—representing all of humankind—who responded, agreeing to help oust the lurking forces." He pauses, smiling wide.

"Once Chaos was expelled from Spheire, the Spirits decided to leave their lands entirely and return to the spiritual plane of Everrealm. Before they departed, however, they granted each sibling a Gift based on their request. We call this historic day, The Granting. It was here that Spheire received the mighty abilities we hone today.

"Our Dragon Lord asked to be bonded to the creatures of this world. The brother who built Indom asked the Spirits to teach him how to form his body into the greatest weapon. The sister who birthed Petrichor asked to be taught the ways of nature's lifeforce, the elements. The youngest brother who developed Loghis asked to obtain complete knowledge. And finally, at the end of The

Granting, the youngest of the five looked upon her siblings. Not knowing what power to request, the youngest sister who would go on to bear Hayvin, asked the Spirits to teach her to be more like them. In a flash, she was swept away to live out her days in Everrealm and that is how the Spirit-Born came to be."

The Sage holds his hands up once more. "Remember where your strength comes from. We were descended from great power. The Discipline will try you—your plight will be against those with whom we've fought and warred. But no matter, whatever differences you may think we have with those outside our borders, remember this. Every Bloodline's might came from a single source."

The Sage folds his hands and steps back allowing Dom Arzen to return to the center.

"Thank you, wise one. Now, clans, let the music begin!" With a cymbal crash, the instruments sound in unison. All the villagers clear their mats from the floor, making a giant dance space at the center. Both the young and old fill it, shaking and jiving to the beat. Tygon winks at me before disappearing into the joyous mass.

I stand on the outskirts, readying myself for the right moment. I'm more of a warmup-first kind of guy; never could understand how some can just jump in so freely. I've got to remember my moves, plan out which ones I'll use, and then—

A gentle hand snakes around my waist, bringing with it the scent of ash-wood leaves.

"Stripes, a small tip. No one you wanna' dance with is going to be standing out here for long. I bet at least one of these young huntresses would like to see if you can back up that fine outfit you're wearing."

I turn to see Lunis standing beside me. My heart explodes before I can utter a word. Ole' reliable—my tongue—swims in my mouth. All I can think is, *"Oh well. Turns out she's way more than you can handle, bud. Hey, feet? Go ahead and flee whenever you're ready."* My ridiculous internal monologue continues. *"Jokes on you, kid. We feets melted into the floor the second she touched you. You're on your own."*

I stammer nervously, not allowing myself to dare ogle the

huntress. I am intentional in my respect toward the beauties of our village. Comes with the territory of having a little sister—I want to set an example of what she should expect from hunters when she approaches allying age.

Still, that doesn't mean I can't acknowledge Lunis's sculpted frame is the purest artwork and a testament to seasons of grueling work.

She's wrapped her toned core in a perfectly fitted tribal gown. It has a black and gray design—an homage to her bonded—and swoops from her muscled shoulders to her hips and down past her knees. Every inch of her teases both power and unmatched grace. Her hair is fuller than I've ever seen it, packed as a bouquet of curls. Whether in Elevation class or heading to the hunting grounds, I've only seen her weaves pulled back. She always looks amazing that way, but tonight her hair is down, framing her honey-hued face. I can't quite put my finger on it, but it's as though she's captured the very look of being caught in the rain. To top it all off, the lightide pendant hangs from her neck. But rather than being tucked away for protection, tonight it's on full display below her neckline. The colored lights around the Hub glint in her gray eyes as she smiles up at me.

Finally, my brain decides to rejoin the party and my tongue along with it. I'm just about to tell her how amazing she looks when a tall, tawny-haired PanLeo steps out from the dancing crowd. He steps right up to Lunis and for some reason, I find myself a bit intimidated, of all things. Maybe because I've always been of average height and he's statuesque in every way. He even looks like he mined his own jawline off the side of a cliff. The hunter completely disregards my existence but has no problem eying Lunis up and down with a quick onceover that only I catch.

"Well, young miss, doesn't look like this kid is going to ask you—mind if a man steps in to do the job? First dance of the night sets the tone for the whole evening, so I'd hate to leave someone like you out here to cool off!"

Spiritless. Shag-faced. PanLeos!

He fits the part of a lion from the Wilds with his bonded's fur flowing like a mane around his shoulders. I can't help but be envious of his effortless confidence in this moment, but I still don't move. Lunis looks to me with lingering hope but allows herself to be led away by the smooth talker. First dances are a customary thing. It's considered rude to decline when someone requests you on the floor. Even I could get asked at any moment and would have to go, but with my luck, it'd probably be Muma who'd give me the invitation. Or Kleo…either of which I'd gladly accept though it wouldn't be the same.

Come on. Move. She's getting away, I scream inside my head as she walks off. Unlike any battle I've had up to this point, the only person forcing me to lose here is me.

With a clenched fist, I march forward and place my hand on Lunis's shoulder. She and the PanLeo whip around to look at me. I clear my throat. "Eh, pretty boy? I might be a little slow on the uptake, but I'm thinking you should find yourself another first dance. This one's been a long time coming. Besides, isn't there a mirror or somethin' you should be shmoozing?"

The tall boy cuts me a squint then holds up Lunis's hand like a trophy as though to prove a point. The huntress lowers her eyeline at him before snatching her wrist back and shoving him off. "Thanks, guy, I'll take it from here." She fires his sarcastic expression back at him.

The wolf-bonded girl lets me spin her around and my arm brushes against traces of dark fur in her garments as we collide. Slowly, her hands slide past my shoulders to clasp behind my neck. The world goes off axis a few inches as she holds my gaze steady. Somehow, the flickering hues of candlelight above look more beautiful here in her eyes. Her scent envelopes me when she leans in and whispers, "I hope your mother taught you to be faster in the field. Just how long does a tiger take to finally make the chase?"

I have no words, just a sheepish grin.

Lunis raises an eyebrow. "Well, consider this chase officially on. You've finally got me, Stripes. Now, what are you going to do?"

Okay. I love her. In every way I can imagine and all the ways I can't. She will always be the one.

I chuckle at her question, remembering Papa's advice. "Lady wolf, consider yourself warned—I'm just gonna' do what comes naturally."

23

Heartfelt

I'd never lie to myself and pretend "natural" is anything impressive to look at. More unhinged stomps and arm flailing than choreographed routine. Sadly, most of it's *around* the beat too rather than with it despite my usual musical sensibilities strumming the balalaika at home. But somehow my manic performance does the trick, just like Papa said it would. Between wild flutters of my head, I can see Lunis barely holding back her laughter. When I point both hands to the sky and throw my hips around in overexaggerated circles, the girl's dam finally breaks. She lets loose the goofiest sound I've ever heard her make and I tease her for it. She smacks me in the gut, a flash of mischief sparks in her eyes. Before I can react, she darts away, looking back at me with a longing expression that begs me to give chase around the dance space. Maybe her huntress skills have something to do with it, but I lose her in the crowd in no time at all. Instead, I'm met with smiles and jives from those around me, but none of them are the person I've put myself out here for.

"Don't tell me you can hunt down a meal but lose me that easily." I whip around to see Lunis has materialized behind me.

"H-how did you?" I blink. "I'll have you know when I'm out there in the trees, I don't have all these people getting in the way of my approach."

She fakes the motion of darting off again with a teasing grin, but instead, twirls back around to connect heart to heart with me once more. We melt into each other's gaze, breathing in the moment. It's a long while before either of us breaks the silence.

Eventually Lunis whispers, "Things got crazy for me before I had the chance to say this but thank you for getting me out of the Domain." I try to hide a blush while she collects her thoughts. "I can't believe what I saw you do out there. There's no way you should've been able to down a Saber—"

"No, please, don't!" I look over my shoulders. "Besides, no one would believe I did that any more than they'd believe a fairy tale. I don't want anyone starting to ask questions—cause the more of those that spring up, the higher chance they'll look into the circumstances behind you getting into the Discipline. I say you earned your spot and we should keep it that way."

Lunis's moonlight eyes fall to the floor with a hint of shame. "Right, but...I shouldn't even be going. I know I had two belts when that Saberhorn found me. My own, and another apprentice's. But when I woke up in the Mender's care, somehow, I had three belts to turn in. I'm not stupid, I know what happened." She fixes her stare on me with a set jaw.

Lunis knows how much I've tried to keep up with her, Tygon, and Zahk growing up. She's a sharp thinker. To her, a crush isn't a strong enough reason to give up my own future opportunities. I can see she expects more depth in my reasoning. But my intentions here are well-founded and I know I've made the only right choice given the circumstances. I simply hope to make her see it that way.

"Lunis...I couldn't take one of your belts. Plus, you were hurt by holding your own against a Saberhorn. I had to get you out. If we both left the Domain without accomplishing the task, I thought we'd both be disqualified for leaving early. So, to me, the answer was obvious. You faced the monster alone first. You earned it."

Her expression softens as she mulls over the logic. "Fine, but I still haven't made up my mind on this. No matter what, don't you get too comfy in here in Praedari. An annual can be a long time, Faylen, so I better see you at the Discipline by the next one." She twirls in a slow turn as the music quiets to a more leisurely tempo. "You know, the other day I finally figured out what I want out of the Discipline…to become someone who can inspire the little ones to dream beyond our village gates." She closes her eyes, having whispered those last words as though saying them too loud would ruin their chance of coming true. "And Fay, on that day, I want you there growing alongside me, not getting left behind here…"

"I promise, I'll do my best while you're gone. I'll do what I can with this new level of power until I can meet you up there in earnest. I hear the Discipline has developed techniques for helping people push into the fullness of their Gifts. I'm counting on it."

She plays with a loc hanging from my temple. "Well until you get there, you'll have to visit in the meantime—that's what I'm counting on. So, don't keep me waiting this time, Stripes." Her hand traces over her collarbone to caress her pendant. "I think I've been doing that for long enough."

At dawn, there's a moment right as morning flowers open their petals to the world. By the Spirits, I don't get it but she smells exactly like this. The warmth of her body coaxes my skin like sitting near the den hearth, and I notice for the first time how full her lips are. Amare, the Spirit of Love, must be working magic between us because I've never had anyone look at me the way Lunis is now. My mind races inside my head. *"Lips, perform chap check now! Breath, be tolerable. Hands…eh hands? No clue what to do with you, so standby!"* Heart snaps back. *"Dude shut up! You're ruining this for all of us!"*

Her eyelids flutter shut and she tugs my shoulders into her. I feel her weight shift just the slightest bit as she lifts up on her tiptoes. I'm finally close enough to taste her air and the room around me disappears. A couple of her curls rush forward to tickle my forehead and she giggles when a loc of mine falls across her cheek.

I am so ready to seal my first kiss.

Before I get the chance, something makes me pause…

A tiny hand tugs on the fringe of my vest. My surroundings crash back into view, and I nearly flinch at the loud music and noise. I crane my neck to look down and see an oblivious Kleo staring wide-eyed up at me. She glances at Lunis, then back at me and her cheeks flush with embarrassment once she realizes what her timing has cut short.

"Um, Faylen? Tygon's outside, and they fired up the smoked roastlet pits. He sent me to get you since they run out pretty quickly. I told him there was no way I was gonna' be tall enough to find you in this crowd…" the little girl stares at the floor, kicking aside a clump of lint with her toe.

Lunis beams a merciful expression at me, then stoops down to give my precious kiss away to Kleo. She whispers something in her ear that I can't quite make out but whatever it is has Kleo grinning from ear to ear. Lunis stands back up and winks at me as if to say, *"Fine, but don't forget, you owe me."* She surrenders my arm to Kleo and darts away into the crowd.

I stand there, watching her go—my mind starting its inner tirade once more. *"Stomach! You traitor! You were in it for those cursed smoked roastlets all along, wern'cha!"*

Kleo pulls me along and I follow her over to Tygon who waves me over excitedly. Once she's delivered me, she runs off mentioning something about Papa buying her more sweets.

This close to the giant dirt pits, the heavy smell of charred meat rushes my nostrils like a flood. The hand-sized meat chunks dangle above a roaring fire and frequently the pitmaster slathers them with an aromatic herb sauce. The brawny man, covered in soot, throws a sand-like substance into sections of the fire every couple of minutes. The powder only sizzles at first, but after a moment, it catches spark, resulting in thick billows of zesty smoke. The cloud plumes upward, collecting onto the herb sauce and instantly caramelizes layers of flavor over the meat's surface.

Tygon dances side to side, making an impromptu beat out of his lip smacks. "Oh boy, I made it just in time to be the first one in line. Sorry I couldn't give up my spot to come get you myself." When my face fails to match his enthusiasm, he prods my ribs. "What's up Fay, aren't you excited?"

I shoot him a devilish look. "Brotya, I was sizzlin' out there on the dance floor way hotter than these slabs here. First kiss man..." I hold up my fingers. "I was this close before your little romance killer swept in and sent my moment packing. So thanks a lot."

Tygon's eyes widen as he chokes back laughter. I peer at him, and his snicker unravels from the back of his throat. After a few seconds wrinkling his face, he fails to keep it together and blurts out a hearty guffaw.

"Bro. Bro! I just. Wish. You could see your face right now!" He manages between coughs. "Okay, okay, all right, I'll be serious. I promise." His cheeks balloon out immediately and he bends over.

Another failed attempt and this time he's howling louder than before. I can't resist joining him while seeing him like this. Sad as it is, even I have to admit the whole thing is kinda' funny—not like he intentionally dashed the already decrepit love life of his younger sibling. If it's this hilarious, heck, maybe I'll have to look out for my chance to do the same to Kleo someday. Keep the freakin' tradition alive.

After a few minutes, we pay for our roastlets and find a quiet place to sit and eat. On our way to a spot, we pass Dourn and one of his kin. The boy still has bandages wrapping his head and crooked nose. I look to see if he'll make eye contact, but even though I'm standing right in front of him, he quickly stares down at the ground and continues to walk on by. Funny, I've seen that exact look on frightened stray dogs.

If that wasn't unusual enough, we hadn't sat down in our spot for more than thirty seconds before a giant bear and his lanky pal have stood in front of me. They unapologetically block my view of the festivities, and I look up to see Borust crossing his hairy forearms while Kip places hands on scrawny hips.

Borust pops a few tar-beans into his mouth before speaking. "I couldn't get him ta' say it too loud, but apparently, Dourn had a run in with a certain cat out in the Domain."

Tygon puts his leaflet on the ground firmly, cracking his knuckles as he begins to rise. I put my hand on his shoulder, keeping my seat.

"Well, can't say I'm confident of what you're getting at, but I can promise that if he *did* run into me, I would've defended myself however necessary. I certainly wasn't going to have anybody *slapping* me around the jungle," I say, raising a suggestive eyebrow at Kip.

He sucks his teeth, seemingly remembering the insults he'd received in the woods. Kip steps forward, thumbing in the direction where Dourn crossed our path moments before. "We just came ta' say that's still our friend back there, but he seems to have gotten a whole new atti-tude comin' outta' dem' woods. So, whoever it was that adjusted it for 'im is good in our books. That's all." The cousins nod, then turn around, strutting back to the celebration. Tygon looks at me in wonder.

"Daaang, Fay, you really set that boy on a whole new life path? Bopped him so hard he's going to have to explain to his kids why they came out lopsided. And you know what he's going to say?" Tygon chuckles to himself. "Uh, this one time. At the Hunter Trials. I put my nose where it didn't belong, and it got stuck that way." I suck in air as he slaps my knee a bit too hard. He chuckles and pops a few juicy pieces of meat into his mouth. Something tells me if he were Papa's age, they'd have been friends growing up—matching square shaped haircuts and all.

I finish my leaflet and wipe my lips. "Brotya, I'm proud of you. I'm glad at least one of us can make it to the Discipline this annual."

Tygon pats his stomach in satisfaction and leans back against a fence post. "Me too, but I sure wish you were coming with the rest of us. It'd have been nice to start this new chapter together."

"You're not wrong, but maybe I needed a little more time in the oven. I've only just had my first taste of real power, and it felt impossibly good! I think I'm gonna' chase that feeling until I can draw it out more consistently."

"If you pull that off, being a couple seasons behind us won't mean a thing. You'll own your classmates, I have no doubt," he says, sinking deep into his lounge spot. "Hey, Fay, can I tell you somethin'?"

I flick a pebble at him to lighten the mood. "Sure, go for it."

He gives me a look before staring back up at the floral pattern formed by the candle lights above us. "I really hope this whole Discipline thing can point me in the right direction. When I'm there, I want to learn what it is I'm supposed to do for people."

"Brotya, what do you mean? You've got a great heart for people. I mean look at how ready you were to stand up for me just now. You're killing it as eldest brother for our kin."

He smirks. "Yea…but I don't know, I feel like with all this"—he taps a finger to his head—"I think maybe there's more I should be doing."

Tygon picks up the pebble I flicked at him and tosses it between his palms. "Sometimes I just find myself thinking about all that mess they show out there in the other nations. And I worry that nobody will be able to do anything to stop it. What type of world does that leave for Kleo then?"

I draw in the dirt with a twig, trying not to envision the worst outcome. "But the Council—they've kept us safe for decades. Even Papa says they've watched over us since as far back as he can remember. Sure, we don't see much of them out here in Praedari, but I sleep well at night knowing because of them, we don't have to worry about the crazy stuff out there."

Tygon purses his lips for a long moment before looking straight at me. "I think that's what I'm looking for, though, Fay. I don't want to only reap the benefits. Whatever they're doing. However they've been keeping Spheire safe. I want in. Sooner the better." He nods confidently. "I won't ever be closer to the Council than when I'm up there at the Discipline. So, to me, that's my chance to show 'em what I can do and how I can help."

I smile, proud that he wants to pursue something so grand. He would. Then it hits me, "But what about coming back to be a Headmaster? Wasn't that what you wanted for so long?"

"Yea, that *was* what I wanted. I figure maybe I can still do that when I'm Papa and Muma's age. But while I'm in my prime and while those Libertas Heirs can still be stopped, I think I'd like to do something to put them down for good." He grabs me behind the neck. "I've got people to look out for, so it only seems like the right thing to do."

The drums sound slowly, signaling that the Selection Ceremony is about to begin. We rush to our feet and make our way back to the hall. Tygon hugs me tight before heading to the stage.

"Thanks for listening, Fay. I couldn't have paid the Spirits to give me a better brotya." He winks at me and runs a hand over his freshly faded haircut. "Don't worry, I'll let you wear my Selection wreath so we can see how it fits for when you get yours! Love ya'!" Tygon runs off into the crowd to fall in line with the rest of the Discipline candidates.

I love you too, brotya. You sure know how to be an inspiration. I'll do you right back here on the homefront and that's a promise.

24

Unforeseen

The stage is packed with a long row of excited apprentices. Each of them revels in the moment, trying to find their loved ones in the crowd. Tygon peers over the audience and finally spots us. He smiles and touches his hands over his heart to say, "Your love rests here" and we all respond in kind. Muma holds up a stick with orange and black cloth tied to the end of it, waving the homemade banner high enough for my eldest to see. Once the cheers reach their peak, the Dominant walks in front of the graduating lineup and raises his hands to calm the jittery crowd.

"Clans of Praedari Village, do you see these fine young apprentices behind me? Has there ever been a more promising group?" His sweeping garments sway theatrically as the man motions toward my peers. He shares a moment of venerated eye contact with each candidate.

"So much of our future lies in your hands and I'm proud you've made it this far in our care. Never forget where your journeys started, especially those of you headed into a world so different from our own."

He waves over his attendants who carry armfuls of freshly woven wreaths. Once they are side by side, the man whips around to the crowd. "I almost forgot! Clans, this may have been the most dangerous Hunter Trials in a generation! I'm sure many of you wonder what trophy the Domain of Bones left us this time?"

Curious mumbles ripple throughout the crowd as the villagers look around the room for some hidden surprise. Dom Arzen signals to the drummers who pound away on their instruments. From one of the alleys leading into the Hub, a team of luggers wrestles with a web of ropes. At first, the crowd is quiet, then a collective gasp filters through the gathering.

"That's right!" the Dominant says. "Apparently, a Saberhorn had wandered into the Domain and made its nest sometime this season. Your brave youth not only managed to fight off one another and mask their aurem for nearly a week—they were also skilled enough to avoid this titan! It was only by pure luck that we found its broken horn, perhaps shattered in battle with another bull. Regardless, we were left with this beautiful token. Another round of applause for our highly trained group!"

Papa elbows me. "Son, don't you worry. It'll be you up there sooner than you can imagine. I fought hard during deliberation with the Dominant and village leaders to get you something for your efforts out of the Trials. In saving that young PanCanis girl, you earned yourself a Pre-Mastery spot." He beams and hands me a wooden stein overflowing with foam.

I take a merry swig, ecstatic for the news. Still, I try to avoid so much as looking at the village's newest trophy. The rich brew of maplecomb mead is a welcome distraction as it washes over my tastebuds with a sampling of spices. Vanilla, cinnamon, honey-milk, and nectarcane all churn together. The last note is the bite of the aged maplecomb. I knock my head back for another gulp, barbarically wiping the froth from my chin right after. Papa laughs as he shakes suds out of his trimmed beard.

"Thanks, Papa. I'm just happy I won't have to stay back in Elevation. I hit a new level of Nodus control out in the Domain, and I need to advance to properly explore it. I'm grateful you made a case for me."

Papa taps his stein to mine, sloshing the amber liquid with a clunk. "That's what Papas are meant for. I may give you a hard time, yes. But there isn't a single night that I lay awake doubting what you're made of. You've got your Grandpa Ravir's blood running through your veins. I know you'll be as much the Silver Fang's chosen as he ever was."

The crowd interrupts us then, bursting into applause. I look up to see the first Selection wreaths being awarded. Dom Arzen places the handwoven crowns on each candidate's head, shaking their hands and saying a few quiet words. With each personalized message, every youth flashes a wide smile. When Tanner is awarded his wreath, his PanVulpis kin nearby erupt into wild whoops. The boy takes the leaf token off his head and kisses it repeatedly before screwing it down tightly over his temples.

Several more apprentices are given their awards, then Zahk takes his stoically. But as soon as Dom Arzen has passed, he's back to being a total goof waving to his kin. Muma Rylia jumps for joy as her son shimmies in place with the earth-grown crown. After a few moments, his eyes find mine. There's a flash of sadness in his expression and I'm brought back to our previous talk about the world beyond Animas. I refuse to let my feelings show through though, displaying only pure happiness for him instead. All the same, I can see it already troubles him not having me alongside during this new chapter.

I run into the center aisle, giving myself a wide berth to imitate our handshake. Zahk's storm cloud instantly melts away once he catches on. He squares his shoulders before copying the steps. At the end, we both throw our heads back for a silent howl-roar combo, beating our chests mad. This upcoming annual with him gone will certainly be difficult, but at least it'll be manageable. After all, distance is no excuse to let a meaningful relationship die, rather it's an opportunity to work harder at keeping the bond intact.

Next, Dom Arzen awards Lunis her wreath. However, before the man can move on, she leans in to speak. A couple seconds go by, and he raises his eyebrows at her. He steps to the side, clearing the way for the young huntress. Lunis strides to center stage and looks over the crowd until the howls and chants die down. She snatches the leafed arrangement off her head and thrusts it into the air.

"I have decided that I am unable to accept this seat to the Discipline!"

The hall breaks out in confused chatter. Lunis holds the pose undeterred until the noise is hushed and she begins explaining.

"During the Trials, I found myself chasing a blooded item through the trees. However, before I caught it, I accidentally ran into the nest of the Saberhorn. Despite my efforts, that giant beast tried to run me through with its horn—almost pulled it off too! I would be dead in the dirt right now if it weren't for a young hunter who isn't up here on this stage tonight."

She takes no time at all finding me and lowers the wreath to point in my direction. The crowd follows until the entire hall is staring at me. I squirm, uncomfortable from the impromptu spotlight.

"Faylen—that little troublemaker from PanTigris—he singlehandedly rescued me from the bull. If it were simple as that, I'd have listened to our elders and let their decision stand. However, seeing the trophy outside has changed my mind."

My jaw drops. She's not going to leave it there, is she? Letting them think I distracted the titan somehow and we made our escape. No, she's going to...

"The Silver Emperor has returned to our village!" she bellows as though her words were a battle cry. "Faylen—with the power of the Silver Fang—saved me by *killing* the Saberhorn. If you don't believe me, the Sage can detect the aurem at the base of that giant horn. It'll be unmistakable!"

This time, the rows in front of me turn completely around. I wish I could melt into the floor right now, because hundreds of eyes study me as though I'm a historical relic come to life. I'm know that in some ways, I'm exactly that—a part of Praedari's fabled tale. Sage Ophis and his attendants rush outside to inspect the supposed evidence. After a few moments, he holds up a hand to Dom Arzen. Lunis nods triumphantly before pumping her arm back into the air and returning to her spot. Silence hangs in the hall before a voice calls out from the crowd.

"Now *that's* a hunter—let's hear it for Faylen!"

The Dominant shouts from the stage, "I'll drink to that!" and the sound of cheering around me become deafening. I'm nearly knocked over several times as friendly faces pat and jostle my shoulders. Then, all at once, every stein goes bottoms up to the timber ceiling.

The crowd eventually settles, and Dom Arzen raises his hands. "Considering this new evidence, the village leaders will convene to deliberate again. Maybe we can come up with a solid reasoning that I can take to the Council—see what they have to say about it. Thank you, young huntress, for pointing that out to us. We would've had no reason to inspect the horn for traces of unusual aurem."

Lunis bows respectfully to the man before winking at me.

The procession continues until at last, the final one is given to my brotya. Up there, Tygon looks the part of a hero from a Nestling storybook. His chest is puffed out, framed by those weighty shoulders. He takes the wreath carefully, making it look like a thin cord in the span of his hands. I think back to his words during our roastlet snack break. If helping the world is his goal, then he'd better watch out. I wouldn't be surprised to see him help lead it someday.

With the final award presented, Dom Arzen steps out of the way and motions to the lineup once more. The room erupts into fanatical sensation as streamers fly through the air and steins are raised above the heads of the crowd. The rows go silent as every soul chugs joyfully. At the end of the toast, Dom Arzen gives a signal. The attendees rush to the front of the lineup and usher the candidates off the stage and back into the crowd. The excited youth walk single file to the outer rows of the Hall. Kin meet their selectees, scooping loved ones up into tightly wound hugs. I smile as Zahk and Lunis are both tackled by their pack. Lunis gets picked up and twirled by her Papa who rambles praises for her integrity.

The last of the graduates trickles in slow succession from the stage. Dom Arzen snaps toward the drumline and they start up into a low rhythm. Sage Ophis and his attendees continue to study the trophy outside, amazed at the aurem hue they can detect. The group furiously scribbles notes likely because this particular life energy hasn't been seen since the last Silver Emperor. Even Orin, the

Spirit-Born, has snuck away from the healer's dwelling and inserted himself into the group to ogle the horn. The young Mender pulls out a magnifying lens and begins examining the cracks in the ivory.

I look toward the stage to see Tygon on his tiptoes, searching for us in the crowd. Our eyes meet and I shout to him, "That's my *brotya*!" He waves both hands and points at the wreath, then to me. He imitates putting it on my head before striking an exaggerated hero's pose. I leave my kin behind to wriggle through the hoard. Closer now to the stage, Tygon and I start throwing out animated muscle flexes at each other. We laugh at our absurdity when he tucks his chin to bulge his neck.

Nope, I take it back. This goof won't be leading anyone ever. A traveling jokester—that'll be his contribution to the world.

Tygon falls back in line with the last few candidates leaving the stage. I continue daydreaming, reveling in this moment. Who knows, traveling jokester doesn't sound like too bad a gig. We could do it together and bring joy to Spheire like no two brothers ever have before. I smile at the ridiculous proposition. But the inner reflection does remind me how challenging our next chapter will be. I don't look forward to the time apart, but I choose to have faith it'll pass in due time.

The seasons have proven by now we can face anything. So long as we've got each other.

Suddenly, a bright flash blinds me from behind the stage and everything goes white. The entire front half of the room is lost behind a wall of light. I feel a rush of movement. I don't know how, but I'm no longer standing where I was in front of the stage. I'm lying on the floor.

How did I get all the way back here? And why is the air so hot?

Vision returns to me in blotches, and while I still don't understand how, the rows around me are a jumbled mess. Villagers are laid out unmoving on the floor, a few here and there stumbling on their knees. My mind faintly registers smoke, but I pay it no mind because I expect the scent of herbs from the roastlet pits outside.

But no…something's different.

Instead, burning fabric and acrid wood are coating the back of my throat. A whole new odor hangs heavy in the air. It's oddly familiar and all-consuming, but I can't put my finger on how I know the scent. Eventually it comes to me, and I remember where it's from. I recall this exact scent from a gathering the village held to honor those who'd passed earlier this season.

That can't be right though. We don't do cremations at the Selection Festival…

I stagger to my elbows and look back to the stage. Where an ornate wooden stage with a colorful tapestry of our village history stood before, wooden shards and tattered fabric have taken its place. What little is left of the stage is being consumed by flames. My ears ring with commotion, but the joy this place held moments before is hauntingly absent. Laughter and excitement filled every inch of this room. In mere seconds, both have been swapped for chilling wails and cries for help. Fear of the unknown drives me into the beginning stages of a dangerously uncontrolled Embrace. However, I don't manage to shift much before clouds of smoke cut the changes from me. Through the haze, I can only manage a single thought.

Where are my kin…

Papa…Muma? Where is Kleo…she was just holding onto my leg before I ran off, wasn't she? Embers rain down from the ceiling and leave fiery bites over my sweat-drenched skin. Despite the blazing inferno, a frigid darkness has caged my periphery like starless winter night. A hoarse cough ravages my chest as the heat wraps its wispy hands around my throat. The roaring flames bathe me in ash, extinguishing the last traces of air from my lungs. I feel claustrophobic, captured by panic and fear. I faintly remember the Third virtue…to never lose control, but my mind doesn't care. It begs my Embrace to save me, despite knowing the awful cost. The tiger's instincts inside are eager to claw out the remnants of my sanity. I've never felt more like an animal than in this moment—the inability to reason is more suffocating than the burning heat.

I try crawling toward the stage where I last saw Tygon, but my fingernails lose their grip in boiling pools of blackened blood. My lower body marks a trail on the floor through the murky soot. I drag myself forward, seeking purchase by pulling on something in front of me. Only when I inch forward do I realize I'm face to face with the twisted form of a dead hunter.

Animal instincts tear at me then, chasing all human emotion away. It rips at my mind worse than the jagged debris cutting into my thighs and knees. The strain becomes too much and before I can go on, a new pain bores through my leg. I twist over to my back to see a burning column has collapsed from the ceiling. My calf is impaled through and through. Pinned to the floor, I can only squirm helpless against the fiery shackle.

I cry out, trying to catch even one desperate glimpse to the front of the hall. There is no movement anywhere on that stage. No response to my shouts. And thus I find there is no hope either. Someone has broken the Fourth and caused unjust suffering. How could this be an accident? There were too many of us in one place for it to be a coincidence. Someone has robbed me of my life, and seasons of learned instinct whisper a terrible truth. I am alone and for all my strength, tonight I'll make passage to Everrealm.

My vision slips away, and I fade away thinking my last...*Tygon, where are you, Brotya?*

25

TWINKLING BIRTH

Sunken beneath the blackness, some part of me wonders what meeting the Spirits will be like. Admittedly, I never imagined I'd ever see them so soon. It feels like ages since I last drew breath, and despite the initial agony, the pain wracking my body eventually melted away. I feel only warmth now and there is an odd peace in the stillness. I've forgotten so much in this moment. Where I am. What's happened to me. The only truth I seem able to grasp is I am no longer in control. Whatever happens will happen. Shoot, it already has—and that's ok.

Faylen...

I recognize that distant voice but allow it to pass into echo. It won't find me here. No one will.

Faylen.

Quiet now. I'm ready for the end. Whoever you are that's calling—come with me if you want.

My name is shrieked into my ears, bringing forgotten pain reeling back to life. Sensation punches through the darkness with no warning, snatching me up from the cozy depths. My eyes pop open and a scream flies out my lips. My leg is no longer pinned, but it hurts more now that the column has been removed. My calf is a twisted mess, but the leg remains intact. My mind scrambles for sense amidst the collapsing inferno and I pinpoint the voice that has brought me back.

"Listen here, Stripes. I'm *not* losing you! Now get up before I really kick you!" Lunis shouts down at me while holding two thick beams on her bare shoulders. Her Embraced form is the only thing standing between me and the crumbling structures above. Flames hiss from the beams Lunis is struggling against, licking at the huntresses' blackened arms.

"Do you hear me, Faylen? Come on, please. Get up! I need you!"

My mind finally latches onto reason and barks simple orders. *Survive! Escape! Live!* I crawl over to my good leg and enter a controlled Embrace. The animal instincts fight for dominance as soon as I access the power. I use the internal war as a welcome distraction to blot out the physical pain.

"Lunis, what are you doing here? I-I was trying to find Tygon. He was right there—"

"There isn't time! We have to get out of here! My pack is outside, and I think I saw your kin too," she yells. The wolf-bonded grits her teeth as the flames covering the pillars hunger for more of her skin. At last, I'm clear from the beams and she can toss them away. Lunis heaves and the wood fall into the debris, kicking up a dust storm of ash and ember.

Lunis sees me limping and rushes over. "Hold on, I'm coming. We're going to have to work together, all right?" With a grunt, she pulls me into her. She fastens my arm over the fur sprouted from the back of her neck. Together, we step off at a steady pace and Lunis compensates for my mass weighing us down.

"I thought I was already dead. I didn't think anyone would find me."

Through coughs she manages a response. "I ran straight inside when I picked up on your aurem. It was faint, but at least it told me you were still alive." Even though my face is covered in soot, she seems to still catch my anxious expression. "Focus. We can't worry right now. I bet Tygon is already out there with everyone else. I didn't detect him while looking for you, but that doesn't mean a thing." She grunts as her fresh burns rub against me. "We've got to think about ourselves now, okay?"

I nod, and we stoop through a small burning archway. The crackling wood around us sounds like a flock of songbirds chanting death hymns in every direction. We limp for what surely is a lifetime, barely avoiding falling slabs of wood. Lunis yelps briefly as a stream of boiling sap paints a stripe down her back. I nearly weep for joy as a whiff of cool air blows into my chest from the opposite end of the archway. As we catch sight of the Hub, hope becomes our only focus. With a final effort, we stumble through the tiny escapeway.

On the other side of the smoldering doorway, we're finally free of flames overhead. Wearing weary smiles, we drink in air, lumbering forward to take a few more steps from the heat behind us. A sudden thunderous snap makes me flinch and my back roasts from a heat wave. Just when I think we're safe from the blast, I feel Lunis's back stiffen unnaturally. I look over to see her face twisted in a silent scream, her shoulders arched. Her eyes bulge as though she's just seen a ghost. Without warning, her entire weight falls into me, and I do what I can to resist falling by splaying out my sole good leg.

"Help! I-I don't know what's going on. Someone help!" I blurt out in horror. My feeble stance doesn't hold, and I collapse to a knee. As we topple over, I cradle Lunis's head into my chest to keep it from hitting the ground. We lie as a heap on the blackened dirt—Lunis's unconscious form revealing a sight that bites my heart like a viper.

A wickedly long shard of wood is sticking out from the small of her back—shrapnel from the fiery explosion. I lurch, thinking of the condition her spine must be in with this jagged sliver jutting out from it. Her unblinking eyes register nothing, the only proof I have that she's still with me is the strained wheezing of her breaths.

Village responders rush to our side, picking Lunis up in their arms. They help me limp over to a huddle where the injured are frantically collected. Close by, a yellow hue pulsates, catching my attention. Orin is bent over an unconscious man, trying to heal him. When the responders lay Lunis next to him, his face loses its color.

"Orin, you have to help her! You have to!" I say, falling out of the responder's grip to Lunis's side.

The boy's hands are shaking and at first, he doesn't reply. I can't help but doubt his capabilities, but after a moment, something registers across his brow. He manages a shaky nod. Then his tattoos glow brightly, and the yellow aura grows in size. He puts his hands together forming a circle above his head. Slowly, he brings the circle down from the center of his brow. The smaller dot tattoo resting between his eyebrows ignites in blinding light. His hands continue down the invisible line, stopping in front of his sternum. A moon-like shape shines as bright as a torch through his robes. He begins to chant but I can't understand a single word. As he meditates, Essence Tongue flows from his mouth at a rapid pace. I stare in wonder as he begins to levitate off the ground and the yellow hue around takes shape, forming a slender vortex over Lunis's wound. A separate tendril connects to the man Orin was aiding before.

A voice echoes in my head, *"It may look impossible, but I promise she shall live. I will sustain her life as is, but she needs to be Restored by the Altis Monks in Hayven's Upper Falls."*

I look behind me to identify where the words came from.

"Silver Fang's own, you seek in the wrong direction."

I turn around to see Orin's eyes remain closed. Yellow luminescence shines like twin lighthouses from beneath his eyelids. Still in his levitating trance, the Mender moves his head as though he were looking at me through his shut eyes.

"Whose voice is that?"

The voice laughs, *"In this moment, I am the boy you know—and I am not. I've studied many things in Everrealm, Hunter...the very tapestry of this world. Now, I am between the threads. I am beyond this place and will keep the girl safe here with me until greater help arrives."* Orin resumes his meditative pose and the voice goes quiet. The tendrils amplify and it's obvious he's gone completely.

I hear a squeal, and Kleo runs up to me, hugging me tight around my neck. "I found him! Muma, Papa, I found Faylen!" she says between tearful sobs. The rest of my kin runs over, and I thank the Spirits. Not one of them is injured beyond a few small burns. Muma and Papa pepper me with questions about my well-being. I wave them off only to be swarmed by more hugs. They finally let me breathe and I have time to ask my burning question.

"Wait, what about Tygon? He's here with you, right?"

Muma's grave face says it all.

"No, son, I've only found you three. Tygon hasn't been spotted yet and we were searching the injured for him when we found you just now," she says.

I stammer an outcry, but my lips have forgotten how to form words. I crawl to my feet. Waves of pain hit me all at once and I feel them all without Embrace to shield me. My steps are a hobbled mess, but I know where I saw him last. Back at the stage. I'll pick up on his aurem there—I'll crawl through the flames if I have to. I *know* where I saw him last!

Papa snatches me back by my vest, locking me in the crook of his arm.

"No! Do you want to die? You cannot go in there, boy!"

I only manage a hoarse cry as I struggle to break free.

Finally, I sputter. "Doesn't look like there's another Spirit-forsaken option! I was the last one to see him." My argument gets cut short by the crackle of snapping timber. I squint my eyes as the Hub is washed over in a giant heat wave—the People's Hall finally collapses in on itself. My mouth is agape as I struggle against Papa's grasp. Vines of spit and mucus fall uncontrolled from my quivering lips and tears dilute the messy flow down into my chest.

After a few minutes, a responder team carries a muscular form from the edge of the ruins. I recognize the aurem trailing from it. "Th-that's Tygon!" I wave frantically for the handlers to bring him closer to us. The team lays my brotya at our feet before running back to the fire. I almost miss the sorrow in their faces as they scurry away.

My mind fractures seeing Tygon's once powerful frame as a mangled mess. Everything is still there, but I've never seen burns like this. The flames were hungry, and they fed upon my sibling like a rabid animal. A gaping hole leaks blood from his side, yet somehow, he blinks at me ever so slowly.

Muma collapses into a heap, shaking at the sight of her eldest son. Papa touches the singed remains of hair on Tygon's brow and Kleo hides in the folds of Muma's garments. My brother's lips move slowly but words have chosen to abandon him. I want to touch him, to let him know I'm here, but I'm afraid to cause him any more pain. With a shriek, I cry out to Orin for help. This time, the boy doesn't move and I refuse to admit that I understand why. No healing aura reaches out to my brother. No inner voice reassures me of his fate. Tygon is beyond Mending.

"Brotya, if you hold out a little longer, we can get you into the healer's dwelling. They have so much medicine in there, I-I know you'll be okay." Tygon looks to Muma and Papa, manages a smile for Kleo. Then he shakes his head at me. My lie isn't near convincing enough. I rip the sweat cloth from my head and press it to his wound. Rather than slowing the flow, the white cloth instantly fills with blood.

"C-come on Ty, please! We've got to get to the Discipline together. We've got to hunt and fight and help people. Together! I can't do this by myself, and you said we wouldn't do this apart—"

Blood bubbles from his lips as he heaves over to his side. I can see his brow furrow with effort under blankets of ash. He points to Kleo hiding behind Muma, then his trembling hand reaches past my shoulder and he looks deep into my eyes. I hear only five words.

"Pro-tect...Kleo."

"Brothers. Never. Apart."

His grip slips away from the back of my neck...

The Hub's smoke trails upward into the night sky. The stone monoliths glow like faces around a campfire. And far above Praedari, a sky full of stars observes our terror. The distant beads of light twinkle in and out from view as though none are strong enough to stay and watch Tygon's eyes go blank. I envy the sparkling watchers above, wishing I too could hide far from here. I scream to those stars—plead with them. *Take me with you, if you please.* Despite my anguish, the sky gives no reply and only the wails around me answer. I sit in the dust and accept the silence from beyond the clouds. I pray the celestial bodies above can at least make room for one more amongst their numbers.

Be kind to him please. My brotya is one of you now.

26

Sowing

The night's fires have finally smoldered into a morning painted ashen gray. Sometime after dawn, a Mender reconstructed my calf and warned to let the new flesh rest. I have already ignored this advice and instead spent the rest of the day trying to be anywhere but our den. It was too much to see my brotya lying motionless beneath linens atop our table. I was more than happy to escape into the woods, running errands for roots, flower buds, and bark—all fragrances to bind Tygon for his burial cleansing.

Now, night has fallen, and I quietly sneak up to our den's treetop. I lay awake for hours, knowing the day's trek should have left me exhausted. Yet here I am, sleep fleeing from me like a startled doe. Another hour passes and even if I could've dosed off by now, the noises of the night disrupt the peace. From the den below, I hear Muma and Papa shouting.

"Jaole, I can't stay here! Look at him…see what they did!"

Papa's voice is steady but clearly pained. "Huntress, our kin needs you right now, we don't have a choice. Our boy needs to be laid to rest. He deserves—"

A clang rings through the grove as a pan collides with a wall. "He only lived twenty hunting seasons! You know what he *deserves*? To be breathing right now! To have enjoyed the rest of his life. My son didn't deserve *this* from some faceless stranger who wasn't even his enemy!"

Muma's shrill voice goes low and only by enhancing my hearing can I hear her muffled words. "What did we ever have to do with any of this? All we do is live and dance and hunt. We've never needed all the world's mess here in Animas—done just fine on our own 'til now."

I hear only silence and picture Papa holding Muma close. He soothes her with a tender tone. "Kura, we will make it through. You and I just gotta' be the constant right now...for each other and for them." I hear the delicate sound of a kiss. "Remember the first child? She was so small—not even an hour old. Yet, I know even now, Tygon will meet her for the first time. The Spirits will see to it."

With a ruffle of fabric, I hear Muma stomp through the den. "The Spirits? The Spirits? Curse the Spirits!" Another flutter of cloth, this time the unmistakable rush of airborne linen. "This is what they left me, Jaole. This is how my son—life from my own flesh—spends his last night in his home. You want me to think of the Spirits when I have to cover him with this?" The rustling ends and I picture a sheet thrown to the floor.

After a few silent moments, Papa speaks again. "I have to go back out to the Hub. Without Arzen, the leaders who are left must do all they can for the village...at least 'til a new Dominant can be named. I'm sorry, my love. The Sage is waiting for us."

Chair legs scratch across the floor. "I know. At least the children are asleep up top. I'll finish the tapestry. But when you come back, I'd better hear a plan. Someone has to pay." Muma's tone turns darker than I've ever heard before. "That killer better pray it's the authorities who finds him first. I along with every mother in Praedari would happily peel that devil down to his bones before he ever made it to the courts."

I let go of my Embrace, unable to bear another word. Huntresses are fierce, but when it comes to their young, they are worse than even mother bears in the Wilds. Out of the corner of my eye, I see Kleo standing over the side of my hammock. She stares at me with a wide-eyed look, her eyelashes outlining the puffiness beneath them. Even her giant curls stick out in a furrowed mess.

"Kleo, how long have you been there? Did the noise keep you up too?" At first, she only nods, staring down at her feet before suddenly snatching my hand to her chest.

"You're it, do you understand? Now, you're really it, brotya!"

I try to understand what she means through her choked sobs, but she only sways from side to side, tiny shoulders heaving deeply. Finally, she looks up with tear-stained cheeks and stabs a finger into my sternum repeatedly.

"I've only got one of you now—so don't you dare let anyone take you. Promise. Promise me that they won't get you too!"

My chest tightens and my lungs struggle to find air. How did Tygon learn to be the eldest, and at such a young age no less? He was naturally good at it. I view the bond between Kleo and me in a whole new light now.

"You know what, kitten? I've got an idea. Let's keep each other safe tonight, okay? Don't worry about anything else, not Muma and Papa, not the village, not even the smoke." I lift the girl up easing her onto my chest like an infant. Her quiet sobs slow their pace until eventually she snores peacefully. I stroke her hair, tucking her head beneath my chin. No worries little one, I might not always be nearby, but I know a place that can teach me exactly how to protect you. I've got power like no one's seen in decades. One day, the Discipline is going to teach me what to do with it. Then, I'll be able to guard this village until I'm crooked and spotted. No one will ever steal away those we love again.

I watch the stars twinkle for an hour more and once I'm confident Kleo won't wake, I carry her to her hammock. I consider also trying for rest but can't bear to be alone with my thoughts right now. Instead, I scale down our tree to find Muma sitting at the dinner table. She doesn't look up from her work when I settle in opposite her. Her hands move in small circles above a pile of twine, but the glazed look in her eyes suggests her mind is elsewhere.

"Is that Tygon's Soul String?" I ask, receiving only slow

blinks at first. Muma peers down at the small tapestry.

"Oh, I suppose it is. Silly me, I hadn't noticed just how far I'd gotten." After a moment of hesitation, her hands begin to move again.

In the dim candlelight, I study the patterns of the cloth circle. The tapestry is hardly larger than Kleo's hand, but the details are unmistakable. In one section, I see an embroidered leaf with several circles sewn into it.

"I didn't know you knew how to weave shapes. That leaf almost looks like it could fly straight off into the wind." Muma's hazy stare finds focus once she registers I'm speaking again, and her fingers stroke the leaf's rugged edges.

"Yes, learned this one from your Nana. Her den is covered in paintings just like this—I once asked her why when I was your age."

I sit quietly, waiting for her to reveal more.

"She told me: 'The fool hoards the seeds of a tree, thinking they will someday grow him a forest. The wise man passes the tree by and appreciates it for simply being. In time, only one of them finds shelter. For only the wise man recognizes it is the leaves, not the seeds, which sustain life.'"

I don't visit Nana frequently enough, but from the times I have visited her seaside den, I can remember the art. Every wall is covered in large paintings of a leaf with four circles cut into it. The holes descend in size, each representing one of Nana's children, with the smallest circle being Muma. At the table now, our huntress weaves a similar leaf with only two circles, one for Kleo and one for me. A faded gray patch is threaded over the hole where Tygon's would be.

An hour later, I have quietly watched her fingers twist several knotted shapes–first a tiger, then Tygon's brown short blade, then a raging river to signify his enduring strength. Finally, she fills the remaining tapestry space with a stump holding twenty-one rings.

At first, Muma's reaction is slow, but eventually her eyes brim with tears as she touches each of the stump's rings. She counts, then recounts, lowering her head as she realizes her error.

She pinches the hem of the last ring and her hands begin to quake. I walk over and hold her weary head in my hands as she tugs on the thread. My fingers wet with her tears when a piercing snip removes the strand from the tapestry.

Muma will never get to see her son make it past twenty hunting seasons.

I kiss her on the forehead and decide it's best to give her some time alone. No sooner have I settled back into my canopy hammock do I hear furious screams and the clatter of pots being thrown. Dishes too shatter against the wood walls. I muffle messy sobs into my pillow as I lament what my world has so quickly become.

At dawn, horns echo through the trees and our village follows their sounding beyond the gates. Those with loved ones to mourn march at the procession's head to the instruments' solemn song. Muma and I walk in step, carrying heaven's youngest star in bundles of white cloth. My thoughts turn back to the night before—I'm exhausted from wrestling with the image of Tygon at the fire's edge. My imagination is usually a ruthless monster, but even it can't outdo what the flames actually did to him.

I distract myself by reaching out to comfort Muma. I place a strand of hair back behind her ear, but she only stares past the stream of villagers ahead. From the circles around her eyes, I can tell she has no more tears left to give. Apparently, a night's worth of sorrow and anger can best even the strongest huntress.

After a few miles on the trail, the horns finally stop at the Birth River. The kin carrying bundles each line up at the banks. I let the edge of the water rush over my bare feet as I stand beside my kin. Once all are in place, we watch Sage Ophis trudge through the current. The elder stops when the water reaches his waist and he turns to the shore, lifting his hands.

"My children, to die is only to be born again into one of life's many forms. Praedari, we gather in these waters to wash away the impurities of our loved ones, thus freeing them to set off onto these new paths." The elderly man pauses lowering his head. "Even as we rejoice the lives of our fallen, we can still recognize the loss. Our village will be left marked by every missing soul."

Of course, how could it not? Fifteen Discipline candidates are no longer among the living. Forty-five adult villagers passed as well. I look down the line to see nine tiny bundles being carried by brokenhearted parents—their Nestlings never stood a chance.

"Finally, children, as you weep for your own, do not forget to remain strong. Our village is now leaderless and though the rights of passage will see that a new Dominant is named, we will remember Dom Arzen as a kind and compassionate father to us all."

At the Sage's signal, a golden bundle is carried out by two attendants. They remove and fold the sheets, lowering our Dominant into the current. The river washes over him, taking with it the layers of scorched blood and soot. Every hunter and huntress lifts their voice in song, our collective tone swelling louder than the rushing stream:

Where- the Ri-ver -flows, where-the-wa-ters-go,
 I-will-meet-you-bro-ther.
Where-the Spi-rits wait, through-the-Star-lit-gates,
 You'll-still-be-my-sis-ter.

The Dominant's body is so far beneath the surface I can no longer see it. Each kin brings their own into the cool depths. I carefully unwrap Tygon—the burns are much harder to look at with daybreak shining over them. With a firm lip, I help lower him under, my throat constricting into the continuing chorus:

And-tho'-the-earth-may-claim-your-grave,
With-this-our-debts-to-her-be-paid,
-So-
Where-the-Riv-er-flows, where-the-wa-ters-go,
We. Will. Follow.

As the bodies are cleansed, rain begins to descend over us. Sage Ophis closes his eyes, raising his head up into the torrent. "Bless the Spirits, even Kyuu weeps with us today." I look around to see several huntresses whisper thanks to the Rain Spirit. Muma stares forward tight-lipped.

After a few minutes, we lift Tygon up. The dark brown of his skin has returned, no longer hidden beneath black and red stains. The procession crosses the river together, trudging for the opposite bank. When we've all made it, Sage Ophis turns to address us once more.

"It is time to sow. According to the Second, what the land has lent us, we must now recompense. I only ask that you do not lose yourselves in this moment. Have your sorrow, yes. But remember Praedari, remember Animas, our Bloodline and Spheire. Our world has wept much these past two nights, yet I fear an uncertain tomorrow still awaits us all..."

He ushers the procession by, patting a different villager's shoulder every so often.

The world certainly did weep and for good reason. Unbelievably, we were not the night's only victims. News from abroad alerted us the following day that multiple incidents occurred. Primitas Village had its market burned down—fortunately, no one was shopping at the time. Two blasts struck in Indom and another in a Hayvin trading town. Of the five disasters, the Sanctum commentators made a point to let the whole world know ours was the worst. Pursuit teams were quickly assembled by the remaining Dominants. Supposedly, they comb the jungle surrounding Praedari and Primitas even now. No leads as of yet, but that didn't stop the metal tapestry's darling—suit lady—from immediately condemning Sanctum's top suspect: The Libertas Heirs. The greenery above us opens up into a field of violet trees. We break off from the procession, and carry Tygon to the PanTigris burial grounds. Tens of thousands of faded tapestries hang in every direction around us. Soul Strings of clan members past dangle from each tree, reminding passersby from whom the tree sprouted. High up on the trunks, colored cords connect the canopies in an interwoven pattern. The lines form a web for each family line, connecting generations old to generations new. As beautiful as the sight is, I only wish I could be here visiting a beloved kin rather than surrendering one.

Kleo yanks on my blouse as we stop at Grandpa Ravir's Soul String. "What is this place called again? I think I've only been here once before."

I help ease Tygon to the ground and turn to crouch at my younger's eye level. "Kitten, this is the Weaving Willows. Do you remember why this field is so important?"

She thinks for a moment, clutching a bouquet of bitterbells in her hands. "Yes, Papa said it's the jungle's way of helping us remember who we are."

Papa walks over and caresses her curly hair. "Don't forget what else I told you. We not only come here to remember who we are here, but to listen for whispers of whom we will be." Papa waves me over, asking me to begin digging.

After a few minutes, a grave two mets deep awaits. We carefully picked a resting spot downline of Grandpa Ravir's tree. I put away the shovel and our kin stands waiting, all looking to Muma to begin the hardest part. New tears find her tired eyes and her shoulders begin to tremble. She barely manages to speak the words.

"I-I am ready to sow so that the land may r-reap."

With those words, she calls out for her Nodus. I carry Tygon beside the soil's vacant depths. Seeing him finally laying here next to his grave, I nearly wretch at the full scene. I'd always wanted to be taller than my brother. When I was a Nestling, I'd chant to the Spirits every night, hoping by morning I'd somehow stand above him. In the end, it never happened, and I forgot my fickle dream. Today, my heart is run through to realize now, my wish is cruelly granted.

Papa turns to us. "Kin, it's time to sow the seed. Kleo, go and find the healthiest looking pods you can from Grandpa Ravir's willow. Muma, will you prepare the enrichments?" He looks to me, and I dread his next words. "Son, can you ready the blade?"

My hands shake uncontrollably as he hands me an all too familiar sheathed short blade. I've seen its worn brown handle a thousand times, strapped to my brother's side. Muma watches in bloodshot horror as I reveal the cold metal. Her mixing bowl nearly wobbles out of her hands as she quakes silently. Papa reaches out to steady her.

"Hush, my huntress, just as we've made it through every other obstacle, we'll fight 'til this one passes too. That's what we promised each other—as your chosen ally, that's what I'll never forget."

The nearby brush shakes and three tigers appear through it. Vai, Muma's Nodus leads Papa's Nodus, Elo, and Tygon's too. My parents' familiars walk up to Muma and Papa and nuzzle them softly. Muma is usually the one to caress her Nodus first, but this time the huntress stares blankly while kneeling on the ground. Vai encircles her protectively, instantly understanding what has happened here. Cil is the last one to join and trots around the group with giddy excitement, trying to find his own companion.

I'm taken off guard when the back of my head is blanketed in warm fur. I look up surprised to see Magnus standing over me considering I didn't call him. Even still, I'm happy he's here. The giant tiger doesn't look directly at me but keeps his piercing eyes on my brotya. The deep thud of the Silver Fang's heart echoes in my ears. He emits a low hum, and I can feel his aurem melt into my own. His breathing holds constant, and in a few moments, the rapid flutter of my heart has fallen in sync with his.

Cil continues to prance around the circle like an eager kitten greeting an old playmate. He sniffs the ground but perks his ears at a sharp growl from his mother, Vai. He follows her gaze next to the hole in the ground and leaps over to it. The young tiger chuffs happily at finding his bonded, blowing strands of hair into Tygon's unmoving face. When the attempts to wake him from sleep fail, Cil butts him gently with his head. Then the tiger goes completely still, listening for a pulse. After several painful seconds, having heard nothing, the tiger finally sinks to lie down on all fours. Quiet moans reverberate in drawn out notes from his chest as he rests his head on my brother's.

Kleo returns with two pods and Papa checks to see if Muma has completed her portion. Her mixing bowl is filled with grounded mulch—a mixture of powdered minerals, bitterbell oil, and Seed Tree bark. She uncorks a thimble of Angel Tears from Hayvin and pours it into the mix.

"H-hurry children, the enrichment has to be laid soon, and the s-seeds sown too," she says between shaky breaths.

Papa nods firmly to me. "It's time."

He and Muma lower their eldest into the hole. I step over Tygon with the short blade in hand. Kleo buries her eyes, bending over into the grass as though to hide from the world. My vision blurs as I find Tygon's fourth and fifth ribs. Every huntress teaches her young to quickly end the suffering of a kill. You learn to slip fast into the animal's heart, ending its pain without delay. When a loved one dies, the practice is mirrored, though the reasoning is different. Rather than to end a life, we do this to begin one. Our sacrifice returns to the land what it gives us so freely. We sow the seeds within ourselves to pay our debts.

I look to Magnus for strength. He lowers his giant head, blinking slowly. *I've already given it to you,* he seems to communicate. Maybe so, but the calm he offered only a moment before is far off now. I know that Tygon is long dead but to do this final act feels like I'm shutting the door on his life…

Like he'll never come back.

My scream is wild as I slip his short blade in. Muma collapses, leaning against Papa's knees, heaving without a sound.

We pour the enrichment into the fresh gash and the mixture turns dark brown as blood pools into it. Kleo crushes the pod shells in her hands and immediately hundreds of hair-like roots emerge, searching out air and nourishment. I press the pods into the enrichment and in seconds, a sprout breaks through, poking out from the incision to breathe. We cover my brotya with blankets of soil until a mound lies over him. The sprig wriggles its way through the earth, reaching the surface at last. Muma ties the Soul String to one of the offshoots that will one day develop into a branch. As the willow grows, the wood will fuse around it and Tygon will be memorialized forever.

I look back at the tapestry detailing the highest marks of his life. Where there should be a sense of rejoicing for the story he created in such a short time, a new emotion bubbles like tar down the back of my throat. I struggle with its unfamiliarity but am won over by its sweet ruthlessness.

Hatred has come to visit me—a welcomed stranger that condemns those faceless bastards. Those dead men who've torched my brother's unwritten chapters.

27

Chasing A Wolf

No matter how bloodied the survivor of sorrow's rapacious bite, time always passes by with the cold look of indifference.

Despite losing a piece of our kin to the Willows, we must eventually return to the cycle of daily life. The shift into normalcy seems impossible at first. The same day as the Sowing, I heard word the Menders had collected the injured and taken them beyond the Wilds. Asking around only got me so far, and though I wish I knew more about Lunis's recovery, I know there are no better hands upon Spheire for her to be in.

A week on from this, Papa and the other village leaders reentered intense deliberation and submitted a unique proposal to the Council. Out of this discussion, not only was I put forward, but eight other Elevation failures were reassessed and presented for Discipline candidacy. Recouping all fifteen apprentices claimed by the blaze would have been ideal, but Praedari's loss was too great to send more away.

Ultimately, the Council only accepted three of the suggested youth—a boy my age from PanHelos, a girl even younger from PanUrsa, and myself. If there are other developments in the village's recovery, I am largely unaware. The few updates I have received came from Zahk during his daily visits to my hammock. Granted, that's only when I let myself be found.

I became a ghost after Muma left with Kleo to visit Nana's seaside den. I spent two whole days alone in the lightide hideaway beneath the Seed Tree where Tygon and I bonded seemingly ages ago. I didn't have the heart to pour water onto the stone tapestry to see their glow. On my second night sleeping beneath the twin moons, I stirred to see a glowing pair of green eyes glinting over my face. Magnus settled around me without a sound, his large form burying me whole in a fortress of gray and black stripes. That night was the first peaceful sleep I'd had since the disaster—but when I woke the next day, the Silver Fang was gone.

Today, a half week later, I lay in my hammock, grinding my short blade against a coarse stone. Some of the other Discipline candidates are off with each other refining their skills with a last few aurem sessions. Others are seeking out advice from their parents, an option I can't indulge since Papa has been resigned to non-stop meetings in the Hub.

Last night over dinner, he told me that the search party had been called off. Eight days spent searching every nook and cranny around Praedari, yet the smallest clue couldn't be found to track the blast's perpetrators. Without any hope, our village was left to mourn as the jungle hid its attacker away.

I sway in the hammock, rocking myself with a single leg. Between strokes of my shortblade against stone, I can hear a new rustling in the leaves. My focus doesn't leave the roof of the canopy until Zahk stoops over my head hesitantly.

"Eh, catboy, this isn't the best look for you. I don't know who was supposed to fill ya' in, but as the best friend, perhaps the job falls to me. You gotta' get up."

I pause, letting the metal edge stop in its groove while trying to think up an appropriate response. *I don't want to* isn't strong enough. *My brother just died* holds weight but becomes more unacceptable as the weeks roll on. I know I should be pressing forward with Discipline prep, but despite my clear reasoning for wanting to attend, the motivation has been difficult to find recently.

I click my tongue behind my teeth. "Look man, this is really hard for me. I kinda' need some time—maybe even some space."

Zahk knits his brow in response. "Well, I'm sure you'd like a little of both, but I can't give you either. Your heart is bleeding. When a hunter is injured and leaking out, you don't stand there and watch. You get dirty, put pressure to the wound and don't let go no matter how much he squirms." He gestures to my unkempt state. "Amio, you are squirmin' something fierce."

I toss my sharpened blade at a nearby target strapped to a branch. The tip whistles through the air before failing to connect. The handle hits with a thud and the whole knife clunks to the wooden platform supporting us with an unimpressed clatter. I look back to Zahk who tries his best to give an apologetic look. With a huff, I throw my head back into my hammock, flailing until the blanket hides my face.

"You know, I think I saw this same look on my little brother Rani just last week. Good thing the younger siblings can get away with that sort of thing."

I keep my head buried firmly beneath my pillow. "Ouch, got to stab me like that?"

Zahk blows an exasperated puff of air. "Actually, I do. I'm gettin' you on the path to recovery one way or another. It's going to take some painful first steps, sure, but you aren't making any progress lying flat in that hammock. You didn't fall to the blast, so it's high time you stood up and stop acting like it."

Wise young wolf. Still, his words sting. I wasn't ready to be the eldest sibling. Then again, I suppose an eldest never has a choice. One day your parents decide to bring life into the world—it's up to you how to interact with it. In my case, with Kleo gone to Avian Village, I haven't had much time to act out the new role. Most days it's only me and this tree.

I poke my head out of the covers. "Speaking of younger siblings, how's Lunis? I miss her already."

Zahk pats me on the shoulder. "Yeah, our kin does too. I

couldn't look for her in the fire since I was busy elsewhere, so I'm just happy she made it out all right."

"Me too. Were you there when the Menders took her away?"

He thinks for a second. "I was. I tell ya', when Spirit-Born use their powers, they don't look human anymore. I think they look like angels."

I pantomime feathered appendages. "Angels? Like with wings?"

Zahk rolls his eyes. "Wait. Spirit-Born don't actually have wings, right? I'm trying to say it's really mystical watching them float there, glowing and all. When they took Lunis away gliding past the trees, I knew she'd be okay."

The young wolf snaps out of his daydream. "Anyway, she's been gone to Hayvin for a little over a week now. I'm sure she's under pretty deep in those Upper Falls. They've got all that Slumberrose after all."

I turn over to get a better look at my friend. I may be having a hard time, but for all my troubles, at least I have resolution. As harsh as the reality is, it still stands—Tygon won't be coming back. On the contrary, Zahk has to balance worrying about his sister and preparing for a new chapter of his life at the Discipline. He catches me staring and cocks an eyebrow questioningly.

"Back up a second, you mentioned you were busy during the fire? Were you injured and I didn't know about it?"

Zahk rubs his forearms a tinge shy like. "Oh, uh, nothing really—I'm glad the village didn't suffer more casualties than it did. Let's say I'm grateful I could contribute to our overall safety is all."

I eye him, wanting to question him further, but the topic clearly makes him uncomfortable. "Fine, amio, let's do it your way then. You came all the way up here, so what did you have in mind?"

He gives me a heartwarming smile that crinkles the edges of his eyes. I catch a glimpse of what he'll look like as a happy old man. "Catboy, we're taking a little trip. It'll be good for you since you've been busy this week doing a whole sack's worth of nothin'."

"Mercy, amio, mercy! Your tough love is hard to swallow."

He tosses a bottle of freshly squeezed dawnberry juice, pegging me in the gut through the covers. "Well, if not me, who else is gonna' get you moving?"

I throw the covers off and hobble at him, ready to avenge my aching stomach. He dashes down the tree like a squirrel possessed before I can grab hold of him. I yell down the trunk, "You really do the most unthinkable crap, you scraggly wolf!"

He takes off in the direction of his grove. "Meet me at the Hub in five minutes. And has someone forgotten my world-famous perspective on the unthinkable? Get outta' that tree before your pinstripes fade all together."

I stroke the pattern of gray and black on the hems of my wrist wrappings and vest. Pinstripes? Okay, somebody's getting punched for that one.

In the Hub, the metal tapestry repeats its series of clips from the week. "Merry stuff," I grumble to myself, watching the chaotic images roll. Two pockets of Libertas Heirs were apparently found in Indom. The images show the perspective of foot soldiers rushing into a series of underground tunnels to extract the scoundrels. After a few loud bangs accompanied by flashes of light, the people inside the hideouts were either dead or about to be. From both raids, only six Heirs survived. They were rounded up, questioned, and promptly sent to the tanks. A segment of further denouncing from suit lady begins as her blonde bangs—trimmed by a new sleek line of red—flail uncontrolled. In today's rant, I wonder how she can read her notes as spittle spews past her face.

"One of you Heirs is going to break. Guaranteed. How frightening is that for you? Hmm?" She tilts her head, her hair snapping to-and-fro like the claws of a mantis. "Your whole plan, your entire organization, everything about you goes up in flames the moment we get the smallest piece of information needed to stop you. You think we won't find out who started all this? You think we won't upend the core of you?"

She rises abruptly, her tall chair rattling on the floor. The footage follows her as she stomps to a nearby window. The maneuver is clearly unplanned by the way the scene shakes. The woman stands at the window with her hands on her hips before the picture focuses again. She bores holes down at us with a pompous look. "This, Heirs, is what you fail to realize. Despite the—admittedly—ruthless tactics you employ, it is effectiveness you lack." Her knife hand makes a sharp line to point to the sweeping view of the capital behind her. "You can never change reality. Everything you do pales against the fact that Sanctum still stands. And know this, you Spiritless cowards—"

The entire Hub stills around me. Every face transfixed with either hope for justice or riddled with uncertainty.

"Sanctum will never fall. So long as she remains, so will Spheire. The Council's power is beyond what you can infect with your hatred and your death. If Sanctum is, the five nations will be also. At the end of it all, the water's embrace will be your only reward."

A few heads nod in the crowd at the promise of judgement for those who'd brought murder upon us. The clip fades, transitioning to the prison courtyard holding the tanks. Only six glass cylinders hold prisoners this time—the survivors of the most recent raids. A boy my age tries to punch his way through the glass, but his shackles easily restrict the blows. The tanks fill quickly this time and soon bubbles stream from his screaming mouth. The whites of his eyes are engulfed with bloodshot streaks—much like the way Tygon's did as he grasped for his final words by the fires. No sooner had the execution begun do the drowning lineup cease their thrashing. The guards torch each Libertas flag in front of their tanks, and its gray and black colors are lost to the smoke. I break away from the screen because I can't pinpoint when exactly these live executions became so much easier to watch...

Zahk finds me and I share what I've seen. He listens in silence, letting me ramble some of the thoughts I've bottled up over the last few days in my hammock. The violence, the Heirs, Tygon's convictions of doing something great outside of

Praedari—all of it spills out until only one thing is left. There's a single admission I've been running from, but the more I hide from it, the more jarring it becomes.

"Amio, I haven't told this to anyone, but there's a fear that haunts me." I walk to sit at a nearby post with Zahk following behind me. "What if I could've saved Tygon?"

The young wolf clasps onto my shoulders, shaking them lightly. "Hey, no. Absolutely not, do not do that to yourself."

I clench my jaw. "Just…just hear me out. When the blast started, the odds were against me, sure. But I was startled, and in that moment, I found neither control nor reason. Instead, only panic."

I close my eyes to return to the setting. "I froze, and the moment took me prisoner. I've never had such an animalistic Embrace. All the senses I could've used to search for Tygon and then escape? Gone."

"Come on, Fay, it's really not your fault, we all—"

"Everyone did more than me, Zahk. During the blast…after it. I mean, just look at this." I walk over to a burned column standing upright from the ground. Marked into its charred surface are the names of villagers lost to the blaze. Below them, large leaves are nailed around them—each with a survivor's name and thanks to their rescuer.

"Maybe Tygon wasn't already doomed, and had I had more control of this new power level, my name would be here among the rescuers. And he'd be at home recovering, rather than in the ground." My fist trembles at my side. "I want to be the one who helps, no longer the one who needs saving."

Zahk's voice is steady. "I mean, I'm sure Lunis is grateful for your help, both in the Domain and in the blast. She needed you to get out of the flames."

I gesture to a leaf one of my kin had written for me with a message of thanks to the wolf-bonded huntress.

"Limping out of a burning building hardly seems like anything when I couldn't protect her from the shrapnel that hit her only seconds later. Overall, I want to do better."

Zahk rubs his arm in the same shy way as before, trying to lead us away from the column. Finally, I call him out. "Okay, man, seriously, what is it? You've been dodgy this whole morning. What aren't you tell—"

That's when my gaze finds "Kleo" written on a leaf with Zahk's name beneath it. I turn to him open-mouthed but speechless. He paces with slow steps and offers a sheepish smile.

"I'm sorry, I didn't want to say anything…it was just something that needed to be done, you know? When I found Kleo, poor thing was rubbing soot out her eyes. No way I was leaving without her. I'm guessing you didn't find out 'cause she was too confused to notice. I dropped her off to safety before she had a chance to recognize me."

"H-how? How did you do it?"

Zahk runs his hands through his thick black hair and the wolf fur lining his vest rustles in the breeze. "Honestly, I don't even remember how. All I know is I heard her screaming and I came, that's it. The blast claimed one less soul and that's what counts. We've got amazing powers—there's no upper limit to how we choose to use them."

After a few moments of silence, he offers me one of the fishing rods he'd brought from his den. "You know, that's the real reason I can't wait to get up to the Discipline. With all the Gifted in this world, I want to learn where I fit into the bigger picture. What could people accomplish if even a few of us came together?"

He takes off as I sit there feeling both inspired and yet very left behind. Zahk has those same leadership qualities that Tygon had. Where do the eldest children pick up these lessons?

We make our way to the Northern Gate and pay the fee for a lushalow berry. I sound the call and after a loud cry, double sets of sapphire wings break through the trees to find us. We climb aboard the Qirin and take to the skies. I watch the air flow through Zahk's thick hair as it whips around his neck. Despite the weight of the past week, unbelievably, he throws his head back in laughter. I'm lucky I still have a friend to help me get through life's twists. He's someone to be caught up to, yes. But he's also the sort of companion I need. If a friend isn't a challenge in some way, isn't it time to find another one or risk ending up being as average as them?

When we've flown some way from Praedari, I scoot up the Qirin's back to yell at Zahk over the rushing air. "Yo, where are we going? This isn't in the direction of Tauris, I thought that was our favorite spot?"

Zahk leans back to shout in my ear. "Right, but you know how I love finding new ones. Don't worry, we're only a few minutes out. By the way, go ahead and Embrace now, you're going to want to be a little sturdy for this."

I almost question him but decide to go along for the ride. It's not until I see flags with snakes on them dotting the swampy jungle below that I jab him in the ribs to get his attention. "Amio! What in Everrealm are we doing in Reptilix Village?"

His shoulders bounce up and down with excitement. I don't need to hear his chuckle to know there's mischief in it. "Well, like I said, I love finding new spots! Would ya' look at that, we're here." He points to an earthen mound rising above the swamps a couple miles from the Reptilix outskirts. Zahk stands up carefully, steadying himself on the back of the giant bird. His legs are covered in a thin layer of wolf fur and his calves flex, helping him maintain balance. He looks at me, winking to indicate his intentions.

"Wait, are you serious? We can't even see the water yet!"

He shrugs his shoulders and laughs it off. "Don't worry, I've been here once before to scope it out. That mound has a pretty large hole at the top."

I peer at the rising wall of earth, barely recognizing the gaping opening. It doesn't help that the mound is concealed beneath a thick layer of overgrowth.

Zahk gives me a thumbs up. "Don't worry! I know there's a lot of brush on top but there's a really nice underground pond right on the other side."

"All right, I guess, but are you sure abou—"

He's already jumped.

I can't believe he actually did it! For a few seconds, I can hear his manic howling as he dives. I look down, truly getting a sense for how high up we are. Scratch striving to chase after my amio. That kid might be on his own today.

The bird continues flying along and I can tell if I don't go now, I'm going to miss the opening all together. I lean forward and after a deep breath, my feet no longer feel the Qirin's back. I open my eyes to see the swamp rising up to catch me. Out of instinct, I hide my face behind crossed arms, the faint stripes painted across my skin offering little protection. With a snap, I'm through the layer of leaves guarding the mound's entrance. I don't slow down until I'm enveloped by a swarm of crisp bubbles.

28

Loose Borders

An hour's worth of flinging lines nets us several large fish from the quiet pond. Zahk was right, this new spot is gorgeous. The walls of the underground cavern climb high, forming the sides of the mound while masking us completely from the outside world. There isn't much light down here either, but enough shines through the overgrowth to keep eerie vibes at bay. A few times now, I've caught myself simply staring at the hues breaking from beneath the water. The fish swimming within move like wriggling rainbows—their scaly reflections bounce off the rocks and twinkle above our heads.

"Amio, you really did a fine job on the fishing spot this time."

Zahk pulls his fishing rod when the line goes taut, and his sparkling catch breaks the surface. He chuckles at the fish's reasonable size. "I think this pond takes the spot for my new favorite. Almost didn't explore out this way since Reptilix is a bit far, but I got the urge, y'know?"

After casting a few more successful lures, we break out our short blades and begin gutting. In slow strokes, we remove the bright scales, whispering our thanks to the pond for its favor. We sit in silence until Zahk stands up to clean his hands.

"So, catboy, it's finally time for the Discipline, eh? Though I wish the circumstances were better, I'm glad they gave you a break so I can keep my friend with me."

"Me too, it'll be nice having a familiar face around. I only wish Tygon were going too. He had so many future plans riding on this."

Zahk dries his hands on his pants leg. "You mentioned he was saying some real deep stuff just before the blast?"

I chew my lip, returning to the last conversation I had with my brotya. The only thing that haunts my dreams now more than seeing what the fire did to him is hearing his hopes echo through my mind. It scares me. If someone with such high aspirations can be whisked away by the Spirits, what can happen to someone like me whose dreams aren't nearly as ambitious?

I finally organize my thoughts. "Tygon was sold on the idea that going to the Discipline was his way of helping others. He saw it as a place where he'd learn to serve with his powers, not just perfect them."

Zahk sits down next to me with a groan—it's not every day we fall a good mile through the skies. "I completely understand how Tygon felt. I know I'm meant to be more…to do more outside Praedari. That's why I can't wait to get out of here."

I shake my head slowly. "See, I don't get that. If this blast has taught me anything, it's that I need to be ready to protect my loved ones against others. I think the Discipline will give me the skills to do that."

I've never seen Zahk take on a more serious expression before he turns away from me. He takes out his short blade and nudges a pebble onto its tip before flinging it upward. The rock fragment arcs through the air and I watch as the whole pond's surface is disrupted by the most insignificant object.

"Fay, let me ask you something. If it ever came down to it, what would you be willing to give your life for? What impact do you want your existence to have long after you're gone?"

I shrug at the question. Life in Animas is generally so peaceful that I've never had to consider that sort of depth before. It's the reason I'm grateful for the Council's rule. They keep us safe, so we don't have to worry about complications like giving our lives for some larger purpose. "Honestly, what are you talking about, amio? We hunt in the jungle. We build, learn, and love here. We've both been safe here for our entire lives. If the world would just calm down, we won't have to answer questions like that. What's there really to die for?"

Zahk's smirk is a failed attempt to hide the flash of disappointment beneath. "I don't mean to be harsh, but considering your loss, I figured you'd be the first to get it."

Heat rises up through my collar and sets my ears ablaze. I'm certainly not ready to hear about morals when Tygon was just cut down by someone without them. Spheire might not always be fair, no. But if Animas, or even just Praedari could stay neutral, that's all my people need to protect themselves. The politics, the complications—all that can stay far beyond our gates. I'll cling to my friends and family instead. Zahk continues before I can say anything more. His voice is hardly more than a whisper.

"Wanna' know why I'm such a traveler at heart? Why I want to see the world?"

"Shoot."

He holds up his hands, flexing his fingers as if invisible claws were at their tips. "This is the Gift our Bloodline received millennia ago. So, what if every Bloodline's Gifts were meant to build up Spheire instead of ripping it apart?"

I immediately picture the fire-into-lightning Weaver we encountered near Tauris Village. "I'm not so sure I care about foreigners right now. Maybe someday, but look at what some outsider did to our village!"

Zahk tightens his lip. "And you don't think that, perhaps, if we looked outside of ourselves more, we may have seen this coming? Maybe even could've had a voice to prevent it in the first place?" He stares at me with fire in his eyes. "We *don't* have a voice out there, Fay. The only one I ever hear seems to be that prattling woman in the Hub going off about the Libertas Heirs. Perhaps we could've reasoned with them—"

I stand up abruptly, kicking rocks up around me. "I don't give a single crap about those Spirit-forsaken murderers! The only thing I want to gain from the outside world right now, is tools how to fight it so I can keep my loved ones safe!"

My voice echoes in the underground cave and Zahk's hides his face. The harsh outburst gives way to silence—made all the heavier by the quiet sway of the pond.

"Sorry, amio."

He shakes his head but is slow to look back at me. "It's fine, Fay. I know none of this is easy for you. But just so I understand, you want to become…a weapon? A tool that someone can easily aim at others?"

I run my hands over my locs before settling back down, clutching my knees to my chest like a lost child.

Eventually, I mumble a response. "At this point, I simply want to be on whatever side feels right. If that means being what the Council needs me to be, fine. Whatever gets us back to the peaceful days before spineless killers ruined everything. I just want simplicity, that's all…"

Zahk's silence says more than words could. He blows out a breath. "Well, if that's your aim, I'll watch your back up at the Discipline. Just…be careful." He pauses, trying to catch my eye. "Look at me, Fay."

I sigh, looking anywhere but. After a moment, I turn to him, and he palms my shoulder in a firm grip.

Conviction smolders like glowing coals within Zahk's dark brown eyes. "If you're going to be a blade, watch constantly who's sharpening you. When it's all done, try not to accidentally cut me down while I strive to become a bridge. Someone has to be willing to connect us to the outside world. I know in my heart a single soul is all it takes to permanently change the way we do things."

Heat rises through my neck again as I feel more frustrated than before. I'm confused. I don't know what's right to feel anymore. Hatred for the people who killed my brother? Anger because no one knows who the real culprits are, only who we suspect? Disappointment for my jaded perspective? After all, Zahk survived the same attack on his home but unbelievably, he wants to reach out rather than withdraw. I realize suddenly that following Tygon was a lot easier than navigating for myself. A shadowy thought has me wondering if his upbeat perspective would have been dimmed following the violence committed against our village had he lived.

In silence, we gather the gutted fish and tie their tails together with cords. Zahk wraps them carefully in leaves and our eyes meet. He smiles encouragement at me. Regardless of the mess whirling inside my head, I've got a good shoulder to lean on. I pray a quick thanks to the Spirits for that.

I startle when two unknown voices ring out into the dim lighting of the underground pond.

"Hey, did you hear that? I'm tellin' you, I saw a Qirin fly right over this area. Nobody from our village better be snooping 'round here."

We freeze in place as a slower speaking, but heavier-toned voice responds. "None of us would be caught dead in the Solemn Vaults. That's one way to tick off the ancestors and wind up at the bottom of the pond."

I wrench my face at Zahk, pointing to the fish in disbelief. He throws his hands up apologetically mouthing, "Sorry, I didn't know!" We pick up the fish and rods and scramble to the outer wall where multiple crevasses lie within the thick rock. We find a small fissure and wade through layers of hanging vines until we reach a clearing on the other side. I hold up my hand. We each still our breaths as the footsteps come closer.

"What do you think? Maybe in one of the tombs?" The first voice says.

I'm too terrified to look behind me to see if we're standing in a catacomb.

"Eh, I think the elders are just being overly cautious. Those old lizards' seen all that mess on the screens and think every little thing is the next attack. I say these tombs are fine, let's get out of here—disturbing the ancestors 'n such."

As my lungs scream for air, the footsteps pass, and we hear the pair finally leave.

We exhale and I hiss, "Amio, that was too freakin' close—"

Bony fingers sink into my neck and my soul nearly exits my chest. I snap around to see a skeleton wedged inches from my face. I yelp but the sound is muffled by wolf-scented wrist wrappings.

"Quiet or they'll be back!" Zahk whispers in my ear.

We duck beneath the hanging skeleton, farther into the clearing. I frantically start packing our goods so we can make a break for it. I almost toss my rod at Zahk when I notice he's too distracted with something else to help out.

"Uh, catboy, you might wanna' have a look-see."

I pay him no attention, too horrified to think what else the tombs could be hiding. Honestly, freakin' Reptilix *would* treat their dead like this. Hanging off the walls like cured meats. Buncha' coldblooded creeps if you ask me.

I reply, "Amio, I'm not coming over there. Now let's go."

A few beats of silence roils my blood and I finally look up to find Zahk frozen, staring into the dark depths. I step over and join him and am immediately dumbfounded.

The room is covered in dust and drab. A few torches cast shadows on the walls, their shifting forms performing a ritual dance on the stone catacomb around us. The burial ground isn't what floors us though—it's the rows of baskets filled with metal cords.

"What do you think all of this is?" Zahk cautiously walks over to the stockpile. I don't react in time to stop him from touching the foreign materials.

"I have no idea." I edge toward a table in the center of the room where papers and books cover every inch. On the top lies a poster reading, "Don't be fooled by false rulers. Bring back the old ways!" Another has a little girl Kleo's age holding hands with a man lifting a flaming torch. He raises the scepter against a podium with four shadowy figures behind it.

I hear a tearing of cloth and see Zahk cutting a hole in one of the sacks stacked along the walls. Before I can protest, he sniffs the material and jerks his nose away. He offers his hand to me, and I smell the sharp smelling powder.

"Isn't that flint? And maybe sparkle sand like they use in the roasting pits? Goodness, that much of the stuff and we'll blow this place to dust on accident," he says.

"We've got to get out of here." I whip around to retrace my steps toward the exit. Before I can commit, a large draping cloth catches the corner of my eye. Something about it is too familiar…memories begin to take shape at the fringes of my mind.

"Wait a minute." I remember seeing these colors, but only ever submerged in water or lit on fire. Zahk, is that…"

He brings a torch to illuminate the gray and black flag. The flames spotlight the face of a heartless angel embroidered in the cloth. Her presence is no less threatening despite her being only a weaving, and my eyes follow her slender form to see a scale being crushed underfoot. Perched on the stitched woman's outstretched hand, an owl watches over the catacombs.

Zahk's voice trembles before he stutters, "H-how in Everrealm…"

The young wolf's earlier words ring in my mind. Apparently, he doesn't need to rush to get to the outside world. Its troubles have already made their way well inside our borders.

The Libertas Heirs are in Animas.

29

Revelation

"Are you absolutely sure about this, boys?" Papa's expression slowly firms as he trades doubt for reluctant acceptance.

We nod and I watch him struggle to process. The tragedy that forever scarred my father's beloved village and stole his eldest, is easier to accept as the actions of an outside force. But having the threat come from a place so close to home is like a mother bear realizing too late that she's made her den near a poacher's camp. Papa paces, rustling the folds of his garments while we confirm our testimony. He closes his eyes, then comes to a sudden halt.

"That means I have to act now. Have to alert the other leaders quietly, but quickly. How many bundles would you say you saw?"

Zahk thinks for a moment, drawing a finger through the air. "There were about six rows of five bundles—each one had plenty of metal cord. The walls were also piled with packed flint and spark sand."

I raise my eyebrows but agree. "Bashtol. Just think how many other blasts they could let loose with all that? What if there are others—not just in Reptilix?"

Papa's cheeks slump into a tired grimace. His hand slowly finds the stump of his arm, and he whispers soft as an evening breeze, "Don't we ever tire of the pain? Why torch peace for some worthless cause?"

Zahk and I share a look. If he's this concerned about one hideout, what happens if there's more concealed within the jungle? Papa seems to understand our thoughts and puts a finger to his lips.

"Say nothing more about this. I'll assemble the other clan heads and Sage Ophis to share the news. If I get my way, we'll have a team of Shrouds at that hideout before sunset."

Zahk's eyes go wide and my jaw drops a bit. I always thought this secretive group of elite trackers to be a myth. After all, erasing one's aurem from complete detection seemed possible only in fables. To further say an entire team claims this ability? It seems like a boldfaced lie.

"Papa, do we really have Shrouds?"

Papa does not share our enthusiasm, and his solemn expression stamps mine out. After a pained look into the distance, he doesn't answer. He turns away to leave for the temporary assembly space—the Pre-Mastery courtyard. When my father looks back over his shoulder there's palpable regret in his voice. "It's a sad thing to unearth the relics of war, boys. You might dig up old weapons from their graves, but it's your children who will run to refill them."

After Zahk leaves for his own grove, I head to the Hub to find the messengers' quarters. Papa asked if I could send a runner to Nana's den near Avian village. The coastal society won't take too long to reach either by Embraced leaps or Qirin, but regardless, he wanted Muma and Kleo home immediately. With the Heirs being so close, I understand why he wouldn't want to risk our kin being separated.

On the way to contact a messenger, I pass the Mender's Dwelling and see it is nearly empty. I poke my head inside and find Orin packing a final set of medicinal vials. The room smells like musty iron and stains on the stone floor explain why. Grooves in the stone are lined with a faded copper hue where crimson rivers flowed barely more than a week ago. The Mender hears me walk in and turns to sit down. With a huff, he leans his back against the wall. I crouch down in front of him.

"Boy, do you look out of it, Sprite."

Orin smirks at the fairy-inspired nickname. "So, you think me magical now do you, Hunter?"

"Well, my best friend thinks you're some kind of angel, but I don't see any wings. Your Gift is a bit *too* beautiful, I'll admit. Maybe some Nestling's bedtime story is missing its wizard."

His fingers trace the luminares etched into his inner forearm. "Truthfully, this village sure could've used a touch of wizard's magic."

With a sigh, he hovers off the ground from his seated position until his hand-woven moccasins can gracefully touch the floor. Orin returns to his work, glass vials clinking while we enjoy a few moments of silent company. I can tell that since the other ten traveling Menders have left with the injured for Hayvin, he's happy not to be alone in the somber place.

I thread my fingers. "I'm sure you've heard every possible thanks from the village, but I wanted to give you a personal one for saving Lunis…twice now."

Orin steps near, offering a hand to help me stand up. His face relates what he's too ashamed to admit with words. For all the healing he's done as a traveler, the blast's traumas were more than he was prepared for. As blood has stained this dwelling's stone foundation, that night's anguish has branded him for good.

In a sudden movement from the boy, I'm surprised to find myself being hugged by him. I'm quick to return the embrace and out of nowhere the familiar weight of tears swells inside my chest. I hardly know Orin, but the pain we've both seen ties us together. The empty vials around us watch in silent witness as two boys weep for innocence lost.

Minutes pass and Orin breaks away, scurrying to stuff the final items into his pack. He doesn't look at me as he dries his face, instead busying himself with a onceover of his equipment. He checks a flat leather pouch strapped to this thigh, counting vials of Angel Tears and other tonics, then secures a tiny scroll dangling from his wrist. He stretches his neck and angles his sculpted chin to the roof, collecting his wavy hair into a short bun.

"Hunter, that she-wolf of yours has certainly got some spunk. I'm glad I could help her. She's bold for speaking her mind against the elder's decision at the Festival and I respect that. I'd keep her around if I were you."

I blush at the remark, trying to come up with a believable denial. I haven't yet convinced myself that Lunis would consider me to be hers, though if asked, I would be her chosen ally in a heartbeat. I try not to be too optimistic. Still, Orin's sentiment is meaningful.

"Sprite, will I see you at the Discipline?"

A streak of lightheartedness returns to Orin's face, a scholar's passion igniting him. "Oh, don't you know it!" He walks around me once more, studying me closely, poking a couple of recovering wounds before resting his hand on my collar. "I'm happy I'll have some friends to learn alongside."

With that, he snags a strand of my hair into a vial and floats away, stealing away out the door with his pack in tow. I shake my head, smiling to myself. Maybe Zahk's leaning in the right direction with this whole outreach thing. There are dangers in the world, yes, but Spheire isn't without her good-hearted people as well. I'm excited to learn alongside that angel too.

Three days passed while I waited to hear an update from Papa. I was there when Sage Ophis chose to let loose the Shrouds upon hearing the news. I was so amazed to catch sight of two shadowy figures leaving the village that I followed them and what I thought were bonded Helos Hounds.

I climbed to a perch in the branches, trying to look for the group of trackers. I didn't notice the huddle of camouflaged Shrouds directly below me until a pair of eyes found me. Despite staring right at them, there wasn't a tinge of aurem to be detected—the team was practically invisible. After a rustle of leaves, I even lost their outlines and assumed they were gone. I darted down from the branches to look for their prints. The only trace I found were six sets of paw prints I've only seen in picture books. Darklings.

I ran for the gate as fast as I could.

Where most animals can be reasoned with, a panther only yields to its Shroud. That alone keeps the clanless pursuers a mystery—no one in Praedari is stupid enough to search the beasts or their Masters out. The encounter left me wondering for the rest of the day…what kind of enemy lurks within the trees that we'd resort to methods like this?

30

THE COUNCIL

Several days have passed since the Shrouds were released and I'm surprised when Sage Ophis calls the village for an impromptu gathering. He informs us that a Council procession is traveling to Praedari, arriving at noon. Apparently, two governing members are set to oversee a judgement.

Murmurs spring up through the Hub as we try to connect the dots. A voice rises above the rest. "A judgment—does that mean they caught him?"

Sage Ophis replies, "That is correct. After watching the hideout in Reptilix for three days, our Shrouds witnessed the same trio entering and exiting. The team captured them, then conducted a thorough sweep of the hideout. Only the trio's aurem could be linked to the room storing the explosive materials. The trackers reported the rest of the catacomb was simply a burial ground."

Gasps erupt, morphing into murmurs, then shouts. "Murderers! Murderers! Spiritless snakes! Dominant Kondur should cut them down and bury them low for the sake of Reptilix honor!"

The Sage raises his hands above the mass, bringing them to silence.

"Ordinarily, crimes of a village would be handled by their leaders, yes. However, due to the increase in violence, especially the similar attacks seen in other nations, the Council has demanded these prisoners be kept alive. This time, they will do the questioning and the judging. Mercy on the captives' souls—their fates are no longer their own..."

Solint finally sits at its highest point and with it, horns sound throughout the trees. Praedari waits with frozen breath as Spheire's mysterious leaders approach. Excited children are made still by their parents, permitted to line the walkways, but only if they remain motionless. Aside from what the scenes from Sanctum have shown, no one knows what to expect. I, for one, have never seen the Council on our soil before.

My first glimpse of the parade is a flash of bright gold. A river of waving fabric twinkles through the Northern gate while glistening banners fly high above the shanty tops to dominate the sky. My generation has been lucky enough to never know war, but as the wave funnels into the Hub, I imagine this to be the scene those conquered by the Council would have witnessed.

Set in the golden center of each banner is an authoritarian emblem. Four sculpted pillars stand side by side, all sharing the same design. Beneath the columns, five distinct Bloodline wreaths submit, dominated by the mighty columns. At the emblem's midpoint, the central wreath is run through by an imperious sword. The woven blade of the sword is lined with precious jewels while the point and hilt are sewn from silver thread.

The banners' extravagance could be mistaken for boasting, as if to say, "Look at the wealth we have." However, I glean a different message from the sturdy pillars and lethal blade's edge. "Ours is an absolute power."

I'm all too happy to be under their protection.

My eyes sparkle as the glimmering wave passes by, marking the way to the Pre-Mastery courtyard. Though we can't see them from the Hub, I know Sage Ophis, his counterparts from the other villages, and the remaining four Dominants are already in place there.

Next, the low thunder of synchronized footsteps rumbles

through the Hub. A sea of soldiers follows the banners, distinguishable by their hardened faces. The militia is clothed in dark, tightly fitted armor with an appearance suggesting both lightness and flexibility. Combat ready men and women stare straight ahead, giving little indication to our presence. Their focus is sharp, and all look as though they're ready to defend a country or storm a fortress—it's up to an opponent to decide which one.

It is challenging to determine which nation any particular soldier is from. The collective erases the individual within their ranks. There are only two noticeable differences amongst the troops—the first being colored waistbands trailing over their left thighs, the second, a half-cloak with intricate embroidery over their left shoulders. Each wearer is a graduate of the Discipline of Peace. Their garments and colors all associate to one of four groups I've seen in the pictures. Small patches over their right bicep designate their ties within the Discipline. Light blue, white and grays cloaks are labeled "Nimbus." Green and blacks wear "Jade" tags. Blood red and whites march past as "Crimson" and the final group, adorned in black, silver and gold trim are stitched with "Umbral."

Over the seasons, I've seen enough news in the Hub to know that the top graduates from each year are handpicked to lead Spheire's only coalition fighting force: The Elite Guard. This standing army is a long-standing tradition from the aftermath of the Great Bloodline War. Watching the ranks of the Council's best trained elites sends shivers down my spine. I can't help but imagine what it would be like to return to Praedari as capable as one of them someday.

After the bulk of the Guard has passed, a smaller contingent is left to escort the rear. Here, at the end of the procession, the grandiose truly begins. I see a sun-kissed woman with a brawler's build and a magnetic smile stroll through the street. She hands out garments, souvenirs, ribbons, and jewelry pieces as she bounces from villager to villager. Their bewildered looks show the recipients are unsure of what to do with the foreign gifts, but the woman beams at them regardless. Every so often she throws her head back in merriment—a thin line of silver traces around her temples to form an Exalted's wreath. Her short-swept hairstyle shifts with her every theatrical move making the woman an instant charm to watch.

When she is mid-way up the street, a horn sounds and an announcer begins, "It is your honor to now be introduced to Exalt—"

The young Council woman, looking hardly older than Headmaster Lujan, narrows her eyes toward the crier. She winds up and nails his mouthpiece with a balled-up souvenir garment from ten mets away. The man falls on his rump, spewing fabric strands from his mouth and her hands go to her hips as she bellows again.

"Heck, as if these fine folks require such an overdone introduction. I am Exalt Baliste, short and sweet." She holds out her arms as though the whole Hub could give her a collective embrace. Unsure of how to react to the leader, some of the Nestlings begin to kneel which prompts a wave of heads to bow. One after another, the throng falls to a knee, but it takes only a few seconds for Exalt Baliste to realize what's happening.

She booms instantly, stomping with a single foot. *"No!"*

I can't tell which truly shakes the ground, her command or the small shockwave from her stepping into the earth. Wide eyes spread through the crowd and the woman notices, holding her hands up in innocent apology. Exalt Baliste swings her arms back and forth joyfully, continuing her stroll through the Hub like the impassioned outburst had never taken place.

From the shade of her darkened skin, it's obvious this Exalted is from Indom. Recalling the images I've seen of the Council, I know the Keeper of the Discipline—Exalt Danika—is from Hayvin. I can't recall the names of the other two Council members, but I'm sure one is from Petrichor and the fourth is also from Hayvin and Exalt Danika's only child.

Exalt Baliste is nearly out of view now but from this angle I can see every muscle in her open-backed garments. There is great beauty in her strength. Where a farm lugger might have pits and mounds of muscle, hers are weaves of twisting fibers. Braided rows seem to lie just beneath her skin, interlaced in tight proximity like the rows of a basket. I'm used to seeing my own muscles ripple with Embrace, but her entire body is in a constant state of latent power. I think of the pressure my skeleton feels when taking on Nodus power. In those first moments, every bone seems to snap before swelling to handle the strain.

Exalt Baliste's frame is compact, like it has adjusted to a lifetime's worth of Embrace. I can only imagine the force bearing down on her skeletal structure. If it were any other race, a body like that would never work, but she's a Warrior of Indom. Rumor has it the whole Bloodline of the Body is like this, though perhaps not to the same degree. I'm more curious now than ever to challenge one at the Discipline for myself.

I look back to the dent the woman smashed into the ground with a simple foot press. On second thought, perhaps that challenge can wait a bit longer.

The final leg of the procession is a familiar sight in that Exalt Danika is not only the most familiar face of the Council, but *the* face of it. If I understand correctly, there is no seniority amongst the four, but she has reigned the longest. In fact, Nana says she is the last surviving member of the original four that established the Council. She's bragged to us youngsters of being in the capital at the founding of Sanctum, when the Council was born. Knowing that, it's odd then that Nana and Exalt Danika look so different in age. Where Nana is a few seasons over eighty, covered in wrinkles and gray hair, Exalt Danika appears as youthful as Muma Kura. I find myself reminded of what Orin spoke into my mind about moving between the threads that make up Spheire's reality...

Exalt Danika floats above the rooftops and ornate streamers linger in the air behind her shoulders. There are no gods in Spheire—we share our life bond with the Spirits, and while we don't deify them, we do revere their role within the world. But if ever there were a picture of a goddess to whom one would bow, the woman above us fits the image perfectly.

Along with her wreath, Exalt Danika wears a heavy looking headpiece that conceals her eyes. The ornamental helm reaches back away from her temples to form a pair of carved antlers. Despite the weight, her back is straight, and she glides effortlessly. Her hands rest in the same circular outline I've seen from our Mender. The luminares tattoos glow, pulsating energy from her forehead to her chest, down six moon tattoos above her wrists, and back again. Every energy pulse sends a low rumbling throughout the Hub.

Beneath the helm, the woman makes no sign of acknowledgement to the crowd. However, I am not foolish enough to think we aren't all within her watch. As a hunter, I know what it is like to sense without seeing and frankly, I feel on the receiving end of this phenomenon now.

Where the villagers eventually stood when prompted by Exalt Baliste, not a single head remains unbowed before the Spirit-Born levitating above us. Her approach is slow—like she left the simplicities of urgency behind in a weaker life, long ago. When she floats above me, I catch sight of her curtain of inky violet hair. A massive smooth disk of dark gray metal floats protectively behind her back. The hovering ornament is the size of a small den, shaped like a full moon but covered in thousands of tiny razors. Orbiting the giant disk in a counter rotating pattern are a pair of massive crescent blades. The glistening assortment hangs lethal in the air, spinning as though it could be dispatched in seconds. I bow, staring at the ground and imagine the decoration zigzagging through lines of hapless opponents while the Exalted floats safely in the background. Her presence is pure intimidation, beyond anything the Hub's images could ever hope to portray. I don't know why, but I catch myself holding my breath as she levitates over my stooped back.

It isn't until later that I realize the pebbles I stared at beneath my nose while she passed quaked until they shattered out of existence.

31

UNTAMED

Once Exalt Danika is well out of view, we flow into the street following the march to the Pre-Mastery courtyard. I find Muma and Kleo in the crowd and guide them through the packed walkways. By the time we arrive, the Elite Guard have lined the courtyard walls, each looking straight on with stoic presence. At the yard's center, both Exalted sit on carved seats—recovered remnants from the People's Hall. Four Dominants and five Sages from our sister villages are seated behind them, ready to observe the judgment. Witnesses from Praedari pack tightly into the remaining space, leaving a central lane open between the rulers and the grounds opposite their position.

I find a spot with a good view, ushering Muma and Kleo next to me. Muma's eyes hold no trace of tears past, instead, she is visibly steeled in preparation to finally know her son's killers. I clutch her hand for a moment, trying to squeeze life into it, but rigid tension is the only response. I glance at the woman's stance. She is only the coldest portions of a huntress now and there exists a certain wiry readiness to her posture.

I wince, imagining how lucky the murderers are to be judged by the Council's hands instead of the furious parents around me.

A pathway leads from the makeshift thrones to two towering boulders with chains and rope at their base. With a signal from Exalt Danika, the Reptillix Dominant, Sage, and clan leaders file in behind one another. They trudge solemnly to the stone pillars. Their eyes look heavy despite the leaders' attempts to walk with a sense of purpose. It's obvious the weight of whatever's to come is clearly cumbersome. A small podium awaits the troop and their leader, Dominant Kondur opens it to remove the contents. At the sight of what is inside, the Reptilix leaders shut their eyes and tighten their lips. After showing initial disgust, the Dominant straightens his shoulders and sets his jaw. Dangling from his grip is a pulplash.

In Praedari, mutual respect is generally such that I've gone many seasons without hearing news of village crime. It's hard to steal when the person you're robbing is a neighbor. Murder then is seemingly unfathomable when a good brawl can settle the outcome of most disagreements. Still, Papa has said before he lived through different times right after the five nations went to war—the invention of the pulplash is proof of that.

The eyes of the clan leaders widen as the Dominant stretches the pulplash's leather core back and forth. Its construction is simple–a short length of woven leather straps with ends tied together into balled knots. Dom Kondur strikes the stone, letting loose a crisp thud. I can tell the purpose is not to break the skin or cause unconsciousness, but rather to bruise repeatedly, to get a point across. With his shoulders back, the Dominant walks the length of the line, handing the pulplash to each Reptilix leader. Most hesitate, but after a brief exchange of words, the clan heads square their frames as well. Justice is not a free gift. Sometimes, its cost is plainly clear—pain.

Exalt Danika seems to observe the scene from beneath her daunting headpiece. Her helm looks on hawkishly, the harsh metal lending her a blade-like focus that fixates solely on the Reptilix lineup. After a submissive nod from Dom Kondur, she calls out in an even voice.

"Bring him."

A hole opens in the Guard ranks and six armored soldiers form two lines. Between them, a pale snake of a man looks around the courtyard as though its light is the first he's seen in months.

His lips are as cracked as his dried skin. Dirt crusted hair is packed around his temples. He squirms against tight bonds constricting biceps to rib cage. When he grits his teeth, I spot viper fangs slicing between his lips. His eyes don't adjust to the scenery until they take on a deep yellow tint. They dart around the unfamiliar area frantically until the man spots Exalt Danika. At this, his composure turns to ice and he sneers. Then he lifts his bony chin to the horizon, deeming the woman unworthy of even his scorn.

Praedari, however, does not share his reservations. "Murderer!" Collective voices chant. "We'll watch you drown for the lives you stole!" Cry others. Rotten fruit, dirt, and trash, fly through the air, building up on the man's skin. Six guards become two as the others return to the perimeter, but neither remaining guard reacts to the commotion.

It isn't until the snake is directly in front of me that I realize I've seen him before. I blink in disbelief, placing him as the same stranger who hissed at me in the Hub on the day I fell to the Gargan-Elk. My blood boils as realization sinks in. The blast had been planned a long time ago and I caught him surveying his target. The man tries in vain to ignore the crowd's clamor, but I can tell his composure is an act. His fear gives off a distinct odor and I have the scent of it now. This is a village of hunters. Every one of us knows this coward's true self.

I flinch back when a screech slices the air beside me. At first, I look down at Kleo—her curly hair bunched against my elbow, as she hides from the sights and sounds. It's only then that I realize Muma is missing. I barely catch her lunging forward from the corner of my eye.

"Share my son's pain!" She spits, reaching for the prisoner's head. His surprise is the same as mine, both of us watching the attack unfold, though too slow to react. The crowd gasps in unison once they understand her intentions. Where their jeers call for the man to suffer by water, Muma means to show the murderer equivalent suffering to Tygon's.

Our huntress drives an oil-drenched cloth, ablaze with fire, into the man's unsuspecting face. She holds it to his brow and immediately his head blossoms with orange light. The flames lick at Muma's skin but her forearm remains unflinching. He falls to the ground, rolling in agony as his scales are taken away by the plume. Muma's eyes are magma, dwarfing the fire's intensity many times over. With a second wild scream, she follows him down into the dirt. I feel Kleo dart behind me to avoid the scene, but the sounds are inescapable. The huntress's fists dominate every inch of the man like rain over a forest. For every strike he manages to squirm from, ten more land in its place.

I look to the Exalts to see Baliste rise from her chair, striking a noble pose, but remaining notably still. Her posture reads that she'll step in to stop the unjust beating, yet her inaction speaks volumes. With her Warrior's speed, I know she could bolt across the courtyard, separating the two before the next fist lands.

Beside her, Exalt Danika gives the first expression I've seen of the woman yet. She tilts her head an inch. Then I see a subtle nod, granting approval. After several moments, the noises of flesh impacting flesh are joined by the crack of bones. Muma brings both her arms up and shatters through the prisoner's shoulder. As his howling reaches a fever pitch, the escorts finally pull Muma off so she doesn't kill the man before questioning. The guards wrench the snake by the neck and toss him to his feet. I watch in disbelief as our huntress continues spewing at the bloodied man.

"The flames only tasted you! They hardly licked your vile skin…but they *feasted* on my boy!" The man snaps his jaw back into place, grimacing at his decimated arm. A snake's tongue flicks over the burn marks on his face, but they are nothing compared to those that still haunt my dreams. With a final howl, Muma refuses to be silenced.

"I hope after they're done with you today, even the Spirits reject you from Everrealm. You'll be a ghost—a buried abomination for all eternity. Even the dirt will forget your worthless name!"

I clench my fists when the beaten man is strapped to the boulder. The pulplash is handed to each Reptilix leader who take turns striking it across his already bruising face. With each crack, they shout "How dare you?" or "Shame upon Reptilix, justice upon you!" After the leaders cycle through many times, the man sinks into his bonds. I think him broken, but what he does next proves me wrong.

Beneath the blood flooding down his chin, the corners of his lips turn up—his eyes concealed by grimy hair.

I shiver, realizing he's smiling the grin of a martyr whose point is only being proven true. Exalt Danika rests her cheek on her fist as though she watches the suffering of an ant. The throng around me, oblivious to the man's eerie joy, raise their voices for revenge. They trade throwing garbage for small rocks, pelting the snake in his bonds. Some of their hands even find Muma, jostling her shoulders with pride for her retaliation.

I watch in disbelief and a tinge of shame as I'm swept up in the mob's passion—my own fingers reaching for a stone. I raise it above my head, feeling one with those around me. In this moment, I hold my brother's justice, I represent his stolen hopes and dreams. I glare at the man, then feel Kleo watching the jagged rock in my grip with wide eyes. I tremble, lowering my arm and letting the stone fall back into the dust. Time blurs as I look from the prisoner, to Muma, to the crowd, and finally the Exalts. The throng's raspy throats, the Warrior's false nobility, and the Spirit-Born's frigid expression all coalesce into a single thought.

Our five nations are not so different. We play at being civil—raising walls to form our villages and cities. We tell tales to pass on our cultures, but this courtyard is the true face our Bloodlines can never hide. We'd be lucky to maintain any semblance of peace if the Council ever lost its grip. This is why I must succeed at the Discipline. It's why I must hone my skills and become a defender of the Council. They will keep my home safe. They alone can keep chaos at bay and safety within reach. Without them, Spheire would eventually descend into madness—without them, our Gifts would go unchecked.

I hold Kleo's head to my side as she shudders at the enveloping outcry. I resolve in this moment to follow the Council because without them...

There is no taming the beasts within our blood.

32

Judgment

Dominant Kondur shakes a fist in the prisoner's face. "Say something for yourself, Phint! You came here to this unsuspecting village and killed nearly seventy innocents. The least you can do is explain why."

The man, Phint apparently, doesn't move, only staring at the dirt.

"If you won't speak for the dead or for yourself, then please, do it for the village that raised you. The Council is fair, but your heartless group has made uncertain times across Spheire." His voice goes low. "I beg of you, don't make them suspect our simple home is something it is not."

Phint's jaw clenches with a surprising tinge of guilt. He meets Dom Kondur's eyes and begins to open his lips. But only a sharp breath escapes, blowing hair out of his bruised face.

"So your lips are sealed then. There really wasn't a reason for this violence, was there? You are just a group of fanatical murderers after all."

Phint sneers, rejecting the notion. He angles his head around the Dominant's shoulders to look straight at Exalt Danika. After fixating on her, he spews a bloody glob into the dirt.

A voice responds from the Exalts' makeshift thrones.

"Pardon, but, I think I'll take it from here, Dominant. I'm convinced you did your best, and I'm certain he was acting without your knowledge." Exalt Baliste accepts Dominant Kondur's grateful bow. After perusing the crowd, she steps forward, strolling to the chained man with easy confidence. Her persona is magnetic and when she reaches Phint, the woman whips around to the villagers, raising her hands like a performer. Despite being a bit shorter than the average huntress, her presence overshadows the bound man, and she directs her attention to her audience as if he'd disappeared altogether.

Her eyes sparkle. "I believe that what we have here is a case of complete misunderstanding. We misunderstand this young man's intentions." She gestures to herself and her fellow Exalted. She spins around to flash him a charming smile.

"Likewise, he too, misunderstands. I don't think he quite captures the Council's resolve. For as much as we've learned over the decades, there's one truth we strive to uphold." The Exalt closes her eyes, folding her hands to imitate modest prayer. "It only takes a single voice to preserve peace."

The courtyard erupts in applause, and she salutes the impressed villagers.

"Now then, let's try to solve our mutual misunderstanding problem, hmm? Surely, you didn't mean to hurt people. I'll bet *you* never wanted to kill anyone. Her Exalted and I are both sympathetic to that." She rests a hand on his unbroken shoulder. "In fact, I think we should match the severity of your fate to that very assessment."

I shirk in confusion, trying to read the expressions of those around me. What is she saying? That he's an accidental murderer? That he's partially innocent and should be treated as such? How do you unintentionally cause a blast during one of our largest celebrations? How was it unplanned in any way that he'd steal our loved ones away?

"Here's where I need your help, Phint. If you didn't want to murder those innocents, then tell me who did?"

A twitch flutters over Phint's cheekbone, and he hides his face when the Exalt leans in to study him. After a moment of pacing, she surrenders.

"Fine, if you won't give me who, then you need to answer for me where. Where are the other two accomplices? The hideout couldn't've been run by just you, not with all the materials hidden there."

I'm baffled once again. Didn't Sage Ophis say the Shrouds found three culprits? If they sent the darkling bonded and they're as persistent as the stories say, there's no way any suspect got away. Why does she need to ask him where they are? I try to fathom the possibilities as she repeats her question, raising her hands to the heavens as though she were sent from on high to help give this man his voice. Phint still doesn't speak, but his brow relaxes slightly. The man has resigned his own outcome, but clearly, he's relieved. He likely thinks even without him, the work can still be done. I clench my fists, watching apathy return to the psychopath.

It's then I catch a twinkle in the Exalt's eyes. Her jubilant swagger shifts into a sudden slither, her grin snaps like the ravenous bulb of a flytrap. Of the two, she's more snake than he ever was.

"Ah, I see. It looks like I'm unable to get a thing from you." She pauses, inspecting the back of her hand. "But since you won't tell me your truths, I don't feel obligated to share mine. Are you sure you want to make this harder on yourself?"

Phint can't hide his puzzled look.

She focuses on him. "You won't get the chance to hurt anyone else. Frankly, neither will they."

With a snap, two ragged prisoners are dragged through the masses. Exalt Danika's headpiece tilts slightly and she and her partner seem to share a look. The crowd begins a slow clap to see the whole guilty party being brought forward for judgment. Phint's indifference evaporates and dread pits his face. The pair, an old man and a girl who Tygon would've been near to in age, struggle against their bonds. As they are fixed to the second boulder, the girl looks at Phint the same way Lunis did when she found me injured in the burning hall.

"You get one more chance, just one, before I make this more

difficult for you, but quite fair for everyone else here." She drives a pointed finger straight for the man's chin. "Where are the rest of the Libertas Heirs and why do you insist on your senseless methods?"

Phint meets the Exalt's eyes for the first time and his lips begin to quake. I hear him whimper, finally murmuring something before he's cut off by the girl. She screams out, ordering him to stay silent.

"Be strong!" she says. "Do it for the cause! We've already laid down so much, sacrificed everything." She nods her chin over the chains. "Our world will be better—Animas will benefit—if we're able to endure just a little longer. I promise. They'll never find—"

Composure leaves the interrogator and Exalt Baliste cackles uncontrolled. "Like I said, you people won't get to hurt anyone else. But, Phint, do you remember what I told you before?" I almost miss it, but the dirt beneath her immediately streaks with webs of tiny cracks. Every intertwined cord of muscle in her arm goes taunt with power.

"As I said. It only takes a single voice to preserve peace."

Before Phint can blink, the Warrior is across the courtyard. In a blur of motion, she strikes, and I hear the sound of chains clattering to the ground. The metal clang is followed by a thud as the top halves of both the man and woman topple into the grass. The Warrior breathes out slowly, rising back to her noble stature and folding her arms behind her. The whole execution required only a single slash of her bare hand. The blow was so quick there isn't a speck of blood on her arm. Even her sleeveless tunic is spotless. It isn't until she's back in front of the sole remaining prisoner that the top portion of the thick boulder slides loose, falling to the ground like a halved apple. It kicks up a dust cloud, but the powerful woman looks on unfazed.

That's the difference in power between Beast Masters and Indom Warriors. Where ours is raw power, theirs takes a different form. They are gods of precise force. Our Bloodline's mightiest may be able to punch a crater into the side of a mountain—she could carve one.

Exalt Baliste wipes a smudge of dust from her neck. "Think what you will about me, but make sure you add this to the list. I take my responsibility seriously, and no faceless group will destroy the peace we're only now able to enjoy. It took so long—decades before I became a member—to grow this stability. So many squabbles, so many pointless border disputes after the Great Bloodline War. The young blossom of peace nearly shriveled up and died."

The man sobs in his chains but the Warrior takes no notice. "Now, that once sapling of peace that was once so feeble has grown tall and bears fruit. The very fruit that will feed our future generations and you Heirs will not poison its roots."

The Exalt strides over to the man and cradles his head. Then she abruptly tightens her grip on his ragged hair. She jerks his eyeline down beneath hers and peers into his soul. Her voice is a soft whisper.

"This is the price you'll pay for the security you're willing to disrupt. Now speak. Do it before your Dominant picks out every other person you've ever loved. Quickly, for they too await your *split* decision."

Phint's eyes dart to the corpses across the courtyard. Shockingly, he still offers only silence as his associates' blood bubbles into the earth. Phint tries to resist the Exalted's handle over his skull. Finally, her patience is lost and she sighs deeply.

"Right, have it your way then. We'll find the reason why, sooner or later. Who knows, you might have been but a lowly pawn all along. Perhaps whoever twisted you into all this never gave you a real purpose, only stories and fluffed up promises."

Phint spits in her direction. "You are a witless bi—"

A backhand echoes through the air, snapping Phint's head back against the stone. His raspy scream slits my eardrums, his mouth sporting far less teeth than before, while his eyes flash manic orange.

"I am your ruler, do not forget it," the Exalt says.

Phint coughs up blood and scoffs. "You...the rest of the

illegitimate Council? All of you faux kings and queens can keep your rule. The lot of you will never find the rest of the Heirs, but you will be gifted their purpose. You will know our wrath."

I fear my own breathing is loud enough to be noticed above the absolute silence of the crowd.

The man surges against his chains. "Freedom demands a price and if that price is blood, we will pay it. If it must be ours that is spilt, we'll offer it. But if it is the nations that must sacrifice, so be it. Either way, we will be the bloodletters until freedom is ours again."

He juts his chin to Exalt Danika, seated in her throne. "Who gave you the authority to rule half a century ago? You capitalized on fear to steal power away from sovereign nations and even now, your actions prove you don't intend to use it justly."

The prisoner wrinkles his lips, glaring between the two women. "Was replacing our leaders not enough? You had to go and poison the minds of our youth, demanding the best of our future grovel at your Discipline of Peace. Doom to the Discipline. It'll be the next place we burn after we drag you into the streets from your high tower in Sanctum."

A wicked smile possesses Phint's blood-stained lips. "Do what you will with me, but I'll sleep peacefully among the dead knowing you damn yourselves. You've taken so much from the nations to build up Sanctum…your precious lamp on a hill. If that abomination can be called a lamp, then you false gods think yourselves the spirit-damned flame to light it."

His face loses the grin, and my insides churn with malice. Kleo, who I'd all but forgotten about, squeezes my hand tightly and I surge with anger at myself. Every villager leans forward, eager to see justice done. I understand, but the collective bloodlust bothers me all the same. We are so hungry for retribution that it's all too easy to forget the ones who need protection. This is the madness brought by having an enemy in the first place. We didn't have these problems before and I'm furious people like him could torch my village's safety. Just let us love, hunt, and live. When did I ask to be a weight in his philosophical scales?

"The problems of Spheire lie in the shadows that your precious rule casts. Sanctum claims all the light because it's as far as your vision goes, but out here? In the dark? Where is your presence?" He throws his brow toward the Elite Guards. "Where were these lines of soldiers before today? We only seen them during a fancy procession? I'll bet you floated in here all high above the crowds too, thinking yourselves beloved rulers."

He pauses, basking in the courtyard's absolute silence, then hisses his next words with a viper's forked tongue.

"Well, I certainly didn't hear nobody cheering when you came."

Exalt Danika's luminares pulse with energy and her hair floats from the aura. Exalt Baliste's nostrils flare. I hope they'll cut this man's speech short soon, carting him off to Sanctum for the punishment he deserves. He's earned the tanks and isn't worthy of any more of our attention.

The prisoner cackles in response to their noted fury. "The Libertas Heirs were born in and live in your shadows. We will remain safe in them too! After all, who are you going to send into the darkness to find us?"

Hardly a breath later, Phint, his chains, both boulders, and the earth beneath them all disappear in a pillar of light. I spin to see Exalt Danika's hands in a circular outline and the space beneath her helm where her eyes must be blazes like Solint. Despite the display of power, I'm even more astounded that her arms never once moved from their armrests.

"That is far more than I care to hear from my enemies in one day," she says.

I see a visibly shocked Sage Ophis rise and bow respectfully to the Exalted. The other leaders, then the throng follow suit. The announcer declares the judgment concluded and the Exalted's departure. The procession reassembles, leaving the courtyard more quickly than it had come. As the crowd files out behind them, Muma hugs me. She sobs as if some weight has been lifted from her shoulders. I'm too lost to share in her emotional reckoning. For a moment, some of the man's words threaten my resolve and I'm more confused than ever. Perhaps we should see the Council's presence around here more often. Maybe it's possible their rise to power ages ago holds unseen consequences today. But once the memory of Tygon's charred corpse enters my mind, my inner fire is refueled. I may not understand all the intricacies of our world or the inner workings between the Five Bloodlines, however, I do firmly believe what happened today was fair and necessary. Overwhelming power like theirs is the only way I can see a path toward preventing this chaos from worsening.

I look for Kleo among the shuffling villagers and find her kneeling at the crater where the man was chained down. She turns to me as I approach, showing her ash covered hands. I sink down to her level.

"Kitten, I know that was quite a lot, but how do ya' feel? Are you proud we finally have justice for those we lost?"

She rips up a clump of grass and tries to wipe the soot from her fingers.

"Well, I guess so, but there's some parts that are hard for me to understand. Sometimes, I have all these questions that I'm not sure I'm allowed to ask."

I tilt my head, stroking her curls. "What do you mean, little one?"

She looks up at me with the face of pure innocence. "First it was Tygon and all our villagers. Now, it's this snaky man. So, when there's a war, does everybody burn?"

Taste leaves my mouth as I try to stammer a response—I've never had to consider war. How do I begin to answer that?

Kleo pushes me to stand up, pulling my hand toward the exit. "Hurry! I want to see the goddess leave the village! Maybe she'll even bless me. I'll pray to her with all my heart that she'll keep you safe at the Discipline." She takes off with me in tow. "Oh, and that she'll remember me when I'm old enough to go to her school!"

Kleo skips along as I steer her away from the half corpses she'd missed being too short in the crowd.

Tygon, what kind of twisted world did you leave me behind in? I've felt more new emotions in this short time than in my whole simple life combined. I think back to our conversation on how he wanted to help people. Walking through the streets, I can't share his hopes. Instead, I am stuck in this confusing space.

We find an empty spot along the Northern Gate and Kleo falls to both knees, clasping her tiny hands together. Soon Exalt Danika floats overhead, her helm never moving from the horizon. This time, I continue to stand, but close my eyes all the same, imagining the way Praedari was before the blast. Kleo grips my elbow, and I hurry to finish my own prayer. I only see the Exalt's back as she is carried away on unseen wings. Phint's mad ravings already seem like a distant memory. If backing the Council gets my world back to normal, if Kleo never sees the scorches of war, I'll follow the goddess to the ends of Spheire and back—starting with the Discipline.

33

En Route
- - - LOGHIS - - -

Althea plays back footage in her head to cross-examine the previous duel of her current opponent. Sixty seconds wasn't a long time to force a submission, but she'd watched the last match closely. Clintis had fooled around for forty seconds out of his allotted minute. It wasn't until the final twenty seconds that he shifted from showboating trickster to cold tactician. She saw now that he'd purposely run the clock so with the last bit of time, his poor opponent would be desperate. Sloppy too. Moments before the shock bands around both their necks were set to go off—consequence for a tie match—Clintis had vaulted just over the boy's head, landing with dancer's grace behind his exposed back. With a familiar *shink,* the pronged needles found their mark, pumping Clintis's foe with his home-grown brew. The smaller boy never saw any of it coming but he fell over all the same, completely paralyzed. All he could do was let his teeth rattle while taking the loser's shock, ending the match.

Althea had no intention to play Clintis' game by similarly authoring her own undoing.

Standing in front of her now, Clintis apparently didn't see the need to shake off his amused expression. His eyes trickle over Althea's stance with the fluidity of liquid gold. She notices his bold stare, estimating that his visual enhancements are likely coated in literal gold to better relay optic signals. She readies her stance as the gilded fox tugs with irritation at the metal band around his neck.

"Ah, Nuke, I can't say I'm too surprised we're the final pair left. What do you say you let me have an easy win? I was hoping to avoid breaking into a heavy sweat before we all pack up for the Discipline."

Althea stands at the ready, mentally plotting approach patterns Clintis might take based off his previous fight. She wouldn't share the temporarily paralyzed boy's fate. Rather, this final win would earn her perfect marks for Electro-Sparring to match her interview ranking with the Crown's Hand. No amount of charm would change her aims, despite the source of said charm being admittedly dashing.

Clintis coos a note louder, "Oh, come on. I'll even save you a good spot on the Sandray if you give in."

She unsheathes her sim-blade, tracing mock tears with the tip of its edged projection. "After you take the loser's jolt, I don't think you'll want me anywhere near you, golden boy."

The referee blows the readying alarm and Clintis slides a razor-sharp bang behind his ear, letting the other one dangle over his daring smile. "My gold's only shining for you, Nuke." A couple of Clintis's female fans cheer his name, waving to him from the sidelines.

Althea cocks an eyebrow. "Apparently not."

Clintis shrugs in response.

The countdown begins and Althea cycles through the first steps of her attack plan. She switches her arm to ballistic mode, but sees her mistake once the announcer shouts, "Match Commence!"

Clintis follows one of several prediction lines Althea had already plotted in the four-met space between them. What she hadn't accounted for however was the added height he'd gain due to those Grade-A nanofiber leg augments. Having never met anyone before with pockets deep enough to afford those higher-grade specs, she didn't have any data on them and had used calculations based on older models.

With him inbound, she scrambles for an escape path, but all too quickly, he's already descended upon her. Her augment must have adapted on its own, since Clintis's sim-blade flickers out when meeting her Boltsteel shield. He capitalizes on her defensive maneuver by sending her sliding on her back as he plants his feet to push off. Althea roll recovers, watching her opponent arc in a graceful backflip. At the apogee of the maneuver, he spins, letting loose two micro-syringes with sniper's accuracy. When he lands on a single foot, the cheering girls go wild, none of them caring Althea had managed to deflect both of projectiles with the back of her buckler.

Forty-five seconds left to subdue the golden fox, time for her own offensive.

She shouts across the dueling grounds. "If I'm as good as you say I am, you're going to have to try a little harder than that, Brother." The layers of Althea's irises spin as she filters through her next options.

Clintis only licks his bottom lip. "I must say, you're far better than what I or anyone else has already said. Which is why I'm not your biggest opponent right now—you are. I just need to move aside and let you outplay yourself."

Outplay this, pretty boy. Althea decides on her tactic. With a surge through her augments, she dashes backward, spraying a pellet blast into the air. Clintis's eyes follow the pellets as they explode, covering his previous leap path in cascading smoke. It's clear that in only a few seconds, the smoke will rain down, becoming a complete veil between him and his target. With his attention above their heads, Althea gently rolls three marble sized rounds onto the ground in front of her.

Clintis smirks, unimpressed by the smoke cloud. He waves a hand over his reflective legs, flexing the metallic muscles within. "Sis, they don't just jump, you know."

He rises up a couple of inches as rugged ball bearings spring beneath each foot. They let loose a high-pitched whirl before the pair of Striders catch, lurching him in a half-circle around Althea's flank. Clintis wields the sim-blade in one hand, unsheathing the pronged syringe from the other. He carves an arc toward her side of the battleground, the syringe catching sparks against the arena floor. The boy shoots beneath the smokescreen just before it has time to fully descend and it's all Althea can do to calibrate her eyes to track his movement.

As Clintis sinks into his approach like a dune skier, Althea detonates the silent rounds her opponent had failed to notice. The three metal rounds fragment, sending magnetic shrapnel sprawling between her and her pursuer. He notices the countermeasure a second too late and dashes right through it. Clintis's leg augments go unstable, his cunning eyes spark with recognition. Hundreds of magnetic particles coat the ball bearings, costing him all traction. His shoulder is the first body part to contact the ground before the adolescent tumbles multiple times, attempting to dive into a controlled roll. Althea watches him fail miserably. Still, she sees him recover just enough to twist in the air and hurl the holographic blade for her head. Fortunately, her eyes had already slowed down the throw by half speed when it was still just a wind-up.

She turns her chin. A miss by one-eighth inch.

Clintis' unruly crash across the floor is cut short once Althea drops a knee into his sternum. The bout is ended once she plunges her sim-blade into his throat, the projection holding steady to signify a kill.

For a long pause, the two hold each other's eyes, chests heaving and augments whirring to stabilize breath. Clintis winks, imitating an exploding sound effect. The victor pays him no mind, rising over the gilded fox like a queen ascending. Althea gives him nothing further—the results speak for themselves. She steps aside, only looking at him once as the boy's collar sparks and he grits his teeth with a grin at every jolt. But Althea grants him due credit, Clintis never yields to her, not even the surrender of looking away.

Althea joins the other two-hundred and ninety-nine Loghis youth loading up to cross the Wastelands. The heat at its outer rim bakes her skin and she wonders how the refugees managed to walk through these harsh temperatures during the Scattering. Then again, she was a little girl when her Protectorate led her on a similar journey. She decides it must've been her Bloodline's proclivity for adaptation—an Arkitech takes pride in crafting their own way. Too bad her countrymen always seemed to be the one forced to adapt. How convenient for the Council to keep their oppression a secret because their offenses are hidden on the far side of a desert.

Skyelle joins Althea's side and reaches for the girl's heavy duffel. When the Protectorate's younger complains about it, she shoulders the bag, waving away the girl's protest.

"You need to save your strength. You already topped the rest of the candidates, so let a Protectorate give her champion a small reprieve."

Althea smiles sheepishly, surrendering the matter. It wouldn't be long anyway, the Sandray maintenance crews were conducting their final checks on the dune traversal fleet. The Sandray formation was always a sight to behold. Each craft wears a polished metallic sheen to reflect some of the deadly heat, but the desert craft also could camouflage to match the terrain. Taking inspiration from manta rays, the cruisers have a sweeping wingspan edged with smooth blades on either side. An elongated tail lends added stability to the already reliable momentum system—six sets of layered treads, streamlined versions of those seen in mining equipment.

At the maintenance crew chief's signal, a notification pops into each student's visual augments, providing their craft and seat number. Althea turns to Skyelle who looks prouder than she ever has.

"I wish you the best of luck, Daughter. I know we've had our trials, but this is how we set our nation back on the right course. So long as you remember the Ethos your mother taught you and that I solidified, you will be precisely what our people need."

Althea cups the older woman's face in her hands, wiping away an unexpected tear. While they had grown close since the young girl's mother disappeared, Althea was never so bold to assume the Protectorate loved her. As Skyelle cries, Althea can feel the entire weight of the woman's pride, hopes, and dreams. Althea can't help but wonder if perhaps somewhere in their time together, she had become a surrogate for the young child she'd learned Skyelle lost during slavery. Watching the woman cry, a sudden realization comes to mind. General Pierce was entirely right—Loghis had paid enough of the bill.

The Sandray engines flare, constricting then rotating in sync as the nozzles expand. Jet streams roar above the bladed tails and the ground rumbles underfoot. With a final kiss, Althea takes her duffel and follows her line to the assigned craft. She ducks under the wing's low profile, stepping inside the craft to strap her goods to the bay floor. Once the fastenings are double-checked, the crew chief wiggles his thumb and pinky back and forth to signal "Go for launch."

Althea finds her seat and buckles in, settling in just before hearing a whisper in her ear.

"Told you I'd save you a good seat, Nuke."

Althea shakes her head and looks over to see Clintis studying her. "It's good to see you too. Looks like the shock ointment did its job."

Clintis rubs his slight neck burns with exaggerated grief.

A weasel-nosed girl across the cabin cries out, "Brother of Intellect, you're hurt!"

She then whips out a canister of therapeutic cream, nearly jumping into his lap with a dramatic show of concern. When Clintis assures her he's fine, the girl hides it away, but not before shooting Althea a death glare. Althea's imperial posture remains undeterred and the girl huffs before crossing her arms to look elsewhere.

Clintis yawns, then leans back to find a more comfortable angle. "By the way, did you see the footage of that Beast Master getting vaporized in Animas? I hate Danika as much as the next Loghint, but you've got to admit she's some kind of powerful. No wonder she's remained in charge." He shakes his head. "Those Heirs need to rethink their strategy. Making enemies out of everyone? How does that play out?"

Althea looks over to him. "I was thinking the same."

Clintis sniffs. "Hey, at least the timing works out for us. I heard that little speech of his too. Potent stuff even if it was coming from a doomed man."

Althea considers for a moment, thinking about the powerful Spirit-Born Exalt. Her voice lowers to a murmur. "And yet here we are, headed to her house. If I were her, I'd have eyes everywhere, especially with this being the first time a new element is being introduced to the Discipline equation."

"Well, don't let it get to you, Sis. I, for one, am excited to see what the other Bloodlines have got. If slowing down the Council or even prepping for war comes out of it, so be it. But for now?" He gives his most charming smile and threads his golden stripe of hair between alloyed fingers. "I'm going to have some fun."

The fleet surges forward and, looking out the rear window, Althea watches Redemption fade into the sand-covered horizon. She closes her eyes, getting comfortable for the five-hour ride. Her mind mulls over the new perspectives she's gathered over the past few weeks, all of them aligning toward a singular purpose. The Discipline is a chance to test her skills and improve a few methods. But it's primarily an opportunity to learn all she can. Whatever obstacles to her mission, they would all be eliminated as necessary.

As they streak through an ocean of dunes, headed for the central terminal of the MagneRail, Althea envisions the Discipline. From the few times she's seen the Redemption projector switched on, even she's found the campus impressive. There may be many things to dislike about the Council, but admittedly, the institution was not one of them. A place to come together. A moment to be the benefactors of the Council's peace, rather than the victims of it. A chance—for once—not to be the isolated Bloodline.

She reaches into her pocket and sets Blooper onto its shoulder mount. After spinning with excitement, the little bot hugs her cheek and begins threading her gray braids. It sings her favorite rain recording and Althea loses herself to daydreams of what she could have seen…of the life she could've lived. Of the country Loghis might've been had the Council never existed.

34

SEND OFF
- - - ANIMAS - - -

"Son, are you all packed up?" Papa asks as I tie a final knot into my satchel. I nod and follow him and the rest of the kin out of the grove. I glance over my shoulder to our home tree and can't help but wonder when I'll see it again. Even the stone tiger's head monolith seems wary to lose oversight of me.

Muma catches my hesitation and gathers me up into a tight hug. "No worries. It'll all be here when you get back." She smiles. "We can watch out for ourselves. All of Praedari will. Don't let worryin' about us keep you kids from succeeding."

I close my eyes and lean in to let her plant a tender kiss on my brow.

We make for the Northern Gate in silence, stirring up only the occasional bit of small talk. Every one of us hopes to avoid the unspoken truth—how hollow the den will feel with both brothers gone.

I clear my throat. "Muma, Papa...you know I could still back out of this right?" Admittedly, it's an option I've given some thought to.

We continue along, my parents searching for the right words. Papa breathes out slowly. "Son, it's not really about what we want. It's about what's needed. The village still needs promising youth like you to help steer us outta' this mess."

"And what about Tygon?" Kleo says stroking my hand. "Someone has to go for him. He wanted it so bad, I think it's up to you!" Muma and Papa nod in agreement and I find myself surprised once more with her awareness at such a young age.

Through the gate, I see our village gathered around its candidates. Loving kin, inspired siblings, proud mentors—their tearful goodbyes ring out from their collective hearts. Even Nodus filter throughout the crowd to meet with their Masters. Magnus finds me and lifts me off my feet once my arms cling to his giant neck. We take a moment to sync aurem and collect each other's scent. The travel to the coast isn't terribly long, but I fear without sufficient connection, Magnus could lose me as he follows under the Qirin's wings.

After a few more minutes of farewells, Sage Ophis rises to the front of the group. A line of excited Qirin flap their sapphire wings, urging us to climb aboard their backs. The elderly man beckons us toward their formation.

"Children, let us set you on your way." We turn to the aged leader, listening to his words.

"So much has happened to our great village over the last few weeks. We've seen times of joy and times of sorrow. Moments of pride and moments of emptiness. Now, your path leads to Sanctum and there will be times anew for us all." He pauses, putting his first two fingers to his forehead.

"Use this moment to find purpose knowing that Praedari will live on past her pains. Anyone can look at our history and see this village has done so time and time again. In the same way that she won't be held back, ensure you aren't either. Engage this opportunity to its fullest."

With these words, kin turn to each other, giving their final embraces. Papa looks me in the eye, telling me how proud he is of the man I'm growing into. I lock his words away for later. With all my flaws, it's all too easy to forget I'm still developing. I know self-doubt will show its ugly face, but it'll only stop me if I let it.

He rummages through the folds of his garments, bringing out

my balalaika. "Son, there's a little something extra for you in this. A token to remind yourself of the potential you've got deep inside." He pats my breast with a heavy hand. I strum a couple chords on the stringed instrument before my hands register something's off. On the back side of the neck, a new trophy notch has been filled in with a heavy gray bone.

I stare at the ivory. "Is this what I think it is?"

"If you think it's a well-earned token, then yes. When it really counted, you alone saved your friend, son. Stick with that momentum, because if a Saberhorn couldn't stop you, what will?" He tousles my locs and I close my eyes and revel in the moment.

Muma steps forward and the huntress hands me a small box. Her eyes are filled with tears before I can even open it, but once I do, I understand why.

"The night Tygon died, you tried to keep him alive just a couple minutes longer. Your Papa and I have seen many friends taken by both hunt and conflict, so it broke me to see the look on your face"— she pulls my stained dancer's headband out of the package, wrapping it gently around my hand—"This was the last thing that touched your brother's blood before he left us for the stars. That means some of his spirit lives on inside of it."

I run my hands over the faded colors. It seems like forever ago that the cloth was white. Now, despite the blood having been washed away, there's still enough crimson to bring back the night's memories.

Kleo yanks me away from darker thoughts and I kneel down to her level. She unwraps the cloth to show a hidden pocket sewn into the middle. I can't help but smile as she reaches around my locs with her little arms. She ties the cloth with a sloppy knot, then grabs both sides of my face and pulls my head over to her lips. She murmurs a prayer to the Spirits, kissing the hidden pocket on my brow.

"There, now there's no way you'll ever lose!"

"Is that so, Kitten? What's gonna' make your brotya such a winner?"

Her hands find the hidden pocket and she pats it gently. "In there are the beads of every charm Tygon ever gave me since I was little. Since you were old enough to buy your own, Tygon never got you any. But me? I'm too poor! I never have any money!"

She pats her handy work. "Since those are from him, I think you need 'em more than I do. I even sent a prayer to Everrealm. I heard Tygon tell me himself it was okay to give them to you."

In Praedari, even the strongest shed tears, so I don't hesitate to cry, melting into my kin's arms. I murmur over and over how much they mean to me. Eventually, I compose myself and wave goodbyes. As I step onto the Qirin, I look back one more time, putting both hands to my heart. They mimic the expression and my chest floods with warmth.

I turn to climb up the Qirin's back and feel a familiar touch.

A wisp of a hand grabs the back of my neck.

I whip around to see who dares imitate Tygon's hold, but there's no one behind me. Zahk is already in front me, strapped into position. Confused, I find my grip on the giant bird. My friend leans back toward me.

"Stripes, here's to a whole new chapter." He holds up a fist and we bump in solidarity.

"Amio, thank the Spirits I don't have to do this alone. Good to have you." I resist the urge to crush him from behind with a tight hug.

"You too, buddy. This will be huge for both of us. We finally get to see the world!"

Just before we soar, Kleo runs up to the beast's wings, shaking a small pouch above her head. She jumps in place, yelping to get my attention. When I call down to her, she tosses the gift to me. I open it and look inside. There are leaflets of cloudberries for packing wounds, lullaby blossoms for healing, and swaddles of bandages. I smile at the sweetness in her heart. I don't expect her to make the connection that I'm going to the campus with the largest Mending corps in all of Spheire.

She cups her hands to shout her love and best wishes before skipping back to our kin.

With a hefty swoop, the Qirin is high above the Wilds. My kin are now waving figurines, then dots, then lost to the jungle altogether. As we pass over familiar places, I thank the Spirits for the good times I've had at each of them. The Seed Tree. The lightide hideout. Even the far-reaching Domain of Bones. I watch the Birth River carve through my beautiful country and I whisper a different sort of prayer.

The Weaving Willows shimmer for a moment and with my head bowed, I give thanks for the hard times too. I rub the back of my neck where I felt the weird sensation, checking for an insect bite. I inspect my hand and find nothing but a small leaf from the Seed Tree in my collar. I hold it in my hand confused, before remembering a lifetime ago when my brotya and I told stories to the sound of thunder.

I'll never be able to explain what happened next. In fact, I doubt I even see it to begin with. But atop the bird's back, I know I'm not mistaken. It's daytime, so of course Solint has overtaken the sky. Yet directly over the lightide hideout, above the clouds, a star blossoms—the same hue as our jeweled collection.

Its light spirals outward in the same pattern as our stone tapestry when Tygon and I would throw water on it. I look down at my hand to see the leaf has disappeared. I look back to the aquamarine twinkle in the sky to find it has vanished as well.

I take Tygon's cloth from around my head and grip it dearly. I close my eyes and breathe deeply. Then, I let loose a proud roar that I hope my brotya can hear from whatever star he's become. Magnus echoes the call from the trees below and I fix the piece back around my head like armor.

I'm ready to face the Discipline.

35

Foreign

After a day of flying, our Qirin circle over a giant rectangular structure facing the ocean. Zahk and I crane our necks over flapping wings to catch sight of the scene below. He laughs, delighted by the masses, foreign vehicles, and ocean waves.

I share his excitement and call out, "Amio, I've never seen anything that was so large, yet man-made in person before! That's the central MagneRail terminal!"

Zahk, being a people person, points with both hands at everything but the terminal. "Catboy, you're kidding right. Who cares about some boring old building? Have you ever seen this many outsiders before? And look at how some of them traveled here!" He motions at rows on rows of odd metal shapes. "What do you think those even are? They look like giant mantas with swords on 'em!"

Seeing all of this at once, I can grasp Zahk's wonder for the outside world—but a voice inside keeps pestering. For as incredible as the novelty is, some influence from down below managed to sneak into my village and take lives away with it. Something urges me to turn around and go right back home. An instinct telling me, in the end, no good can come from opening up to this giant world.

I quiet the dissenting opinion, choosing to instead revel in the moment. It's interesting to see the other Bloodlines' reaction to us.

As we swoop to the earth, I notice many gape at us and we do the same to them. Sand and sapphire feathers fill the air but none of the foreigners run. When the Qirin touch ground, hundreds of hands try reaching out to touch their wings. It's all we can do to keep the Qirin calm while we feed them their tribute. Finally, the birds are satisfied, and they storm off, lost once more to the clouds.

The Praedari join a section in the crowd with other Animas candidates. Beast Masters of all shapes stand ready to punch their ticket to a new future. Some practice familiar combat moves, others talk to their bonded. It isn't until I sit down with Zahk that I realize the potential problem awaiting due to the incoming stampede of our own village's Nodus.

"Hey, have you seen our bonded? They were nearby and I'd hate to scare every—"

A collective screech breaks out from the far side of the gathering and a rift of fleeing youth opens up. The other candidates can't get out of the way fast enough as a drove of predators skulk from the perimeter. Magnus only has eyes for me, and I watch him stride head and shoulders above the hoard. When our bonded reach us, our greetings are typical, but the looks of those around us are varied. Some watch in awe as tigers rear up on hindlegs. Some twitch with unease as bears tumble the ground with their partners. However, the expressions toward me and Magnus are the most shocking—I only see faces of fear.

Magnus, of course, doesn't help this at all. He stamps the earth, pacing in a close circle around me. His focus scans the surrounding throng. No matter the Bloodline, the Silver Fang stares the candidates down with equal measure and after marking his turf in massive footprints, he finds the back of my head with his chest. I hear the roar start as a rumble in his chest, but even I don't expect the volume that follows. Magnus stands over me, letting loose a primal thunder that quakes the dirt. From my periphery, I can see even the ocean waves turn back from the sound. He issues a challenge and when it is unmet, the roar cuts, leaving the masses in silence. He sinks to his haunches, yawning to show off fangs that are nearly half my height. The Silver Fang licks his snout and stares down at me before nudging me with a kitten's nose.

Great, I was going for a low profile, but sure, let's do it your way.

As if to confirm I definitely won't be hiding anytime soon, electricity crackles through the air nearby and I catch a familiar sight. In robes of sky blue and alabaster white, Ilysia floats high above the crowd. She looks down her nose at me, and when our eyes meet, she smirks the same cocky grin from the lake near Tauris village. She channels the electricity around her, letting a lightning bolt flash through her body and into the ground. The display earns a distasteful growl from Magnus. This time around, I press my shoulders back and stand my ground in the face of her power. I'll show I'm not afraid of the lightshow.

Admittedly, my bravado falters a bit at what happens next. She begins a freefall and lets herself comet to the earth. I notice Zahk beside me and see his face wretch in horror as she plummets uncontrolled. Frankly, my expression is no better as my mouth flies open.

When she's only a met from the ground, she spins, bringing her arms into her body. I spot a bright orange glow within those arrogant eyes and her body lights on fire as she tunnels into the dirt. The grounds are quiet for a second until the whole area erupts into a vortex of flame looking as though a small meteor has landed in front of us. Ilysia ascends coolly from the impact zone, her long black braid trailing behind her as she surveys the onlookers around her. Bored with them almost instantly, she flies straight for me with a grin and long tails of smoke float out the corners of her lips.

When she's hovering face to face, Magnus towers over us, but she pays him no mind. I try looking unfazed, but my palms sweat heavily. She locks me in her focus and juts her chin well into my bubble, but her whisper is only meant for me.

"You might've impressed everyone else here, but let's see if you can back up that kitty's roar. Consider this a 'challenge accepted,' fur-face." She watches my features twitch, well-aware the crowd around us is spectating too. She whips around, smacking my nose with her braid. Flame ignites beneath her feet and she blasts away, winking at Zahk a moment before she carves the sky.

The boy gawks after her in complete wonder.

I roll my eyes. "Wow, Amio, you were some help back there. Huge thanks." He doesn't respond. I knock him in the shoulder. "Bro, seriously. Pick your mouth off the beach before some critter finds a new home there."

Zahk huffs then straightens out before smacking me back.

"Stripes, she's so cool, man. Remind me how she knows you?"

I crane my neck so hard it almost snaps. "You can't be serious, her? Of all people? Trust me, you don't *want* to know her."

He shakes his head. "I dunno' Faylen. She kinda' spicy." He imitates her hand motions, as if he too could suddenly weave flame.

By the Blood, it takes so much will-power not to slap sense back into his head.

Before I can go off on him though, a voice calls for the crowd's attention from atop the rectangular structure. A short man with a thick beard slams a hammer twice his size into the roof he's standing on. A slender woman with epaulets of raw gems and sleeves of rough stone covering her arms stands beside him. Every few seconds, she nods her head and with each one, a column of earth springs up through the crowd.

The man calls out again, "Shut! Your! Faces!"

There isn't another peep.

He rests the head of the giant hammer with a thud. "Good, looks like we can get some quiet from you dillies yet!"

The pair step forward onto a floating miniature island the woman forms out of nowhere. This time, the woman speaks. "I am your Maven, and this is your Ward. Don't worry about names, you won't remember them right now anyway. Commit this to memory instead—

Candidates—your male overseers, Wards. Female overseers, Mavens."

The Ward raises his heavy weapon with one hand. "Dillies, you'd better be paying attention down there!"

The island descends to ground level and the masses spread to make room for it. The Maven raises her voice again. "Fix your attention here to the front. Exalt Danika, our glorious Keeper, will now deliver you privileged selectees a message." With a flicker, a column of blue light fans out above the crowd, taking the giant shape of the ruler.

"Candidates, congratulations on your accomplishments to stand here today. You bested friends and familiars alike to arrive at this very moment, truly shedding the cloaks of your mediocrity." Light blue tendrils of her hair float in the air, hanging over the assembly.

"Now, together we will begin a new chapter. One necessitated by the atrocities of conflicts past but written by your futures. The Discipline of Peace must hold true to its name, so I encourage you"—she glides a tree sized hand above a Bloodline clothed in metal on the other side of the crowd—"dedicate yourselves to shaking loose the shackles you've worn your whole lives.

"I have charged your Wards and Mavens with moving you beyond the simplicities of nations, villages, clans, and tribes. In fact, the Council is so committed to the need to come together, that I've called for the brightest of Loghis to join us for the first time ever."

I crane my head to see the metal wearing group—apparently the Loghis candidates. Zahk and I scramble to Magnus's back for a better look.

"Amio, the Bloodline of the Mind is so different from us. Why do they dress like that? Metal on their arms? And legs? What happens when to their clothes when it rains?"

Zahk points to a girl in the front row. Her long gray braids weave together like a river, joining at a point and flowing just above her waist. I can feel her poise from here and her face signals fierce determination. If the prowess of an elder huntress could be painted onto a younger form, it would look exactly like her. I find it difficult not to stare at the Loghis crowd. Hearing so many rumors about their Bloodline growing up, I'm having a hard time forming my own first impression.

Zahk whispers in my ear. "Is it just me or do they look like an army?"

"Glad one of us said it. I hope I can go a while before winding up in the ring with one of them."

The Exalt presses on. "Yours will be a generation of trust. No one is exempt." The crowd shifts as Bloodlines with complicated pasts eye one another. The Council leader scans the hoard, echoing the line with different emphasis each time, finally booming a clear order with the last repetition.

"Yours *will* be a generation of trust. *No one* is exempt. The Discipline will not only give to you but take from you as well. You will bathe its floors in sweat, and its duels will require your blood. We will put you in the care of senior students who've been where you are now. They, along with my trusted Wards and Mavens, will demand whatever else you're able to give."

Chills run down my spine as I think of every day I ever slept in. Of every time I ran in the middle of the Elevation pack so I wouldn't have to set the pace or get called out for trailing. Papa's countless speeches loom larger than the Exalt's shimmering face. He reminds me of the possibilities I could have if I'd only get out of my own way. I look over to Zahk who holds his head high at the challenge. Ready as long as he gets to work with new faces.

I envy him. I'd never slacked off completely, but some days I didn't feel like being defeated by a potential I feared I'd never live up to. On those days, it was just easier to act like I had no potential at all. Tygon rarely corrected me on this and I thought it was because he was being nice—now I see he hoped I'd grow to correct myself.

Above us, the woman finishes her introduction. "Finally, keep in mind you will be tested by the Gifts of those standing beside you now. We have the Mending Corps to aid you, but don't be surprised if not everyone makes it to graduation. Your seniors are no strangers to injury and death, so my advice to you? Become strong and don't die."

Many of the Animas candidates drop their jaws. My eyes dart to the other groups to see their reactions. Indom's Warriors and

Blade Dancers thud each other's chests, howling at the absurdity of being brought low by death. Petrichor's Weavers are too composed to read. Hayvin's Spirit-Born chatter in Essence Tongue before collectively bowing their heads in a silent prayer. My intimidation is reinforced when I spot the Loghis candidates. Most of them smirk up at the ghostly image. I know that expression. It's the same one I make when I get the jump on an easy kill.

Exalt Danika holds her hands up, and the luminares tower over us like the point of a Saberhorn's ivory. "I look forward to seeing you in the Discipline's halls. Be a generation of trust. No one is exempt. Your hardest Challenge begins now!" In a shimmer of light, the woman dissipates into a single thin beam.

"Stripes, I'm declaring myself ahead of you in ranking already."

I raise my eyebrow, wondering if Zahk heard some secret from the speech that flew over my head.

"Yeah, she said she wants us to be a generation of trust. So, dibs. I trust you first. Boom, test passed. I'm the man."

He flexes, touting his miniscule victory. I shake my head at the goof. I wish Tygon could've made it here too. But in his stead, I won't slip back into my lazier habits. I'll do it for him, for Kleo, our kin, and the village…and especially for Lunis.

Before I move to join the lineup for the ride beyond the sea toward Sanctum, I snag Zahk unexpectedly and bring him in for a hug.

"Thank you for not leaving me to do this by myself," I say.

He holds the embrace for a moment before grabbing my shoulders to nod with confidence. "Let's show 'em what we Praedari boys can do."

With that assurance, we move inside the massive terminal. We join some of the other Beast Masters, surrendering our Nodus for their own MagneRail where they'll meet us at the Discipline. Not every Beast Master elected to, but we were given the option to have our bonded join us during our studies. Apparently, the institute has an enormous free-range estate where the animals will stay while we are occupied.

I pet Magnus and he plows me to my rump with the weight of his head. We share eye-contact and I scratch over the bridge of his nose. He licks me in return, sliding me up to my feet with coarse taste buds. A deep chuff bellows from his chest as he laughs at my new hairstyle, freshly remade in his tongue's image.

We climb aboard the MagneRail and Zahk and I find a comfy booth. The deep seats swivel, making it easier to look out the window. Our car is packed with a mix of people from different nations. The car fills up with excited chatter and laughter, and Zahk's cheeks rest in his hands as he listens to the collection of accents.

"I just can't believe there's so many differences on this train and yet we're all speaking the same language. If that doesn't speak to some kind of shared origin, I don't know what does. Only the Discipline could put us back together like this," he says in wonder.

The doors close and I feel us rise slightly. Out the window, I can see we're no longer resting on the tracks but hovering above them. I lurch backward in my chair as the car jolts forward in smooth acceleration. We leave the terminal and hurtle over the waves below—the beach behind us grows small and is soon overtaken by stretches of blue.

We watch the sea for half an hour before Zahk curls up for a nap. He makes me promise to wake him up once we are close enough to see the Sanctum limits. I open up my pack and bring out a sheet of parchment. As the sloshing waves blur into one uniform body of motion, I look in the direction we're traveling to see a glint of purple on the horizon. At first, I think it's the my brother's star trying to reach out to me again, but the shimmer doesn't twinkle. It remains inexplicably constant in the distance.

I spread out my parchment and sit back to find a more comfortable position. If this next chapter is going to be a new leaf for me, there's one last thing I need to do to flip it over completely.

36

UNDER

Dear Lunis,
The last few weeks after Tygon's sowing have been...different. My mind is in a million different places, meanwhile my heart wishes it could be in only a few. One of those places is in the Upper Falls with you. I hope you're recovering all right. Who even knows how long you'll be under? By the time you get this, I bet I'll be a Discipline expert, giving your scraggly brother a run for his money!

I've decided to try my best and make some long overdue changes. I feel like the better version of me has been standing in the tree line, watching a fool plod through the grasslands for a kill. He's seen me waste both time and opportunity for many seasons and I don't want that anymore. I'm calling him to join me in becoming the best Faylen I can be.

I'm scared though—glad Muma taught me to admit that instead of hiding it. I'm an eldest son now in addition to an older brother now. I'm not used to being the trailblazer. I'm used to having an obvious set of footprints to fall behind. But now...now I've got to get it right. Kleo needs me to look out for her. I just want to get back to the old days where her only concern was what to do with all the flowers little boys like your brother Rani kept giving her!

Anyway, I'm trying not to let the big world out here intimidate me. *In my dreams, I still feel the explosion and burns, but I'm trying not to let my demons keep me hostage. Be safe up there, Lunis. I pray every night that the Spirits keep you from those seeking to do more harm. Maybe I'll see you sooner than we think. I hear the Council might accept an extra group of students soon to offset the lower numbers after the attacks. They say it could be an accelerated first study year for the geniuses in every nation. You're the smartest apprentice I know. You're a shoe-in.*

Well, let me wrap this up. I need to poke Zahk before he breaks his neck sleeping. Honestly, how does he sleep at that angle? Maybe I'll get some rest too. Oh, and I'm taking old advice from Tygon's book and gifting you something a long time in the making. I hope you'll wear it. And...let's talk when I see you next. I've got a few things I need to say. No worries, we'll be miles away from any sisterly interruptions this time.

  Yours, More than you know...
  Faylen

I fold the parchment carefully, enclosing a bracelet around it with nervous hands. She won't be able to recognize this one from any specific shop. It took a whole three days to untwist the twine of my bracelet stash and another three to weave a line of tiny lightides into a spectrum of colors. I miss Lunis so much and I hope I've crossed her mind too.

I run my hands across the pearly white tabletop to crease the letter edges before sealing it with a touch to my forehead. As I repack my satchel, my finger runs up against Kleo's pouch. I stroke it and chuckle at how unnecessary it will be where I'm going. With a loving sigh, I decide to attach the medicinal supplies to my belt anyways. When I finish, the train's blinds dim and I'm thankful for the lowered light. It'll make sleeping easier since I'm really feeling a snooze coming on.

I trace my fingers along the bright white marble table and almost reach over to thwack Zahk. His neck is hanging at an awkward angle from the table's pearly surface. Instead of waking him, I cradle his heavy head, propping it up against the window.

Wow, is he out of it.

"Zahk you better not topple over again. That position can't be comfortable."

I plop back down and watch him drool over the light red tabletop.

As I begin to dose off, a sour tinge hits my nose. I know the smell from somewhere. It reminds me of something Orin once showed me—of a PanVulpis I once met too. I crank my head around, squinting my eyes to see if either of them is nearby. After a few heavy coughs, I give up searching, cozying up on the blood red tabletop where Zahk snores away. I count the candidates in our car, chuckling at their bobbing heads. My eyes are unusually heavy, and I realize how draining the day has been. I need to rest, same as all these other jokers, or I'll be the only guy who was too stupid to sleep while he could.

I'm almost comfortable but curiosity rouses me when I look more closely at the glass door separating our train car from the next. A voice repeats a message, and I see a shimmering face. At the glass, I see Exalt Danika's ghostly image from earlier. It flickers back and forth, repeating her closing lines.

"I look forward to seeing you in the Discipline's halls. Be a generation of trust. No one is exempt. Your hardest Challenge begins now!" The words echo loud in the silence of the sleeping car. I lean a shoulder against the metal door and poke at the glass, watching her image distort where my finger slides. I chuckle when I place a massive bulge right over her forehead. She looks like a grazing—

A slam startles me from the other side of the glass and a girl looks frantically through it. Her features are sharp and elegant; every angle of her face is like the cut of a rare gem. I recognize her immediately—the poised Loghis girl I saw standing at the front during the introduction. Her eyes find me, and I'm confused by their appearance. I thought the reflection of Solint on the waves was tricking me before, but she really has little lights in her eyes. They're like nightflies, or maybe the moving pictures back in the Hub.

She yells at me and bangs on the glass with a metal bat on her arm. Where did she get a bat on a train? Weird. I can't make out much from her until a strike cracks the glass, splitting Danika's face into two separate images. The halves flicker different images, making her face look eerily inhuman complete with a third eye. I back away from the loony Loghint. I have no intention of getting in trouble for glass she broke. When I turn back to my chair, the whole room is dark red. The sour smell is thick, and I cough even more than before. I catch a familiar whiff, but it isn't until I'm on my hands and knees that I fully remember. I've felt this sort of drowsiness before, though not nearly as potent.

Slumberrose.

I stagger to the cracked glass to see if the sculpted face is still there. I peer through the cracks to see she's gone unconscious, her head resting on a crown of thick gray braids. Uncontrolled, I wretch and slump to the floor, barely able to lift my head. My pulse is dropping fast—did someone rig the train somehow? I try to Embrace. I picture Magnus and my kin. Faint stripes appear when I think of getting up to protect Zahk…of living to teach Kleo.

The attempted Embrace doesn't last, and I think of all the things I should've done. I taste Lunis's breath on my tongue. Why didn't I just kiss her when I had the chance? From the floor, I look up at Exalt Danika. Now, she's split into several shifting faces as her speech plays back. I fade away with my eyes still open, convulsing atop the broken glass.

The Keeper's voice is distorted, but I finally understand her words. The message sounds so much different than before—

"D-Do… Don't Die."

"Tr-Truuuu… Trust. No one."

Your Greatest Challenge Begins Now.

Author Note

Dearest reader, thank you for reading my debut novel and exploring the world of Spheire with me. I hope these pages have left you with a single thought: you are empowered! This was a core belief I used throughout the eight-year journey of this novel—from organizing my first mood board on PowerPoint in 2018 to the copy you're holding now.

Are you looking forward to the next title? I hope in the time it takes to get it out, you will mentally return to scenes from this book and find hope. Perhaps imagine yourself as one of the Bloodlines (or take my online quiz to discover yours!) These small moments of escapism can be the difference between making it through a low point and losing the will to press on.

Toward the beginning of the pandemic, I reached one of these low points myself. The journey to publishing this title stalled significantly. The market seemed to whisper there was no room for my book or its main character. But in the same way Faylen felt something raw and powerful just beneath his skin, aching to be seen, so too did this story claw restless through my mind. I have to thank my publishing team at Mountain Brook Ink (especially Tim and Mrs. Miralee) for coming alongside me when all seemed lost.

You will reach similar challenging spaces in life or perhaps you're in one now. My ask is that you do not give up. Whether that be looking up into heavenly places for the answer as I try to do, or turning to those nearest to you, do not stop moving forward. Momentum qualifies the living.

Finally, use this book as a reminder to invest in what you love! Think back on the hobbies, interests, and skills you had growing up. For example, I exist at the juncture between a love of books instilled by my mother and an obsession with anime. I used the latter to revamp my interest in books, searching out titles that felt like anime in book form. I was heavily inspired by Jay Kristoff's, *Nevernight*, as well as Pierce Brown's *Red Rising* and Neil Shusterman's, *Scythe*. However, it was once I added the secret ingredients imagined from *Naruto* and other shonen titles that I truly found my unique style for the first time. You too have the ability to dissect your interests and create something new. I, for one, can't wait to see what you'll gift the world!

See you for Book 2!

www.ingramcontent.com/pod-product-compliance
Lightning Source LLC
LaVergne TN
LVHW011927070526
838202LV00054B/4530